THE SCARS

THE HURT TRILOGY BOOK THREE

EVA BIELBY

KEEP IN TOUCH WITH THE AUTHOR

Visit my website online:
https://www.evabielby.co.uk

or
Join me on Facebook:
www.facebook.com/eva.bielby/
or
Join me on Twitter:

https://twitter.com/AuthorEva69

ACKNOWLEDGMENTS

I would like to take this opportunity to thank my son
and daughter for their never ending support over
the last few years, and now The Hurt Trilogy is completed.
I love you both to the moon and back.
Also, I would like to thank many of my friends
and author friends from around the world,
who have given me constant support, encouragement,
and advice, whether acted on, or not!
And again, a special mention goes to authors Ian Grant and
Mel Comley!
Thank you all for making this journey
an absolute pleasure.
Eva xx

CHAPTER 1

The instant I opened my eyes, I was in a panic about the time. Fretting in case I slept later than intended, I rolled over to see the alarm clock. Although with my black-out blinds the room was still dark, I could see from the luminous pointers it was just past ten in the morning. I cast my mind back to the events of yesterday. First was the shock of Ruby's arrival on my doorstep complete with her huge suitcase and secondly, the one with the biggest impact; Ruby revealing why she'd turned up unannounced and distressed.

I sat up in bed, straining my ears for any tell-tale noises and wondering if she was awake and downstairs yet. If she was, I would need to get out of bed. She couldn't be left alone with her own thoughts for too long.

I made my way downstairs to find her already sat at the kitchen counter, chin in her hands, tear-stained eyes and staring directly ahead, almost trancelike. Eventually, she looked up and acknowledged my presence.

"Did you get any sleep at all, Ruby?" I enquired hopefully and gave her a smile.

She slowly turned her head to face me.

"Precious little."

"That makes two of us, sweetheart. I'll get us both some coffee. We've got serious talking to do."

"Urgh! Do we have to? I really just want to forget about it. I want it to go away, Helen."

Her eyes filled up with fresh tears and she stared down at her hands, wringing them together. I didn't reply to her comments, but busied myself with the kettle and two coffee cups for a few minutes.

I placed a cup of steaming coffee in front of her and deliberately sat down to face her so that she was forced to make eye contact again.

"You are going to have to help me out here, Ruby. I don't know what you want me to do. I have no wish to upset you in any way. In fact, that is the last thing I want. I could...if you want me to, organise for you to have an abortion, no problem. I was in a similar position to you just a few years back and with that same decision to make but..."

I paused for a few seconds, carefully considering my next words and giving Ruby the chance to digest my revelation.

"I must also ask myself what David..." I hesitated a little. "...what action your Dad would wish you to take..."

I watched her eyes widen in shock as it finally sunk in what I just dropped on her. Somehow a smile didn't seem to be appropriate after my announcement, so I gave her arm a squeeze of encouragement.

"You? Pardon me, Helen? Did I...did I just hear that correctly or was I imagining what you just said? You... you had an abortion?? How? When? Who?"

"I think it's important that you should tell your Mum, Ruby! It's vital..."

She was quick to cut me off. I could see that the preoccupation with her own predicament was forgotten for the moment as her face was full of concern for me.

"Helen, what happened? Why did you...you know?"

My stomach lurched as the reality of my own misdemeanour became prominent in my mind.

"Okay, I'll tell you! It happened during my uni years. I'd been away from my apartment for the week staying with my Mum. My Dad suffered a heart attack and I needed to go home. A couple of weeks later, once he was better and back at home, I returned to my apartment to discover Gavin, my boyfriend and my best friend sha...ermm...at it...in my living room. I was devastated. I threw her out of the apartment straight away, quickly followed by him with his black bin bags full of clothes. I quit uni the next day and went home, just like that."

I watched her face and body language as she was taking it all in. From time to time she looked away and stared at her hands nervously. If I was correct in my thoughts, she was embarrassed. I continued with my story.

"After a month or so, I realised I missed a period. The first pregnancy test I did showed that I was pregnant. I was mortified. I was taking the pill and had been doing for some time, but I think a course of antibiotics ruined its effectiveness. The pregnancy was confirmed by a doctor a few weeks later. I considered my situation carefully but an abortion was the only option for me at the time. Like you, I had studying and a career to think about. It was a horrible and heavily emotional time."

"Oh, Helen, I'm so sorry. It must have been horrendous for you...to find him and her in the way that you did. What did your parents say?"

In a desperate attempt to avoid answering her last question lest she would want to follow suit and try to wriggle out of telling her Mum, I carried on talking.

"I was broken-hearted about the whole Gavin and Bobbie scenario. She had been my first best friend and I loved him *and* her so much. I also felt disappointed in myself. And dirty…I felt dirty. Not long after the termination, the mental health issues started; constant washing, my hands in particular, cleaning, scouring and the rest. My father came with me to see our G.P. I was diagnosed with O.C.D. and referred to a clinical psychologist who recommended that I should undergo cognitive behavioural therapy. I didn't see the therapy through. I'm okay these days…most of the time. But it doesn't take much stress to trigger off another episode. I doubt I'll ever be completely free of it."

She stared into my eyes, her lips moving but she clearly couldn't find any words. I sensed she was perhaps struggling to search for the right words; comforting or appropriate.

"It's okay, Ruby! I know. There are no words."

She lowered her eyes again and at last she showed an interest in the still steaming liquid in her cup. Her hand went around the mug and she took a few sips.

When we started the conversation, I hadn't intended speaking about my past for so long. What we really needed to be discussing was how she planned to break the news to her Mum, *not* the raking up of my past. Watching her carefully, I realised in that moment that she was going to be a tough cookie. She was strong willed and I saw the defiance in her eyes. I continued to watch her as I drank my coffee. Her eyes glazed over once again.

"The decision is a bit easier for me. At least I don't have a broken heart to contend with. I don't feel anything for him… Andrè. He was just…fit."

I smiled at her, masking the anger that ate me up inside when she mentioned his name…the hostility I felt towards him.

We finished our coffee in silence, but for the loud, attention-seeking purrs from Harry, who was wrapping himself around our legs, desperate to get his message across. 'Hey, humans, get my breakfast please!'

Some half hour later, the cat had been fed and Ruby and I had both eaten breakfast which was the standard quick fix of cereals. With our second coffee of the morning, we made ourselves comfortable in the lounge. Ruby, remote control in her right hand was channel hopping eagerly, perhaps hoping to find a distraction. Determined to keep her on track, I blurted out.

"You've got to speak with your Mum today. You can't let this drag on sweetheart, as it eats away at you."

She looked in my direction and much to my surprise, she stabbed at the 'power off' button on the remote and placed it back on the coffee table. Releasing a heavy sigh she replied in the flattest tone ever.

"Yeah…yes. I know that!"

"Good. When will you do it?" I asked, trying my best to sound cheery instead of being too pushy.

"I'll do it this afternoon. I need time to psyche myself up."

I stood and turned away from her hoping that she wouldn't see me when I gave a massive sigh of relief.

CHAPTER 2

*A*fter constantly observing Ruby, coupled with checking my watch for most of the afternoon, four o'clock arrived at last. I sat next to her and saw the look of defeat in her eyes as her fingers tapped out her mother's phone number. I recognised Heidi's voice answer at the end of the line. Ruby put the call onto loudspeaker so that I could hear her Mum's contribution to the conversation. Whether it was a mother's intuition I didn't know but somehow, despite hearing Heidi's sobs at the beginning of the exchange, she did not seem to be too shocked or even phased by her daughter's news. With Ruby's wild reputation of late, perhaps the revelation hadn't come as that much of a bombshell to her.

When asked by her Mum who the father was, I was startled at Ruby's flippant reply, "Oh, just some boy I met." In those few seconds I waited in dread of her answer in case Andrè's name would roll off her tongue. I think I was afraid that Heidi would try to lay the guilt on me had she discovered that the said 'boy' happened to be my neighbour in Paris. However, I was quickly realising that Heidi was not the type to lay blame on anybody.

"I know what I need to do, Mum. I have my studying and career to think about. I can't have a baby at my age."

Ruby's eyes glistened with fresh tears as she stated the obvious. Through the loudspeaker, I heard Heidi's voice falter for a few seconds as she considered her daughter's words.

"Is Helen there, sweetheart?"

"I'm here, Heidi. Sat right beside her."

"I don't know what to do, Helen. I've never been in a situation like this."

I didn't relish the thought of explaining my past indiscretion over the phone and had no intention of doing so. I um'ed and ah'ed for a few seconds before deciding on the most sensible answer I could come up with.

"Look, why don't you come over here, Heidi? I think...I hope I may be able to help. If you'd like me to, that is?"

There was a slight hesitation from down the phone line and it struck me that she might think I was invading on what was really a mother and daughter dilemma. I glanced over at Ruby, who seemed to be cringing at the thought that her mother might come over. She gave me a resigned look and shrugged her shoulders.

"Yes, I will please, Helen. If you don't mind? I just want to put my arms around my daughter and hug her to death."

I leaned across towards Ruby and before handing back her mobile, I altered the status off loudspeaker. She could at least have a few private words with Heidi and give her my full address. Leaving her to it, I headed for the kitchen. I had no appetite and suspected that Ruby wouldn't feel much like eating either so I plated up some snack food.

Two hours later...

I heard the front door bell ring downstairs, immediately followed by Ruby's footsteps on the wood flooring in the hallway. She told me after finishing up the earlier call, that her Mum would be arriving around six o'clock, so I purposely made myself scarce so that they could have a few private moments together.

I had no desire to eavesdrop, but nevertheless I heard Ruby unlocking and opening the front door. Nothing but silence followed. I felt like sobbing, knowing how hard it would be for the pair of them. I could picture her crying silently on her Mum's shoulder and Heidi in turn hugging her daughter tightly and succumbing to more tears herself. Shortly after I heard them go through to the lounge, I could hear them talking in low voices and much as I was curious about what was being said, I also didn't want to know. I needed a distraction for a while. For want of a better idea I undressed and headed for a shower.

The shower proved to be a good escape for a while and I relished the heat of the water. I imagined the liquid to be washing away all my troubles as I vigorously sponged every square inch of my body, taking my time and delaying the inevitable which I knew would be happening at some point soon. Heidi would want to speak with me as planned earlier. I pondered, not on Ruby's dilemma but how I would feel when we finally met. She used to be David's wife, and she had 'had' David long before I knew him. It crossed my mind that I might feel jealous of her; after all, *she* had managed to *have* a life with him, something which I never got the opportunity to do. After I felt they'd had plenty of private time, I turned off the shower and towelled myself dry in a bit of a rush. I found some smart, casual clothes to wear. I needed to dry my hair and get some make-up on my face to at least try to look half-presentable. I previously saw a picture of Heidi and from what I could recall, she was a very stunning lady, though I couldn't now picture her face.

I sat in front of the dressing table mirror in a hurry to get my face on...I didn't want to look over made-up. Always believing that a first impression is important, I wanted to look natural. A moisturiser with a hint of foundation, some light blusher, mascara and neutral looking lipstick. I carefully monitored the results as I applied each and reasonably happy, I started to dry my hair. I had a feeling it wouldn't be too much longer before I was summoned downstairs. As I brushed my hair, my emotions started to take over again and I could do nothing about the feeling of nausea that crept up into my stomach.

"HELEN? Are you coming down soon?" Ruby's voice came from the bottom of the stairs.

Oh my God, this is it! David's ex-wife is waiting to meet me!

That's all I could think about! Not the serious fact of Ruby's unwanted pregnancy and possible imminent abortion...I was more worried about what David's ex-wife, *not* Catherine and Ruby's Mum but David's *ex-wife*, was going to think of me!

"Two minutes, Ruby! I'm just finishing drying my hair and throwing some clothes on". I shouted back.

Three minutes later, I was satisfied with my hair and quickly dressed in the denims and casual, classy T-shirt I got ready after I showered. I took a final look in the full-length mirror of the wardrobe; a long, deep breath and slowly headed down the stairs.

"Helen! How lovely to meet you at last."

Heidi folded her arms around me almost as soon as I entered the living room. She hugged me fiercely and whispered in my ear. "I am so, so sorry!"

"It's so lovely to meet you, Heidi!" Tears welled up in my eyes as I felt the warmth and compassion through her hug. "But what are you sorry for? You have nothing to be sorry for, I assure you."

She gently pushed me back from her hug and through her own watery eyes, looked directly into mine. I was busy taking in her stunning looks; her neatly cropped blonde hair, cheekbones to die for and perfect white teeth. She was beautiful.

"Helen, first and foremost, I've wanted to tell you for a while how sorry I am about David. Sorry that you found each other and he was so cruelly snatched away from you. It was heart-breaking that you didn't actually get to *be* together after falling in love. When David told the girls and I about you prior to his death, my heart went out to you. And that you didn't know until after…I can't begin to imagine what you have been through…I…"

With another deluge flowing down my cheeks, Ruby watched the pair of us in silence and reached for the tissue box from the coffee table before offering it in our direction. I offered them to Heidi first before plucking out a couple for myself. Dabbing at my eyes, I tried to get some words out but struggled.

"But I only…" I started, then, "David was…"

Heidi quickly cut in, clearly understanding the emotions I was feeling and I tried to speak again but my mouth was opening and closing with nothing coming out.

"Please let me finish, Helen. I have other things I want to say. I want to apologise for Ruby's behaviour when the girls came over to Paris to stay with you."

From the corner of my blurred vision I spotted Ruby's face. She cringed, turned scarlet with embarrassment and looked away from us.

"Oh no! Mum, don't, please!" she begged.

Heidi ignored her.

"No, Ruby! It needs saying!" After a swift glance in Ruby's direction, she turned to face me again.

"That disgusting behaviour from Ruby was unforgive-able and I am sorry that Catherine had to cut short her visit too. She would have loved to stay…but it wasn't possible in the circumstances. I hope you understand, Helen?"

I nodded my head.

"But we..."

"Yes, you got through it, but it was a nightmare for you and Catherine at the time. Anyway, enough about that. Thankfully, it's in the past. I also want to offer my apologies for Ruby putting you in this position...with this...*situation*, for Heaven's sake. Will you ever be able to forgive us, Helen?"

My head was spinning. A minute of high speed flashbacks; being with David, reading David's letter, the horrendous, drunken Ruby in Paris, Catherine's tears, André carrying her up the stairs, my conversation with Bill Douglas, Simon's shock that I fell in love with David and that David loved me in return, Ruby arriving on my doorstep and pregnant, the revelation that André used her...and Heidi being here, standing in front of me.

"Should I make us coffee, Helen? I think we could use some!"

Ruby looked pale and small despite her stature, her voice meek and barely audible. As quiet as she was though, it snapped me back to reality and realising that I couldn't stand here looking... (how do I look? I feel 'punch-drunk'). With a desperate need to do so, I took charge instantly.

"No, Ruby. I'll do it, instead of standing here letting my emotions take over."

I headed to the kitchen, resolving to get a grip of myself. Getting the cups and saucers in order seemed like a major task, but eventually the kettle came to the boil and I was heading back to the living room, feeling determined to get back on track to where this conversation needed to go.

"So...tell me if any decisions were made while I was upstairs getting ready. What's going to happen?"

I shot questioning looks at both Ruby and Heidi. Ruby

shrugged and looked at her Mum for help, maybe hoping Heidi would step in. She obliged.

"We've discussed it all, Helen. We agree that the best solution is for Ruby to have a termination. Do you think the same? Please feel free to be honest as we both value your opinion, don't we, Ruby?"

Heidi looked at Ruby with concern but also, I felt the concern was coupled with pride. I sensed that she was proud that her youngest daughter had been doing some growing up recently.

"Yes! We do." Fresh tears gathered in Ruby's eyes now. "Helen, I just want you to know that I am genuinely sorry for everything I have put you through...*really* sorry! I truly value your concern, your opinion and your advice. Dad was right about you."

It was a beautiful compliment she paid me and I was overwhelmed with emotion. I wanted to hug her tight, but her mother's arms were wrapped around her. I watched the pair of them together, remembering the many occasions my Mum did exactly the same for me. A mother's love!

"Okay. I don't know exactly how much Ruby has told you about me Heidi, but I'm going to tell you. I went through a termination a good few years ago. My parents didn't even know about it. I organised everything myself."

Heidi looked at me. She looked somewhat shell-shocked, mouth and eyes wide open as her daughter had done earlier. Clearly, Ruby hadn't disclosed anything about my private life.

"By the way, my parents died in a tragic accident, not too long ago. It was before David died."

I felt the need to explain about Mum and Dad although it wasn't relevant to what I was trying to say. I carried on, not waiting for any input from either of them.

"I met Gavin not long after I started university and we fell in love. It wasn't long, just months, before he moved in to my apartment. We made plans for our future together; even plans to maybe go and live in New York some day." I sighed, a dark heaviness descending on me. "I received a call at uni one day. Dad had suffered a heart attack, so I rushed off to be with him in hospital. I stayed with Mum the whole time until he was back at home and sufficiently rested."

I suddenly felt I needed to speed it up, as I was starting to relive the nightmare once again.

"When I returned to my apartment I let myself in and found *him* and my so-called best friend. At it, they were...in my apartment of all places. Unwise I know, but I quit university and returned home to live with my parents...and to get a job. I couldn't have coped with staying where I was. A month or so later I discovered I was pregnant."

"You didn't need to tell us all this, Helen. That was private and your own personal Hell! But I am sorry that you went through that alone."

The concern was there again in Heidi's voice. It struck me again that this lady was beautiful, inside and out.

"No, I needed to tell you. The reason I couldn't tell them is...I couldn't bear to see the disappointment that I would have seen on their faces. What I'm trying to say when I can get the words out, is that I can help. If you want me to, that is? I went for a consultation and then later to a private hospital not far from Harley Street. I was in and out in a few hours."

"Would you mind...really? I don't know how to go about these things. Should Ruby see our G.P. first or not? I don't know what to do."

I explained to them that I hadn't seen a G.P. I only dealt with the clinic, attended for a quick consultation and was given a date for the procedure. I'd only needed to wait for three or four days. Ruby listened with interest, and dread too

I guessed. I think the assurance that there were no long delays grabbed her attention.

"You will need to call the clinic yourself, Ruby. Oh, no you won't! You're still under eighteen. I keep thinking of you as much older. You will need your Mum to make the appointment for you. There will also be a deposit to pay at the consultation. And I've no doubt your Mum will be accompanying you? I think that's wise, just in case you're feeling a little groggy afterwards. I was…I remember it well."

She gave her Mum a shy look, almost apologetic, then gave me a questioning look before stating,

"I would like you to be there as well please, Helen. Would you mind?" Then she quickly asked "You don't mind, Mum? If Helen could come too? Is that okay with you both?"

Heidi watched me carefully, awaiting my reaction. I wondered if she was hoping I would go for some moral support. I didn't need to think twice about my reply.

"Of course I will, Ruby. But only if that is okay with your Mum."

"Helen, of course I would like you there. You've been through it yourself. And if I'm totally honest, I feel a little out of my depth with this. First thing on Monday morning I will call the clinic if you can give me their number please, Helen."

I hadn't kept the number for the clinic. I never felt the need. After quickly thumbing through the phone book, I wrote down the number for the clinic I'd used on a 'post-it' and handed it to Heidi. Ruby asked if it was okay to stay with me until everything was over. She looked to her Mum for approval, and although I sensed that Heidi would have liked Ruby to go home with her, she agreed.

She left shortly after, with big hugs for Ruby and promising to call us with details on Monday after she contacted the clinic. As I was about to close the front door behind her, she turned around and smiled.

"I can see why David fell for you, Helen. I really can. Kind, warm, intelligent, caring, beautiful, compassionate…and dark. He always loved dark hair."

She fiddled with her cropped blonde locks briefly, beamed at me, evidently amused, and she turned and walked away. I was stunned.

CHAPTER 3

I closed my eyes so I could focus better on the wonderful sensation my body was experiencing. He teased me enough already during our foreplay. He was using his tongue and his fingers and succeeded in tantalising every nerve ending in my depths…they were like a raging fire. I sensed he was ready to go inside me and penetration could not happen soon enough. I craved and longed for that moment; incensed with the anticipation for the pleasure that I knew would come.

He was knelt between my legs and with my eyes still closed, I visualised him staring at me intently whilst he massaged his cock in preparation. My body tensed, waiting eagerly, though I was fighting hard against the temptation to open my eyes and be further teased by watching his actions; his gentle rubbing of his swollen muscle. It wouldn't be long now.

The back of his hand brushed against my inner thigh and I held my breath…any second. Then it was there. His bulging cock nudged into me and I delighted in the sensation. As he bit hard into my breast, he edged deeper into my dampness.

"Tell me what you want, Helen. Tell me."

I opened my eyes and stole a quick glance at his handsome face. I gasped for air in delight as he thrust into me; struggling to breathe as I gazed at his muscular torso and his strong arms. *I'm so lucky. He's mine and I love him so much.*

"Do whatever…you want…to do. I'm…all yours. Make me cum…a hundred times…over."

He leaned forwards and moved in for a kiss and as his lips touched mine he bit into my bottom lip. The bite came simultaneously with his hardest thrust and I wanted to scream in the eroticism and sensuality of the move. I closed my eyes waiting for more.

He stopped for a moment with his cock buried deep inside me. The throbbing was intense. I opened my eyes to see why he stopped thrusting, fearing that he was about to cum. My attention was drawn to a movement in the corner of the room. Someone, I couldn't see who but it was a female, sat on a chair watching us as she masturbated with a giant dildo while she watched on, perving at the pair of us.

"Fuck her up the arse. I need to see that." She urged.

Contact with him was momentarily lost. He climbed off and rolled me over.

"NOOOO!" I shouted out in utter terror. "I don't want to do that!"

Before he could start nudging into my backside, I flipped myself over to face him, my pregnant belly making the move clumsy. Horrified when I saw who was about to ram into me, I screamed once again.

"GET OFF ME! I don't…want to be fucked…by YOUUU!!"

My eyes were drawn to the corner again…a different room this time. David and Ruby watched on and the disgust on their faces matched how I felt. I could tell they didn't like this man. Their expressions showed nothing but contempt and pure hatred. I started to cry and the tears kept coming. There was a memory coming back to me...an horrendous recollection.

With loud sobs I opened my eyes, for real this time. There was nobody in my room, no pregnant belly...my tears were real though and my pillow, wet.

I cried more with relief as it dawned on me that I'd been dreaming; ghastly memories that intruded on my sleep. Unwanted hallucinations which served to remind me of the two men...unsuspecting fathers to two unwanted pregnancies...Gavin and André.

Feeling agitated, I got out of bed and straight into the shower. I felt tainted and I wanted to scour my skin clean. I scrubbed for what seemed like an eternity...and until my skin was raw.

It wasn't a dream that I'd be relating to Ruby.

CHAPTER 4

I got up well before dawn, and feeling completely drained. I paced back and forth in the kitchen, my nervousness for Ruby overpowered all other thoughts. Before I had the chance to get coffee on the go, she appeared in the kitchen. She looked as washed out as I felt. She headed straight towards me, arms outstretched in search of a hug. I held her close to me for a few minutes in silence and pushed her bedraggled hair out of her face. Although I felt the urge to weep for her, I fought those emotions and gave her a weak smile.

"Just a few days and it will be done with, Ruby. Then you can move on with your life and concentrate on your studies."

"Were you able to move on, Helen? Did you...have you ever had any regrets about...you know?" The tone of her voice gave me the impression she was almost pleading for me to give her the answers she wanted to hear.

"Yes, sweetheart! I *was* able to move on. It wasn't easy and I won't pretend otherwise. I think the thing that gnawed away at me the most, was my guilt. My parents always hoped that they would be grandparents one day and I denied them that. Now that they are gone, well...they didn't get to be grandparents, did they? That's the hardest part for me. But then, as far as Gavin's concerned, I have no regrets whatsoever. I wouldn't have wanted to bring up a child single-handed. I couldn't look a little baby in the eye each day and see nothing but Gavin's betrayal. That would have continued throughout the baby's life. I couldn't cope with that."

Pouring our coffee into the cups, I felt her arms around my shoulders and she kissed me on the cheek. "I'm so sorry, Helen. I've dredged up your past and I can see those things still hurt. You don't have to come with me if it is going to cause you more pain, seriously."

"I'm coming with you, Ruby. You want me there and I am going to be there for you. I don't know for sure but I feel that's what David would want. I feel it's the right thing to do. Besides, if helping you through this brings you some comfort, then something good has come from *my* termination. It's helping me be a help to you...if that makes sense? I know what I mean anyway!" I laughed. I noticed some of her tension seemed to have eased. Her shoulders didn't seem as taut when she joined me in trying to bring a little humour into the moment.

We sat watching breakfast T.V. for an hour or so, but I noticed every now and again that she was nervously twisting a tissue around her fingers.

"Would you like me to come with you to the consultation, Ruby? If you do, I'll phone the office and say I'm not well. Not very professional in my business I know, but on this occasion needs must. I'm going in late as it is. I'm staying here until we hear from your Mum."

She considered for a minute or two, toying with an answer, twisting her mouth from side to side and eyes darting all over the place before they looked directly back at me.

"No. I don't think so. I think I'll manage that okay. I'll have Mum with me. As long as you are there on the day… that's the important bit. I'd love that. I really can't thank you enough, Helen, for everything you've done….and *about* to do. How could I *ever* have been so horrible to you? I'm ashamed of myself. I don't deserve you."

Her emotions started to get the better of her again and I didn't want her to bring any more negativity into the equation.

"Please don't ever think like that, Ruby! You were in a bad place at the time. Those dark places have haunted me many times too. None of us can accurately predict how things are going to affect us. I reacted differently to you, but it could so easily have been the opposite for both of us. You have nothing to be ashamed, neither do I. We don't have any reason to berate ourselves. I'll always be here for you. At the outset it was because *David* wanted me to get to know you both. But things have changed. Now I will be here for you because it's *me* who wants it to be that way."

Her tears dried up in no time and nothing further needed saying.

Just after nine I called the office. When Christina's cheery voice answered the ringing after a couple of minutes, I told her that something had cropped up and I would be in the office at some point before lunch.

We didn't have too long to wait for Heidi's call. It was nine thirty when she called with the news. Ruby's appointment was for three thirty pm later in the day. They arranged to meet up at Oxford Circus tube station at three o'clock, giving them plenty of time to walk the short distance to the clinic. Before I headed out at ten to catch my train, I asked her if she would be okay by herself. She gave me her reassurance that she would and said I wasn't to worry.

Once I took a seat on the train, I plucked my phone out of

my handbag and checked to see if I had any messages from the last couple of days. I noticed that there was several from Simon.

Hi Helen, I don't know what has gone on with your house guest, but I hope it isn't anything too traumatic. Simon x

Helen, I hope your guest is doing okay. Hope her stay isn't causing you too much trouble. Hugs. Simon xx

Hello Helen. Do you know yet how long your guest is staying? I'm not pushing or anything like that. I just want to know that you and she are both doing okay. Simon xx

The most recent read…

Hi Helen. Please get in touch as soon as you can. I've been getting rather worried about the pair of you. Just let me know, however brief your text is. Love Simon xxx

I quickly typed out a text in reply.

Hello you. My house guest is Ruby. She's David's youngest daughter. It turns out she's pregnant. We're okay. It's getting sorted. I think she will be staying another week or two. Helen xx

Half an hour later, I was back to it and settled down to start finalising a few client accounts that had been left on my desk for approval by the technicians. Ted popped in to my office for a quick catch up chat. Besides a few client matters, he also informed me that Nina was given the all clear by her consultant and would be coming back to work. She would be returning to the practice in a couple of weeks; part-time for a couple of months until she eased herself back into full-time hours. It was brilliant news. I was thrilled for her that the cancer was caught in time. As our client numbers were steadily on the increase, we would need Nina's expertise. Since her sudden departure, Linda Brownlow's workload had landed on everyone else's desks and we were over-stretched most of the time.

Christina and I popped out for a short while to collect

sandwich orders for some of the staff. By the time we returned it was a short banter in the kitchen and then back to it. As I sat down to pick up where I left off, my mobile bleeped out a text notification. It was from Simon.

Oh my word, Helen. What a shock for you. What a shock for her! How did you deal with that? Glad you're okay. Hopefully, I'll get to see you soon. Text me when she's left please. Simon x

The text left me in doubt whatsoever…he was getting desperate for sex. He was going to be disappointed though. I had no intention of meeting him just yet. Ruby is my priority for now and there's something else that I need to attend to once she's gone home. I tapped out a quick reply.

Hi. Well it won't be happening just yet for a while. Once she's gone home, I'll be flying out to Paris. I have some important business there. Helen.

I barely put the phone down and the swiftest reply ever from Simon pinged through.

What? Why do you have to go to Paris? Do you want me to come with you? Simon x

I bristled at his need to interfere and I could feel myself getting wound up. My hands were shaking as I re-read his last message. Selfish bastard. His needs at the forefront yet again. With my irritation building I flung the phone across my desk and it slid over the surface and onto the carpet. I knew I needed to ignore him before I said something I might regret. My face still burning in anger some minutes later, I got up and stomped off to the kitchen, doing my utmost not to slam every door behind me in disgust. Before I realised what I was doing, I started making everybody a drink. The action calmed me to the extent that I stuck my head into reception to ask Christina what James usually has to drink and how he liked it.

Get your head sorted, Helen!

I didn't intend to take it too far though. Once all the drinks were ready, I asked her if she would oblige where James was concerned and take the cup of tea for him. I told her not to reveal to him that I made it.

The rest of the day passed by at a reasonable pace. Eventually I replied to Simon's last text.

Hi. No, you can't come with me. I'm going to sort out the bastard who made Ruby pregnant – my ex neighbour. I'll be gone a couple of days. Helen x

My backlog was such that I could have done with working late, however, I was keen to get back to Ruby and find out how the consultation had gone. Hopefully, she would have been given a date for the procedure to take place. As she wanted me to be there on the day, I needed to get the time off logged into the office diary.

It was five forty when I walked in through my front door. I could hear music playing, Bon Jovi. I smiled to myself, her taste in music for someone much younger was pretty similar to mine. Obviously, having heard the front door close, she flung the living room door open and greeted me with a sort of half smile. I could tell immediately that her burden was eased.

"I'm half-way through cooking us a meal. Helen, it's all organised. It's happening on Friday at the Chelsea and Westminster Hospital. I'm so relieved it's getting done. Mum said Catherine wants to come along too, for a bit of extra support. What do you think?"

She blurted it all out, without pausing for breath and it took a few seconds for everything to compute in my head. Once it registered, I took her hand and lead her to the sofa. We sat, and still holding her hand, I looked deep into her eyes.

"Okay sweetie, we'll all be there for you, but I don't think they'll like having three of us sitting around waiting all day.

Whilst…whilst it's… being done, we should maybe go out for a coffee and some lunch or something. You won't be allowed to leave there until later in the afternoon. I'm pleased Catherine is coming. That is lovely of her. See how lucky you are…having a sister to look out for you? I missed having a sibling. Treasure her, Ruby. She's one in a million…and so are you! You never had any need to feel you have to be more like Catherine! Everybody needs their own identity! You are *you*…and very much loved."

It seemed to be a constant round of tears and hugs since she turned up on my doorstep. It was good for her…and me too! All part of the healing process that was taking place. We both cried several times that night, but at least they weren't tears of despair and misery!

At one point during the evening I was in a bit of a turmoil when Ruby asked me if she could stay with me on the Friday night and the whole weekend after her termination. Much as I enjoyed her company, I worried about what Heidi would feel. I didn't want her to think that I was encroaching on her territory or that I'd pushed in any way for Ruby to stay longer. Eager to put me at ease, Ruby called her Mum and also let me speak with her for a few minutes. Apparently, Ruby already mentioned to Heidi before the consultation that she wanted to return to mine…just to enjoy a last weekend with me before going home. Catherine also told Heidi that she was hoping to come and stay for the weekend too. Heidi, in no uncertain terms assured me that it wasn't a problem and couldn't thank me enough for being there when Ruby needed me but I suspected that she would prefer to have Ruby back home. She seemed not to have an ounce of malice that her daughter sought me out for a shoulder to cry on. I feel so much admiration for her…David's first wife! It struck me that she is one of the nicest ladies I have ever had the pleasure to know.

After arranging to meet up at eight thirty on the Friday we finished up our call. Heidi, accompanied by Catherine, would be waiting for us. I felt sad about the whole situation and my heart lurched. Ruby would be in the operating theatre, while we would be lunching and maybe hitting a few shops to fill the time in. Knowing, through my personal experience, how she would be feeling when Friday arrived, was a sobering thought with which to end the day.

CHAPTER 5

riday morning was on us all before we knew it. My week just whizzed past at Mach 3. The workload of every staff member in the office seemed never ending. Needing to keep one step ahead in readiness for my day's leave, I worked late on both Tuesday and Wednesday evenings. I wasn't sleeping too well as I found it increasingly difficult to switch off. As it was the eve of her abortion, I was fretting about Ruby until well past three am. I knew her emotions would be all over the place, today probably more so than ever before. Much as she has the support of her Mum, Catherine and myself, it doesn't offer a great deal of consolation to what she will feel inside...and what she is about to go through. Three am was the last time I looked at my alarm clock before nodding off.

After only two or three hours of restless sleep, I felt drained and there was nothing I wanted to do more than turn over and disappear back into the land of the semi-comatose! The pointers on the clock ticked around to five thirty and I groaned out load, knowing that I needed to get out of bed before sleep grabbed me once more, but into a much deeper state. I dragged my feet from bed to bathroom. Standing beneath the hot flow of the shower I closed my mind and tried a little meditation; anything to stop myself dwelling on how the day would unfold. Whilst brushing my teeth ten minutes later, I heard tell-tale sounds of activity in Ruby's room. She was up a little earlier than what I hoped. My main worry was that she hadn't slept, because if she hadn't I don't have much confidence in her being able to keep her emotions in check. It would be a long day if that was the case.

She emerged from her bedroom as I was at the top of the stairs. I guessed correctly. She looked wiped out...but there was a determination about her. Her eyes had dark rings around them yet there was no lethargy present. She seemed to possess an eagerness to get the day over with.

"Morning, Helen. It's here, it's getting done today. I can't wait for it to be gone." She bestowed me with a wan smile.

"I know, sweetheart. I felt just the same when my day arrived. Not long now." I returned her smile. "We'll have a girlie night tonight with Catherine. Hopefully it well get us back on track."

"Wish I could turn the clock forward." She uttered, sounding a bit subdued.

With as much enthusiasm as I could muster to try to give her a bit of a lift by injecting some cheer into my words. "Right...let's get some coffee on the go. But no breakfast for you, liquids only."

Between getting up and until it was time for us to leave, she didn't have much in the way of conversation to offer. She evidently wanted to be quiet and left to her own thoughts and I respected that. I didn't have any wish to try to draw her into meaningless chitchat that she had no wish to partake in. Yet there was still a strange animation about her. No dragging her feet across the floor and everything she did had purpose to it. She ran up the stairs when she noticed it was time for her to get showered and dressed.

Shortly after I heard the flow of the shower cease upstairs, I heard her calling me.

"HELEN?" It sounded urgent. I rushed through to the hallway, a little concerned.

"Yes? What's matter, Ruby? Are you okay?"

"I'm fine...honest. It's just...do I need to take anything with me? A change of clothes or anything?"

I smiled up at her. "No, you don't need anything. Your clothes aren't going to get dirty, sweetheart. What about a little make-up for when it's time to leave the hospital?"

"Right, yes. Thanks!"

She hurried back into her room and before she closed the door behind her, I heard her muttering to herself.

"Okay, you've totally got this, girl!" She was geeing herself up and there was no mistaking the conviction in her voice.

Fifteen minutes later, we were on the train and heading to meet Heidi and Catherine outside the hospital. We sat in silence for most of the journey with Ruby staring straight ahead, lost in her private thoughts. Somewhere near the last minute or so of our journey, she quickly grabbed my hand. I turned to her with a smile, but she was still gazing straight down the aisle...at nothing in particular. It was an indication that she was seeking moral support. I held her hand tight in both of mine and gave her a tight squeeze of the reassurance she sought. Feeling sad for her, my eyes glazed over but I blinked them away, determined not to let her see me upset or worried.

When we reached Heidi and Catherine near the hospital steps nobody said a word. I respectfully stood back a little while her Mum and sister embraced her in silence. At that point she finally succumbed to a few tears, but the strength and determination were still evident. She held herself high and emanated a strong resolve not to break down in any way. I realise that she is much tougher than I at first, gave her credit for.

Seeing her like that...those few seconds when I saw the *real* Ruby, I also recognised myself and exactly who I am. Having always thought of myself as precocious, prissy...and weak, I saw the *real* me. It all fleetingly rushed through my mind; the bullying in school, my own abortion and how alone I was at that time, my so-called husband, the death of my parents, my O.C.D., the abusive clients, and my beloved David's untimely death. I always felt broken and that I never truly 'belonged'. I'd done things I wasn't proud of but basically, I was a good and honest person. I struggled and fought through the lot. Despite everything, my loved ones were in my heart forever and I have beautiful memories to be thankful for. But for a few abrasions and mental scars, (*the* scars), I came through it all almost unscathed...and here I am, being a support to David's daughter. I now know that I am far stronger than I ever thought possible.

I stepped forward as Heidi gave a quick 'it's time' nod to Ruby. I felt flushed with pride for her. I folded my arms around her and whispered.

"Nearly there. You're going to be fine!"

Without any doubt I knew she would be. She hugged me back before breaking away. Catherine and I watched as Heidi took her daughter's hand and gently led her up the steps. She would stay in the hospital with Ruby until it was time for her to go down to theatre. Catherine and I would meet up with her in a short while at a coffee shop in the next street.

As we sat waiting for the waitress to bring our cappuccinos, Catherine's eyes filled up, and I watched the tear drops spill down her cheeks. It hadn't escaped my notice that she had been tight-lipped from the moment I saw her. She hadn't displayed much in the way of emotion, which was likely for

Ruby's sake, so her tears didn't come as a surprise. I reached forward and held her hands in mine.

"This is all my fault, Helen. I should never have let her go off by herself that afternoon in Paris. I should have made her come out shopping with me. I'll never forgive myself."

No sooner were the words out of her mouth, she started sobbing even more. I touched her cheek lightly and then lifted her chin up making her meet my eyes. Through her tears, I saw the desperation and anger towards herself. She held my gaze only briefly before stealing her eyes away from me and back down into the coffee that arrived a few moments ago.

"Catherine! Catherine, look at me, please!" She slowly raised her face and her eyes looked into mine once more. "That's better. Listen, this is *not* your fault. No way. You can't go through life feeling you are responsible for Ruby's actions and mistakes. Everybody makes mistakes in life. God only knows, I've made more mistakes than you'll ever know. But no-one other than me was responsible for them…just as you're not to blame for Ruby's. Does your Mum blame you for this?" I asked of her.

"No, she doesn't. She would never do that!" She answered vehemently.

"Yes, I already know that, Catherine, and Ruby doesn't blame you either. She has admitted to me that nobody's to blame but herself. I know who I'm blaming though…the father! That no good piece of shit is going to get it in the neck from me very shortly, trust me!"

There was the inevitable question in her eyes, but I didn't elaborate. The subject was dropped and we moved on to discuss our imminent weekend and making some plans.

Heidi joined us within the hour and dismissed the idea of sitting down and joining us to have coffee.

"Let's hit the shops please girls. I don't want to sit around thinking about what Ruby's going through. I need some sort of distraction...."

Catherine and I looked at each other. "Okay, let's do it." We replied almost together and simultaneously reached down to grab our handbags off the floor.

Many shops and a tasty lunch later, and with hardly any bags in our grasp, the intention of us all was apparent. Each of us made purchases for Ruby, but nothing for ourselves. Amongst other things, Heidi purchased a cute wooden sign. Its message was simple: *To my beautiful Daughter, You are unique. Never change. I love you unconditionally and with all my heart. Love Mum xxx*

It was so pretty and the words with their significance said it all. She would adore and treasure it forever. Catherine's gift to her sister was a new Michael Kors handbag and I bought her a large glass paperweight which contained a purple heart and a white feather with the words 'In my heart, forever!' I was instantly drawn to it when I spotted...as if guided by David himself. I hoped she would like it. After a last drink in a quaint little coffee house, we headed back to the hospital ready to collect Ruby.

We didn't have to wait too long. A nurse summoned Heidi to take her along to the ward. Ten minutes later they were back, Ruby arm in arm with her Mum. She gave us a glowing smile, the tension in her shoulders of a few short hours ago was gone.

"It's over. I can get on with my life now, can't I?"

My heart went out to her, her relief blatantly obvious. I was relieved and pleased that her nightmare was finally over. As we walked down the street, Heidi turned to Catherine.

"You'll have to come back home with me, sweetheart. You need a bag for the night."

"Oh yes. I got it packed this morning." She turned to face me.

"I'll see you shortly, shouldn't be much longer than an hour or so!" She turned back to Heidi.

"Sorry for leaving you alone, Mum!" Heidi gave her a weak smile, though I saw the sadness in her eyes.

"Heidi? You're going to be alone?"

My guilt hit me in an instant. She was here today for her daughter, and I was taking the pair of them back to my house, when all she probably wanted to do would be to be there for Ruby and keep watch over her after the traumatic procedure she just endured.

"I'll be alright, Helen. Richard is away on business for a few days. It's nothing, really."

I made my mind made up in instant, I blurted it out before I had chance to think too long and hard.

"Erm...then come with us, Heidi. Come to mine and be with your girls. It makes sense. That's if you don't mind...and it doesn't feel a bit weird to you? I've only got three bedrooms, but there's a twin. You can share with Catherine, or if you want to be with Ruby tonight, Catherine can have the room that Ruby's been using." I watched her face for a reaction, and it seemed like forever before she replied. Catherine and Ruby stared open-mouthed, probably in disbelief at what was unfolding in front of them.

"Helen, how kind of you. Are you absolutely sure? I would hate to feel like I was put..."

"It's not putting me to any trouble whatsoever, and I'm one hundred percent sure. It's either that or the girls come home to you. I know they *should* be with you. I don't want to be guilty of stealing them from you this weekend when I know that you would rather have them with you."

Her face broke into a warm smile. I could see the gratitude there. She hugged me and placed a lingering kiss on my cheek.

"Thank you so much, Helen. How thoughtful of you. I would love to."

This was surreal! The strangest, most peculiar sort of surreal and I couldn't quite believe it. David's first wife and two daughters were staying with me for the weekend. After a few seconds I snapped out of my stunned silence, trying to act as normal as I could possibly manage.

"So what happens now?"

I addressed the question to them all. It was Heidi who replied.

"Simple, we all go back home to ours on the train and then I'll drive us all over to Maida Vale. I can throw some things into a bag for myself...it won't take me long."

I was still in disbelief as I turned the key in my door just short of an hour later.

Well, this promises to be a weekend with a difference!

CHAPTER 6

*A*rriving at Heidi and Richard's home after we
walked the short distance from Kensington High
Street, I was stunned by its beauty. It was a very large and
desirable residence. I had a rough idea of the cost of a prop-
erty in the area and was impressed. As much as good fortune
shone on me, thanks to my parents and David, Heidi's ex, I
suddenly felt like the poor relation. That said, I've never been
particularly materialistic so I quickly dismissed the thought.
Heidi has obviously done well for herself having met Richard
and therefore married to a millionaire yet again.

She unlocked the front door and pushed me in ahead of
the three of them, and proceeded to fuss about and make me
welcome. She showed me where everything was in the
kitchen and asked if I wanted to make us all a drink. Nobody
seemed interested in another drink so I stood admiring the
kitchen layout while she headed up to her room to grab a few
items for the weekend. After a few minutes she called me
upstairs and gave me a quick tour once she'd packed her bag.
Every room boasted something unique about it and the
décor was amazing. She had so much and yet the airs and

graces that usually came hand in hand with such affluence were absent from her personality. Heidi is as down to earth as it is possible to be; she exuded compassion, warmth and humility.

Catherine's bag had already been left in the hallway, so once I had my tour we were good to go. Ruby's demeanour had changed and she seemed a little quiet but I could see no signs that gave me cause for concern. It was to be expected that she would be feeling a little thoughtful. When her Mum asked if she was okay she replied that she was looking forward to our girlie weekend. It didn't take too long before Ruby and I were loading Heidi's car with the bags. She suddenly glanced up and laughed. Heidi was descending the steps with two wine carriers.

I laughed and shouted at her.

"We won't need you to take up space in the car with those, Heidi. I have a pretty good stock of wines and spirits. I also keep a stock of Fosters for when the girls are staying."

She grinned back.

"Well...perhaps just one then. I'll take the second one back in the house." I shook my head in amusement.

"Mum's always been scared of running out of things... anything at all. You should see the toilet roll cupboard!" Ruby declared.

"You've got a cupboard for toilet rolls?" I asked naively.

"Take no notice of her, Helen. At least her sense of humour has returned."

Catherine chuckled. Understanding I'd just been had, I tut tutted at myself in disgust before joining in with their laughter.

Twenty minutes later we arrived at mine. We climbed out of the car, removed the bags and I carefully guided Heidi as she reversed into my double garage. It was a bit of a tight squeeze and she had to scramble over the passenger seat to carefully get out without scraping her door on the garage wall. We entered the kitchen through the side door from the garage.

"Heidi, Catherine, make yourselves at home. Take your bags up and I'll have a look in the freezer and see what we can have for dinner."

"What? Oh no! You're not spending the weekend cooking for us all, Helen. None of us are. It's a special girlie weekend. I won't hear of it. My shout...we're having takeaway tonight, because Ruby needs to rest. Tomorrow night, we can eat out, somewhere posh! I know I'm sounding a bit controlling and bossy, sorry. I just think we all need to let our hair down after...after today. Everybody agree?" Heidi asked of us all.

I was grateful for her input as I didn't really relish the thought of cooking.

"Well, yes. It sounds like an excellent plan to me! I'll make us a drink while you all decide whether it's Chinese, Indian, Italian or whatever. I could eat any of those but we'll go with the majority. I'm happy. Heidi, do you want coffee or something stronger?"

"A coffee...then let's hit the hard stuff! It's been one of those days. We deserve it."

By the time coffee was made, we reached a unanimous decision; a variety of Indian cuisine that we could all dip in to. Catherine called the number on a menu she found in one of my kitchen drawers and placed our order. There was a rather awkward silence while we sipped at our coffee. I wasn't sure exactly what thoughts were running through their minds, but what had crossed mine, was what Ruby endured that day. It was almost like we'd gathered for a party, with plans for drinking and having fun. Somehow it felt wrong, dreadfully wrong. I found myself scanning her face a little too often and hoped she hadn't noticed the fact. Perhaps Heidi and the girls thought that this scenario was a little surreal and that was the reason for their silence...to be staying for the weekend in the home of their Dad's last lover with none other than their own Mum. It was a rather unusual situation, but then again, Heidi had no axe to grind with me, nor I with her. I wasn't able to tell exactly how they were all feeling but maybe each individual's lack of conversation was for entirely different reasons. The only quiet I could fully comprehend was that of Ruby. She had a bloody good reason.

It took forty five minutes for the delivery to arrive and in no time at all we were sat around the dining table tucking into the scrumptious Indian fare, and at last...chatting. The awkward silence of earlier had passed. Catherine and Ruby both had the obligatory can of Fosters to hand, Heidi was halfway down a bottle of red and I was on my second G & T. The drink certainly helped transition us into what was a much lighter atmosphere.

After a while, David's name cropped up in the conversation and though I was taken aback, I should have known that it would be inevitable. I was aware of Heidi watching me carefully as we listened to some of the stories the girls related. I don't know whether they half expected me to be upset but I coped with it fairly well. It was a pleasure to learn more about him; his generosity, his warmth and kind, caring nature...everything he bestowed on me too. Knowing Heidi as I had come to do over the last few days, it didn't surprise me that David chose her for a wife all those years ago. It said a lot about me too. Clearly, David looked for his own qualities to also be present in his life partners. It was a great comfort.

We remained at the table for a little while after we finished eating and presented Ruby with the gifts we purchased for her. As I expected, when she saw the wooden heart sign and its message, she was on her feet and straight to

Heidi's side immediately. She hugged her fiercely. She both cried and smiled through the opening of her presents. She did the same to Catherine and I. She loved all of her presents, but I could see she was embarrassed too.

"Thank you all so much. I don't know...how disgraceful of you all to be shopping while I went under the knife! No, seriously there was no need to buy me presents, much as I love every last one of them. The best thing you could do for me is what you're doing right now. You've all been so supportive today and the horrible days before. You're all here with me for the whole weekend and that is the best present ever!"

We were in tears at that...hugging Ruby, hugging each other. It was the warmth of the whole thing. Probably for the first time in my life, I didn't feel like an outsider. These girls were my family, and I considered Heidi to fall in that bracket too. I could sense that David was giving us his full approval. It felt right.

Ruby only drank the one Fosters all night and by nine thirty she'd gone to bed leaving us all to our ongoing bonding session. I suspected that she felt like having some 'alone time' to go over and accept in her mind what was done...the ordeal which she'd gone through earlier in the day. The rest of us exchanged unspoken, knowing looks as Ruby left the room. Even Heidi, concerned as she was, knew to leave her alone for a while.

Heidi and I chatted, occasionally stopping to recharge our glasses while Catherine sat cross-legged on the floor, busy on her mobile and playing with Harry. I couldn't fathom whether she was playing games or frantically messaging friends, but eventually she tired of it and threw the phone over her shoulder onto the armchair against which her back was propped. She reached to grab the remote for the T.V.

"Can I see if there are any films we could watch please, Helen?

"Feel free sweetie, there's no need to ask. See what there is, if there's anything interesting maybe we could watch too, unless your Mum is happy to keep chatting of course?" I enquired of Heidi.

"Don't worry on my account, either of you. I'm easy to please."

Ten minutes later we settled down to watch "The Edge of Reason", second film in the Bridget Jones series, but half an hour before the film ended, Catherine yawned constantly and disappeared off to bed. We watched the film until the credits rolled and with Heidi's nod of agreement, I switched the television off. She was warm and entertaining and I was happy and comfortable in her company. The conversation drifted free and easy from one subject to another. We talked about her marriage to David, how it came to end and that naturally led to my own relationship with him. I was a little guilty of rushing through my answers. The most difficult part was having to gloss over a few white lies about how we met. I wondered how David explained that one to Heidi and the girls when he told them all about me. In the time I had spent with Catherine and Ruby they never disclosed exactly what he said to them all about me. I made a mental note to pick my moment and ask Catherine one day.

It took longer than an hour to relate the story of my nightmare relationship with Anthony; his horrible parents, the tragic deaths of mine during that time, his sexual tendencies and the drug thing which subsequently led to his imprisonment. I'd already told her the story of Gavin and my abortion. She was easy to confide in and before I realised what I was doing, I blurted out the story of the girls from work and our night out at the Lamb and Flag. Seeing my tears when I told her about his rape of me during the early hours of the morning, she moved closer to hand me the box of tissues. She shook her head in disbelief.

"Oh my God, Helen. What a bastard. You've had enough crap to last you a lifetime…and then to lose David. I don't know how you've ever found the strength to carry on. Life is unfair to us all at times, but you've gone through more heartache than most. Bless you." And with that she hugged me close to her, and kissed my forehead.

With the easy way in which we conversed, we hadn't noticed the time slipping away, two thirty five am. We giggled like schoolgirls as we tiptoed up the stairs, trying not to wake Catherine and Ruby. However, one of them was awake.

"Night Mum, night Helen!" Ruby shouted out.

We exchanged glances and realised that she had probably laid awake for hours reflecting on her traumatic day. Heidi gave me a questioning look which I read to mean 'Should we go in?' I gave her a nod and waited as she went in first.

There was dried tear tracks down both cheeks, but she was sat up in bed trying to read.

"Do you want some company?" Heidi asked her. She nodded back and Heidi lifted the duvet and pushed her way beside the girl, putting a comforting arm around her shoulder. I grabbed a large throw from out of the bottom of the wardrobe, wrapped it around myself and sat on a chair beside the bed. However, Ruby didn't want conversation, she just needed the company and comfort from her mother. I sat for a while and decided to leave Mum and daughter to have some quality time.

On the Saturday morning, Catherine and I were first up. We sat around in the kitchen waiting for the others to come down. It was mostly Ruby who we chatted about. Before too long, Heidi came down and joined us. I made a fresh pot of coffee and we started to throw some ideas into the mix of how we would spend Saturday afternoon and evening. I was happy to do whatever the majority vote came up with, thinking that a lovely walk in the countryside might be their choice, but we would make a final decision on what Ruby wanted to do when she finally came downstairs. The weekend was about her after all. Anything that would seem normal and make her happy was fine by the rest of us.

Once Ruby was up at eleven, showered and dressed, we sat around in the living room with coffee and toast asking her what she preferred to do. I should not have been surprised by her answer, as Heidi and Catherine had predicted what it would be.

"Please can we go into the city for a mega shopping sesh? And I mean…*mega!* Let's spend a small fortune. I want some new clothes and bits and pieces. *Pleeeaasse?*"

Catherine smiled at her. Being a practical type like her dad, she was not a shopping sort of girl, but as a one-off I could see that she would make an exception to the rule for her little sister, especially this weekend.

"I don't really need anything, but I'm more than happy to see you all having a good spend. Let's do it. We'll do some retail therapy until the shops close and then can we go down to Docklands and find somewhere nice to eat? Are you all in?"

The decision was unanimous and with our plans for the day finalised we started to get ready to go and catch the train into central London.

What an afternoon it was. We started with a snack in a little bistro opposite Harrods before finally hitting the famous store itself. For someone who wasn't big on shopping, Catherine was the one who came away from there with more bags than the rest of us. The January sales were still on, so maybe she just liked bargains. Our visit to the store took up a fair amount of time, but we still managed to hit quite a few of the designer shops around Knightsbridge, which added to our combined baggage. We were laden down and decided to take a taxi down to Docklands rather than risking the tube with our purchases. It meant that we would also need a taxi to get back to Maida Vale, but that wasn't a worry.

After wandering around the place for half an hour we chose a restaurant where neither of us had eaten before, Plateau. It was situated in Canada Square and was a French/European eaterie.

They boasted an extensive menu which made it difficult for us to choose. After changing our minds a few times we all selected the grilled Queen scallops for our first course. For main courses, Catherine and Heidi selected sea bass with fennel and Ruby and I opted for Romney Marsh lamb cutlets with Korean spices. The food was exceptional and the service was amazing. The desserts rounded off the meal nicely and as I was tucking in rather enthusiastically, my addiction to sweet food obvious for them all to see, Ruby stopped me dead in my tracks with a question which stalled me for a moment.

"Helen, I've been meaning to ask you…when I turned up on your doorstep that day…you know which day…who was the guy who left? He seemed nice."

Her question totally threw me and I stuttered, struggling how to answer it.

"Oh, sorr…sorry Ruby. The…shock just flooded back through my head. Seeing you standing there, looking heart-broken. I'll never forget it. That …that man was Simon…*is* Simon. He's the guy who first introduced me to your father. He's been a great support to me since David's death. I would still be living the life of a hermit…holed up in my apartment in Paris if it wasn't for him."

All eyes were on me expectantly as I ran each line

through my head a couple of times before letting the lies spill from my mouth. Simon hadn't been around at all for the six months I had been in Paris. It was only because he needed to speak to me urgently regarding Anthony that he called me. I continued telling the story.

"As it turned out, Simon was prosecuting for the Crown in the case my husband was involved in with the other scumbags. I had to come back to London to go through things with him in readiness for the court case. He told me that I was doing myself no good at all hiding from the world. After a couple of trips back and forth between London and Paris he made me see sense. Ted Hopkins, my senior partner at the practice also coerced me into returning to work. I'm grateful to them both for their friendship. They've been amazing. I should never have ran away in the first place. I would have had more support over her."

"Is this the lawyer, Simon Banks, Helen?"

She caught me by surprise, I hadn't envisaged her asking me that. I hadn't thought for a second that she would even know him.

"Yes, the same one. That's him."

"I met him a couple of times at functions I attended with David. He's nice enough, but what a womaniser, isn't he?"

I forced a couple of laughs at the comment, but I was still feeling uncomfortable and uneasy with the fact that she knew him.

"Yes! Yes, he can be. I think once you put him in his place a few times he actually respects you more for it."

Heidi howled, clearly finding it hilarious and I joined in, hoping it would provide me with cover for being economical with the truth. I was grateful when Catherine provided a distraction by pointing out a famous celebrity and his equally well-known boyfriend at the far end of the dining room. The topic of Simon was swiftly forgotten. As Heidi settled the bill, a member of staff took us to a room at the side of the kitchen where they had kindly stashed our shopping bags earlier so that clientele and waiting staff alike wouldn't trip over them throughout the evening.

It was just after ten fifteen when we arrived back at Elgin Mews. Once Heidi and I were armed with gin and tonics and Catherine and Ruby with a Fosters each, we made ourselves comfortable with our shopping bags in the living room, unpacking our day's purchases and showing off to each other. Catherine (who had excelled herself with her bargain seeking skills and made the most purchases) and Ruby were chatting and in unison came out with a suggestion.

"We should have a fashion show. Let's see how we all vote on our purchases."

"Okay, let's do it then. Is that okay with you, Helen? It's your house after all and it's already looking like a bloody department store in here."

I laughed.

"It'll be fun. I'm up for it."

We had a fabulous time, taking off, trying on and showing off our purchases. Everything was given the seal of approval. I don't think any of us made a purchase that we didn't like. The only items I left hidden at the bottom of a bag were some new underwear. We all purchased underwear but some of mine was a little too naughty to show off. I didn't want the girls to think the wrong thing. They would have been correct if they had, but I didn't want them to guess that I was involved with any man.

Ruby disappeared upstairs about half past eleven and looking at Heidi and Catherine, I think they were thinking the same as I did, that she had disappeared up to bed without a word. Five minutes later, she was back down wearing pyjamas and carrying a pillow and the duvet off her bed.

"Ruby? What…?"

"I just want to get comfortable. I hope you don't mind, Helen?" She asked looking very sheepish.

Heidi looked at me dubiously before starting to speak her mind.

"Ruby, I don't think that's…"

"Nonsense, Heidi. I think Ruby just got me to thinking it's not a bad idea. I'll go and get my peejays on too. These denims are killing me after that meal. Anyone care to join us both? Catherine? Heidi? Come on, let's camp out. We've got booze and nibbles."

They looked at each other, shrugged their shoulders and probably thought that Ruby and I had lost our marbles.

"There's plenty of duvets with covers on in the wardrobes. Help yourselves. Let's do something different."

With that we all scattered to our bedrooms and ten minutes later, we'd cleansed faces of make-up, donned peejays and brought down duvets and pillows. We giggled around the kitchen like school girls, gathering up crisps, nuts and easy snacks and carried them through to the living room with drinks and glasses. For a while we watched a chick flick…Dirty Dancing to be precise but as the drink took hold we started getting quite raucous. Heidi was letting her hair down and I loved it. The more I was getting to know about her, the more I liked her. She was just so natural and normal…no airs and graces which one would have expected taking into account where she lived and how much money she and Richard had. She was no snob and was certainly up for plenty of fun.

Ruby and Catherine, seeing as their Mum and me were getting drunk took advantage of the situation and started asking us both about secrets from our younger days and some of the things we got up to in our teens. Did we ever smoke weed or take ecstacy…questions like that. There were times it got quite personal…like asking how old we were when we lost our virginity and had either of us ever been caught by anyone when we were having sex. Like Heidi did, I made a few things up to keep them amused. And their constant questions certainly kept me amused.

"Did you really get caught in your Mum and Dad's bathroom, Helen? Gosh I bet you were for the high jump?"

We never stopped laughing, but Heidi and I both made them wait a while before telling them the truth.

"Damn! You had us fooled there, Helen," and "Mum, I didn't realise you were so naughty."

We were thoroughly enjoying ourselves. We played some silly games as well. Ruby asked if I had Trivial Pursuit, but it was quarter to four when she asked, by which time most of us were too far gone to be able to answer trivial pursuit questions. Catherine was the first of us to give in to sleep, shortly followed by Heidi. They were at opposite ends of the sofa and there seemed to be a large mound of bedclothes on the top of them. They would be bound to wake up too hot during the night. Ruby was giggling quietly so as not to wake them up.

"Should...should we go to sl...sleep too...too...Helen?" She uttered between yawns. "I don't want to wake them up. It's been a long tiring day, hasn't it?"

"It sure has. Have you enjoyed yourself? I've thoroughly every minute of it Ruby. I love you all to bits and I've loved having you all around me this weekend. It's just what I needed. At times like this I really wish I had a sister."

I was already on a folded duvet on the floor and Ruby came over to give me a massive hug. She fell asleep in my arms. I silently let a few tears fall. My emotions were running riot and I knew I was going to miss them all terribly. When Heidi and Catherine were leaving on Sunday afternoon, Ruby would be returning home with them. I felt a massive wrench in my gut. She had been staying with me for over two weeks. It was going to be pretty quiet.

On Sunday we were up and about reasonably early considering our lateness to settle down the previous night. After a lovely brunch prepared by Ruby, we drove out into the country and spent a wonderful few hours walking and having some fun. I was making the most of my time with them as I wasn't too sure when I would see them next.

It was gone seven when they left my house and not only Catherine and Ruby but Heidi too, promised to stay in touch. She held my face in her hands for a minute, looking me deep in the eyes.

"Helen, don't ever be a stranger, please. I have really enjoyed staying with you this weekend, and having my girls close to me too! I want you to come and visit us in our home too! You'll always be welcome. Just give me a ring when you fancy a night out or even if it's just some company you want."

I felt very weepy at their departure. Despite the fact that Ruby had her abortion on the Friday, it had all been put to the back of their minds for now. My mind was torn…missing them but I was on a high as well. It was one of the happiest weekends of my life and I hoped there would be further opportunities to spend time with them.

CHAPTER 7

*A*lthough I originally told myself I would return to Maida Vale to see Helen in a month's time, I suppose I knew back then that my resolve would eventually weaken.

When I saw that girl arrive on Helen's doorstep with a bloody great suitcase, I was extremely pissed off about it, even though it didn't necessarily have to mean much. I had to remind myself over and over again that it didn't automatically follow she was there for an extended or more permanent stay. She was a teenager after all and kids fall out with their parents constantly. Maybe that's what the problem is...and if so, true to form she would likely return to her parents in a couple of days, if not the next morning. Perhaps Helen will have talked her into going home.

The night I witnessed her arrival, I felt cheated out of my long awaited chance to make a move after month upon month of persistently stalking Helen. Once I arrived back at my apartment I wasted valuable hours asking myself the same questions repeatedly. Who was she? A younger sister? I couldn't recall whether Helen even had a younger sibling during our years at school, but if she was a sister there must be fair age gap between them. Perhaps she was a friend! I quickly talked myself out of that one, thinking that she was a little young to be included in Helen's circle of friends. After a couple of hours turning these thoughts over and over in my head and adding to my personal agony, I started with a headache. I tried to switch off from my inner confusion and resorted to watching some film on Freeview which resulted in me staring through the T.V. screen instead of paying attention to it.

The film didn't appeal to me after all and after twenty, or at a push twenty five minutes, it went steadily downhill as I let thoughts of Helen and her guest creep into my head yet again. After a spark of genius I came up with yet another theory...the visitor could perhaps be a work colleague.

The major factor that was causing me more than a little mental turmoil was the man who left Helen's house shortly after the girl arrived. Who exactly was he? I felt more than a twinge of jealousy eat me up every time I allowed him to enter my head. Surely he would be too old to be a lover of Helens and somehow it didn't sit well with me that he could possibly be her father. If my gut feeling is correct though, he's definitely not her father...he can't be.

Time after time I gave myself a severe bollocking whenever I let the image of him creep into my mind, if only to try and block out the green-eyed monster in me. I could be completely on the wrong track with all my mixed up thoughts and I hope there is a simple explanation for everything.

As I waited for sleep to arrive, I started to make plans to travel to Maida Vale yet again. I couldn't wait for a whole month. First and foremost in my mind was that I needed to know whether the visiting girl was still there. It was eating away at me with a vengeance. I couldn't concentrate on my job. I am totally incapable of relaxing on an evening. Something has to give. My pacing around the flat is making me dizzy.

I ruled out travelling up there on a night after work. It's January, nights are still dark. The girl could be holed up in Helen's house all week without ever showing her face outdoors. Trying to think logically, I toyed with the fact that women in general usually *enjoy shopping trips on a weekend. Nodding to myself at my own ingenuity, I decided it had to be a Saturday. If the young woman was still at Helen's surely they would do something on a weekend that would be typically girlie. I felt pretty confident that by the time I completed another 'watch', I would know if she was still there or not.*

A few days later...

Saturday arrived at last, and when I opened my bedroom curtains I wasn't impressed to see the weather. It was raining like a fucking bitch. For fuck's sake! Why today of all days? I sat mulling it over in my mind while I drank my coffee. I couldn't take my eyes of the persistent trickles of rain down the outside of the window. I felt a deep depression setting in. At times I could hear the wind howling and what should be a gentle pitter patter increased in volume until it sounded like heavy hailstones beating at the glass. The longer the weather continued to hammer it down the more I leaned towards abandoning my plans completely. Two minutes if that, of standing on Helen's street corner and I would be piss-wet through. Unlike being stationed outside her office, there were no shop doorways in which I could stay dry and remain covert. I pictured myself on the journey back home on the train absolutely drenched, it wasn't appealing to say the least. There was only one thing to do, I would have to forget about it for today...unless...

It was the only option if I wanted to go today, I would drive over there in the car. I know it's a bit of a gamble. I would more than likely struggle to get parked anywhere in the area, but at least if I'm fortunate enough, I can keep an eye on things and manage to stay dry. I wasn't thrilled about making the journey. I hate driving within the Greater London area, but on this occasion I need to. I started to get myself ready.

By the time I left home, the clock had ticked away towards eleven am. I started feeling a little dubious as it occurred to me, that if it was too fucking wet for me to stand and keep watch on a street corner, it would be highly likely that it was too wet for two ladies, as may be the case, to head out to the shops.

I'd been on the road for ten minutes or so and it struck me how light the traffic was. The weather was probably causing a major issue for some and I could empathise with them. Not a lover of driving at the best of times, especially in city centres, and then with the windscreen wipers on top speed...well, it was one of my worst nightmares, and here I am, living it!

Just before setting off I entered the specific post code for Elgin Mews South. Although I knew the area well enough from many years ago, I was unfamiliar with which roads are one-way and which aren't. I was relying on the satnav to safely guide me as to keeping on the right side of the law. The only thing I knew for certain was that I could not park down the little cobbled street itself. I could drive down it and come out of the other end, but I didn't really want to take the risk. Mulling these thoughts over in my head as I drove, I could feel the stress building and tension was settling in in my neck and shoulders. I was going to hate this latest mission, I just knew it.

Driving up Elgin Avenue, I started indicating left into Randolph Avenue, before my satnav had even instructed me. Randolph Avenue is where Maida Vale tube station is situated. I had come to know it well of late. As my car came adjacent with the arch leading into Helen's street, said satnav announced 'you have reached your destination'.

"Sure I have...but where to park? Answer me that if you can!" I uttered out loud as I kept on driving, or to put it more accurately...crawling...down Randolph Avenue.

I allowed myself to get so wound up thinking about my current plight, it had escaped my notice that the rain had stopped. The worn rubber of my windscreen wipers started making that horrible screeching sound across the glass that suddenly alerted me. I chanced a look up at the sky for a second instead of scouring the street for somewhere to park...the clouds had gone and there was a beautiful blue sky. I smiled to myself. Now if only I can find some-where to dump my bloody vehicle, I can go and take up my semi-resident spot on the corner near the arch. I carried on driving down the road until I reached Sutherland Avenue, realising that I could turn left, then left again down into Lanark Road, and back onto Elgin Avenue. Hopefully, I can find somewhere to park around this block.

Before I had chance to curse each of the individual roads for having no available parking, I was back to where I started my tour of the block - Elgin Avenue. Indicating left once more and turning into Randolph Avenue, I was instantly distracted. Helen was just coming out from under the arch and the blonde girl was with her. They were being followed by a tall, blonde woman who from a quick glance, I guessed would be a good deal older than Helen. There was a dark haired girl walking with her. I carried on driving, taking a long lingering look through my rear view mirror. I saw Helen and the girl turn round to face the other two ladies. Some-body must have said something funny as I noticed they all started laughing. All four were seemingly together. "Damn it! FUCK it!" In seconds they disappeared out of my view due to the cars parked at the kerb side. I had to keep on driving down the street.

More fucking things to further cause me confusion. What is going on here? Are they all staying at Helen's house? If so...for how long? The only slight consolation was that my parking dilemma was now no longer an issue. I switched the CD player on...some-thing to attempt to find a distraction and keep me calm. I now needed to concentrate on driving back home and the roads are suddenly laden with fucking traffic.

"FOR FUCK'S SAKE!" I yelled out loud and banged my hands on the steering wheel. For once my anger wasn't aimed at other drivers!

CHAPTER 8

"*How* come you've delayed your visit to Paris? I thought you would have sorted the bastard by now. I was surprised to get your text. Of course I wanted to come over for the night. I feel honoured. I thought I was out of favour again." He barely paused for breath.

He just knocked on the door, barely gave me time to open it and walked in before being asked. Furthermore, was already being his usual irritable self, as was his way. I pulled him further into the hall so that I could close the door behind him. *Hellfire!* I didn't want anyone in the neighbourhood to overhear our conversation. The sarcasm in his voice when he said 'I feel honoured' summed him up. Most of the time he just didn't fucking think. I could feel my heart start to race but with anger rather than horniness.

"At least do me the courtesy of getting through the door and letting me close it before looking for a row. You'll have my neighbours curtain-twitching. You're being an arrogant shit, Simon. I thought you would be pleased I asked you around? If you're going to be obnoxious, you might as well just g…"

He'd been in my presence for less than sixty seconds and was already giving me grief.

"Helen! I'm sorry! Calm down, I didn't mean it to come out like that. I was a little frustrated and fucking narked to be honest. I had to go about cancelling my hotel booking. I wouldn't have bothered with the hotel if I'd known you delayed your plan to fuck off to Paris!"

I could see that he was trying his best to keep the irritation out of his voice in an attempt to calm me, but then blamed me for him having to cancel his hotel booking. I felt anything but calm. I gritted my teeth. Not trusting myself to speak, I walked through to the kitchen to pour some drinks but the way it was going I was likely to kick him out before giving him the opportunity to even have a glass of red.

"Helen, please let's not be like this!"

I thought I left him standing in the hall but he followed me through. Before I got the chance to uncork a bottle of wine, one of his arms was around my waist. With his free hand, he pushed my hair from my neck and began kissing and sucking on it in a very provocative and sensual manner. He knew my weaknesses…every last one of them. The b*astard!* I went from furious to wanting him in a split second.

He whispered close to my ear.

"Babe, I want to fuck you so bad. It's been ages, my cock has never had such a long boring time and he's desperate to be where he likes it best… buried inside your wetness! We're going to have just one drink and I'm taking you up to bed… No. I'm going to fuck you down here…fuck your brains out! Does that sound good, sweetie?"

Carry on sucking my neck right in that spot and you won't even get a drink, buddy. I'll have you fuck me on the kitchen floor!

My arms were out to the side, one hand still clutched the bottle of wine. I carefully placed it back on the counter. My hands were shaking as I experienced my first waves of sexual desire in…fuck, had it really been only three weeks? I pushed a hand behind my back to edge between his body and mine; to push gently against the front of his trousers. He was already semi-hard. My body shuddered in anticipation. I wanted him; positively ached for him.

"Oh baby! I can tell that sounds good to you. Can you feel my cock getting hard for you? You want me to fuck you! When? Right here and now? On the kitchen floor? Do you want me to fuck you hard with your bare arse slapping on the cold tiles? Tell me you want it. Tell me what you want… and I'll happily oblige." His voice was next to muted; almost whispering those last few words and his breathing became laboured. "Tell…me!"

"Please…Simon!" I gasped, ripples of excitement coursing through my stomach and in my pubic region. God knows, I wanted him bad!

"Please…what…Helen? Tell…me…"

He pulled me around to face him. One hand proceeded to unfasten my blouse. With the other, he edged his way up my skirt and between my thighs. I opened my legs for him to make it easier.

"Plea…please…Simon! I want…you…to…to fuck…me! Now!"

I shuddered in pleasure as his fingers forced a way into my warmth, his tongue entered my mouth simultaneously. He pulled it back out demanding to know more.

"Good! That's so…fucking good…baby! But…tell me… what you…want!"

He tormented me…tormented me in the way that I love best; verbally! It never fails to turn me on. I love hearing his dirty words and what they do to me. I craved his cock. My warmth and dampness needed him inside me in every way possible.

"Please…fuck me…fuck me ha…"

A judder from me, my nerves, every one of them alight. I closed my eyes, savouring each tingle of my orgasm as it arrived. He hit my g-spot during his probing and I soaked his fingers with cum. It felt phenomenal and I wanted the feeling to continue but I groaned in frustration as he withdrew his fingers. There was a brief moment of beautiful pain as he bit into my right breast. As his movement suggested, he unfastened and lowered his trousers and boxers. I started to kneel so that I could take his cock into my mouth. He pulled me back up by one arm, clearly not wanting it. Once I was upright again, he pulled roughly at my panties and tights, yanking them down my legs to my ankles.

"No, Helen! You…can do that…later!" He lowered his voice to a growl, his breathing steadying for a moment. "Right now, I'm going to bury my cock in you. I'm going to fuck you so hard, you're going to be screaming, sweetie."

I let out a desperate groan of disappointment. I wanted to gaze at his length and anticipate…imagine the beautiful specimen thrusting in and out of my warmth. I felt the wetness pool between my legs.

"Si…Simon, please?" I begged.

"Later… sweet cheeks. Get on the floor. You want me to fuck you hard and I'm going to…and then some. Scream for me, angel! Cum for me! Scream when you cum. It turns me on to hear you scream."

He took me in his arms and lowered me to the floor, shoving his cock hard into me without any guidance as his weight descended on me. He thrust furiously. I savoured every hard push as his cock touched the top of my depth. I clenched tight around him with every hard shove he made. He was driving me wild. Our desperate moves were clumsy, our mouths searching each other's, my hair frequently in the way and I was constantly trying to pull strands of it out of my mouth as our tongues cavorted and danced together in the throes of our wild and desperate fucking. His pace started to slow but became more intense; he almost stopped and then thrust even deeper and with more force. The fingers and thumb of his right hand rubbed frantically at my clit and my stomach ached with need. The feeling inside me was intense, my mind racing ahead in anticipation of my next release.

"Now...scream...out loud...for me...Helen. Scream...loud....and cum. Cum...all...over...my...cock!"

His words were punctuated with every deep, hard thrust he made. My clit was alive, the nerves inside of me taut, then quivering...my body juddered and I screamed at the top of my voice as I let go...my cum drenched his dick...

"FUUUUUU---UCK MEEE!"

I felt his release just seconds later and my orgasm continued...my body jerked in ecstasy during each of his manic thrusts. His groan was almost as loud as my scream. We lay there breathless for the next five minutes, spent. I flushed with pleasure, still waiting for my orgasm to fully dissipate. He held me tight to him until our gasps once again steadied to more even breathing. I smiled up at him, my eyes feeling heavy, and I wished we managed to get upstairs to the bedroom. My bottom started to feel the chill from the floor tiles as it penetrated my skin. I shivered.

We didn't speak. He dragged himself into a kneeling position before pushing himself up and getting his lower clothing back in order. Groaning with fatigue, I took myself upstairs to get showered, remembering my lack of sleep of both the Friday and Saturday nights. Even Sunday hadn't been much of an improvement. I was desperate for sleep and the prospects of that luxury were not looking particularly good for tonight.

I flopped down on the sofa fifteen minutes later in what I can only imagine would look like...a slump. He handed me a gin and tonic. He was wearing a puzzled look on his face.

"Sweetie? What's with the frown? Are you sulking? What have I done now?"

I screwed up my face and gave him a twisted grin I didn't feel.

"You haven't done anything. Well, you pissed me off when you arrived but I'm over it. No! It's not you. I'm knackered after my weekend with the girls, and I slept like shit last night. Oh…and add to that, it's been the day from Hell in the office. A great day. Not!"

I shocked myself at the selfish outburst, and regretted it instantly. My cheeks began to burn with embarrassment and I uttered a "Sorry!" As weak as it sounded to my own ears.

"Babe, I'm sorry to hear that. Would you like me to go? I will, if you'd rather be alone and then you can get a good night's sleep? I'm sorry about my irritability when I arrived on your doorstep. I am. I've added to your woes."

He stroked my hand, kissing my cheek gently at the same time. I softened.

"No. Stay please! Sorry, I lashed out. You haven't added to my woes at all. You had me in the kitchen…not so long ago, remember? I needed that. Probably more than even you realise. It was good…but maybe we can better it later?" I offered.

"If I stay, I'll cuddle you until you fall asleep. You're shattered and I'm not that selfish that I would deprive you of sleep, Helen. I know you *think* you can a do a second round, but…" I didn't want to hear anymore. I wanted to lose myself in him again. I cut him off, rather rudely.

"No. I…"

"Yes. You! You are going to sleep. I've fucking seen you this tired…remember the court case? I was hard on you then, too. The subject is *not* open for debate Helen! You are going to sleep tonight. Anything else can wait…and it's no good looking at me with those sad doe eyes. Close your mouth. I don't want to hear another word. Finish your drink. I'll bring you another. Then…*bed!*"

I smiled, bossy as he is, it was hard not to. I felt such a rush of affection for him, my bossy, obnoxious, yet caring, fuck buddy.

We sat down to watch, or rather *he* did, some traffic cop re-runs, his favourites for some crazy reason. I was staring at the screen but not interested. I could feel his eyes studying me; felt them burning into me and I guessed there would be more questions. I wasn't wrong.

"Helen, you're not watching T.V. so stop pretending and go up to bed. I'll come up shortly. You're too quiet. It's unlike you."

"I'm okay, really."

"Really? Well, if you think that 'I'm okay, really' is going to get you laid again you're sadly mistaken, Miss Rushforth."

"No, no! I wasn't thinking that. I *am* actually drained. No, I was just mulling things over. I don't want to go to work ever again."

"Now, that's being overly dramatic, Helen. Isn't it? Come on, bedtime!"

He led the way and I wearily followed him up the stairs. Ten minutes later he was as good as his word. Pushing my back into him, we lay like spoons, his arms tight around me, and I relished the comfort. He was swelling up next to my bottom, but for once I didn't act on it and neither did he. Sleep came easily to me. I closed my eyes and was gone, but not before hearing his rhythmic breathing in my left ear. His hand lost hold of my left breast and fell onto my side.

CHAPTER 9

I *'ve been running various ideas through my head for the last two weeks. Ideas as to what is going to be my next move. I'm no further forward though...no idea what the fucking hell to do. I berate myself every day for letting the woman get under my skin. I don't know how much longer I can go on with these fucking ludicrous notions of mine. I need a result...positive, negative or otherwise!*

Every day I rack my brain for possible explanations as to who the guy is who left Helen's house when the girl arrived. I have carried on until the point where it drives me crazy, wondering who the other woman and girl are. What are they all to do with Helen? How long do they plan on staying for? It's mainly the guy who I'm puzzled about. The jealousy I'm feeling about him is insane; it gnaws away at me. I've got to stop thinking of him as Helen's lover. That thought makes me want to vomit and on one or two occasions, I have.

I've allowed my obsession to get so bad that I made more than a few fuck ups at work too; fuck ups that I can do without. Nobody knows about the mistakes so far and I've managed to cover them up and put things right. Several times it has meant late nights in the office for me. It won't be long before someone starts to ask questions. 'Why is he putting so many extra hours in and yet he's not getting through the work any faster?' 'What the fuck is he doing in his extra hours?' It's a ridiculous situation. I've been working during my extra hours, that's what I've been doing; putting right what I've fucked up during the day.

I considered making an appointment with my G.P. I need to do something as a matter of urgency to get myself calmed down. Either that or I need to make a more conscious and determined effort to keep Helen out of my head during working hours. It's going to be a mammoth task.

I'm obsessed with her, I know I am. I acknowledged that months ago. People would call me a creep if they knew; a perve, an oddball. Stalker too! Yes, I'm stalking her, but I'm no fucking creep and certainly not a pervert. The truth of the matter is I want to be with her, I want to fuck her again...make love to her. Every night I go to bed and live my dream before I sleep. I'm fucking her and she is fucking me back and loving every second of it...taking my length and relishing ever last inch. She loves it, she can't get enough! Besides being obsessed with her, something else has gradually crept into the equation over the last few days. I know I'm in love with her. That realisation has also dawned on me. The thought scares me half to death. I know I'm going to end up hurt if I don't go about it in the right way. I need to take my time over it and plan my next move carefully if I want it to work.

CHAPTER 10

Two weeks had flown by since Ruby's termination and the lovely weekend when they all stayed at my house. Despite the trauma that she had no doubt gone through, we managed to enjoy our time together.

Work continued to be as busy as ever with January being a heavy month of tax assessments. Christina being Christina would break the monotony from time to time when she sensed things needed livening up. She played the odd practical joke here and there, and enacted the drama of some of her family moments which she related to us all with such hilarity. There was impromptu moments of her bursting into song (which she knew not to do if clients were present in the building) and her unrelenting wittiness and sarcasm too, all served to brighten our days when the office at large, seemed a little too dull. It was unprecedented, having a character like she was, around.

Despite the relentless workload on my desk, my mind was running on fast forward thinking about my rapidly approaching Friday night flight to Paris. I booked a hotel for the first night, but planned on staying in my apartment on the Saturday. I wasn't without my concerns; the biggest which would be managing to get up the stairs to my flat without being spotted by André. I didn't want him to see me before I was ready to tackle him. I couldn't have him notice me first and come anywhere near my flat. When it came to our confrontation it had to be in his space, where I could leave after I'd done what I had to do, rather than struggling to get him out of my apartment. I lost count of the numerous times I fought to get my mind back on track to my numerous daily tasks. Gemma, Leanne and the others too came out with varying remarks.

"You okay, Helen? You're looking a bit preoccupied."

"Wake up, Helen. You're miles away."

"If you need to talk…"

I suppose they're just showing concern and perhaps a little worried for me. They watched me go through the O.C.D. issues following the death of my parents and close behind that the devastating events of my marriage break-up so they were sure to worry. I still kept my secret though and they didn't know about my brief relationship with David or my heartbreak after his death. I was quick to put their minds at ease.

"Seriously, don't worry. I just have a little private matter to attend to this weekend. I'm not looking forward to it, but it won't take long to get sorted. Nothing too drastic."

They were pacified.

"Okay, you know we're here for you! Don't ever forget that."

I took a small case in to work with me on the Friday morning and once finished for the day I only needed to walk around the corner to the tube station. Getting off at Paddington station, I took the brief walk to London Paddington from which my next train was the Heathrow Express and a direct one to Terminals 2 and 3.

My short flight departed at a few minutes before nine pm and touched down at ten twenty. I got a cab to drop me off at the Paris Rivoli hotel. It was just after eleven when I checked in. I'd used the place a couple of times before. It was just around the corner from my apartment and would be convenient for Saturday morning.

The only things I bothered to unpack were my little bag of toiletries, make-up and clean undies. I got straight into bed after a quick cup of tea. I already had a couple of glasses of wine on the flight and needed to be up at a reasonable time.

As I laid there hoping sleep wouldn't take too long, I started rehearsing a script in my head, wording and re-wording what I planned to say to Andre, but on waking after a decent sleep, I had no recollection of the script. In my mind I gave a silent prayer, hoping appropriate words would come at the right time otherwise I would have to 'wing' it.

Knowing that André was not an early riser, on a Saturday morning in particular, I knew I had to get to the building, up the flights of stairs and into my apartment before eight thirty. It was seven thirty when I checked out of the hotel. I didn't bother with breakfast in their dining room. I called at a delicatessen en-route and picked up fresh milk, bread, chocolate croissants and one or two other items. When I left the apartment to return to London a few months back, there was a fairly good stock of tinned and non-perishable foods in the kitchen cupboards. I wouldn't go hungry for the weekend.

Good luck was on my side and I passed nobody on my way up the stairs. I heaved a sigh of relief when I closed the front door behind me. By ten minutes to eight fresh coffee was brewing and I buttered myself some toast to go with it. In the living room, my plate and mug on the still covered coffee table, I removed the dust sheet from the comfiest arm chair and made myself at home, be it only for the short visit I intended it to be. I switched on the T.V. but left the volume muted. If and when André walked past my apartment at any point during the day, I didn't want him to hear any noise; anything that would give him an inkling that I was 'home'.

Determined not to spend the whole day getting worried about how things would go between us, I buried my nose in a book. There was no shortage of reading material, mainly books that Mum and Dad had brought over on holiday, but there was also a number of mine too. For most of the morning, my choice for a read was a book from a Patricia Cornwell series. It kept me engrossed. I broke off only once to wander through to my bedroom and make the bed up with fresh linen. Whilst doing this, I experienced some brief flashbacks to when I, on a few occasions shared the bed with André. I tried not to let the thoughts traumatise me too much. I pushed them to the back of my mind and reminded myself of the only reason I was here, Ruby...and the way he used her.

I picked up my book again fifteen minutes later and soon got back into the story. It blotted out the traumatic thoughts of seeing André tomorrow. Rumblings of hunger started and my concentration deserted me. Checking the time on my mobile, I saw it was just after one in the afternoon. I ventured through to the kitchen, careful to open and close the cupboard doors softly so as not to be heard. I busied myself for a few minutes making scrambled eggs on toast. I froze on the spot when I suddenly heard a door slam closed. It had to be his front door as there were no other apartments on this floor. Then I heard the distinctive sound of someone heading down the stairs. I stayed where I was until the person had gone and took my lunch through to the living room. I tucked into the food, eager to kerb my hunger pangs of a few minutes ago.

No sooner had I finished eating, my phone started to vibrate. Simon's name was on display. I panicked momentarily, a little worried in case I was heard talking by anyone on the stairs, or to be more precise, André. Remembering that he'd gone out, I answered the call. He didn't give me chance to speak.

"Hello, Sweet Cheeks!" He greeted me, before bombarding me with questions, barely drawing breath between each. "Where are you? Have you seen him yet; André? Are you alone? Where are staying?" And then. "You should have let me come with you."

I raised my eyes to the ceiling, humming quietly under my breath, letting him ramble on...until he must have realised what he was doing.

Finally.

"Are you there, Helen? You're not saying much."

Am I not? I wonder why!

I sighed in frustration in the knowledge that I was letting him wind me up again.

"I'm just letting your verbal diarrhoea run its course. Yes, I'm here. There's not much bloody point in me even trying to speak while you're in full flow."

"You haven't answered any of my questions yet!" He grouched, arsey as always.

"You haven't given me the bloody chance...yet!" He was such an irritating bastard, though I couldn't help but smile.

"So, answer them then! Damn you, Helen!" I could almost imagine him grinning to himself as he feigned irritation.

"Right! I'm here...in Paris, as you already know. I spent last night in a hotel and tonight I will be ensconced in my apartment. Yes, I'm alone! Why wouldn't I be? And no, I haven't seen the twat yet. What else was there? Ah, yes. I didn't need you to come to Paris with me. I can sort out my own battles, thank you very much. Why would you want to come with me anyway? It isn't exactly going to be an exciting weekend."

"Don't get fucking smart, Helen. It doesn't suit you. I only thought that... that..."

I got the distinct impression that he was struggling to come up with a valid answer. There was something else though; a 'pissed off' sort of attitude, maybe resentment, I couldn't fathom out why he would feel like that. Not wishing to prolong that discussion, I asked him how his week had gone and chatted briefly about my week at work. I also managed to establish that he was phoning me from outside the gym; just about to go in for a change, instead of the usual calls when he was leaving. All in all we ended up chatting for forty five minutes and as I hadn't heard any more footsteps on the landing, I assumed André was still out. Thankful that I hadn't had to spend the phone call in a whisper, I realised that not only had Simon's part of the conversation dried up, but I was finding the small talk to be hard work...I wanted to get back to my reading.

"Okay. When are you back in London?"

His voice had taken on the attitude again...his best arsey voice. He didn't even say my name or the 'sweet cheeks' thing, something was niggling him. So I answered briefly, and with attitude, as he had.

"Late Sunday night!" I almost snapped.

"Okay! Will I see you next week?"

It was a game now; who could be the rattiest?!

"You might! You might not! We'll see!" I grinned to myself as I spat out the words, knowing full well that he would be getting worked up; getting a taste of his own medicine.

"Bye then!" He didn't bite back but the call ended abruptly. He'd disconnected me in his annoyance.

I sat for half an hour puzzling over his attitude; wondering what the hell I'd done wrong. It was clear that he didn't like the fact that I was here in Paris, but what the hell? He knew my reason for coming over. He was aware that I was going to tackle my neighbour, and the need for it. Just what was his problem? I was starting to let a bit of anger creep up on me and taking my mobile, I threw it across the room in temper. It made a terrible clatter as it crashed noisily into the recessed bookshelves before dropping softly onto the thick carpet. I jumped, hands over my mouth in shock. The last thing I intended was to make a noise of any description and risk André hearing me. Sighing with relief at the fact that he was not at home, I picked up the phone and curled up once more in the armchair. I took a few deep breaths and closed my eyes for a few minutes, slowly bringing myself back down.

I fell asleep. When I next opened my eyes, the first thing I noticed was that it was dark, both in the living room and beyond the window. I dragged myself up and across to the side table near the window. I closed the curtains and switched on the lamp. I had been asleep for several hours. It was gone six. I didn't feel particularly hungry but knew I should have a snack of some description because I fancied a couple of gin and tonics. Opting for the easiest solution I could think of, I 'nuked' a couple of chocolate croissants, taking care to turn the microwave off at the socket before it had chance to 'ping'. I poured myself a gin and once more returned to the living room, making sure that no light was on in the hallway. With a slight headache, I didn't feel inclined to pick up my book again. I pressed the remote and brought the 'sleeping' and muted T.V. back to life. I found a Sky News channel and sat for an age watching the news headlines as they scrolled across the bottom of the screen, but I wasn't taking them in. Thoughts of Simon and his strange attitude started preying on my mind again. Time and again those thoughts went backwards and forwards through my head. I just couldn't get to grips with the idea that he was so keen to come to Paris with me. I told him why I was coming and that I wasn't planning on it becoming some sort of holiday break. All I could put it down to, was that he imagined we could have a marathon weekend of shagging. But why? It's not as if he ever went long without. So many questions that I didn't have an answer for. My head started to throb again.

By nine thirty I was in bed. I hadn't heard André return to his flat. I wasn't sure whether he would have returned whilst I slept the afternoon away. Remembering what I could about his lifestyle, I somehow doubted it. I figured he was out for the day drinking and unlikely to be home until much later. Propped up against a pillow, my third gin and tonic on the bedside table, I picked up my book and got back into the story once more but my eyes soon became heavy. I switched off the lamp, put my book down and curled up. I slept for a few minutes and on waking again, my mind started another round of questions; yet another theory about Simon's behaviour just hit me out of nowhere. Unless I was totally wrong, I think he's jealous! I let this crazy notion flit backwards and forwards in my brain for quite some time, talking myself out of it one minute, then reverting back to it the next. I honestly couldn't think of any other logical reason. That idea unsettled me somewhat. He is a married man and he's having an affair. That's what shag buddies do…they have an affair. We had this conversation back on Christmas Day. I know he loves his wife and I am his bit on the side, so jealousy on his part? It somehow didn't fit! I didn't want to think about what it might mean. I turned over and tried to settle back to sleep, but to no avail. It was well past four in the morning when I succumbed.

Waking at eight minutes past ten, I got straight out of bed and headed for the kitchen. Last night's gin and tonics had left my mouth feeling dry. I needed a glass of water and a couple of pain-killers. I sat at the kitchen table and pondered on the day ahead. It was going to be a long one; more waiting about until four o'clock, when if all panned out well, I would go and knock on his door.

Not wanting the long wait to drag out unnecessarily, I decided to go through my wardrobe and some of the cupboards around the apartment to see if anything could be sorted ready to throw out. By mid-afternoon I was thankful to have been busy. My little chore resulted in two bin-liners full of clothes from my wardrobe but the most rewarding bit, I found some family photographs in a box in what used to be, and always will be, Mum and Dad's bedroom. The box of photographs was my best distraction yet. I filled an envelope with some favourites and put them in my handbag to take back home; one of them a favourite of mine for the last ten years. All three of us were sat on one of the benches alongside the Seine, me in the middle, Mum and Dad's heads up close to mine. It was taken on a long summer night when we walked back home after having a meal in a local restaurant. We were so happy that night. I cried silently for a while as I shuffled through the snaps. Finishing up, I replaced the lid and returned the box of photos back where I found it.

Just before three thirty I packed my toiletries and make-up back into my small suitcase and at the last minute added a couple of favourite tops that I had not taken when I was last here. I threw out what I hadn't eaten of the fresh food I bought yesterday and washed up the few dishes. I paced backwards and forwards between bathroom, bedroom, kitchen and lounge trying to keep myself occupied for the last few minutes. My mouth was dry and a nervous churning began in the bottom of my stomach. I was dreading seeing André again and though I didn't relish having to do what I was about to do, I knew without a doubt that I would see it through.

I placed my suitcase and handbag just inside the front door. When I returned it would be to grab both bags and get the hell out of here. Everything else done, I popped into the living room and threw the dust sheet back over the armchair. I didn't know if or when I would be coming back. I didn't dwell on the thought as I was ready for action.

When I knocked on André's front door my heart raced and my cheeks burned. I considered what would possibly happen in the next few seconds. If he slammed the door in my face it would be game over. I didn't want that though, I needed him to answer my questions. I wanted retribution for Ruby…and David too. I heard a key turn in the lock and quickly grasped my hands together in front of me to steady the shaking. The door opened and he was there in front of me. His eyes opened wide in surprise.

"Hel..Helen?" He stammered and almost staggered backwards in his shock.

"Hello, André!"

We stood there speechless, staring for what seemed like an age, but must have only been ten seconds, if that.

"What…? You…you'd better come in, I suppose."

He stood back and made room for me to enter. I walked in and hesitated for a second. I didn't know where to go so I stood and waited for some indication from him.

"Erm…go…go through to the living room. I'll get you some coffee. Don't…don't mind me, but I think I need a stiff drink."

I could see that he was shell-shocked, and suspicious too. He didn't know where to look, but obviously didn't want to make eye contact with me.

"Go ahead…it's your home."

He muttered something and I watched as he hurried away

down the hallway to his kitchen. I headed through to the living room and assumed it would be okay for me to sit. I plonked my backside in one of the armchairs and started to shake again. Rubbing my hands down my face I could feel it burning. I took some deep breaths to calm my racing heart. I had to stay focussed if I was to do what needed doing. I couldn't do it if I let myself give in to a panic attack, for fuck's sake.

André seemed to be taking forever to make one cup of coffee. I sat nervously fiddling with my watch strap and wondering what was keeping him. I guessed he was having a couple of swift drinks before coming back to face me. Somehow, knowing that he was probably feeling as nervous as I was, that thought seemed to bring about a change in me. The deep breathing was helping me and I knew that when he came back I would be up to the job in hand. I couldn't wait to get it over with and be on my return flight to Heathrow.

My stomach turned with a violent lurch as he disturbed my thoughts. I hadn't heard his approach. He was back. He handed me the mug of coffee and in his other hand he held a glass of whiskey. For a fleeting moment he met my eyes as I accepted the drink and went over to sit on the sofa. I watched him carefully as he gazed into his glass, refusing to meet my eyes again. We sat in silence for ages. I couldn't say anything... he had to be the one to start it. I sipped at my coffee but my gaze never left him. He raised his eyes from his glass eventually and turned to face me.

"Why, Helen?" He asked, his voice sounding full of emotion.

"Why what, André?" I challenged him.

"WHY? WHY DID YOU FUCK OFF LIKE THAT? IN THE WAY YOU DID? YOU DIDN'T EVEN...EVEN HAVE THE GUTS TO DISCUSS IT WITH ME!! CAN YOU

IMAGINE? DO YOU HAVE ANY IDEA HOW I FELT AT THAT TIME? EH?"

He had been quiet up to now, so the shouting startled me and I winced in surprise, my body tensing.

Determined that there would be no more shouting until the moment arrived when I was going to scream back at him, I deliberately kept my reply quiet, hoping the softness of my voice would calm him down for the time being.

"Because, André! Because I needed to have a life. I wanted to get back to my career, my business partnership. My existence in Paris was not the life I wanted…and what we had was not a relationship…not on my part. It was a friendship that got out of hand. I was extremely fond of you, you know that. But it could never have been forever. It would never have worked out between us. I wanted more. I wanted to return to my life in London. I'm sorry, André. I know that I went about it all completely in the wrong way, and I'm sorry for that. Sorry that I had to hurt you in the way that I did."

It worked. He calmed and I saw the hurt, still evident through his facial expression; the humiliation I had caused him. His eyes showed it all, they had a distinctive watery appearance. But there was also, defiance.

He opened his mouth to speak and the words didn't come. He closed it, but seconds later, it opened again and the words came spewing out.

"You're wrong, Helen. We could have made it work. Eventually, you have put that…that grief you were going through, behind you. You just needed more time. You would have loved me in the end, if you had just given us the chance. But you resorted to…running away for fuck's sake. Have you always run away, Helen? You ran away from England to come to Paris in the first place, didn't you? You ran away because you couldn't face people. You can't run forever, you know. Exactly what is it that you are running from? I think you're trying to run away from *you*…correct me if I'm wrong, but I think I'm right when I say that."

I stared back at him, hoping my face gave away nothing about how I was feeling inside. I could feel my anger building; furious at the fact that he was maybe closer to the truth than I had realised until he pointed it out to me. He was also wrong, and despite the real reason I was sat with him in his apartment, I even started to feel a little sorry for him. He was slightly deluded in thinking that I could ever love him. Time will eventually heal my grief over David's death, even I know that. But to ever end up falling in love with André and become life partners…that had never been on the cards and never would be, and certainly not now! I anxiously watched his face. He was fighting another emotional outpouring, biting on his bottom lip, his hands wringing together nervously and trying to blink away the moisture in his eyes.

"I've been drinking heavily since the day you left, Helen… as you can see."

He picked his drink up and gave a nod to the glass of whiskey, smiled at it, then jerked his head around to face me again.

"I haven't even had another woman since that day. Look what you've done to me, Helen."

My anger was only fractionally below boing point, his bare-faced lie the final trigger. I needed to get out of his flat before too long; do what I need to do and go. I was not going to have him laying some fucking guilt trip on my shoulders because he couldn't get his act together and stop throwing drink down his neck as if it was the answer to everything. I placed my empty cup on the floor, and stood up…ready for what I was confident would happen next.

He also got to his feet and moved towards me.

"Helen, you…you can't leave yet. We need to talk. I…we can…"

His words tailed away as he moved into my space, and without even extending his arms out to touch me, he leaned in and brushed my cheek with his lips, whispering my name.

"Helen."

It happened so fast, his lips were suddenly on mine, kissing me passionately.

Not long now! Stay calm. Keep strong. You've got this!

I didn't respond at first, but my inner voice succeeded in calming me and a few seconds later I was kissing him back, sharing his passion, knowing it was wrong of me, but I urgently needed to play the game.

Nearly there. It's nearly over! Please, touch me, André. I need you to touch me...now!

My plea was answered. In an instant his arms were around me, pulling me tight towards him. Needing to hurry things along I reached up to hold his face in my hands, and he kissed me more urgently and forced his tongue past my lips and into my mouth. The fingers on his left hand raked through my hair and his right hand cupped my left breast. It was now or never.

Shocking myself with the force I managed to summon and the speed at which I acted, I raised my right knee up and into his nether region with sheer brute force and knocked the breath out of him. He crumpled to the floor in a heap, grasping his balls tightly. I could see the pain in his eyes as he gasped. He stared up at me, mouth and eyes gaping wide open in disbelief and fury as he struggled to breathe.

"You...you...fu...fucking...bitch! Lead...leading me on!" He gasped, the pain still evident in every word. "WHY?"

"WHY, ANDRÉ? YOU EVEN HAVE TO FUCKING ASK?" I screamed down at him, his body creased up on the floor. "I'LL TELL YOU EXACTLY WHY! YOU FUCKED MY STEPDAUGHTER, YOU DIRTY BASTARD! THAT'S WHY!"

"SHE'S…NOT! NOT YOUR FUCKING STEPDAUGHTER, HELEN!" He was attempting to get onto his knees now and still clutched at himself in agony.

With my throat hurting from the harshness of my screaming, I lowered the volume and spat back at him.

"No. You're right. She's not. You thought she was my little sister at first. But whatever she is to me…SHE'S DAVID'S DAUGHTER!" I took a deep breathe before continuing my attack. "SHE'S DAVID'S DAUGHTER AND…AND…I LOVE HER! WHY ANDRÉ? TELL ME THAT, BECAUSE I NEED TO FUCKING UNDERSTAND WHY! WAS IT TO GET BACK AT ME? YOU WANTED TO GET BACK AT ME FOR LOVING DAVID? YOU WANTED TO DO THAT BECAUSE I LOVED DAVID AND COULDN'T LOVE YOU? OR IS IT THAT YOU WANTED TO GET BACK AT DAVID? YOU HATE DAVID BECAUSE I LOVE HIM!"

"Stop…stop…screaming, Helen. You'll…have everybody… in the…block up here. No. I didn't…didn't do it…to get back at…you…or David. I promise you that. I'm not that vindictive. What do you take me for?"

He managed to push himself up from his knees and flop back onto the sofa.

"She was here. She was attractive…and up for it. That's all. It was no attempt on my part to get back at you. We both wanted sex. It happened. End of."

I had said my bit; achieved what I set out to do. I didn't take any pleasure from it. He looked pathetic sitting there. My only consolation with the whole scenario was that I had paid him back for having sex with Ruby. The shock of what I just achieved returned and my hands shook once again. My whole body trembled and a sickly feeling rose up from my stomach and into my mouth… as if it was the distaste of all that had occurred in the twenty five minutes or so. I was ready to leave. I reached the door to the hallway and turned around to face him for the last time to utter my parting shot.

"By the way, André. Your child was aborted two weeks ago...yours and Ruby's!"

I'll never forget the look of pure horror on his face; deathly pale. I closed the front door and left him to his thoughts.

CHAPTER 11

*N*ot long after our first mid-morning coffee of the week, Ted rang my extension.

"Helen, can you pop into my office in, say half an hour? You haven't any clients booked in, have you? We're having a brief meeting…you, Jim and myself. Is that okay? I've a couple of minor matters I would like to discuss with you both."

I closed my eyes and sighed quietly in despair, trying hard to keep a tone of irritation out of my voice.

"Yes, okay. Will do!"

I put the phone down and gave an audible sigh. I was knackered. I flew back in from Paris the previous night and hadn't arrived home until twenty past eleven. To top it off, I spent half the night running the scene at André's apartment back and forth in my head, feeling guilty one minute and happy in his discomfort the next. I wasn't really sure how I felt about the whole charade, but one thing I did know was that I was desperate for sleep, which finally happened an hour before my alarm went off…seemingly much louder than usual, and scaring me half to death. I jumped out of bed before I was fully awake and sat for what seemed like an age, waiting for the dizziness that followed to pass before I could even think about getting in the shower and ready for the day to begin.

The last thing I wanted to hear was that Ted wants me in a meeting with bloody James Mortimer. Fuck it! There was nothing I could do but see it through, and in the hope that I wasn't expected to contribute too much.

When my half hour of dread passed by, I made my way along the corridor to Ted's office and tapped lightly on the door.

"Come in, Helen!"

Walking through the door, it became apparent he'd known it was me as James was already sat there.

"Good morning, Helen." My God, did I want to wipe that stupid looking smirk off his face and if that wasn't bad enough, he added. "Crikey, you look rough!"

"Morning, James. Thanks for the compliment, I'm sure." I bit back, my hackles up before we even got started.

I sat down just as Christina knocked on the door and entered with a tray of coffee. Ted smiled up at her and she beamed back at him then grinned over at me before quickly making herself scarce. She'd completely ignored James.

"Right then, let's get started. I want to discuss Christina with you today. As you both know, up to now we haven't done anything about replacing Linda Brownlow, since she… erm…left our employment."

I noticed a swift flash of annoyance pass across James' face, as Ted continued.

"You are also both aware that our number of clients continues to rise. I know my shorter hours have added to your burden *and* to that of the other staff. Nina will be returning soon, as *you* already know, Helen. She will start back on reduced hours and gradually build up to full-time as hopefully, her health continues to improve. I've also, just this weekend, received a phone call from Cindy. The baby's birth is imminent and normally she would have remained on maternity leave, but she is eager to come back to her reception duties after a month. Her sister has just made it possible for her to do that; she recently opened up a nursery."

He paused and looked to James and I to see if we had any comments to make. James obliged.

"So where does Christina fit into all this, Ted?"

"Yes, quite. Christina as you know, has been temporarily covering Cindy's role. I like the girl. She has previously worked in busy accounts departments, doing both sales ledger and purchase ledger admin. Now whilst we don't offer those roles here, the skills and knowledge she has attained is a good basis for her to learn book-keeping. I want her to take up Linda Brownlow's old role, learning as she goes, along with your guidance, Helen. If she wants to study for A.A.T. then that would be a bonus and I would be more than happy to put her through the qualifications with the Hopkins Partnership paying for it, of course. Do either of you have any thoughts or input on the matter? Helen?"

He faced me, grinning and no doubt already expected what my response would be.

"Ted, I'm more than happy with that as I think you already know. Christina fits in well. She's intelligent, funny, polite with clients, efficient and...noisy at times, I know! Everybody gets along with her; staff and clients alike. I know for a fact that she was dreading having to leave us. She'll be thrilled!"

"Excellent! Jim? What are your thoughts? Anything to add?"

James turned to scowl at me briefly, somewhat rattled I suspect, before giving his reply.

"Well, I think our Helen here, has all but sold you it, Ted!"

Twat! What was with the 'our Helen'?

"However, I agree that she has skills to offer. I just hope she can prove to be as efficient as Linda was in that role. Plus, I think we could *all* play an active role in her training and not add the *whole* burden to Helen's workload."

What an arsehole!

I was furious, but not wanting Ted to see my anger with the heat rising up my face, I looked down at my nails, stayed tight-lipped and didn't deign to comment further on James' response. Trying to give the impression that he actually *cared* about *my* workload. I could only imagine what Christina's response would be if she knew he was already trying to muscle in on her training before it was even underway.

Looking us both in the eye to see if there was to be any further input from one or the other of us, Ted brought the matter to a close.

"Helen, would you please be so kind as to bring our decision to Christina's attention? I think it will make her day."

I nodded, delighted with the thought of breaking the good news to Christina.

"Okay, we're agreed then! Now, the subject of training leads me nicely on to the next matter. I have received some correspondence about a taxation seminar that is to be held in roughly six weeks' time; in Manchester. Following the recent government changes to business taxation, we have now received printed information. However, at this seminar there will be a more, shall I say, in depth and comprehensive look at some of the finer details. I shall be out of the country at that point, but I would like both of you to attend. The duration is one and a half days, which will require a one night stay. The first session starts at one o'clock on a...a Wednesday I think it is. Jim?"

James shot a look in my direction. "Well, I can't see any problem."

Ted also stared at me eagerly.

"Helen? You have no family ties, so I'm assuming that's okay with you too?"

Not knowing what else to say and knowing it was expected of me, I uttered.

"Yes. That's fine, Ted. I'll…I'll go."

For fuck's sake! No! It wasn't fine! I didn't want to go anywhere with him!

"Okay! Good! Helen, I'll email you now with the date and details. Can you sort out accommodation for you and Jim, please? Jim, I'll leave it to you to sort the journey out. Right, thank you both. I had better rush now. I'm meeting up with Hilary for a spot of lunch and I've a few things to attend to first."

As we approached the door James reached it first, opening it wide and standing back to let me through, half a smirk plastered across his face, as he nodded me to pass through.

"It'll make a pleasant change from being cooped up in the office won't it, Helen?"

I read so much meaning behind those words. I was seething, boiling with rage and I had to swiftly summon a large amount of self-control just in time to stop myself from slamming my office door behind me in anger.

CHAPTER 12

*A*fter the meeting with Ted and James, the first thing I did when I got back to my office was summon Christina in from reception to inform her that if she was happy to accept, The Hopkins Partnership were offering her a permanent position as a trainee bookkeeper. Her reaction came as no surprise. She jumped up and down with her arms outstretched. She knew of course, not to be noisy with Ted not having left the building yet.

"Oh my God! Oh my God! Oh my God! Wow! Thank you, Helen. I'll thank Ted when I next take his coffee in. I'm so excited. I didn't want to leave you all. I love it here."

I couldn't help but chuckle at her joyous bouncing.

"I'm glad you're thrilled, Christina. Of course, you'll have to take care of the reception duties for the next month or so until Cindy is back at work. Also, if you would be so kind as to cover reception duties when she takes her annual leave. You can still do your book-keeping work from the computer in reception."

"Oh. Yes, that won't be a problem. I'll actually miss some of the clients when I'm ensconced in Linda Brownlow's old office...up all those stairs. When will my training be starting, Helen? And who'll be training me?" She asked eagerly.

"Okay. Well, I thought I would start your training next week. As you've still got to cover reception, I can come and sit with you a few hours each day and start you off on some of the basics. You've already got an extensive knowledge of sales and purchase ledgers so that is excellent basic knowledge. Most people who start out as trainees don't have that kind of practical knowledge and experience. Obviously, you know that everything which gets posted to those ledgers also has a corresponding entry on the nominal ledger. First of all, we'll delve a little further into nominal ledger work that you won't have covered, like trial balances and journals. Is that okay?"

"Yes. That's fine!"

"There's something else which I should perhaps forewarn you of. James Mortimer suggested that to ease the burden on me, he would also play an active role in your training. I am going to try to discourage that if I can possibly do so. I know it's not something you would relish the thought of. Take it from me, it won't be happening if I can do anything about it."

She grimaced, as I knew she would. Her face soon broke into a smile again though and her eyes sparkled in her excitement. I got the impression that nothing was going to dampen Christina's spirits for some time to come, not even the grim thought of receiving training from James Mortimer.

"Well, if it has to be that way, so be it. I'm made up. I really am. Thank you, Helen."

"It's my pleasure. At least *something* good came from that meeting this morning. It's been great news for you. Unfortunately, it wasn't such good news where I'm concerned."

She tilted her head on a side and the smile disappeared to be replaced by a worried expression.

"Why? What's matter, Helen? What happened?"

"Let's just say, when you leave this office in a few minutes time, my next task is to book a hotel in Manchester for James and myself. Ted wants us both to attend a taxation seminar there next month and it involves a one-night stop-over. It's really made my day, I can tell you. *Not.*"

"Oh shit. Poor you. I can imagine it's your worst nightmare, Helen! What are you going to do? Does that mean you will have to endure his company on the night then? You know, dinner and drinks until bedtime?"

I glared at her. Up until the point she just mentioned it, that thought hadn't even crossed my mind. My dread doubled in a split second and I gave a loud sigh of exasperation.

"Oh bloody hell! I hadn't thought of that. Thanks for bringing it to my attention, Christina. Put it this way though...*not* if I have anything to do with it. I'll order room service and watch a film in bed. He can do whatever the hell he wants to do as long as it doesn't involve me."

"Good luck with that. Right. I'll go and leave you to get on with your hotel booking."

With that, she stood up and left my office. I cast my eye over the email that Ted as promised, had just forwarded. I wanted to find out exactly where the seminar was to be held and the paperwork informed me it was at the Hilton in Deansgate. It made sense to try and get accommodation there, unless it was fully booked up with seminar delegates. It would certainly be easier than having to leave the Hilton. The alternative was to travel with him to another hotel after the seminar and then do the return journey back to the Hilton the following morning.

I browsed the internet looking for the hotel phone number. When the young lady on the bookings line answered, I gave her the dates of the seminar and informed her I wanted to book two double rooms.

"It doesn't matter if the rooms are not together, so whatever you have available."

I crossed my fingers, even the ones holding the phone. There was a lengthy silence while she was obviously checking the bookings.

"We're pretty booked up with seminar people, but you're lucky. We only have two rooms left…and they're together on the fifth floor. Is that okay for you?"

I told her it was and promptly smacked my forehead with the heel of my hand in frustration.

Is that okay? It'll bloody have to be okay, won't it?

I gave her the details for myself and James followed by my business credit card details. Two minutes later it was done. For the first time ever, I found myself silently cursing Ted for putting me in this preposterous situation. Although he'd never commented, I feel sure he was aware of the constant tension and niggles between James and myself. Being a man who liked eternal harmony in the office, I was surprised that he never made a point of mentioning it, if he was indeed aware. Resigned to the fact that I was stuck with the situation, I made a promise to myself to try a little harder in James's company, particularly when Ted was around. Entertaining the thought that he was aware of the reality, I think he would be disappointed if James or I allowed the animosity to continue.

Making a resolution to start being pleasant to James going forward, I took a deep breath and called his extension.

"Hello, Helen. You must be psychic. I was just about to call you. How can I help?"

His voice sounded oily. So much for my intention to be nice. Already I was tense and on my guard. I imagined his face at the other end of the phone, probably that bloody smirk plastered across it as always. I bristled.

"Hello. I was just ringing to tell you that I sorted out the accommodation for the seminar. We're staying at the Hilton...that's where the seminar is being held."

"Excellent. Like I said, I was just about to call you. I've looked into the cost of train tickets and it would certainly be cheaper for us to go up in my car, unless of course you want to drive us both there. No point in taking two cars anyway. I figured it was also going to be too much hassle with the train. Both of us needing to get taxis to the tube stations, then on and off tubes, for me at least, until we arrive at King's Cross. I've no doubt it would mean taxis both ways, to and from Manchester Piccadilly, I think. More trouble than it's worth. Is that okay with you? I'll pick you up. We're going to need to leave yours by half past seven to allow us plenty of time. The seminar starts around lunchtime."

Oh, what? Four fucking hours sat in a car with him, both there and back! Bloody Hell Ted, I could do without this.

My mind was working overtime. I felt sick in the pit of my stomach. He couldn't fail to wonder why I took so long to say anything, but I finally managed to speak.

"Okay. Yes, I should imagine it's a nightmare with tubes and taxis, like you said. Are you sure it won't be a problem to pick me up?"

"No problem at all, Helen. Just let me know your post-code nearer the time."

"Will do. Thanks!"

I put the phone down. The first thought running through my mind, illogical though it was, was that I didn't want him to know where I lived. Then I chided myself at the stupidity. James could look at the staff records anytime he wanted if he was that desperate to know where I live. He'd worked at the Hopkins Partnership for quite some time now, so if he wanted to, he could have paid me a visit if he'd ever wanted to try and follow up on the events that have occurred between us in the office. Next, I had to remind myself that the telephone call of a couple of minutes ago was fairly amiable. I really didn't have any valid reason to be negative as he'd been helpful and polite throughout the conversation. His dismissal of the train, tubes and taxis was a fair point too. I needed to get a grip.

I struggled to concentrate the rest of the day. I left work early and went to catch the tube back home.

CHAPTER 13

ingering the sex toys on my bedside cabinet with one hand and the fingers of his other exploring my warmth, Simon looked turned to face me, waiting for a decision on my part. I groaned in despair.

"How about this one, sweetie? Your Christmas gift from me? I know it's your favourite."

I stared through him, not fully agreeable with what he was asking of me. Truth be told, I wasn't feeling much enthusiasm for any of the toys. I wanted his cock straight away, but clearly he was wanting to prolong the fucking session.

"Hmm. Whatever! I'm not bothered, Simon. Truth is I would just rather have your cock inside me. I want it hard and rough."

I gave him the best sensuous smile I could manage in the hope that my revelation would excite him. I understand him so well. He loved to indulge in enthusiastic wild sex. He always referred to it as 'fucking my brains out'.

"Well, I can do that if you want, honey. I just thought you might like to play a little? Like…sucking my big dong and making me harder still, then I could shove it hard into that delectable little pussy of yours and feel you cum all over me. I want you nice and wet for me."

I wasn't paying the slightest bit of attention. I was concentrating on the tendrils of excitement that crept through my nerve-endings and on the verge of an orgasm that just wasn't happening.

"Simon, I'm waiting to cum and it's just not happening. I need you to stick your cock inside me, now."

He stopped poking around and stared at me intently as if I'd lost my mind. After thirty seconds of inaction, I took charge. I pushed him over onto his back and straddled him the second he was in position. I grabbed his cock and pointed it into the appropriate direction before lowering myself on to it. Immediately it slid in as far as it would go, I rode him furiously, moaning with each move I made. Then it was there. I released my cum with a scream of pent up anger.

"Fucking hell. You nearly bent my cock double there, sweetie. Go easy."

I still wasn't listening and after taking a few seconds to catch a breather, I continued to ride him, working my anger away and getting lost in the moment as another orgasm had me in its grasp.

"Seems...like you're the boss...tonight. But are you going to give me the chance to get you to squirt it out for me, babe? I'm kinda feeling a bit out of it. I love your enthusiasm, but there are two of us here."

It crossed my mind that I was being selfish and that wasn't usually my style. I couldn't help it. I needed to get rid of some anger and it felt like this was the only way. He placed both hands on my waist and before I realised what was happened he rolled the pair of us over in one deft move until he was on top. However, he changed his mind and quickly climbed off.

"Roll over, honey. I'm going to fuck you doggy style. You wanted hard and rough, you're going to get hard and rough."

I got onto my hands and knees and lifted my bottom into the air for him.

"Okay. Do it then. Rough as you like! I'm ready for it. If I scream out, just keep going, right?"

I felt his swollen cock nudge into my arse.

"*No*. NO! You're not doing hard and rough in my backside. I can't cope with that. I want it in my pussy!"

He was fast to pull out the inch or so of his cock that he'd managed to push into me and without wasting another second, rammed hard into me and my forehead was hard up against the headboard. His arms were around my hips, fingers playing a dance over my clit and it felt like heaven. His thrusts were as hard as I had ever felt. I screamed out loud as I was rocked with a massive orgasm.

"FUUU..CKING...HELL!" I gasped, the wind knocked out of me. I was struggling to breathe but it was amazing.

"Cum for me...you little beauty. Drench...my fucking cock...filthy bitch. Keep...screaming and...I'll fuck you... even rougher."

"FUU...CCCKING...DO...DO IT!"

A few more thrusts and he groaned loudly...a disappointed groan.

"Fucking...cumming. I...didn't want to."

"GIVE...IT...NOW!"

Suddenly, he stilled, cock shoved to the very top of me and I felt it pulsing as he released his cum, buried deep within me. Feeling the pumps so vividly it set forth yet another release for me. I juddered violently and my insides tingled in delight.

Shortly after, as I lay in his arms, he whispered.

"Fuck me, Helen. Is something wrong? You seem...angry. Have I done something to upset you again?"

"No. It's not you...for a change!" I laughed, my earlier anger considerably reduced.

"What's matter then? Tell, Uncle Simon!"

"Urgh! Don't. I don't like that. It makes this whole situation between you and I sound pervy."

"Sorry! Forget I said it, right. I just care about you and I want to know if anything's wrong."

"I'm tired again, that's what the matter is. Busy at work, sleeping like shit and a few other minor things beside. Oh... and add to that, I'm now informed I have a seminar to attend in Manchester with bloody James Mortimer...arrogant twat! I don't want to go to the fucking seminar with him. He's a fuckwit. There's no getting out of it...short of death that is. HIS...not mine!" I gave a false laugh at my pathetic sense of humour in the moment.

"My advice to you is just to put it out of your head until it happens. Then you just keep your distance from him for the two days. Simple solution, sweet pea."

I gave him a sympathetic smile, he just didn't get it. If only he knew my true reasons for dreading the journey. Then again, he wouldn't would he? He hadn't a clue and wasn't likely to, of the brief history between James and myself. My biggest worry was the situation I might find myself in away in Manchester. Those thoughts terrified me but certainly no more than I was scared of me and what I might end up getting myself into. It was going to be dangerous ground.

CHAPTER 14

I *made my mind up days ago, and here I am again. I'm going to follow Helen once more when she leaves her office for the day. My intention is to keep about fifty yards behind her as she makes her way down to the underground station. As I destroyed my baseball cap a few weeks back, I frantically searched for some suitable headwear in the depths of my hall cupboard. Amongst all the old coats and boots, the only thing I could find to stick on my head is a black beanie...actually, it's more a knitted woollen cap for fuck's sake. Thanks to my careful planning, I have a few day's growth adorning my chin and top lip. I doubt she'll recognise me and I seriously pray to God that I'm right. Having been so run down lately, due mainly to my lack of sleep, a few spots have appeared on my face...not the bloody greatest look I've ever sported.*

Standing here again in this fucking doorway, I'm frustrated as fuck and feel like I'm starting at the bloody beginning. It was as cold back then as it is now. My feet feel like they don't belong to me and my hands are that frozen they've gone white. I pulled my coat on when I left work and dug deep into the pockets to find that my gloves are no longer in them. I've tried cupping them together and blowing some warmth into them for the last fifteen minutes but to no avail. Watching the main door of the building where she works, I have to push myself back in the corner of the porch way as a man emerges. It's the guy in his forties; the one who I'm convinced was responsible for upsetting her a few short months back. From the shadow of the porch I kept my eyes on him fearing he would cross over, but he stayed at the opposite side of the street. He went in the opposite direction to which she usually takes. There was something about him I didn't care for. The way he walks has an arrogance about it. He struts; so much cockiness about him. I couldn't imagine Helen would like such arrogance in a man. A vivid memory hit me and I was disquieted for a minute. My face flushed with guilt remembering the time I tried to force myself on her. Hopefully, she'll find out that I've changed since those days.

Fortunately, I didn't have long to wait in the cold. She came out of the door roughly ten minutes later, accompanied by two other ladies. They all stood shivering together while Helen locked the door. They didn't hang around beyond that and I could see they were saying their goodbyes. One headed in my direction, but damn it all...the other one, a shorter lady I've spotted before, linked her arm in Helen's and walked arm in arm with her in the direction of the station. I waited until they turned the corner together, before hurrying up the street after them. I watched as they entered the station together, and felt more than my normal level of frustration. Christ, how much longer of this...this CRAP could I endure? Staying at a distance where I could keep them in my sights, I watched as they fed their rail tickets into the machine and walked through the barriers together. Knowing defeat when I recognise it, I left the station and made my way back home. There was really no point in following her back to Maida Vale at this point in time. I'll make further plans.

CHAPTER 15

idweek, I had plenty of work I needed to catch up on. Having been rather busy with Christina's training for the last two to three weeks the work had started to build up on my desk and it was getting to be quite a backlog. I decided to take an early train and get into the office for eight am. That would give me at least an hour to get some of my own work done before I spent some more time with Christina.

It turned out to be a good call. It slipped my mind that she had a dental appointment and wouldn't arrive at the office until after ten o'clock. I made a coffee at ten minutes to eight and went straight to my office to attack the pile that seemed to have multiplied overnight. During that time I needed to use the photocopier in reception and the damn thing was playing up. I fiddled about for ten minutes, opening and closing the drawers but couldn't seem to stop the paper getting snagged up. The thing was incessantly bleeping error messages at me. Gemma was the first in the office and had a quick look but she couldn't manage to sort it either.

"Not to worry, Gemma. When Christina gets in, I'll get her to phone the copier company."

She went up to her office, leaving me to it. I switched the paper trays around and used a different one so that I could carry on with what I was doing. I finished up and left a post-it note for Christina on the reception desk.

She gave me a quick call when she arrived.

"I've called the copier company. They'll be out sometime this afternoon. Is that okay? It was the soonest they could offer."

"Yes, that's fine."

Giving it some thought, I decided to carry on with signing off the accounts. I'd already finalised a small stack but was eager to get through the rest of them.

"I'll tell you what Christina, if you have anything else to get on with this morning, I have plenty to do. How would it be if I came through to sit with you this afternoon?"

"Okay. I've plenty to keep me occupied until then. I can carry on with those spreadsheets you got me started on yesterday, if that's alright?"

I assured her that it would be fine and buried my head back into the accounts. By lunchtime, I was satisfied with my mornings work. I'd almost caught up.

Christina was making great progress too. She was really getting to grips with her training, full of enthusiasm and enjoying herself having been placed in a position of trust. I sensed she was going to be a tremendous asset to us. By three o'clock we were ready for afternoon drinks and just as Christina was about to get up to go to the kitchen, the front door opened and a rather attractive young man came in and announced he was the engineer to fix the copier.

"Okay. That's the little beast over there."

Christina, polite as ever, pointed to the offending

machine in the far corner from the door. "Can I offer you a drink?"

He gave us both a winning smile. "Yes, I would love a coffee, thank you. White, one sugar, please."

"On its way."

She gave me a beaming smile and a wink behind his back, and tilted her head in his direction. A look that indicated that she found the guy to be 'hot'. I grinned and nodded back. He was hot. Not my type, and far too short for me, but nevertheless she was right, he was attractive. His rolled up sleeves displayed impressive biceps and with a matching six pack; clearly he was a gym goer. No doubt he was used to admiring looks and attention from the ladies at the many companies his business visits must take him to.

I'd never known Christina be so fast with the coffee making. She almost tripped over herself as she rushed back in, slopping some coffee onto the tray as it tilted a bit precariously.

The guy turned out to be really sweet and he chattered away while he worked on the copier. From the twinkle in his eyes, he enjoyed flirting with the pair of us and seemed to love the attention he was getting. There was no urgency about him and he seemed in no rush to get the machine finished and go to his next call. Christina, hidden from view behind the computer screen kept smirking and tilting her head in his direction when he had his back to us. James Mortimer walked through the front door, back from visiting a client. His eyes went straight to the engineer before turning to face us. He hesitated for a few seconds, realised we were involved in a conversation with the engineer and just had to say something.

"My word, you have got a lot on today, Helen!"

I glared at his back until he left the room. Christina saw my displeasure.

"Don't let him get to you. He's not worth it, Helen."

His blatant sarcasm left me reeling...and after I had been trying to make the effort. I got back to our ongoing conversation and put him out of my mind. My phone rang and it was a client calling so I took the call. The conversation didn't take above a couple of minutes but during that time I heard a text buzz its arrival while I was still talking. I guessed it would be from Simon and once I ended the call with the client, I put my mobile back on the desk and totally forgot about the message. The engineer guy chatted on in his friendly manner. It was a pleasant distraction. We managed to establish that he was called Carl and he had a two year old daughter who he clearly idolized. I couldn't understand why but throughout our conversation with him Christina kept giving me the odd scowl and pointing to my phone. At first I didn't understand what she was getting at but then I remembered the message. I think she was trying to say that I should check the text I received. I ignored her. If indeed the text was from Simon, I was not going to open it with Christina in close proximity.

She carried on, almost drooling as she chatted to Carl but every minute or so she gave me such dirty looks, indicating my phone in earnest. I picked up the phone and swung my chair to face her so that she wouldn't be able to see over my shoulder when I opened it. I stared at her, my mouth and eyes wide open. I couldn't believe what I was seeing; a text from Christina which simply read 'my vulva is twitching'. She took one look at my face and her mouth creased up. She ran from the office, holding in what must have been the biggest guffaw ever to be held back. Trying to maintain my composure, I was left speechless when Carl asked me.

"Is she okay? What was that all about?"

All I could think of to reply was "We're used to her, Carl. She has some very strange... she's weird!"

99

He looked puzzled and deep in thought. Somehow I think he cottoned on that there had been an exchange between us which was to do with him. It was ten minutes before Christina dared show her face again. Even then I could see she was having some sort of internal struggle. I gave her what I hoped would be my fiercest 'don't you dare do that to me again' type of look. I think we embarrassed him between the two of us, because after that our banter ceased, he got on with his job and the photocopier was finally fixed.

Once he left, Christina and I had an uncontrollable fit of the giggles. I couldn't believe this woman and how she had the capability to make me behave in such a juvenile manner. I regularly heard the other girls laughing on many occasions. They always seemed to emerge from her office with tears of laughter rolling down their cheeks and shaking their heads in disbelief. I remember before I took off to France that, although I loved working for the Hopkins partnership and with the staff too, it had always been a happy place to work but nowhere near as lively as it now is.

It was Friday before we knew it and I was looking forward to Leanne coming over to my place for the night. She confided in me earlier in the week that her parents were away for the night celebrating their silver wedding anniversary and although a friend normally stayed with her in their absence, she wasn't able to on this occasion. She made several calls but without a result and she was dreading being home alone, even though she was approaching her twenty first. Empathising completely, I invited her over for a quiet supper and said she could stay for the night. She'd always been good fun and I was looking forward to her company for the night.

We left work together when all the others had gone. James had disappeared ten minutes ago so the only one left to walk out with Leanne and I, was Gemma. We said our goodbyes to her and after I locked up, Leanne grabbed my arm and we hurried off to the station.

We ordered delivery of pizza and fries. I had a few gins while, as Catherine and Ruby usually do, she chose to drink Fosters. We had a pleasant evening and I was glad she wasn't alone and afraid at home in her parent's house. We spent a lazy Saturday morning sat around binge watching a drama that was showing on catch-up T.V. As she was going out on Saturday evening with some friends, it was past two when she left. I was alone again; alone with my thoughts of the upcoming Manchester seminar with that prick.

CHAPTER 16

I drank my way through half a bottle of gin before staggering up the stairs to bed. I fully expected to spend half the night fretting about having to endure the company of James Mortimer for four hours or longer on our drive to Manchester. Fortunately, luck was on my side and the two paracetamol I swallowed down with my last glass served me well. It was a miracle. After roughly six and a half hours of quality sleep I managed to wake up without a hangover.

I scurried around the kitchen with my head spinning. The stress kicked in again as I got organised and filled Harry's self-feeder. I hoped it would last him until I arrived home. I sat at the breakfast bar having my first caffeine fix and my stomach started to churn with anxiety. I forced myself to eat some toast hoping it would settle the queasiness.

Having rushed around earlier to be ready in plenty of time, I cursed myself. I now had well over half an hour to wait with nothing else to do but sit and allow myself to get embroiled in an attach of the jitters. My overnight case, handbag and coat were in the hallway near the front door, ready since the previous night. All I had needed to do this morning was to add my hairbrush, toiletries and make-up which I'd done when I came downstairs.

I manically plumped up the cushions on the sofas, wiped the worktops with antibacterial spray and twisted my hands nervously, all several times over. I allowed several unsettling thoughts pass through my mind on repeat. How would we manage to be civil with each other for roughly forty eight hours? Maybe I would watch a film later and shut myself in my hotel room so I didn't have to spend time with him. Bloody hell, I hope he doesn't try to belittle me in front of others attending the seminar. God, I'm dreading the journeys there and back; two lots of four hour silence. Would we speak at all? If so, what would we talk about?

While processing these thoughts, I had a solution. I hurried through to the lounge and grabbed a book I was in the middle of reading.

Reading might be a good idea, I won't need to speak to him!

I glanced through at the kitchen wall-clock; one minute to go before he would be here to collect me. Giving my sleepy pet a quick stroke as I passed his bed, I went through to the hallway and unlocked the front door. Peering out into the street after opening the door, I looked to my left just as James's BMW turned into the cobbled road. I cringed, my stomach felt like a nest of butterflies. Stepping briefly back into the hall, I grabbed my case, coat and handbag, then locked the door as he pulled up alongside me. He jumped out of the car beaming.

"Good morning, Helen! How are we this morning?"

The same condescending grin he always had was plastered across his face. I hated it. *Fucking smug bastard!* My good manners coming to the fore as always, I returned the greeting without a shred of sincerity.

"Morning!"

He opened up the boot and grabbed all the things out of my hands to stow away.

"No, James. I want the handbag in the car with me!"

"Oh, okay!" Without taking his grinning eyes from mine, he offered it back and almost let it drop. It was only due to my swift reaction of snatching out at it that saved the bag from falling onto the cobbles.

"Ooops! Sorry! Clumsy of me."

At that he turned away, the broad smirk still present. Things didn't bode well for a pleasant journey. I got into the car and closed the door with a resounding slam which I genuinely hadn't intended to do. His grin disappeared and he shot me an evil glare.

"For pity's sake, Helen! What has the car door done to you? Leave it on its bloody hinges."

"Sorry! I didn't mean..." I let the words tail off knowing he wouldn't believe me.

I considered the exchange of words so far and stared straight ahead for the first hour or so. Listening to the rousing tracks that Classic FM were playing I began to get bored watching the traffic weave backwards and forwards between all three motorway lanes. I reached into the foot well for my handbag and pulled out the book I brought along. I could feel James's eyes boring into me. I opened the book where I left my marker and made a conscious effort to get back into it. I could have predicted it; I knew it would be his cue.

"You know, there's an alternative to reading, Helen. You could actually *talk* to me."

I kept my head down and buried in the book, though my eyes weren't focussed on the pages. Suddenly irritated at his intrusion, I snapped back.

"Well, you've shown no interest in starting a conversation

up to now, James. Besides, I would prefer it if you kept your eyes on the road."

"My eyes *are* on the fucking road, Helen. I don't need to take my eyes off my driving to listen *or* to speak." His reply was a barely disguised snarl.

"See what I mean? If this is the most interesting conversation we can have, griping and point scoring, well it's best if we don't bother, I think."

I watched his hands grip tighter around the steering wheel, knuckles turning purple.

"Fine! Have it your way. I'll just drive in silence. As you were."

I was bloody seething, biting the insides of my cheeks until they hurt and then my left foot started a nervous tapping which I knew would instantly rile him. I needed to get a grip. Just as I expected it to, this was turning into a nightmare already. If I didn't calm myself down I wouldn't be taking anything of use away from the bloody seminar. Within making a sound, I closed my eyes and practiced some deep breathing techniques for a couple of minutes. It took effect almost straight away and feeling my annoyance gradual fade, I read. I got engrossed and the time seemed to fly past. James didn't utter another word until I became aware that the traffic was getting busier. We were on the outskirts of Manchester.

Turning off the music system, he tapped a few buttons on his telephone and activated the satnav. He turned his head slightly in my direction.

"Nearly there. Another fifteen minutes or so." He paused for a few seconds before adding, "I need a drink."

Trying to be helpful, I offered him the unopened bottle of water which sat in the centre console.

"Not that sort of drink! We'll need to eat soon anyway so I'll be able to have a beer or two."

"But I already told you, there is a bit of a finger buffet and drinks provided before it gets under way. We haven't time to go off anywhere else."

"I'm heading straight to the bar then. You suit yourself."

Feeling his eyes burning into the side of my head, I turned away to gaze out of the side window. The weather outside had turned and it was drizzling. Within a few minutes, rain pelted down with a vengeance and the friendly female voice of the satnav lady was suddenly gone.

"FUCK IT!" I nearly shot through the roof of the car as James rapped his hand hard against the dashboard. "Fucking satellite signal's gone. Pissing clouds!"

"Oh! Have you any idea how to get us there without it?" I asked tentatively, almost afraid to speak.

"Haven't a fucking clue. God, I could have done without this. Time's running out."

Realising that my phone would likely be no use either, I decided to offer a suggestion to the predicament; the old-fashioned method.

"Do you have a road map? They usually have city maps in the section at the back. I could try to direct you." I offered, tentatively.

"What good would that do me? I don't know which streets are one-way, do I?"

"Fine! Just get us there, James. I'm done!"

My face flushed with anger and my hands started shaking. I closed the book, returned it to my handbag, and watched all the pedestrians rushing around, hoods up or umbrellas held aloft as the deluge continued to fall. For another twenty or twenty five minutes I listened to his unrelenting expletives, excessive sighs and exasperated banging on the steering wheel. I didn't dare tell him, in case he hadn't noticed, that he had driven down the same street of retail outlets three times…or that the seminar would be starting in twelve minutes.

"Ah! Got it!" he shouted triumphantly. "It's down this street."

I was glad that I pre-booked the parking. At least we didn't need to drive around searching. He easily located a vacant parking-space. Once parked he jumped out of the car, barking orders at me.

"Come on. We need to run. I'll come grab the luggage later."

We were the last to check in and as James gave our names to the person sitting at the door, my eyes scanned the conference room for a space. It already looked full and there were no seats available near to the front. Finished with the check-in lady, James offered me one of the shiny folders she'd given him, together with a lanyard attached to a delegate badge bearing my name. He pointed over my shoulder.

"Quick, Helen. There's three seats together over there, second row from the back. On your right, look."

My heart sank and I rolled my eyes to the ceiling. Four hours with him in the bloody car and now I was stuck with sitting next to him again. Hurrying over to the row he pointed out, I plonked myself on the furthest of the three seats, dumped my handbag on the one immediately to my left, leaving James with no option but to take the aisle seat. I turned to face forward, but in my peripheral vision noticed his scowl, first at me and then at the offending handbag. Fortunately, he never got the chance to comment as the first speaker took the stage, offering her greetings before commencing the lecture – 'Inheritance Tax – Important Changes.'

At three o'clock and with the first lecture out of the way, the speaker announced a refreshment break. James was on his feet ahead of me.

"Sit down, Helen. I'll bring you a drink. Coffee…or tea?"

I sat back down.

"Thank you, James. I'll have a coffee, please!"

I grabbed my phone out of my handbag with the intention of logging on. However, I watched as James joined the long queue at the refreshment table. The line moved slowly along for a minute and I noticed him tapping on the shoulder of the guy in front. The man spun around, his mouth and eyes opened wide as he clearly began to recognize James. Some serious back patting and hand shaking ensued as they talked away animatedly and laughed, with a little too much volume. People were turning to stare at them. I'd seen enough.

My attention was taken up by my phone vibrating and by the time I read and replied to a couple of texts from Simon, a cup of coffee was thrust into my hand.

"Thank you, James." I looked up at him. "Who's your friend?"

"Well, that's what I was just about to tell you, Helen. That's Chris Owens. He was a great friend of mine through our uni years. We started together and finished together."

I glanced across to where the guy was about to take his seat a few rows back from the front of the stage. He was busy chatting amiably to a lady who occupied the seat adjacent to him. They were both smiling; laughing at times.

"Where's he from?" I asked, in an attempt to show an interest.

"Bristol. He's got his own practice now. Anyway, you can chat to him later. I've asked him to join us for dinner, since he's also staying here."

My jaw dropped in shock and desperately thinking of a way to back out, I decided to be honest about my intentions.

"*Us*? But I was going to watch a film and maybe order some room service."

"Oh, come on, Helen. Don't be unsociable. You don't even have to talk to me if you don't want to. Talk to Chris. He's great fun and very entertaining. Better than shutting yourself up there in your room all alone, surely?"

I gave a heavy sigh without answering and sipped at my coffee. The next lecturer had already climbed the few steps to take the stage.

"Good! That's decided then. You'll enjoy yourself."

The bloody nerve of him!

I made a valiant effort to show a little enthusiasm for the lecture, 'Capital Gains Tax – Your Responsibilities', yet in my head I was counting the hours until I would be back home. Chris Owens or not, I felt nauseous at the thought of sitting through a meal with, let alone an evening in James Mortimer's company.

After a long and boring two hour session, the speaker finally left the stage. James turned to me with a sickly sweet smile.

"Right then. Are we heading to the bar for a couple?"

Somehow, I should have been prepared for it, especially after he never got the lunchtime beers he was desperate for.

"You go if that's what you want to do. I'm heading to the swimming pool for half an hour before I get ready for dinner."

"Swimming pool? You should have told me there was a pool, Helen. I could have joined you. Never mind. We're meeting Chris outside the dining room at seven thirty. Make sure you're there or else I'll come looking for you."

He walked off heading in the direction of the bar, no doubt for pre-dinner drinks with his uni friend, Chris.

After fifty lengths of the pool I felt invigorated. The borderline headache I felt coming on as I left the conference room had almost disappeared. The gentle exercise had been calming and refreshing. I reluctantly admitted to myself that

109

the time would pass much faster by going to eat with James, with the wonderful Chris in tow. Hopefully, it shouldn't be too bad. I knew I would only brood in my room and probably end up not watching a film at all. I hoped Chris was going to be as entertaining as James portrayed him to be. I tried hard not to harbour any thoughts as to the contrary.

As things turned out my fears were groundless. When we met outside the restaurant, James introduced me to Chris as his co junior partner at the Hopkins Partnership. Watching him carefully throughout the evening, I took in every detail. He was positively charming throughout. Having only seen him from a distance in the queue for drinks earlier, I had thought his hair to be brown, but closer up it was more...not ginger but a rich auburn colour and his very dark eyes shone with a wicked and mischievous look about them. He was extremely charismatic. I couldn't be sure why, but James was also being extremely polite...and funny too. It crossed my mind that perhaps he didn't want to be outshone by his buddy, but hard as I tried to find fault I struggled to find anything amiss with James's behaviour. He'd even shown himself to have impeccable manners.

When we moved from the restaurant into the lounge bar, James found us a comfortable and fairly private corner. When the pair of them came over with our drinks from the bar, James sat on my right hand side and Chris was on the opposite side of the table facing the two of us. It was amusing to listen the banter between the two of them. Alongside my amusement, I was trying to get over the shell-shock of finally being able to see another side to Jim; his comical quality.

Halfway through the evening, James's left arm gradually crept around the back of me, yet remained firmly on the wooden ledge; not touching. He maybe he sensed that I'd assumed a more relaxed demeanour. The smile never left his face, especially on hearing my laughter at both his funny persona and Chris's jokey ways. Though I remained a little suspicious of James, I was thoroughly enjoying even *his* company. I started to feel a little giddy as the clock ticked around to eleven.

The bar was staying open late but the three of us all agreed that, as the lectures would start at nine o'clock the following morning, we needed to get some sleep if we were to be up and ready for breakfast early enough. We set off to the lift and I struggled a little to keep my balance so pulled off my high-heeled sandals and carried them. The mix of gin and tonics and the wine with our meal had got the better of me. Chris left the lift on the third floor, bidding us a cheery 'see you soon.' The lift doors slid closed behind him and it set off again up to the fifth. As I tottered along ahead of him James stayed close behind. We reached my door first and he caught me by the arm as I struggled with the key card.

"I've enjoyed your company tonight, Helen. It's been nice to see you laughing and letting your hair down. Would you join me for a nightcap in my room? I'll raid the minibar. Please say yes. It would just round the evening off beautifully."

I felt incredibly drunk and giggled hysterically at his suggestion. His face swam in and out of focus and that too held me in some morbid fascination.

"Let…let me get this right, James. *You* want *my* company…*mine*? For a nightcap, right?"

I laughed out loud as my third attempt to insert the key card failed miserably.

"Yes. Just one little drink, Helen. Here…let me help you with that card."

The door opened easily for him and I made to cross the threshold.

"Helen? What do you say?"

"Okay, okay. I'll be there. Give me ten minutes. I'll freshen up and…brush my teeth. I'll be there. You'd best not be messing with me again, James."

I screwed my eyes up in an attempt to look menacing.

"I promise you. No messing about, Helen."

I closed my door on him without saying another word.

Stumbling about the room for five or ten minutes, I started to wonder what the Hell I was doing. All I could remember was that I was supposed to be doing something; going somewhere. I filled the mini-kettle at the bathroom sink, returned to plug it back in and switched it on to boil. I felt the need to freshen up so headed back into the bathroom and stood there for five minutes, head bent low over the sink bringing handfuls of cold water up to my face. I slowly started to come round and caught my reflection in the mirror. My eyes were back in focus. Then it all came back to me, James invited me for a nightcap…quite some time ago.

I quickly brushed my teeth and freshened my make-up. I picked my sandals off the floor to put them on but ended up flinging them back down near the door. I wouldn't need them just to walk next door to James's room. It must have been half an hour since I told him I would be ten minutes. Maybe he would be asleep, but I hoped not. Memories of the evening came fresh into my mind. It was a long time since I'd been out in male company and I'd thoroughly enjoyed myself, it had been an excellent night. I would never have believed it. I made sure to remember the key card as I headed to the door. I tiptoed the five metre walk to his room and knocked ever so gently.

CHAPTER 17

I stepped into his room and immediately felt uneasy. I came along willingly but now regretted that I agreed to a nightcap. He'd pressured me and I was too drunk to resist. As soon as I was through the door and turned to push it closed, I was aware of him coming up close behind me. Seconds later, I could feel his breath on my neck. I squirmed. Some fast thinking on my part was a must. How could I make my excuses and get out?

The door closed softly and with an air of finality (or maybe that was my imagination) behind us. I turned quickly where I stood and his face almost touched mine, his mouth found my lips. Feeling repulsed, I pulled my face away and pummelled on his chest with my fists.

"James, get the *fuck* off me, this instant! I only agreed to come here for a last drink. We've had a fairly pleasant evening and got along fine together for a change. Please don't spoil it!"

He smiled lustily, his hands firmly around my waist.

"Come on. Don't give me that please, Helen. You know

what has passed between us in the office. You're no innocent party in all this. You're as guilty as I am. You want me as much as I want you. Otherwise, why agree to come for a drink, when you knew what would...*could* happen?"

Puzzled myself about that, I struggled to find some words...any words that would get me off the hook.

"W...wanted, James. Want-ED. Past tense."

He leaned in again to kiss me again, whispering as his lips neared mine,

"Really, Helen?"

Our lips barely had chance to touch. I grabbed his wrists tightly and thrust his hands away from my waist. I shoved him hard in the chest and backed away a little.

"I told you already. *Get away...*"

Trying to get the message across, I took a few steps towards him and gave another but more forceful shove at his chest. He staggered backwards, and looked down in an attempt to regain his balance. Having made a successful job of remaining firmly on his feet, he gazed back at me with what I thought to be, a drunken leer.

Our eyes met. This time, I saw the longing in his which mirrored my own, trying hard though I was to deny it. With my right hand I grasped a handful of shirt and tie and roughly pulled him up close me.

"...away...from me." I whispered, seconds before planting my lips hungrily onto his mouth. His tongue delved between my lips in seconds and I allowed mine to willingly play along.

From what I could remember of the taunting sessions back at the office, we never kissed. Still gripping tight onto his shirt and tie, I kissed him back, my pure wanton desire increasing. It was intense...like a raging inferno was building up inside of me. My tension left and I relaxed, falling into the fire; letting it consume me, wanting it never to end.

I released his shirt, and placed my hands on his chest. Through the fabric of my blouse and bra, I could feel his hot palms as they covered my breasts. His lips broke away from mine and his sexy voice teased me as he whispered in my ear; his breath tickled like a soft breeze.

"That's my girl. Let go. Enjoy yourself, sexy Helen. My God, you are just…so fucking *hot*." He lifted me off the floor and scooped me up in his arms before carrying me over to the bed. In feeble protest, I pummelled on his chest with each step he took. He kissed me again before placing me gently on top of the duvet.

He knelt over the top of me on his hands and knees. It seemed like an age as I was oblivious to time, but it must only have been minutes that he gazed down at me from his position. His eyes burned in to me. I sensed that he was trying to read my thoughts…and I was failing miserably at keeping him out. I was leaving my soul fully exposed and letting him in my head as I came under his close scrutiny.

I tried to penetrate his mind too, but I was defeated. I didn't know anything about him and something wasn't stacking up. How could this man with questionable morals have picked me up in his arms and laid me down on the bed like he had done…tenderly? Inebriated though I was, I was fully aware of everything, yet still puzzled. The guy didn't even like me for fuck's sake! Recalling my humiliation on the occasion he left me wanting and naked in my office, I asked myself 'Why?'

I was jolted back from my thoughts as he spoke. It seems that without intending to, I voiced the word out loud.

"Why? Because you are fucking gorgeous. You are what every man wants in a woman, Helen. Surely you don't need me to tell you that?"

His breathing was laboured; his excitement and arousal undeniable.

"I'm going to take your clothes off. I can't wait to see you naked again. Remember when I saw you naked in your office? I was cruel to you that night. Cruel to myself too. I wanted to fuck you so badly, Helen. Right over your desk... with you bent over it. You are intoxicating. I wanted to fuck you all night. I knew that if I once put my cock inside you we would be there all night...so I left. We've got all night here...I don't have to go home tonight, Helen. Neither of us needs to go home."

I gazed blearily into his eyes, hanging on to his every word...each hypnotic word, watching him, hardly able to take it in. I was mesmerised and suddenly realised he was removing my dress. His arms were behind me unclasping my bra, and I was powerless to stop him. I didn't want him to stop. He was being a gentleman; treating me like a lady. A shiver rippled right down my spine as, bra unclasped, he pulled it free, his fingers grazing my skin as he did so. I tried to speak but no words would come. Letting the bra drop to the floor at the side of the bed, his fingers moved to the top of my panties, slow little movements to pull them down and he let his thumb trail lazily across my tiny Brazilian strip. I sighed heavily, thinking back to those two occasions in the office when he left me wanting, remembering how badly I wanted him, how aroused he made me...how hard he was.

"James..." I pleaded.

"Don't talk, Helen. Just lay back. I'm going to fuck you tonight...all night. I'm not going to run out on you this time, there's no need. We are both going to get what we have been wanting all along...each other. You've wanted me to fuck you, haven't you? I *know* you have."

"Yes...yes I have!" My words were barely a whisper.

"I'm going to remove my clothes and lay next to you naked, Helen. In the semi-dark. We're going to explore, you can explore my body this time. I'm going to enjoy that."

He reached over to turn off the bedside lamp. By doing so, it left one thin sliver of light from the unclosed bathroom door to throw only a little illumination into the room. I felt too light-headed, but could make out his movements near the bed as he sat and removed his clothes. I was filled with a sudden desire to see his cock. I tried to remember if I saw it during our previous antics. I leaned over the bed, eager to have a look but his dark outline against that sliver of light formed a shadow. I groaned and shuddered, the anticipation building, both in my mind and within my warmth. We had time tonight. I wanted it to go slowly…to last. It crossed my mind whether it would be possible for me to cum without penetration, without him even touching my body. No sooner did I entertain that thought, my whole body shuddered with an overwhelming orgasm of a different kind. I gasped, barely understanding what was happening, a small amount of release pooling underneath my bottom.

"Whoa, girl! Phew!" His hand reached out of the darkness, feeling my wetness. I tried to focus on his smile, it was hazy. It occurred to me that I might be dreaming.

"Wow! I've got to fuck you now…you're wet for me already! Was that nice, sweetie? If you can cum like that without me touching…what can you do when I'm fucking you…*really* fucking you?"

"Not…not…yet, James! I want…" I pleaded again.

"Patience, Helen. It'll happen. We've got all night to fuck. You'll be surprised, angel."

He allowed me to rub my hand down his cock a couple of times, his girth and length felt amazing. He watched the movements of my hand on him. I was on fire and the flames lapped eagerly at my body. Perspiration was forming on my forehead…and my breasts. And finally, his cock slid slowly inside of me, his thumb rubbing furiously on my clit and it was there, another violent orgasm…and so intense. My eyes rolled back into my head and my stomach quivered at the prospect of what was coming. He felt big inside me. I tensed my muscles around him and pulled his face down to mine. Our lips met and he thrust his tongue deep in my throat, coinciding with the thrusts of his cock. I was driven wild. I pulled his buttocks further in, making him go deeper still, my fingernails digging into the skin of his buttocks. He thrusted harder.

"Raise…your pussy…when I thrust. Raise it…to meet me."

His voice was hypnotic. I did as he asked and thrust my pelvic region hard at him as he did the same within me.

"You…are…fucking…*amm-aaazing*, babe. Do you know that? *Wow!*" His words excited me once more, his words, his thrusting cock…thrusting harder. I gave a loud scream as the next orgasm caught me in its greedy grip. His hand was over my mouth in an instant, whispering in my ear gently so as not to alarm me.

"Shhhhhushh, Helen. Shush! They'll have us thrown out of here."

I bit into my lip, letting the scream die along with the orgasm's last throes. Our wild thrusting ceased as he attempted to silence me, but then his hand was gone from my mouth and he placed both hands on my hips, coaxing me to move.

"Roll over! Climb on top! Ride me."

I straddled him, my excitement escalating once more. His arms tight around me, he pulled my torso closer to his chest and the feeling of him inside me changed. I could feel his tip nudging my cervix. He filled my complete depth. I flung my head back and moaned as the tingling brought about my next orgasm.

"Ohhhh! Fuuuuck!" I stilled my movements, closed my eyes and revelled in every second of my release. I became aware of his tongue as it swept lazily across my rear entrance, then pressure being applied, a finger slowly edging its way inside. It was beautiful. My body quivered in delight as my dying orgasm came alive again.

Yet something didn't feel quite right…I was still inebriated and his face was next to mine…

CHAPTER 18

*H*is teeth bit into my neck and for a second I was caught up in the sensuality of it. The next second I couldn't comprehend why a tongue played over my butt; how he was feeding his cock into my arse when one of his hands stroked and nipped at my breasts. His other hand played between our genitals, stimulating my clit. It couldn't be so…but as fast as I opened my mouth to protest, I closed it. There was someone else in the bedroom, someone who, as my body jerked violently with another climax slid the intrusive finger out of my butt. None of it made sense and yet, I was too far gone to try and fathom it out. James was still thrusting into me relentlessly, but my arse was being penetrated by a larger intrusion, easing in gently at first followed by torturous pain. It was off the scale excruciating. I was oblivious to all else but the burning sensation and it hurt so bad I felt as if I would die. Finally, it started to register with me what was taking place. I tended.

"I…what's…?" I heard my own voice. It sounded distant.

James stroked my hair and tried to pacify me.

"Helen, I forgot I asked him for a nightcap too. He's

taking a fucking liberty here, but it's up to you what happens next, babe. I can stop this right now. You say the word. If you say 'stop' it ceases this minute and it will be just the two of us."

"I…I…stop! No! Don't…stop."

This was a new sensation to me and through my drunken fog I was curious enough to want it to continue.

"Is that a 'stop', or a 'don't stop', Helen?" James asked, "You're not making yourself clear."

"I…it's…don't stop."

"Okay, baby! You're the boss. You decide what happens or doesn't happen, you understand?" He stroked my hair again, soothing gentle stokes.

"Ye…yes!" I felt James' chin dip over my shoulder; a nod to someone, perhaps.

"Okay! Relax those arse muscles, Helen! Take me deeper. Come on, you can do it! It'll make it more beautiful for you."

I stiffened in that second with the pain…and the shock from hearing that voice – it was Chris who whispered. I was incapable of speech as he edged further in and the pain intensified for a minute before it became an extraordinary mixture; extreme pleasure coupled with the piercing pain. It was fierce; strong, agonising and yet utterly sensational. I was in unfamiliar territory, floating in a dreamlike state and the agony of seconds ago became insignificant; feeling my all-consuming bliss and self-indulgence.

They whispered all the while, one in each ear, one voice and then the other. They were distant voices urging me on, goading me through such extreme orgasms as one rolled into another; repeated explosions.

"Cum, baby…"

"Do you like being fucked up the arse…? You do…"

"Keep coming. Drench my cock, baby!"

"Fuck! You're a dirty girl."

"You're so fucking wet…"

The voices were subtle as if it was my imagination, yet I heard all the words clearly. It was as if I was removed from it all, not a part of my own body. They settled into a rhythmic thrusting, James fucking me hard at the front, and Chris's cock pounded into my butt. The rhythm was strangely comforting and helped me cope better with the pain, the powerful prolonged orgasm; the blowing of my mind in an experience that was unprecedented, at least, to me. My body jerked and bucked. I shuddered and couldn't control it. One of them held my head still as I was twisting and turning it in frustration, struggling to cope with the ferocity of the throes.

"Easy, baby!"

"Helen? Helen, come back to earth, babe!"

"Nearly there! Almost!"

"You want to go to Heaven, Helen?"

I heard the words so clearly this time, not too far away. I whispered the words that were on my lips.

"Yes, t..take me to…Heaven! I want…want to go…there, plee-ease."

The voices faded again. I couldn't hear their mumbled words, the brief exchange between them, but then I was back in the middle of them; sandwiched between the two. The thrusting grew wilder and the strange evil pain returned.

"Are you ready for us, Helen?" James asked me.

"Ready, baby? We're going to fill you with cum."

With that, they both stopped thrusting and pushed deep inside me. Their stilled cocks throbbed in unison; swollen in capacity and throbbing as they awaited their flow. A thought flashed through my mind as to both of them having erections to be proud of. What happened to the old theory that intoxicated men couldn't achieve or maintain a hard on? Jim and Chris had smashed that notion into dust. The pain I thought couldn't get any worse reached a crescendo and I screamed out again in agony and ecstasy as they both shot cum deep inside me. I climaxed on yet another level.

"Oh, fuck me! Helen!"

"Wow! What…in…the fuck…was…*that?*"

I was beyond answering. Exhausted and stinging everywhere, all I could do was shake my head in amazement…and disbelief. We laid there peacefully for a while, our breathing gradually returning to normal. I smiled to myself in the dark, still trying to process what happened. The next thing I knew, James was now behind me his hands stroking my face.

"Open your eyes, Helen. Don't go to sleep, babe!" It was James.

I moaned, waking a little, and aware that both pairs of hands fondled every inch of my body. Chris bit into my left shoulder enthusiastically, as fingers entered my swollen folds and his hard-on lay heavy against my belly. James's arms encircled my body, his fingers pinching my nipples painfully, his erection sitting between my butt cheeks, poised and ready for more action.

"You haven't time for sleep, Helen. Not tonight." Chris whispered, "You're going to get fucked…all night."

"Yes, babe. We want to show you the time of your life. Fuck you to within an inch of your life…and then some!" James promised.

"Fuck you until we have no cum left."

"Do you want us to show you better this time, Helen? You won't think it possible but we can do better can't we, Chris?"

Dirty words from both of them. I was flabbergasted to realise that despite my weariness I was becoming aroused again. My energy level was at an all-time low, all I could do was lie there and let what was going to happen just…happen. I closed my eyes tight, powerless to resist, but the anticipation coursed through my body. Hands left me for a moment and my body was moved into position. I was being rolled over on to my tummy and pulled further down the bed. One of them lifted me by the hips and I felt pillows being stuffed under me raising my bottom into the air. My head was being supported, something was being put into place to cover my eyes. I didn't know what it was, some soft fabric, so I guessed it to be a tie. Fumbling taking place at the back of my head as it was being tied; pulled tight. Somebody's fingers were trying to keep my hair from getting caught up in the knot. There was total silence for quite some time; no hands, no whispering, nothing!

My mind was in overdrive. I was being driven crazy in the anticipation and I fast-forwarded in my mind what was about to occur. Then my head was being gently lifted again, someone was on their knees in front of me and proceeded to rub their cock over my lips. Parting my lips, I welcomed first the head and then the shaft into my mouth. He started to thrust to the back of my throat and a tongue entered my pussy, which instantly stung due to the recent onslaught in there. I turned my head away, letting the stiffness fall from my mouth.

"Shower...I..." I groaned. "...need...shower!"

It was James who whispered back to me from down there.

"No, you don't, babe. This is dirty. I like dirty. Enjoy!"

I reached out for the cock and shoved it back into my mouth. I clenched my lips tight around its length and sucked hard as he thrust forwards and backwards and almost down into my throat. As James started fucking me with his tongue once more, he lightly stroked over my clit, twiddling, rubbing until my nerves were on edge, tendrils of excitement coursing up to my tummy. He knew I was ready to cum. He quickly withdrew his tongue, scrambled up the bed between my legs and rammed his cock hard into my wetness as the orgasm exploded. Unable to scream out due to Chris's cock fully stuffed into my mouth, the scream inside my head was deafening. Whether he intended to or hadn't expected to, his cock twitched and Chris spurted cum to the back of my throat as my orgasm subsided. I struggled for breath and had no option but to swallow his salty cum, gagging as I gasped for air.

James carried on eagerly thrusting deep into me, his fingers still rubbing furiously at my clit and I was totally engrossed in the sensation. Chris it seemed, had gone and I couldn't help but feel disappointed.

"Is it...dirty...enough, babe? Tell me...what...what you want. I want to ...hear it...from *you*. Tell me...how *you* want...fucking. Tell *us*. We're more than...happy to oblige."

"I...I want.." I started, but he cut me off.

"Wait, Helen. Tell us...both together. He's...back now."

I closed my eyes behind the blindfold, inwardly sighing in relief, raw anticipation taking over. James slid out of me.

"Tell us now, Helen. What do you love best? Don't be shy."

I felt as if I was living a dream. It didn't feel as if it was me, or did it feel real. I couldn't understand how it was happening or that I felt at times detached from it, even though the orgasms were like electrical currents and the pain so harsh. It was staggering.

"I...I want...to be fucked by...fucked by...both of you. At...same time – your cocks...both in me."

"Where, Helen? Tell us where you want our cocks. Let us hear it." James demanded to know.

"I want...you...to fuck...my arse, J-James." I moaned.

"And me?" asked Chris. "Where do you want me to fuck you, Helen? Say that word for me. Say it. I'd love to hear you say it."

"My...I want you...fuck my...my cunt...now." That word that I detested so much came freely from between my lips, but in this wild and crazy sexual abandon...it didn't feel particularly wrong for some reason.

James pulled away the pillows from beneath me and I heard their soft thud on the floor. Chris grabbed my hand and pulled me down onto the carpet.

"Straddle me, Helen. I want you to feel my cock all the way up to the top."

Seeing nothing because of my blindfold, I felt around in the dark to locate his cock and I carefully guided it, inch by inch through my soreness. He pulled my upper body close to his chest and bit into my neck. I tensed myself again, the joyous apprehension of waiting for the sensitivity and glorious pain when James would nudge his length into my arse. I started to ride him like a maniac, vigorously grinding my clit tight against his pubic bone, needing...*wanting* to cum. But I was missing something, I hung back; I had to wait. I told myself repeatedly to wait...I had to wait for James.

As if my wish had magically been granted, I felt his tongue flick across my puckered entrance; slowly, enticing, teasing and stimulating...pushing me into the abyss. Then he was nudging into me with the head of his cock, right at the onset of the next vigorous orgasm to rock my body. A hand was placed tightly over my mouth to smother the noise as I yelled out in that confused mingle of ecstasy and pain. My head started to spin wildly and I feared that I would lose consciousness. I started to float again and right at the point where I couldn't take any more of the oversensitivity, I was brought back to reality with a forceful slap on my right butt cheek. James and Chris both pulled out of me as the second slap came. Chris leaned forward, stretched out his arm and slapped hard at my left cheek. As the spanking escalated to full-on, Chris rammed his cock hard into my mouth to stem the scream that was building up inside. They were hurting me, yet I welcomed the pain, welcomed the shivers and gasped at the impact of it all. Another flow released, I marvelled at the orgasm not born from penetration.

126

In seconds they were both kneeling either side of me, first one cock then the other gently fucked my mouth in turn. Their hands raked all over me, prodding and poking every orifice, causing more smarting and tenderness. I revelled in it…every beautiful second of it.

"Baby, are you loving it? Tell us you're loving it." James wanted to know.

"Un-fucking-believable! Awesome!" Chris growled.

"I…I…" I was gasping for air with James's length still in my mouth.

"Do you want it to stop, Helen? We're going to fuck you some more in a short while. Do you want us to make you cum again and again, sweetie?"

"No! No…stopping. Kee…keep fucking…me!"

The rest of the night passed by in a blur. Crazy, manic fucking which at times I felt partly detached from; the pleasure all-consuming and *real*. There were several more occasions when the feeling was as if I had left my body and I began to wonder if subconsciously I was willing myself to do that to keep the pain levels somewhat muted, therefore bearable.

I woke up in Jim's arms just after seven am after having slept for less than ninety minutes. Chris was nowhere to be seen. I felt Jim stir and I turned over to face him. His eyes opened a little and his face broke into a smile.

"Jim?"

"Hmmm?"

"Was…was all that…?" I asked, finding it implausible that I was laid next to *him*, a guy I hated…and after the nights' unexpected developments.

"Real? Yes, of course it was real, Helen!" He folded his arms around me again. "Now go back to sleep. Let's have another half hour."

I sighed heavily, closed my eyes and wanted nothing more

than that half an hour's sleep, then opened them sharply two seconds later as he sat bolt upright in bed.

"Helen! You call…you called me, Jim!"

"Shut up and go back to sleep, James!" I chided him.

I was unable to eat breakfast and sat through the day's seminar in a daze. Every part of my body ached. I shuffled about in my chair repeatedly, such was my discomfort down below. With James on my right and Chris on my left I wasn't really paying attention as the voices of the day's four lecturers droned on in the background, my eyes seeing nothing. I managed only one small sandwich at lunchtime washed down with a glass of water. The afternoon session was a short one, thankfully.

By five minutes past four, James and I said our goodbyes to Chris and walked back to his car. Once I was in the passenger seat, I was about to pull the car door closed and James appeared there, thrusting a thick navy jumper into my hands.

"Here you go, Helen. Fold this up and put it up next to the window. Sleep. Rest your head on it."

Before I had chance to thank him he pushed the door closed and was climbing into the driver's side. I smiled across at him. He smiled back, a genuine smile that sparkled in his eyes. I slept. In what seemed no time at all, I felt a gentle squeeze on my right arm.

"Helen? Helen, we're about twenty minutes away from London. I thought you might like to start waking up now?"

"What? Hmm…okay."

I removed his jumper from the side of my head, gradually shifting myself into a more upright position. His eyes were straight ahead, staring at the road intently. I watched him carefully for a few minutes until I noticed that he was shuffling uncomfortably. I looked away, sensing that it was my stare he found unsettling.

"Jim?" His name rolled off my tongue again. "Can I ask you something please? Why do you hate me?"

His head snapped round to face me, mouth gaping, then his eyes were back on the road again. Breaking hard just seconds later, he turned the steering wheel sharp left and the car came to a grinding halt in a layby.

"Helen! I have *never* hated you. I *don't* hate you. What makes you say that?"

"I...just the way you have always been with me, Jim. You've always appeared to be...arrogant...even, angry towards me."

"Oh, Helen. That manner of mine! It was never about *you*. My hate, if that's what you call it, was for myself. I hated myself."

"But...why? Why would you hate yourself? Help me understand, please?"

He reached forward taking both my hands in his, eyes boring into mine.

"You may find this hard to believe, Helen, but I have *never* been unfaithful to my wife...until last night, that is. She on the other hand, has had several affairs. I have wanted you so badly since the day I first met you. Wanted you so badly at times that perhaps I did hate you a little, but not as much as I detested myself. I knew that first day, Helen. My need for you was so bad that it was almost inevitable that I would have you one day. I sensed it in you, too. I couldn't get you out of my head no matter how I tried. You wanted me in the same way, I knew that much, otherwise those...*attempts* at the office would never have happened."

He was waiting for me to respond and I didn't know what to say for once. I didn't feel the need to confirm that what he suspected was true. I looked down at my hands held tightly in his, desperate to avoid his gaze. I felt as if he wanted...I don't know what it was that he wanted me to say. He gave my hands a shake and pulling one of his free, he brought it up to my face, tilting my chin up to face him.

"Helen? What...?"

Rather abruptly I found myself blurting out my last question; the thing I had to know.

"Last night, Jim...you, Chris. How? Had you planned that earlier in the evening? Did you two work your way through uni having threesomes together? Because it seemed..." He cut in, not giving me chance to finish the question.

"No, Helen. I swear. We never did that before last night. Like I did with you, I asked him to my room for a night-cap, that is all. But you arrived first and...and we were alone. I didn't give him a second thought once I was alone with you. I had you to myself and I wanted you so much, you looked so stunning. I completely forgot about Chris. After we got started, well we were rather drunk to begin with, I saw him come into the room. At first I thought he would leave, yet when he started removing his clothes I...I didn't stop him because I wanted you to have a night you'll never forget. I wanted to make up for...you know!" He smiled again and I had to look away to try and hide my embarrassment.

"I guess the three of us had a night we'll never forget. But...it can never happen again, Jim. You know that, don't you? We have to work together, amicably I hope?"

"Yes. I know, Helen. Let's just accept right here and now that it was a one-off. I've probably got you out of my system now."

He kissed me passionately and I enjoyed the feel of it; sensual, yet undemanding. It was a kiss without any further expectation. Ten minutes later he pulled the car into my street and we said our goodbyes, quickly this time before he drove away leaving me stood on the doorstep watching his brake lights before he turned left out of Elgin Mews.

CHAPTER 19

*H*aving responded to the couple of texts I received from Simon while I was at the seminar, I hadn't expected to feel the way I'm feeling right now. When he pestered me yet again asking when he could see me next, I gave him my honest answer; 'I don't know'. During that first evening after the seminar, I had no idea that I was going to be sandwiched between James and Chris indulging in a mammoth mind-blowing fucking session for most of the night.

I felt extreme impatience, bordering on outrage towards him when the first text of the day arrived.

Hi H

When can I see you? I'm needing a sexy fuck buddy fix.

Hugs

SS the LL

Fuck him!

I hadn't arrived home until late and the sleep I thought would be inevitable never happened. I twisted one way, quickly followed by the other, when I first got into in bed. I tried hard not to think about what occurred in Manchester, but there was no way I was going to be able to switch off from it. I never experienced anything like it in my life so there is little wonder. The pain, the excitement, the disbelief and the feeling of pure bliss just consumed me for the umpteenth time. It was a vortex of mixed emotions that I somehow knew I would never experience again. I could still feel the aches and bruising I sustained so it was real enough. I was reassured to still feel the physical, as it was that which made me finally accept that it *had* all happened for real and it hadn't been a figment of my imagination.

The main factor that ate away at me though, more so than being fucked by two men at the same time, was how I felt throughout the double penetration experience. Feelings that I was floating and had left my body behind. The pain and the intensity had still been there. I experienced both and yet while my mind was seemingly on another higher plane, the whole feeling of the physical was dimmed. I shuddered as I let the thought of it all pass through my head on a continuous replay. It disturbed me. As pleasant as it felt to be floating, it hadn't scared me at all. But once back in my physical body, and with time to process it, I was more scared than I would ever admit. Could I have caused the out of body experience to happen, to enable me to cope with the pain levels? Was it my subconscious or my conscious? I didn't have anybody I could ask because of the dubious circumstances that brought it about…plus it was private. I couldn't tell anyone about the sexual experimentation that took place; it was unmentionable. Was there more to me than meets the eye? It was a nice feeling and it fascinated me. I began to wonder if it was possible to do it again. I had to find out…I needed to know.

Having just suffered through two nights with next to nothing in the way of sleep, I cringed as I tapped my reply to Simon, knowing he would be less than happy.

Hello you

I'm sorry, but right now I'm struggling to stay awake. I didn't sleep on Wednesday night because I was fretting again, then I didn't sleep in Manchester because of him. I suppose I was letting him wind me up again. I seriously need sleep. I'm going to suggest one night next week. I can't function right.

Hugs

H x

Thinking I'd best get stuck into some work, I put my phone on silent and tucked it away in my desk drawer so that I wouldn't be distracted by the display. I knew I couldn't cope with any irate messages from Simon throughout the day. It was becoming all too predictable with him. I say no to him and he gets arsey. Every time it resulted in me getting wound up and then I don't get anything productive done. I needed to shut him out for the day.

Christina called in sick first thing. She was suffering from a sore throat and had no wish to bring any bugs in and have them circulate around the office for the rest of the staff to fall foul of. Gemma, Janet and Leanne were taking turns to run reception in two hour shifts. The other ladies were out of the office attending audits. Since they were all otherwise occupied, I decided to do my bit to help. I went to the kitchen to do the mid-morning drinks. Ted was still away.

As the kettle noisily came to the boil, I felt a hand on my shoulder and almost jumped in shock. It was Jim. He was taking a risk.

"Good morning, Helen." He lowered his voice to a whisper and I had to strain my ears to hear the words. "How are you?"

"Good morning, Jim. Yes, I'm fine, thanks. Nothing a couple of good night's sleep can't fix. I had no sleep last night." I smiled, his hand was still on my shoulder.

"Are you alright? I hope so. I really do."

He looked from me towards the kitchen door, evidently fearful of anyone overhearing our conversation. I was wary too. It was common knowledge around the office that we had not got off to a great start and I didn't want to arouse any suspicions as I'm sure he didn't either. He continued to whisper.

"Well, I feel guilty as fuck, but then that's no more than I deserve, I suppose. At least you have nothing to feel guilty about. I'm glad you're single."

I could hardly believe what he just said. He didn't know about my fuck buddy so as far as he was concerned, I had nobody in my life to feel bad for. It was inconceivable that he didn't realise exactly what I had to feel guilty about.

"Don't I, Jim? Nothing to feel guilty about? What about your wife? Do you think I don't feel guilty about the fact that I pretty much fucked her husband for a whole night?"

It was his turn to be shocked at my little outburst.

"Shh, Helen! Keep your voice down. I really am sorry. I hadn't given that aspect any thought whatsoever. Probably because I've got enough guilt for the pair of us. I didn't mean to be flippant."

I gave a heavy sigh as I looked him in the eyes. He kicked the kitchen door closed.

"I know. I know you weren't being flippant. It's okay."

He folded his arms around me and held me close to him, whispering yet again.

"I'll learn to live with my guilt. I just want you to know that I enjoyed myself so much that night. I'll never forget it and I don't want to."

"Yes, me too, Jim. I…I…"

"What's matter, Helen?"

"It's…I've something to tell you…ask you sometime."

"I answered already. Truthfully."

"No. Not that. I know you did. It's something else, kind of not related. I need to talk to you."

"I've got clients all afternoon. Some other time, or is it urgent? We could stay back until everyone has gone home."

I held my breath for a while, tempted. But I couldn't put myself in that situation ever again. He knew that too.

"No. It can wait. Maybe next week? I can come to your office if that's okay?"

"Okay. I'll check my diary and give you a buzz when I'm free."

We both jumped and broke away from each other as a door opened somewhere down the corridor. He made to leave.

"I'll bring your coffee down shortly."

"Thanks, Helen."

By the time I took his coffee he had a client waiting in reception so I didn't hang about. He winked at me as I placed his cup on the desk. My heart melted.

The time ticked closer to five o'clock. I opened the desk drawer and pulled out my mobile. I was amazed to see a calm reply from Simon.

Okay sweetie.

I'll call you Monday night when you're home and we'll take it from there.

Hugs

SS the LL x

So he could be nice when he wanted to be. I smiled. There was no way I could have him visit me for rampant sex sessions with the recent hand marks still fading on my arse cheeks…and the soreness that needed a good long soak in a 'lavender oil' bath.

CHAPTER 20

$\mathcal{M}$y weekend was without a doubt uneventful. On Saturday morning I took my third soak in a relaxing bath, feeling at last that my body was recovering nicely after the sexual onslaught by Jim and Chris. I looked forward to when the aching and soreness would be fully healed. Hopefully, after I've fully recovered I'll be able to rid myself of the action replays which flit through my mind probably more times than is healthy. I didn't fear the replays so much now but lived in dread of letting thoughts of astral projection, the out-of-body experience thing that I was fantasising about, play havoc with my mind. It was a mystery that held a great fascination for me.

I busied myself catching up with jobs around the house and then settled down to read the second half of a book...the same book that travelled with me to Manchester and back, still part unread. During Saturday afternoon Ruby called me for a catch-up and after we shared our recent snippets, mainly her college news, we rounded up our chat and she passed me over to Heidi for a minute. The news Heidi was most excited about was that Catherine has a young man in her life and was hardly ever home. Her voice overflowed with happiness. Apparently, it's serious. He's called Gary and he's going through his final year in med school. I was thrilled for them all. Catherine has never been one for going out and socialising and boys always seemed to be far from her mind.

It was lovely to speak with Ruby. According to Heidi she was back to her old self...the Ruby before I got to know her. She was socialising with friends again and thoroughly enjoying her studies once more. I knew without a doubt that she would excel beyond her own expectations.

Heidi and Richard were taking a long-earned break and heading to the Indian Ocean on a cruise in the next few days. I was quite envious. Had David still being here, I would have loved to be able to do just that...take wonderful long luxurious holidays together. But the best part...to make wonderful memories. I have precious few memories with David...but though small in quantity they are more valuable for that same reason...too few of them. Heidi and Richard's forthcoming holiday brought home to me the sadness that I'm not part of a proper relationship. I have no-one to go and enjoy special times with.

I spent Saturday night brooding too much, as usual, about many things. Harry curled up on my lap as I indulged in a couple of drinks and got into a new book; not the well-travelled one. It's strange how he always seems to know when I'm feeling a little morose and loves to snuggle up close and inflict his contented purring and warm personality on me.

Sunday turned out dull too. The highlight of my day was heading out for a much needed food shop. Other than a few pleasantries with the check-out assistant, I received no phone calls or visitors for the remainder of the day. By eight o'clock Sunday night I was looking forward to Monday morning more than normal.

Come Monday, Christina was back at work and thankfully her sore throat hadn't progressed into nothing more than a severe head cold. She brought in the first coffee of the day with her usual beaming smile, but she lingered longer than she normally did and I got the impression she had something to say.

"Come on, Christina. Out with it. There's a reason you're hanging around. Have you got something to tell me? There's usually a purpose when you stand there with that expression on your face."

She grinned, acknowledging what I'd immediately suspected.

"Well...the seminar, of course. How did it go with you know who? How was the journey? Did you bury his body on the moors on the way there or the way back?" She gave a raucous laugh. I touched my finger to my lips in the hope of shushing her.

"Christina, keep it down, please."

I should have realised, should have *known* she would want to know that, after all I hadn't exactly been very professional in not keeping my dislike of him from her or any of our circle of friends. I racked my brain furiously for something to say. I forced a laugh and spoke in a low voice, although I could feel myself colour up.

"Okay. On the journey there, we barely spoke more than a dozen words, because he was in a bloody grouchy mood. During the journey back, I slept almost all the way until we were fifteen minutes out of London."

I would have been happy not to offer any further information but she had her determined face on, coupled with the solid stance that told me she was going nowhere. She would relentlessly push for more details.

"What about on the night? Did you have to endure his company for dinner and drinks? I could imagine that would be..."

Although I wasn't keen on being rude by butting in, I needed this little tête à tête over, so in a rush to end it, I cut her off.

"Yes! I did! James had a best friend from uni attending the seminar. I was coaxed into...or rather, *told* that I would be joining them. I was dreading it, but I have to say it went better than I thought it would. Chris, his friend, was very amusing and I saw a side to James that I didn't realise existed. All in all, I enjoyed the evening. He was much nicer to know. I think we've got more respect for one another now. I'm hoping that we've made progress and there shouldn't be any further animosity between us."

From the look on her face, eyes and mouth open wide, she was more than a little surprised to hear that.

"Oh, right! Well maybe it was a good thing Ted sent you both."

"Yes. As it turned out, I think it was for the best too. We all need to get along in the office."

I got the impression that she was satisfied. She left me alone and returned to reception. I was a little perturbed by her quizzing though. I got a feeling that there was something being left unsaid. It unsettled me.

Just before lunch my phone started vibrating and I saw straight away that it was Simon. I expected him calling much earlier so I was beginning to think maybe he wasn't working in the city after all. I snatched up the phone and answered.

"Hi!"

"Hello, sweetie. Is it convenient? Nobody around?" He asked cautiously.

"It's fine. Nobody with me right now."

"Are we on for tonight at yours, Helen? It might be eight o'clock before I get there. Just want to get some notes written up for another big case I have on in the next day or two. Is that okay with you?"

Fortunately, my body had recovered. The long soaks in the baths over the last few days had worked their magic and soothed all the aches and pains away. I felt excitement course through my body. I was ready for some hot sex again...with my fuck buddy this time.

"Yes, that's fine. I can't bloody wait. If you were here right now..."

"Ooh! That eager, huh? You shouldn't have said that. I've now got a hard-on."

I could well imagine he did, horny bastard. We said our goodbyes and I hung up. I coloured up, guilt suddenly descended upon me and I felt my cheeks burn bright. Why was I feeling guilty about cheating on a married man!? I let those thoughts play through my mind for a few minutes before getting stuck in to attack the buff folders stacked on my desk.

With Simon not arriving until later, I took the opportunity to have a leisurely soak in the bath. I lay there for ages, topping up the bath with hot water from time to time and letting my mind just wander off back to 'the night'. It had reached a stage where it felt as if I was just reliving what was an erotic dream, even though it was undeniably real. Was it because I seemed to leave my body that made my memory of the event now seem surreal? I didn't understand it and though at times I was excited to recall what had been one of the best nights of my life sexually, the thoughts of leaving my own body still had me shuddering. It felt weird to think of it as an out-of-body experience, and yet it had been far from unpleasant. I still needed to find answers from somewhere, yet it was hardly a conversation I was going to have with Simon.

An hour disappeared in no time. I towelled myself dry and picked up my watch from the bathroom counter...ten minutes to seven. I wasn't exactly about to be rushed but I wanted to take my time doing my make-up and hair. It was essential to me that I look my best. I want to compensate for having made Simon wait a long time to see me. It crossed my mind that there was also an element of wanting to alleviate some of the guilt that was eating away at me. I found a brand new set of underwear and an electric blue silky kimono. Taking a look in the full-length mirror of my wardrobe, I was happy. I kept the make-up to a bare minimum and used a hot-brush to put waves in my normally straight locks.

It was five minutes before eight when I recognised his knock on the front door. I held back the laughter when I saw the shock on his face as I opened the door. Clearly he hadn't expected me to be so scantily clad.

"Oh, my God! Why do you always have to look so fucking inviting, sweetie? I was hoping for two or three bevvies before we…erm…but I…"

I gave a noisy snort of laughter.

"Well, go ahead and have those bevvies as you call them. This body is not on offer right this second. I could use a couple of gins myself, so you're going to have to exercise some self-control for a couple of hours, Mr Fuck Buddy!"

He stepped off the street and into the hallway. After closing the door he wrapped his arms around my waist, pulling me up close to him. He kissed me softly on the lips and instantly, I felt his need in that kiss. One hand moved from my waist and rubbed over my breasts. I wanted him badly but I quickly pulled away the offending hand and rapped him hard on the knuckles before letting go. I got the distinct impression that he thought we would be heading straight upstairs. Leaving him standing there, I pulled free and headed through to the kitchen to pour us a drink.

"Just make yourself at home and switch the T.V. on if you want. I'll bring the drinks through." I shouted, seconds before

I realised he was right behind me as I poured two good measures of gin into each of the glasses I put ready earlier.

"So the seminar can't have gone too badly then? How was the journey…or more appropriately, journeys?"

I hoped not to have this conversation, tonight in particular. I briefly told him the details on the phone a few days ago. I had the third degree from Christina earlier in the day and didn't want it again. My stomach lurched and I racked my brain to try and turn the conversation around quickly. This was not an ideal time to be discussing James Mortimer. I didn't want to constantly have these memory joggers; to be persistently reminded of that night and my massive indiscretion with Jim and Chris. It was certainly not conducive to what I hoped would be a night of sexy shenanigans with Simon. I hadn't even answered his question and I already let the guilt creep in to my head.

"You're miles away, Helen. Was the question a bit difficult?" He laughed at his own attempt at sarcasm. I scowled at him before answering.

"Sorry. I think I told you the other day. We barely spoke all the way there. He got in a mood when the weather turned bad and the satnav couldn't pick up a signal. We drove round and round and only just made it for the start of the seminar. The journey back was…well, I slept all the way until about fifteen minutes out of London."

"Oh, yes. I remember you saying. What about the seminar itself? Are you fully updated on the new tax rulings? What did you do on the night?"

Bloody hell! I wish he'd stop with all the fucking questions.

I managed to get a grip and answer them as fast as I could, hoping that once I did so, he would drop the subject.

"The seminar was in as much depth as it is possible to go with taxation but boring at times. When we finished the first afternoon's session, I went for a swim. A friend of his from uni days was there too. I was told by them that I was to join them for dinner and drinks. The friend seemed quite an amiable sort of guy. I think maybe the gins relaxed me and helped pass the night. It was pleasant enough. I didn't have to contribute much to the conversations as most of the banter was between them. That about sums it up."

"Well I'm glad you got through it. I know how much you were dreading it. Now, do you want to watch something on T.V. for a while since you've told me to keep my hands off you? What would you like to watch?"

"I'm not bothered. Just find something you want and go for it. I'm quite happy to sit here and sip my gin and unwind after today. It's been pretty hectic as always."

I watched as, glass in one hand remote in the other, he did a fair bit of channel hopping looking for something to catch his interest. He eventually settled for a courtroom drama that, according to the T.V. guide, was almost a third of the way through. It didn't take him long to get to grips with the events that had occurred. He became engrossed and didn't realise that I was watching him. He kept rubbing one hand over his shaved head. His facial expressions as the facts of the murder became apparent were hilarious. For half an hour or so, I watched bits of the drama but still cast plenty of glances in his direction. I imagined him as the prosecutor on T.V. taking apart the murderer's story. I knew he was brilliant at his job.

By the time I finished my third gin and tonic and Simon, his fourth, the programme finished and he flicked the buttons searching for news headlines. Once he found what he was looking for and had devoured the day's news, he stood up and took my empty glass along with his own, through to the kitchen. I thought at first he was topping the glasses up again but he came back through to the living room empty handed.

"Are you ready to go up, Helen? You've made me wait all this time, but I'm ready to fuck you now."

The butterflies started in my tummy. I relished the idea and couldn't wait.

"Yes, I'm ready too."

He took my hand and hauled me up onto my feet. He turned the lights off behind us and we made our way upstairs. Simon used the bathroom first and when he was back in the bedroom, I went in. As I stood at the vanity unit brushing my teeth he came up behind me and lifted up the back of my silky gown. His hands were on my butt cheeks straight away. His fingers slowly crept around my hips and edged their way into the front of my panties.

"Fuck me, you're wet already, sweetie. I knew you were ready...but wow."

He turned me round to face him and his tongue was between my lips in a second and pushed to the back of my mouth. I let my tongue dance around with his as I enjoyed having his fingers explore my depth. My hand searched for and found his throbbing hardness. I pushed his tongue free of my mouth and bent forwards to take his cock between my lips. It felt amazing. His hands raked through my hair as I took him to the back of my throat, my hands fondling his balls.

"Oh baby, you're eager. I could fuck you right here and now, but I'm going to take you and lean you over the bed. You're getting it from behind."

His hands raised my head away from his cock and he led me to the bed. Nothing further was said. He gently pushed me over the end of the bed as promised and his fingers entered me again. It was heaven. In no time at all, his cock pushed its way into me from behind. I gripped tight onto his length with my inner muscles and already I could feel it pulsating as he started to pound away at me. One finger played over my anus, taunting me. That movement acted like a trigger and before I realised what was happening, it wasn't Simon fucking me. I was back in Manchester being used and abused by Jim and his mate. The thought induced an immediate response and in seconds I experienced my first orgasm of the evening. It was pure ecstacy, my body juddered uncontrollably and Simon urged me on.

"That's my girl, your cum is right down the length of my cock. You must have been ready for that, sweetie? It's been too long, hasn't it?"

"Mmm!"

I drew myself back into the here and now, trying to be a part of the time with Simon. I felt as if I just betrayed him again. He hadn't brought about the last release of cum…it was my recollection of how I felt with Jim and Chris that prompted the orgasm. I felt ashamed as he continued to thrust into me like a man possessed. As a result, I could feel tension settling throughout my body.

After half an hour I 'came' several times and he must have sensed that I was tiring.

"I'm going to cum, Helen. Can you manage a last one? More of your cum over my cock? I love it when you're so fucking wet."

"I'll see what I can do, since it's you. Leave it tight inside me. I want to feel when you're pumping into me. Actually no! Would you like to cum in my mouth tonight? I would love you to do that. Let me taste your cum for a change."

"What the lady wants the lady gets."

He started furiously thrusting into me then I felt the telltale twitch of his imminent orgasm. He pulled out in a rush. "Quick, Helen. I'm going to cum now!"

I stood up quickly and sat at the edge of the bed to take him into my mouth and it wasn't a second too soon. As he pushed in between my teeth, I felt the first spurt of cum dribble down my lips. I looked him in the eye as his cum continued to pump.

"God! Do you have to look at me with eyes like that? You're such a fucking tease, Helen."

It didn't take him long to fall asleep. His arms were around me only seconds before he started to snore. Where I was concerned, it hadn't been Simon fucking me; Jim was at the forefront of my mind.

CHAPTER 21

For the last hour or so, I'd stared at the same spreadsheet on my computer screen, lost in thought. Both the text and numbers were blurred; merged together. It might well be a page of Roman numerals or hieroglyphics for all I could see. None of it made sense. I was trying to make a conscious effort to glean some sense from them, but my mind was not sanctioning it. I couldn't understand why my head wasn't functioning and had decided to play games with me. I must have a heightened awareness of my own bloody heartbeat. At times I give great gasps to take air into my lungs and my stomach alternates between knots, butterflies and a disgusting sickly feeling.

Why me?

It isn't as if things have been difficult at the practice. With the tension gone between James and myself, I actual enjoy being in the office these days.

Ruby called me the previous night and it had been a pleasure to have a really great catch up with her. She's been back in college for a good few weeks now and told me she's feeling more focussed than she has done in a long time. It was reassuring to hear that and I'm made up for her. I know if David's watching down on her he'll be proud.

Things have been ticking along well with Simon too. We meet up most weeks and he hasn't made me angry for a while so that is something on a positive note. All in all, things are fine in most aspects of my life, so I'm baffled as to why I'm regularly getting these strange days when I seem to re-run the whole shit-show of my latter few years. It's like a film or drama being played on fast forward, skipping some sections to then rewind back to the skipped parts. I'm not a willing participant in this so why does it keep coming back to haunt me? I hate the feelings of panic it brings with it. At times I'm afraid; feeling the irrational agitation.

This morning though, my thoughts seem focussed on death; the tragic death of my parents and the trauma surrounding David's death. Sometimes I'm so lost amongst it all that I shed a few tears and dab at my eyes, only aware of it sometime later when I spot the soggy tissues in my hand or on my desk. I'm terrified of anyone in the office seeing my distress and have it escalate into a mass panic because 'Helen's having an episode again'. That is the last thing I want. I've caused them more than their fair share of worries about me.

Thankfully, there was a knock at my office door. I was grateful for any form of distraction.

It took seconds for panic to set in and self-conscious, I reached for tissues again to dab at any remaining moisture around my eyes. I hoped that whoever was outside my door wouldn't notice what I was certain would be my puffy, tear-stained face.

"Come in!" I hoped my voice didn't quaver too much as I uttered the words.

Christina walked in, looking distraught. It was unusual for her to wait. Normally she would rap on the door as a warning and then walk straight in, unless she knows I have a client with me. Her hands were trembling and her lips quivered as she tried to speak. I stood and rushed over towards her.

"Christina, what's matter? Out with it."

My words were a signal for her to start bawling her eyes out and everything else followed in the form of verbal diarrhoea. Feeling rather concerned, I folded my arms around her for a quick hug. I led her over to one of the chairs in front of my desk.

"Sit down, Christina! Right, spill!" I urged.

"My husband is working away this week, and my son and daughter are almost killing each other every day. I'm sick of getting these fucking migraines; it's been six years now I've tolerated them. My sister is in one of her 'I feel sorry for me' moods again..."

She said the words in a whiny tone which, knowing Christina's talent for mimicking, would be a quality impersonation of her sister.

"...and right when I could do with her help it's all about *her*. I've been spending oodles of money lately and now my car is going to cost a small mortgage to put right. One of my closest friends is being very judgmental and opinionated about everything I do and...."

I stopped her mid-flow by offering her the box of tissues. She pulled out two or three one after the other, and using them all in a wad, blew her nose rather loudly, like everything Christina did.

"Oh, Christina. I think I would..." I offered.

"But you don't understand. There's worse to come...much worse. I can't do this bookkeeper role, Helen. I just can't. I've messed up the set of accounts I'm working on. You'll be furious when you see what I've done."

At that her sobbing became more profound, as if she thought she'd committed some heinous crime.

"Christina, let's get the accounts issue out of the equation first. It doesn't matter what you have or have not done, it can always be put right, so take *that* factor off your list of worries right now. It's only a bloody spreadsheet and everybody makes mistakes at work. Over the years, I've made enough to match 'War and Peace' in volume. I soon learned not to stress over them. The more you panic about one mistake the more cock-ups you make. Come on, you know this is true. Let's not have any more talk about you not being able to do the job, right?"

My words had the desired effect and her sobs died away.

"Thanks. Thank you, Helen."

"I will pop up in a while and take a look at what you've done. We'll see where it went wrong and put it right... together. Now, I don't know how I can help with your other problems but you need to talk to your husband. Are you sure it's not the migraines that are making everything else bigger troubles than they really are?"

"It...it could be. I'm suffering from them too much lately. I will admit though, I was more mortified by my mistakes at work than anything. I just want to be good at this job."

"And you are good at your job. We wouldn't have offered you the position if we didn't think you were capable."

With that she brightened, gave me a beaming smile and got up to leave. As she reached the door she turned around and gave me her parting shot.

"Thank you. One more thing...it's been nice to see you much happier lately, Helen."

Maybe it was her personal nightmares that prevented her from noticing my earlier upset when she arrived. She obviously hadn't spotted the bin full of wet tissues or the state of my eyes. It occurred to me that I must have improved where hiding my feelings is concerned. As it turned out, it was Christina's traumas that turned the mood around after my woes, which paled in comparison to hers.

On checking her work, there was nothing other than some transposed numbers, probably typos, in the spreadsheet that caused her unnecessary distress. We had it sorted in the space of fifteen minutes and Christina was back to her usual chirpy self.

My own lack of output that morning prompted me to work late and get up to date. If there's one thing that I hate more than any other on the work front, it's getting behind when the pressure and volume are overwhelming. A three hour session on top of my working day and the heat would be off.

By five thirty, everyone except James had popped their head around my door to say goodnight, but he's never in the habit of saying goodbye anyway, so I wasn't concerned. Once I heard the last person turn the key in the front door I grabbed myself a coffee and headed back to my office. With sheer determination I got stuck into my work and managed to push the demons to the back of my mind. After a couple of hours of pure concentration I'd made great progress. The not-so-urgent emails which had built up for a couple of days, I read and replied to. The pile of buff folders that awaited my attention was half what it had been. The stack of 'actioned' folders increased. I would leave them on Cindy's desk ready for tomorrow. When I heard a gentle tap on my office door I was startled as the office had been peaceful for a couple of hours. I froze, petrified for a few seconds until Jim popped his head around the door. He smiled apologetically when he realised how shocked I was.

"Sorry, Helen. I didn't intend to make you jump. I hadn't realised anyone was in the office but me. I was going to get a drink and saw the light coming from under your door. Can I get you one?"

"Phew!" I heaved a sigh of relief, though I still trembled. "God, you scared me for a second. I thought I was going to have a coronary. Yes, thanks. I'll have a coffee please, Jim. I've got about another hours work."

"Coming right up!"

He left my office to disappear down the corridor and minutes later, came the noisy clatter of cups in the kitchen. As he made a cautious entrance balancing two steaming mugs, one in each hand, I smirked as I saw his facial expression; overly exaggerated and intense concentration. His eyes focussed back and forth between each over-filled mug and he had an unopened pack of Jaffa Cakes dangling dangerously from his mouth; his teeth holding tight on to one end of the plastic sleeve.

"Thor…you mi' fanchy a schnack." He struggled to get the words out between his gritted teeth.

He placed the coffees on the desk, deposited the pack of biscuits and sat down in one of the comfier chairs. He apologised again for scaring me and asked if it was okay to stay for a chat. I didn't see it was a problem while we drank our coffee. The conversation was easy, friendly and mainly about business; new clients we'd taken on, the recent government mini-budget, staff matters and general day to day snippets. There was no trace of our old rivalry and I enjoyed his company. Once he finished his coffee, he placed his cup on the desk and walked around to stand close to me. I watched in fascination as he placed a hand on top of mine, folded his fingers around it and pulled me up into a standing position. My heart raced; like the palpitations of earlier in the day, but these speedy beats were for an entirely different reason. His presence excited me.

"Jim! Please. We said we wouldn't…"

My flow of words was stemmed in a second, his lips making urgent contact with mine. I kissed him back though my head was warning me against such reckless actions. He held me rigid in his arms as we kissed and I recognised the familiar need for him. I wanted him; I'd always wanted him. Since that night away, my need for him had increased at a staggering rate.

"I know we did. I can't, Helen. I can't stop wanting you. I'm sorry! But I want you to myself this time. Just you and me...no third party. I've tried my best to keep a distance. It's easy when the staff are around but tonight...finding that you were here in the office...just the two of us again. I couldn't help myself. If you don't want me, say so and I'll leave you alone, I promise."

He wants me! He still wants me! Can't he see how much I want him?

I kissed him again, determined to demonstrate my need to him. In a furious wild fumble we peeled each other's clothes off. I was aware of my work being swept aside off the desk, along with the two empty mugs. After sweeping me up into his arms, he placed me on the desktop on my back, my head making contact with the keyboard. I arched my back as the head of his cock forced its way into my warmth and we were soon at it again, my arms tight around his neck. He stroked my hair with one hand, cupped my chin with the other all the while as our tongues thrusted and twisted together. It was electrical; I'd come alive again. We were oblivious to our surroundings. There was a kind of gentle tenderness to him screwing me and it drove me crazy. I thought of his words that night we returned from Manchester when he explained that he never hated me after all. He was scared that if we started having sex in my office he would want to fuck me all night and not go home. In no time at all, I orgasmed and he became still.

"Phwoar! I can....I love that you climax so often. I love that I make you so wet babe, but it's all mine this time. No sharing. Just you and I."

Removing the hand that stroked my hair, he placed it on my cheek. He held my face as he stared into my eyes. His steely grey eyes sparkled wickedly.

"Turn over, babe!"

He shifted his body weight from me as I rolled over on the hard surface and slid down a little until my feet touched the floor. As he pushed hard into me, his thumb swept over my anus; taunting me. My thoughts transported me back to the night in Manchester and me being sandwiched between the two of them. I realised I was holding my breath, waiting for the double penetration that rocked my world that night but wouldn't happen again. No sooner had I let the notion into my mind, his sweeping movement came again and I experienced a surge of energy through my body. I closed my eyes, savouring every second as I climaxed again. My vocal moans were making him thrust harder into me and he was breathed heavily into my right ear.

"Babe! Tell me you love me screwing you. Now. I need to hear it. God, I waited too long to fuck you like this, Helen Rushforth! It's all I want to do. Feel you cum, have your cum all over me, again and again."

I wanted him to keep fucking me forever but know that it's not possible. I needed him badly, again and again. We frantically changed positions. He sat on the edge of my desk and kneeling on the floor between his legs, I took his beautiful cock into my mouth. He said my name over and over; it rolled off his tongue and his voice made it sound beautiful. I was overwhelmed with how deliciously naughty it was to be fucking in my office; everything about it. I cried as he grunted first and let his cum pump into my mouth. He tasted good.

He joined me on the floor and we spooned right there, naked. I was emotionally drained. My eyes glazed over as I wept silently. We lay there in silence for what seemed like an age; he stroked my hair with one hand, his other arm tight around me and holding both my hands in his other. After a while he pulled my body around to face him. What started out as just a long kiss escalated and our need was reignited. We stayed on the carpet and this time, it was with double penetration from behind. He edged a finger into my backside as he shagged me doggy style. My body shook as I entered a multiple orgasm like the ones a month or so ago. Once he 'came' he started to talk...about the subject that was supposed to be not mentioned by us again.

"You loved it that night. Having two cocks inside you...it made you wild! Would you like to do that again? To be fucked by me and Chris again? One up your rear and the other in your pussy? Would you like to do that once? Tell me. You were intoxicated. Me and another guy...or him? Whatever you want, I can arrange it? I like fucking you when it's the two of us, but I can sort it if you want? I want to give you the thrills you love, truly I do."

His questions were overwhelming me. He mentioned it and it almost sent me into convulsive orgasms at the thought. The pain was absent, but I ached...ached from just wanting him inside me forever. I lost control of my body in that moment. I juddered, moaned, screamed and felt his hand over my mouth.

"I love it when you scream for me, Helen. It makes me want to take you to the country and fuck you in a field in the middle of nowhere, where you can keep screaming and I can yell out loudly when you make me cum. Imagine Chris and I fucking you in the middle of a field. Fuck me, you'd howl your lungs out. Tell me, babe! Please tell me I can sort it out to do it again."

I nodded, unable to speak and I imagined the Heaven. The way I felt…I needed to experience it all again. It was all I dreamed of these days and it crossed my mind whether it would be possible for me to enjoy a normal sexual relationship with one man as a permanent partner. I told myself it was a phase I was going through; a novelty that would wear off …at least I hoped it would. But at this moment in time I craved it.

"Yes… sort it, Jim!" I gasped as we climaxed together. We lost track of time. After I'd been being laid in his arms for ten minutes, I checked my watch.

"James! Fucking hell…it's almost eleven. I'm sorry. You should have gone home earlier."

"Okay. I'm taking you home, Helen. There's no way you're getting on the tube alone at this time of night. My car is around the corner."

He was dressed first and picked up the files he pushed off my desk what seemed only a short while ago. I dressed and took the mugs and unopened biscuits to the kitchen. When I returned to the office I checked that it looked exactly as it always did when I left for home.

We walked down the street and around the corner to where his car was parked. He placed his arm around my shoulders and turned his head towards me several times, checking to see I was okay. He kissed me on the cheek but nothing further was said.

When he pulled into Elgin Mews, I didn't know where my words came from, but I uttered them nevertheless.

"Jim, I thought Manchester was a one off. I thought we got it out of our systems. Your wife…"

"Don't spoil it, Helen." He reached over and placed a finger over my lips as the car crawled to a stop in front of my house. "I don't want to think about it. You're an addiction. I want more of you!"

Thinking that we'd been caught up in the moment, I vowed that things would be different in future. There would be staff in the office. We would strengthen our resolve once more.

"We'll speak tomorrow then. Thank you for the lift, Jim."

He leaned across and kissed me before I climbed out of the door and then he was gone. I fumbled in my handbag for the house key and let myself in. I headed straight up the stairs to brush my teeth and get into bed. My head was hurting. We promised the last time was to be the final one. How could I have let it happen again? He was right about one thing...he said I was an addiction, but so was he to me. Fear was creeping into my thoughts. He's married and it feels like I'm in dangerous territory. This has the potential for causing problems in the office as well as in his private life. I only hope that we are both professional and mature enough this time to not let that happen.

Surprisingly enough, I slept well. The office session; the reason for my depleted energy.

CHAPTER 22

I was awake early, refreshed and with all the
bounce of a kangaroo. I was on a high; a feeling I
hadn't managed to attain in a long time. I sang and danced
around the kitchen as I completed the morning's pre-work
tasks. I hadn't eaten since lunchtime at work the previous
day so there wasn't pots to load into the dishwasher which
made a pleasant change. As demanded by my hungry feline, I
gave him breakfast before taking the garbage out to the
garage. I watched him wolf down his food, trying to recall
whether I'd made much impact on my work before Jim made
his appearance in my office.

Once on the train and determined not to lose myself in
delicious thoughts of the extra-curricular activity with Jim, I
took out my book and tried to read for a while. With it being
rush-hour it was an impossible task. The only seat available
was an aisle seat next to a very large lady and I was uncomfortably seated with half my bottom jutting out into the aisle
along with my elbow. The passengers coming to and fro
knocked into me as they passed by. It was frustrating. I

sighed and returned the novel to my handbag. With nothing else to do I indulged in a bit of people watching; trying to distract myself from invasive thoughts of the previous evening. At last the train pulled into the station.

Turning into the street, I was surprised to see Jim come around the corner at the far end. Even though we were some distance apart, I saw his face light up and he gave a discreet wave with one hand, leaving his arm unraised. I arrived on the doorstep seconds ahead of him and my hand already placed on the door handle. He came up close and reached around me to place his hand over mine in a bid to prevent me opening the door. I noticed him cast a quick glance down both ends of the street before he whispered in my ear.

"Come into my office when it's coffee time. We need to speak."

I looked him in the eye, wondering what was so urgent, even though I already had an idea what he wanted to discuss.

"Helen? Please!" He hissed.

"Okay, I'll be there. Ten thirty then."

He looked out into the street again. Evidently we weren't in danger of being seen as he placed his lips softly onto mine; a quick peck. I was astonished that he would take such a risk in close proximity to the office. We didn't know whether Cindy was just behind the door in reception but we walked in together and saw that fortunately, she hadn't yet arrived.

As coffee time approached, I heard Cindy open the door from reception and head to the kitchen. My office door was slightly ajar and in no time I heard the kettle coming to the boil. She came and popped her head around my door.

"James tells me you're having a meeting and I'm to take your coffee down there Helen, okay?"

Very resourceful. Make it general knowledge that we're having a meeting, hence no interruptions. I have to admit, I like his style!

A feeling of disquiet crept into my tummy. This was definitely not going to be a discussion about business, I knew that much. My head started to spin. Had last night been another 'one off' after all? How was this 'meeting' going to end up?

I heard Cindy come back down the corridor and close the door to reception. It was quiet again. I headed down to Jim's office and gave a little tap with my fingertips before I walked in, double-checking that the door was firmly closed behind me.

He smiled and got up, coming straight over to me. He put his arms around me and kissed me full on the lips. It was very sensual; a lovely greeting. I pulled away quickly, knowing that anyone walking past would expect to hear voices, not silence. Rather reluctantly, I pulled out of his hold and hissed quietly at him.

"Don't do that here please, Jim. It's not right." He grimaced, knowing it to be true. Nodding at me and sitting down again, he indicated the chair opposite him.

"Have a seat, Helen."

"Thanks. What's our meeting about, Jim? What's it for?" I asked, though I knew exactly why. He didn't need to answer, but he did.

"Helen, you know why." He lowered his voice to a whisper again. "Last night, I asked you about doing certain *things* again. You said yes, and that you would like me to organise things so we can do it again. Have you changed your mind or do you still want that to happen?"

As I sipped at my coffee, I looked into his eyes, not allowing myself to break that contact. I tried hard to read what he was thinking; to know precisely what was on his mind, but his eyes gave nothing away. I wished we were alone in the office again. It was going to be difficult to have a whole conversation of this nature in whispers. I made a mental note that if there was anything we could say that wasn't a dead giveaway, I must try to speak in a normal voice. Whispered voices overheard by staff bore the potential to be misinterpreted, even though on this occasion, being misconstrued *wouldn't* be the case.

"Jim, when you asked me those things last night I thought...I thought that it was in the heat of the moment. Perhaps it helped turn you on and it was done to heighten the experience for me...for us *both*? I can't get to grips with the idea that you actually mean it?"

It was his turn to give me an intense stare and I felt as if I was being scrutinised.

"You agreed at the time, Helen. You said yes. Was that done to heighten the experience for me too...or is there a chance that *you* actually mean it?"

I looked away from him. I knew I couldn't search my heart for the answer while under his spell. I focused on the desk lamp while taking some more sips of my coffee. I didn't have to search hard, but I already knew what my answer was. I just didn't want to be under the influence of his intense gaze when the words left my lips. As I took so long to answer, he broke the silence first.

"Helen, whatever your answer it doesn't matter to me. I love it when it's just the two of us, like last night...but if it's what you enjoy, and I know you do, I'm okay with sorting it out simply because I know it makes..."

"Jim, you don't have to explain. I said yes last night, and today...my answer is the same. I want it to happen again. I'm deadly serious."

We made eye contact once more, no smiles, just a serious acknowledgement and understanding of what we were both saying; what we were agreeing to. It wasn't even at the planning stage but I could feel shivers of excitement move throughout my body. I trembled, shaking my head in disbelief at our outrageous plan.

"You can change your mind at any time, Helen. I saw you shiver there. Does it scare you?"

"I'm not scared. No! Why would I be scared? The last time I was…well, it was like being on another planet…in a way. I'm not ashamed to say I loved every minute of the night."

He leaned forward over his desk, resting his chin on his hands and fixed me with his stare.

"I know you did. I loved seeing you…elated. When we put the blindfold over your eyes you lost any inhibitions you may have had. Was it that you enjoyed the anticipation; the not being able to see what was going to happen next? I'm just trying to understand what it was all about for you."

I put my fingers to my lips, hushing him. He wasn't speaking in anything more than a whisper but I wanted silence for a minute; to listen for any hint of a noise in the corridor. No movement, no noise, everybody obviously in their offices getting on with their work. I felt a tinge of guilt.

"We shouldn't be having this conversation here. It's too risky."

"Nobody's around, Helen. Stop worrying. Don't feel guilty about holding a conversation with me in the office. Think about what we did here last night. Now that *is* something to feel ashamed about."

He was right. We both had plenty to feel guilty about and the conversation we were having now was pretty low on the list of the things we were culpable of.

"Okay. Get to the point, please. We've got work we should be doing."

"Yes, I know." He sighed. "Just tell me who, sweetie. I have Chris's mobile number. We promised each other to stay in touch. Do you want it to be him or someone else? I can arrange something…even somebody else if you'd prefer it?

Or do you think I should ask him? Do we invite him along somewhere and see if…if he's up for it again?"

I didn't have a clue what the guy's thoughts had been after Manchester. His behaviour was perfectly normal towards us on the last day of the seminar. I suddenly remembered Chris was single and didn't have anybody to answer to like Jim did. But for him to be purposely told 'Helen and I want a three-some again and we want you to join us'. It didn't feel right; as if we were making assumptions.

"Yes. I think it's got to be him again. He joined in without being asked didn't he, so it's something I think he's done before. But please don't tell him. I can't explain why because…I don't know."

My body was on fire just having the conversation. Already I felt the dampness in my panties. I stood up to leave and whispered to him once more.

"Please, Jim. We can't have these conversations in the office again. How am I going to concentrate for the rest of the day?"

He followed me to the door and with one hand holding tight on the door knob he pushed me against the wall and kissed me, grinding his swollen cock into my pubic area. I wanted him. I was addicted. I just couldn't say no.

For fuck's sake!

"Feel that, sweetie. I get excited too. I'll let you know what I can sort out. Give me a couple of weeks."

"Well, whatever you sort out, don't send emails or mention it in the office, please!"

My day's work was ruined. The amount of catching up I did the previous evening was to no avail. The pile of folders awaiting my approval grew to its previous size throughout the course of the day.

In the middle of the evening, I was laid on the sofa deep in thought when my phone rang. It was Simon calling. With my finger poised over 'accept' I considered carefully on whether to answer but I didn't bother to swipe 'accept'. I ignored it until the ringing stopped. He was the last person on my mind. I wanted to enjoy my thoughts of Jim without being distracted by anybody. Simon would have to wait if he wanted my company.

CHAPTER 23

*S*ince our questionable little 'meeting' in the office, two weeks flew by and I was still waiting to hear back from Jim. During our working day, we'd seen each other several times in the corridor but there hadn't been any real opportunity to talk; there was always somebody within earshot. I didn't want to go to his office for yet another meeting. I'd already noticed the staff raise their eyebrows at our new politeness and amiability towards each other. Neither of us had any desire to make things look too cosy between us.

There was loads of missed calls on my phone; calls from Simon which I was hell bent on ignoring. After most of the times he tried to ring, he followed them up with periods of furious texting.

'Helen, why are you ignoring my calls? What have I done this time?'

'Sweetie, please text me back. I need to see you or hear from you at least.'

'Helen, answer your fucking calls!!'

I was panicking in case he turned up at my home. Not that I had anything to hide if he did, but I didn't relish the thought of him descending on me unannounced. Though I think the world of him, and probably always will, he isn't what I need right now. On a few occasions I considered telling him that our 'fuck buddy' status was finished but I couldn't bring myself to do it. It isn't in my nature to be nasty to him. He's a brilliant friend and he *does* care, but I need to get this...this...I don't even know what it is with me and Jim, but I need to get it out of my system. Somehow, I can't see myself having threesomes for the rest of my life. I'm annoyed that I've allowed myself to get sucked into a relationship with yet another guy who's married. Where Simon is concerned I'm not too bothered because many times he's admitted to me he's a consummate cheat. He made it clear that if it hadn't been me, then it would be someone else, even though he's confessed that he loves his wife deeply. It's different where Jim is concerned. Some years ago, he did love his wife and she abused that love by relentlessly cheating on him. He told me that he never considered cheating on her, at least until I came on the scene. How true that is I don't know but I feel as if I'm the only one to blame, just by being me.

On Monday afternoon, the ninth of May, I was working in Christina's office giving her some more tuition when Cindy called from reception; one of my clients had popped in to see me for ten minutes asking for some advice. I gave my apologies to Christina and promised to return in fifteen minutes. I went down to my office and called Cindy asking her to send Mr Howard along. As I returned the phone to the cradle, I spotted a post-it stuck to my computer screen.

'I'll text you later. I found something. X'

I was shocked for a second or two. It was Jim's writing. I didn't have time to concern myself with what he sorted though. There was a knock on my door and Mr Howard walked in. After a twenty minute chat with him, I joined Christina again to resume the training session. The rest of the day was pretty uneventful and I left the office on time for a pleasant change.

It was six o'clock when the promised text finally arrived; it was a link to a website. I clicked on the link and was stunned to see a picture of a beautiful one bedroom country lodge complete with hot-tub. It stood alone in the middle of nowhere. The nearest village was five miles away according to the travel directions, with the closest city being Bristol, at fifteen miles away. I imagine the fact that Chris lives in Bristol was what prompted him to search the surrounding countryside for a suitable place to stay.

Ten minutes later, the next message arrived.

'What do you think to it? Nice, huh? Cheryl and Jack are going to her parents for two weeks at half term. We can drive down after work on Friday. I can get Chris to join us on Saturday. I get you to myself for the first night.'

I answered immediately. The excitement had already started to course through my body and I shuddered in anticipation. Three weeks was a long time to wait; the pleasure… and the pain.

'Sounds fantastic. How will we escape from work? I need to bring a small case.'

I received a quick reply.

'I must get home. Don't answer this text. We need another meeting. X'

I spent all evening contemplating how work would be for the next three weeks. I had to keep avoiding him at all costs. The whole plan would drive me to distraction. I suppose two weeks had passed quickly since our last 'meeting'. To have another meet up in the office would have to go unmentioned to any of the staff. I needed to release some sexual tension that night when I went to bed, thank goodness for the sex toys. It didn't fully hit the spot but it had to do for the time being.

I disappeared into Jim's office first thing the next morning. Nobody saw me.

Before closing his door properly, I didn't engage my brain before blurting out the words straight away.

"What have you said to Chris?"

"I haven't mentioned anything. I told him I was having a weekend break in the Bristol area and did he want to come over for a few drinks on the Saturday night. He said yes. I told him he'll be on the sofa." He gave a little laugh and added. "He didn't seem to mind."

"Okay. It's fine for you. Your suitcase will be in the car. How do I get around bringing mine in to the office?"

"Come on, Helen. Stop seeing problems before they arise. It's easy. You're going to a friend for the weekend. Once everybody has left the office you head around the corner to the car park with your case. I'll follow you a couple of minutes later. Or I can leave before you, it doesn't matter which. Nobody will have a clue, trust me."

He made it sound so bloody easy, yet I knew he was right. I couldn't help feeling over cautious. The nerves started to creep in and I shuddered. It felt downright deceitful. Feeling the guilt about our shady little meeting I got up to leave. He stood up and came towards me again but I shot out of the door before he had the chance to try and kiss me. I didn't need sexual tension creeping into my day like it did the last time. I went back to my office and buried myself in the deep pile of paperwork.

For the next few days I was harassed by more texts and missed calls from Simon. Realising, as I should have done days ago, that he would carry on regardless, I replied to one of the texts.

'Simon, please leave me alone for a while. I'm busy. Sex is the last thing on my mind right now as I have some things I need to sort out in my head. Please have some respect. I will contact you when I sort myself out. Helen x'

I should have expected it, yet it still angered me that he thought he could make everything right as always. Another message arrived and this time after reading it I switched my phone off. I had no wish to engage in further conversation with him.

'Okay, sweet pea! Anything I can help with? Always here. Love Simon xx'

I allowed the guilt to eat me up as usual. I was treating him badly and I couldn't help but feel sorry for him.

The following Monday was my birthday and as is usual on staff birthdays, most of them gathered in my office after morning coffee and gave me presents and cards. I was aware of Jim hovering in the background, and each time I looked over he gave me a wink. He didn't have a card for me but I knew the flowers that arrived shortly after nine with no card, were from him. I never mentioned to him when my birthday was, so I assume that at some stage he'd looked in the personnel files in Ted's office. He stood in line like the others to come over and give me a hug, saying in a voice loud enough for everyone to hear.

"Sorry, Helen. I hadn't realised it was your birthday."

I politely offered my thanks with,

"It really doesn't matter, James. Don't worry."

Letting my eagle eye scan quickly around them all as he hugged me, the only person to have watched this exchange from the corner of her eye was Christina. I didn't miss the slight smirk as she averted her eyes.

CHAPTER 24

When I walked through reception tugging my little case behind me, Cindy, together with Nina and Janet, who were stood around her desk raised their eyebrows and smiled knowingly.

"Ooh, Helen! Going somewhere nice for the weekend? Who's the lucky man?"

I'd been just about to answer when the door to the corridor opened and Jim walked in. I gave him a blank stare and turned back to the girls.

"As if! Sorry to disappoint, girls. There is no man. Just an old friend from my uni years. We're heading into the country for a break. Nothing more exciting than that, I'm afraid."

But they were having none of it.

"Aww, come on Helen. You've had flowers delivered twice now, including the ones on your birthday…and now you're going away and being overly secretive. You expect us to believe you haven't got someone in tow?"

Jim didn't stick around in reception too long. I guess he thought that his presence might make me feel uncomfortable in light of the awkward questions being asked.

Whether he stayed or not, I couldn't feel any more uncomfortable than I already did. It felt wrong to be deceiving them. I was lying to my friends. I suppose it goes with the territory when you're doing something that feels wrong. I left reception cringing inwardly. Jim was half in and half out of his office as I headed down the corridor to mine. He gave me a wink and a reassuring smile before going in to his room. I sighed as I dumped the case in a corner of the office.

It seemed as if the working day would never end. Thankfully, I had given two hundred percent for the last few days and I had left myself very little to do that I could be distracted from. I spent most of the day staying out of Jim's way and stared at the computer screen lost in my daydreams. I wondered if he was feeling the same. As guilty as I felt I could not stop the state of euphoria that I was lost in.

At five fifteen I stood to the side of the window in my office, keeping a discreet watch on everyone leaving for the weekend. I saw Gemma and Cindy leave together with Christina following two minutes later. Ted had already left the office at lunchtime heading off on a golfing weekend up North. The young trainees would be heading straight home from their week's audits. It seemed as if the last two were going to take forever. Surprisingly, Leanne was much later than normal, as was Janet but just as I was about to call Jim, I heard the front door close once more. I dashed to my place by the window to see them disappear. Two minutes later, Jim appeared in my doorway.

"Are we ready, Helen? Shall we do this?"

He grinned expectantly and came over to where I was standing, my nerves kicking in in a flash. He folded his arms around me and kissed me on the cheek. I felt an extraordinary sensation swoop over me. My heart rate elevated. Any guilty thoughts I'd nourished were gone.

"Yes. Let's get on our way. You go first, Jim. I'll lock the front door."

Releasing me from his hold, he patted my bottom playfully before heading through to reception.

"See you shortly, sweetie."

I took a few deep breaths to try to regain some composure and followed him down the street. I couldn't help but look behind me every few seconds. I feared someone may have forgotten something and turned to come back to the office. Jim would be in the car waiting by the time I arrived at the car park.

He laughed as I opened the car door.

"What took you so long? Second thoughts?"

I smiled and he leaned over the console and gave me a slow and meaningful kiss.

"Do I look as if I have second thoughts? I wanted this, right? I told you that. I want it very much, Jim. Do you?"

"Yes. I want *you* very much. I'm going to enjoy having you to myself tonight, Helen. Right, let's get out of here."

From what he told me earlier in the week, it would take us the best part of three hours to get there if we stayed on the M4. The plan was that we would stop off somewhere to have something to eat, though. If he remembered to do so the previous evening, he'd planned on putting a supply of alcohol into his car. I wasn't sure that I wanted to drink tonight but I knew I would need to consume some alcohol on the Saturday. I very much doubt I would find the courage to be an active participant in a menagé without drinking beforehand.

Until we stopped off for food at a motorway services, there hadn't been much conversation between us. I don't know why James was quiet but I was letting my private thoughts and anticipation run away with me. When he parked up I can't remember being so sexually charged. I would have happily got him to take me into the back seat of the car and fuck me there and then. It's a blessing that he seemed to have more self-control than I did.

The food in the services wasn't brilliant but at least we ate enough to stave off hunger. We were soon on our way once more and this time I got the feeling we were only indulging in idle meaningless conversation to keep our minds off the forthcoming activities the night held in store.

It was gone ten o'clock when he pulled the car alongside the decking which belonged to the lodge. The place was in dense blackness. There were no lights to be seen from any nearby buildings or homes, so I assumed the information was correct; the lodge stood miles from anywhere. He told me which plant pot the key would be under while he grabbed both our cases from the boot of the car. I soon located the key, unlocked the door and reached around the wall trying to find the light switch. The whole living/kitchen area was soon bathed in a subdued amber light. It was stunning, cosy and tastefully furnished. I stood gazing around, taking in every detail as Jim came up behind me and hurriedly dumped both suitcases to one side of the door.

He took my breath away as he swept me off the floor. Keeping me cradled in his arms he kissed me, passionately at first and more demanding as our mutual need grew. He gently lowered me back to the floor and proceeded to unfasten my clothes. I followed his moves urgently, being careful not to tear too wildly at the trousers of his suit.

He kissed around the back of my neck and whispered in my ear.

"Helen, let's take this to the hot-tub. I'll go grab a couple of towels from the bathroom."

Although it was almost June, the night was chilly. We hurried over the decking wrapped in our towels and quickly hauled the cover off. We shed the towels and climbed into the water. It was Heaven. We sat giggling for a few minutes, kissed each other wildly and indulged in some serious foreplay. It was wildly erotic to say the least. We explored each other's bodies on and off and splashed around in between times. It felt good to be having fun with nobody around to judge us. We giggled like pre-school children on a first ever dip in the paddling pool. Water poured down my face and I leaned over to grab a corner of the towel to dry my eyes. When I turned back to face him he was playfully waving his cock about under the water and watching me for a reaction.

"If you think I'm going to perform an underwater blow job, you're sadly mistaken, Mister." I laughed as I scolded him.

As I attempted to lower my body back into the water he grabbed me by the thighs and ran his tongue slowly across my folds. I carried on lowering myself until his head was submerged. He stayed in that position as long as he could, but emerged coughing and spluttering.

"Go on, Helen, be a devil. You know you want to."

The challenge was there in his eyes, willing me on. I stared hard into his eyes and took his cock into my mouth before lowering my head under the water. I pushed its full length to the back of my throat but sadly, I swallowed too much water as he had done two minutes beforehand. I emerged, somewhat traumatised by the intake of water into my nose and mouth. Showing concern that I was okay, he rubbed and patted my back until I stopped spluttering. Pulling me towards him, he parted my legs until I precariously straddled him on the narrow seated part of the tub. He rammed into me and it felt amazing. I tried hard to ride him but it was frustrating; we kept losing contact. After just ten minutes in the tub Jim climbed out, towelled himself dry and held the other towel out for me as I stepped out. He wrapped it tight around me before hurrying us both across the decking.

As cosy as it was indoors, he went over to the fireplace and found a box of matches in the hearth. Five minutes later the log burner was nicely aglow.

"I want to fuck you right here, babe. In front of the flames! Go and grab the duvet from the bed. I'm going to the car to get the booze."

"Let's do it then! I'll get the duvet."

By the time I returned from the bedroom, he was back from the car with the drinks. With the duvet over the top of the fireside rug I knelt, head bent over close to the flames, until my hair was steam drying. Jim poured drinks, placed the two glasses on the side table and sprawled on the duvet. He reached out for my hand and pulled me down to lie next to him. We laid like that for some time, doing nothing more than kiss in the firelight. I was suddenly struck by how romantic it was. There was no desperation or urgency and I had no wish to rush things. With the whole night to ourselves, it was my intent to enjoy every second with him.

After we'd kissed for a long time, he asked me to turn over and face away from him. I fully expected him to ram his cock into me from behind, but he didn't. Instead, he placed his arm around me and did nothing more than cup my breast. It was cosy, warm and comfortable; ecstacy. I felt safe and content just to be in his arms. My eyes started to close as I watched the flames of the log fire flicker. It was hypnotic; on the borderline between awake and asleep.

I jumped, snapped awake as I felt him kiss the back of my neck. One of his fingers played in my hair which was still damp. He twirled and un-twirled it around one of his fingers. His other hand still cupped by breast. He tweaked my left nipple in a teasing manner.

"Helen?" His whisper was barely audible.

"Uh-huh?" I was surprised at how sleepy my voice sounded.

"I lied to you earlier!"

My ears pricked up, I was instantly wide awake. I wondered what he was about to say. I dreaded hearing what it was he supposedly lied about. The seconds ticked by before I answered.

"Did you indeed? About what?"

"I said I was going to fuck you!"

"You did. So…now you're not going to?"

"No."

"*Why?*" I asked, my question indignant. I was taken aback.

"Because, Helen, I'm going to make love to you instead. That's why!"

It took a while for his words to sink in. I struggled to get my head around what he said. I'd been in this situation on a few occasions and usually it didn't bode well. The heart and head battle started again; they were never done being at war with each other. Thinking forward to the Saturday, Chris would be arriving. If things happened according to plan, if he was tempted again, it would be the pair of them fucking me at the same time. Jim wants me to himself tonight.

If he wants to make love to you, then let him! What's not to like about the idea?

I didn't respond with words. I rolled over to face him and trailed my fingers across his lips before letting him kiss me. His eyes never left mine. I could see the desire in them…and something else. I couldn't even believe I was in his arms and yet here we were and he was about to make love to me. The guy who I once hated, the guy who I thought had detested me. Alone together, naked in front of a log fire. I was over-whelmed. I wanted this more than anything else in the world.

His moves were slow. His hands gently stroked my skin

and held my face. He paused the kisses and his eyes bore into mine, never wavering. I gazed back at him and sometimes I'm sure I saw the disbelief in him, too; almost a dreamlike state. My heart was on fire...the feeling so intense.

He finally broke the long silence between us.

"You are beautiful. I can't take my eyes off you, Helen. It's not you're your beauty though...I can't explain. There's something about you that...I don't know...that *excites* me...in a way that I've never been excited before."

I laughed softly.

"I think I've noticed!"

He was insistent.

"No, Helen. Not in the way you're thinking. Yes, I admit I've wanted to fuck you since I first set eyes on you...but there's more to this than wanting sex with you."

I should be scared by his words; terrified at where this could possibly be heading, but I'm not. I searched for reasons for the opposite. I don't feel frightened. I felt deliriously happy and my heart raced, yet I sensed I needed to end the conversation quickly.

I moved my right hand down between our bodies, letting my fingers trace the path over his belly before I took hold of his erection. He had been hard all the time we'd laid there. He gasped as I held his cock...then smothered my lips with his. He moved one hand down and placed it on the top of mine. Together we guided his cock into my warmth. We both drew a sharp breath in that deep contact and further arousal. Our breathing became laboured but we enjoyed the moment without further movement. He pulled me closer to him and folded his arms around me as tight as he could. It was a powerful and passionate moment when he thrusted into me; slowly at first before he settled into a deep, steady rhythm. It was pure ecstasy. It didn't take me long to climax, a slow intense release. I cried with joy.

We lost track of time. I got lost in the depth of his eyes. He kissed away my tears and smiled every time I climaxed. He enjoyed witnessing my pleasure. It was plain to see, he was lost as I was. The excitement coursed through my body in pleasant waves of indulgence. When I noticed that he seemed to be tiring, his acknowledgement of the fact came at the same time; his thrusts became more urgent, faster and faster until he stopped. I felt his cock throb inside me before he let go and released his cum, prompting yet another intense orgasm for me.

We didn't move, we curled up in each other's arms and gave in to sleep right there. When I woke it was just before two am. I felt chilly. The fire must have died over the last half hour or so. He scooped me off the floor, and threw the duvet cover we had been laid on over his shoulder.

"Let's go to bed, Helen. The fire's dead and the heating's gone off. We can sleep some more."

I wasn't awake enough for conversation, so I nodded. The coldness of the bottom bed sheet had the reverse effect on us though. After trying for ten minutes to slip back into the land of dreams, I was wide awake and so was he.

"You not sleepy anymore, babe?" He whispered, his hand stroking my hair.

"No! Not! Can you think of something to do to make us tired?" I asked, hopeful.

"What would you think?"

He didn't even give me chance to answer. My lips were covered by his no sooner were the words out of his mouth. We made love again, but it wasn't for long this time. Mentally, we were enthusiastic but our bodies hadn't recovered from earlier. Our movements came to a slower rhythm and stopped. He held me tight in his arms and within five minutes I felt myself drifting off.

CHAPTER 25

On Saturday morning after we drained all the coffee in the pot, we took a shower together before heading back to bed for another love-making session. I slept better than I have done in a long time following the previous night's sessions. Jim also appeared to be super-charged and raring to go. We were far more energetic and, as well as the passionate love-making we indulged in some wild and dirty screwing. As we showered for the second, Jim brought up the subject of Chris's impending visit later in the day.

"I suppose we should head into town somewhere and get food of some description, Helen. No doubt he'll want to eat, and you and I can't survive on making love all weekend. We don't have to put any great effort into it. What do you think? Buy some top quality ready meals and a bit of salad to go with it? Maybe a dessert too? We've got plenty of drink. I've got more in the car. I only brought a small amount in last night."

He was right. I felt ravenous and as if on cue, my stomach growled in agreement.

"Yes, it's an easy option and I don't want to cook. Are you sure we've got plenty to drink? I'm going to need it tonight."

He was quiet for a few minutes before he answered.

"I'm sure you'll be fine, sweetheart. You coped last time, but you were a little drunk, I suppose. No, correct that. You were extremely drunk, but I want you to be happy with what we're doing, that's all."

I lost myself in thought as Jim drove us into the nearest town and he must have sensed something was eating me up.

"Babe, are you still breathing? You're so quiet." I jumped when he spoke, shattering the silence.

"Uh-huh! I'm…yes, I'm still breathing."

Other than casting me a few worried looks, he didn't push it any further. My head was spinning again. I didn't want to let on to him how worried I was about Chris's visit. The session in Manchester wasn't planned; it just… happened. This time Jim and I planned the whole scenario; Chris was coming to the lodge without knowing that I would be there. In a way it was presumptuous to expect him to want to be involved. It crossed my mind that he was also very intoxicated that night; we all were.

While we were out shopping, Chris called to say he would be arriving sometime before six. The panic started to set in again. When Jim mouthed 'Chris' before he answered the call, I'd hoped he was calling to cancel. My head went into overload and I couldn't understand why I was feeling so het up. I'd wanted this; relished the thought of being fucked by the pair of them again. It was a mind-blowing experience and one I thoroughly enjoyed…so why I was getting stressed I couldn't begin to imagine. Within ninety minutes our shopping for the evening meal was done, along with a few breakfast items for Sunday. Once back at the lodge, we put the food away. My hands were shaking uncontrollably. After putting away the food shopping, I poured myself a large gin and asked Jim if he wanted to join me.

He came up behind and kissed me on the back of my head before guiding my hand with the gin bottle. When he tilted the bottle back, his glass only had half the measure I had poured for myself.

"I take it the nerves are kicking in, babe? You'll be okay. Don't go too mad with the measures. You want to be aware of everything that happens, don't you?" He smiled at me before heading for the sofa. I followed and slumped down next to him.

"Yes, I'm a bit edgy. A couple of my measures will relax me a little. I'll go steady after that."

The plan was to get the meals in the oven once Chris arrived, eat and then have some more alcohol. Jim suggested we should all go in the hot tub together later, as maybe that would set the mood for the evening.

We both became aware of the car approaching in the same instant, it was just before six. I felt as if I was going to vomit as I heard the slam of the car door. Jim headed out to greet him and they walked back into the lodge carrying what could easily have been a week's supply of drink. I was waiting at the door and for a fleeting moment, I saw the raised eyebrows when Chris noticed my presence. His mouth broke into a massive self-satisfied smirk. Even though Jim hadn't told him I was going to be here, I'm sure in that instant he'd realised exactly why Jim had invited him over. Between the grin and the sparkle in his eyes, I could tell he was going to be more than delighted to take part in our raunchy shenanigans.

"Hello again, Helen. How lovely to see you."

"Ermm. Nice to see you too, Chris."

The meal was lovely and the conversation came easy. It was just as humorous as it had been the evening in

Manchester, but for some reason I wasn't letting go this time. I had to force myself to laugh when the conversation demanded. I was tense and the humour wasn't hitting the spot. Thinking that it would make it easier to enjoy myself, I went back to the larger measures of gin. Eventually I was giggling along with them, but unsure whether I was chuckled at the right moments or not. Jim was watching me intently. I could tell he was a little worse for wear but he hadn't consumed his liquor to the extent that Chris had. My mood changed and with every passing minute I was rapidly feeling eager to get things started. I jumped up and started to remove my clothes.

"Okay then, who's for the hot-tub? We can take our drinks outside and put them on the table."

Chris gave what I assumed was an enquiring glance at Jim, who seemed a little bewildered. It looked as if he was feeling the effect of the alcohol.

"You up for it then, Jim? The hot-tub?" He enquired.

Jim was deep in thought, watching me as I unfastened my bra.

"Huh? Oh yes, hot-tub. Of course. That's why I booked the damn lodge so let's use it."

It was chilly outside on the decking, like it had been the previous night. I hurried to remove the cover and get myself immersed in the hot water. Jim followed me out carrying our drinks and for some weird reason, with a tie draped over his arm. Chris had both hands full with his bottle of red and a glass. Jim sat at one side of me and Chris on the other. For the first ten minutes or so we carried on drinking and chatting. Removing the glass from my hand, Jim reached over and placed both his and mine on the table. Chris's eyes never left the pair of us as Jim started to kiss me and slip his hand under the water to stroke my pubic area. He stood up to reach over, ridding himself of his glass too. Sitting back down, he reached an arm around me and started to caress my breasts. His move must have spurred Jim on and I felt two fingers thrust into my pussy as his thumb trailed back and forth over my clit. I shuddered in delight.

"You lucky girl." Jim whispered in my ear. "You get to be fucked by both of us again, and so soon. It looks as though Chris is eager too."

The last glass of gin had tipped me over the edge. I felt giddy and out of control. I laughed out loud but had no clue as to what I was laughing at. No hands clamped over my mouth this time. We were miles from anyone. I took Jim's cock in my left hand and Chris's in my right and rubbed them slowly up and down. They didn't need the stimulation, they were both rock hard. I was turned on in a big but drunken way.

"I'm soooo lucky." I sang at the top of my voice. "I get to have two cocks fuck me at the same time. Come on, guys. What you waiting for? Make me scream!"

I knew it was my mouth speaking the words but as I heard them, it seemed as if they were distant; coming from further afield. A feeling of unreality. To demonstrate my ability I let out what I guessed would sound like a blood-curling scream. I watched Chris's face and laughed. He cringed.

"Babe, you've got an impressive scream. At least there's nobody around to hear you." Jim leaned closer towards me and whispered again. "Helen, shall I blindfold you? We're going to play for a while. No fucking just yet, right?"

"Yesssh...bl...blinefole me." I slurred the words and giggled at how sloshed I sounded.

Jim reached for the tie, fastened it at the back of my head, everything became black. One of them stood in front of me and placed their cock on my lips while the other had one hand in front, fingers poking in and out of my pussy and one hand behind, a finger nudging its way into my arse. I remembered the bliss of those weeks ago; it came back into my head like a deluge. As yet I wasn't filled with any notable girth but it was arousing. Wiggling my backside with their thrusts I brought about a vivid orgasm.

Contact was lost for a moment and with the waves sloshing around in tub, I knew they'd shifted position. Different fingers played in my warmth this time, therefore the length in my mouth was someone else's. I was fascinated. An arm was moving between my body and…whichever guy. Groping around, I traced the arm down and discovered that whoever had their cock in my mouth was the person doing the fingering of my pussy. Whoever it was behind me was poking inside my arse. I clenched my muscles tight and squirmed about in a frenzy until I was ready to orgasm.

From my dreamlike trance, I heard Chris's voice.

"Fuck those fingers, honey. You're insatiable. Cum on my fingers."

It was incredibly dirty and horny. Though inebriated, I was charged up and didn't want my energy to wane. Starting to soar, I was heading towards my happy place. Rather abruptly, I was back to earth; the hands and cocks were gone. Somebody gently guided me out of the hot-tub. I imagined it to be Jim. He placed me on the decking and took my hand to lead me back through the patio doors into the warmth. I felt a waft of cold air as I was guided in the direction of the fireplace. I guessed it would be Chris, throwing the duvet onto the floor for us.

Jim, I think, scooped me into his arms and knelt down before placing me onto the duvet. It was all guesswork but I didn't care who was doing what, it was just so erotic, and extremely dirty; carnal. I revelled in my own bravery and willingness to take part in what was about to happen. I was rolled over and lowered onto a cock that immediately started thrusting into me. Hands groped at my breasts and squeezed my nipples hard. I let out a massive gasp of shock. A tongue trailed over my arse and pushed in a little way. The anticipation escalated and I waited patiently for another cock to nudge into me, but it didn't come immediately. The fingers probed and the tongue swept over time and again. I wanted to stay in that position and allow myself to fucked in whichever way possible. I was swept away in the moment and lost track of time.

Finally, it happened. The second cock nudged painfully into me before a steady rhythm was found. I screamed the house down as I released my cum. Nobody hushed me or covered my mouth. It was the exquisite pleasure coupled with pain that I had grown to love.

"Baby, you're wet for us. Scream away. Lose yourself. Let go of your cum."

Jim's words urged me on, yet they seemed empty…like a pre-recorded script. His voice lacked enthusiasm. I reminded myself how drunk I was and decided not to analyse, but to trust in my enjoyment and the sensations. The next thing I realised, I was floating again; feeling the extreme pleasure that was filling my private area, the pain was in the background, bearable only because of the intense pleasure.

"Hell, this chick enjoys being fucked, doesn't she?"

I was out of my body again, the voice of Chris coming from who knows where but I answered it, my voice slurring with the drink and the feeling of being high.

"Yessh…b…being fucked…not…nothing better."

The thrusting carried on until the cock in my arse suddenly pulled out. They changed my position and then swapped places I think. Cushions were pushed under my hips and someone knelt in front of me and thrust their cock down my throat as I was rammed into from behind. Fingers poked into my folds at the same time. Whoever was inside my backside was thrusting as if in rage. The floating feeling stopped in an instant. I was back in my body, having suddenly decided that this was not what I wanted anymore. On my return, the pain ravaged the whole of my lower body. I screamed and pulled the tie down under my chin to look up into Jim's face, my eyes wide open in fright. His face softened and he acknowledged my discomfort by stroking my hair and my cheek.

"Okay, okay babe. It's fine. Chris, this is where it ends. Helen is uncomfortable. We stop right here and now."

He pulled out of me and stood up. The pain was gone at last.

"Sorry, Helen. I guess we took it a little too far. Do you want me to go, Jim?"

Jim stood up and sighed. He pulled me from the floor to stand next to him and picked up the duvet to cover my nakedness by wrapping it around me.

"No, mate! You've been drinking. There's no need for you to leave. I invited you over here. Nobody's blaming you."

"Are you sure?" He looked over at me, waiting to see if I had anything to add. "Helen?"

I didn't get the chance to answer as Jim hurriedly led me towards the bedroom.

"We'll just go to bed. You've got the sofa, mate. There's a pillow and another duvet in that cupboard in the corner."

"Cheers! I'll say goodnight to you both then."

Jim hesitated a little, maybe thinking what else it might be appropriate to say, but he kept it brief.

"Night, Chris!"

With that said, he closed the bedroom door behind us. We showered quickly and brushed our teeth before spooning up together in bed. His arm was tight around me and he kissed me on the back of my neck and stroked my hair again. He seemed to have a fascination with my hair. I loved it…it was soothing. I didn't have any words for what had happened, so I kept quiet. I was safe, warm and comforted. I sensed he was thinking of something to say, he kept giving a sharp intake of breath as if he was about to speak. Finally he did.

"Helen? Are you okay, darling?"

I hesitated a little, unsure how to explain how I felt. The words came to me but somehow I knew he would get the wrong idea.

"I'm okay. It…it was…the intrusion I didn't like."

"But I thought you loved anal? I thought it was your ultimate pleasure?"

"I do. I didn't mean *that* intrusion, Jim. I meant intrusion as in…intrusion into what is private between you and I. I wanted it to stop. It didn't feel…right. Sorry!"

"Yes. I wanted it to stop too. In fact if I'm to be completely honest with you, I didn't want it to happen again. It's my fault. I should never have allowed it to happen the first time. You have no need to be sorry."

I found it difficult to believe that he had wanted to call it to a halt. I thought it was a big turn-on for him, after all he hadn't stopped Chris from joining us a month or so ago.

"Why? Why did you want it to stop? I thought you enjoyed it because it usually makes me happy." I asked, keen to hear his reply.

He was quiet for what seemed like an age. I started to get suspicious of his motives but finally he spat it out.

"Why? Because I was fucking jealous, babe! I want you for myself. That's why!"

I rolled over to face him, not knowing what to say. I wished he told me earlier and we could have avoided putting ourselves in the situation again. I placed both of my arms around his neck and kissed him, feeling so fond of him. With his arms around my back he pulled me tight up to him, as was becoming a habit. He seemed to love that closeness, that feeling as if we were melting into each other.

I whispered, not forgetting that Chris was in the living room at the other side of the bedroom door.

"I had misgivings about tonight, you must have realised. I was dreading it, particularly after our amazing night last night. I just wanted it to be you and me again, Jim. I hoped Chris wouldn't turn up. If only we'd spoken earlier. We could have spent the night to ourselves again."

"Let's get some sleep, sweetie. Hopefully, he'll leave by lunchtime and we can have the place to ourselves until we leave. There's no rush. The lady who owns the place told me that nobody else is booked in, so we can leave when we want."

We kissed briefly and although our hands roved up and down each other's bodies, it was nothing more than teasing. We were drained.

When we woke up and quietly made our way through the living room to the kitchen, we saw that there was no reason for us to whisper. There was no sign of Chris. The sofa didn't show any sign of having been slept on. Looking out of the window to the parking area, Jim confirmed what we already suspected.

"Yes. His car's gone. I bet the stupid bastard drove home after we went to bed. He was legless. What a tosser!"

We ate a leisurely breakfast of chocolate croissants and coffee, before showering and going back to bed. We made love a couple more times and by four o'clock we'd packed up the car and were on the road. The journey home was quiet. Jim appeared to be deep in thought like myself but it was a comfortable silence. Had it not been for Chris's arrival at the lodge it would have been a perfect weekend. Our love-making had been surreal and I had regrets that the weekend was over. I felt that we had come to a turning point in our relationship. I sensed that Jim also knew it, yet those sentiments were left unsaid.

When he pulled up in front of my house, he leaned across the seat to kiss me. I pulled back and looked him in the eyes. I didn't want him to go home and I knew his wife was not at home. She wouldn't be returning home until late on Saturday.

"Jim? Can I ask you something please?"

He laughed.

"Well, since you've pulled away from my kiss it looks like you're going to ask anyway. Fire away!"

"Will you stay with me tonight? I want you to. I don't want you to go home."

"Oh, Helen!" He sighed heavily.

I wondered what was coming and I closed my eyes, dreading the knockback…which didn't come.

"I would love to. I can ta…"

"No. Don't say it. I can't come in to work with you on Tuesday morning. Someone from the office might see us. I'll go in on the train, like always."

"Okay! You win!"

I was thrilled to have the chance of more time with him. I knew I was going to find it tough trying to keep the smile off my face once we were back at work.

CHAPTER 26

*T*uesday morning came around all too soon for us. We said our goodbyes privately, in the garage. I opened the door and watched him drive out into the street with a heavy heart. I sobbed for a minute, chided myself and headed to the station five minutes later.

My anxiety reached an all-time high as I considered the situation at the office. I knew we had to keep our distance from each other. Since the seminar, there had already been raised eyebrows at our new found tolerance and politeness to each other. We certainly couldn't be seen to be any more than two people who once felt a certain animosity towards each other which had now progressed.

Much as I wanted to sit and relive many moments from the extended weekend in his company, I didn't have time. I contented myself to keep busy and promise myself that I could dream to my heart's content once I arrived home from work.

Christina came down to my office to go through one or two accounting issues with a client's figures she'd discussed briefly with me before leaving the office on Friday. She brought her coffee in and made herself at home. I sat and listened to her describing the hilarious antics of her weekend away with friends. Eager for her to get back on track once we finished our coffee, I tried to bring her attention to the profit and loss account issues.

"Right, Christina...where were we?"

"Hang on. You haven't told me how your weekend went. You must have had a good time, you're in an unusually good mood."

I faked a hurt look before laughing at her facial expressions.

"Are you saying I'm usually in a bad mood, Christina?"

"No. Not at all. It's just that you're unusually chirpy this morning. Did you go out, you and your friend? I bet you pulled. That's it, isn't it...you pulled?"

I couldn't help but feel amused at her terminology. It was as if she always knew though. I couldn't keep the smile from my face and the more I smiled it seemed to convince her all the more that I had been up to no good.

"Christina, stop it, please! I had an amazing weekend...a great catch-up with my friend. We had lots to drink...but there's nothing more to tell. I have not 'pulled' as you so charmingly put it. Sorry to disappoint you. Now let's get on with this please. I've got appointments all afternoon."

"Loud and clear. Sorry, Helen."

I smiled. Pacified at last, she gave the matter her full concentration as I explained why she was having the issues with the P & L spreadsheet. As the time ticked towards lunchtime, my landline phone started to ring. I answered it to find it was Cindy calling from reception.

"Helen, can you pop through, please? There's a delivery for you."

I was puzzled. It was extremely rare for me to receive parcels at work. I hadn't ordered anything either for myself or the office that I could recall. I got up to head through. Some of the girls were leaving to go for their lunch breaks. Christina grabbed her coat from the cloakroom and caught me up in the corridor. We walked through to reception together.

I was stunned. There was an enormous and very beautiful flower display sitting on the corner of Cindy's desk. It was massive and took up quite a lot of space on her desk.

"Those are for me?" I asked in disbelief.

"Yep. They're yours!" Cindy confirmed.

"Wow! Who are they from, Helen?"

"Crikey. Who did you impress at the weekend?"

The girls all um'ed and ah'ed over the flowers as I searched amongst the stems for a card.

"I don't know! There's no card with them."

Perhaps disappointed not to get an answer that satisfied their curiosity, Gemma and Leanne opened the door to face Jim as they were leaving. He had a couple of packets from the local bakery in his hand.

"Oooh! Nice flowers, Helen. I would say you've got an admirer. Who's the lucky guy?"

With that he gave me a wink, carried on through reception and down the corridor to his office. My heart skipped a few beats. I quickly scanned the faces of the remaining staff hoping that Jim's wink had gone unnoticed. I carried the blooms through to the kitchen to stand them in some water before I returned to my office.

My phone rang. As I expected, it was Jim.

"I think you'll need a lift home tonight, Miss Rushforth. You won't be able to manage that flower arrangement on the tube. What do you think?"

"The flowers were from you?"

"Well, who else might send you flowers? Have I got competition that you've failed to mention, Helen?"

I laughed.

"No competition at the moment!"

My thoughts quickly turned to Simon. He would still be seething that I'd not been in touch with him. I knew I would have to deal with him sooner or later, but at that moment I didn't want to think about him.

"Do I get to take you home tonight then…along with your new front garden?"

"I don't know, Jim. It makes sense I suppose, because I'll never be able to manage the flowers."

"Is that the only reason? Because of the bloody flowers? Helen, I'm hurt!"

He sounded anything but. I smiled to myself knowing that he was enjoying the drama immensely.

"James, stop it! I'll let you take me home. Shall I cook something for dinner?"

"Are you flirting with me, Helen? Trying to get me alone again? This is becoming a habit. And you called me James! Do I take it I'm in the bad books again?"

"And I'll keep calling you James if you persist in being irritating!"

"Okay. Then I'll let you cook me dinner. That could be an adventure!"

Throughout the afternoon, a few of the girls were still enthusing about my flowers, and with the sheer size of the arrangement one or two of them offered to drive me home. I thanked them all, but said I needed to work late. I also assured them that I'd be able to manage as there would be fewer commuters on the train after seven o'clock. I'd been rather devious as I knew the later hour would deter them from pushing to help.

Ten minutes after the last staff member left, Jim walked down the road to collect his car. He pulled up directly outside the office door. An hour later we were sat at the kitchen counter digging in to a swift meal I threw together, nothing more exciting than chicken stir fry with bean sprouts and mixed salad leaves.

"This is delicious, Helen. I'm loving it."

I raised my eyebrows.

"You're easy to please. I'm no cordon bleu chef. It's a stir-fry, Jim. There's no need to be so patronising!" I chuckled as he eagerly forked the food into his mouth.

"Well, I thought if I was really complimentary to the chef, she'd offer me more than a cup of coffee!" He grinned cheekily and winked.

"Are you suggesting what I think you're suggesting? Because if…"

"No! I was merely hoping for a nice glass of red. Unless of course something to satisfy my hunger for you is on offer too?"

I didn't answer. I stared hard at him trying to read his thoughts. My stomach did a massive flip. Worry started to plague me. We were getting too comfortable with each other. He was turning into a habit and one that I didn't relish the thought of. He was married. I could feel a broken heart waiting for me again. I tried hard to reason with myself but yet again, I was powerless to resist.

"If you're asking if you can stay with me again…then…?"

"I wasn't but…if you offer me some wine, I won't be capable of driving home, will I?"

"Then stay, by all means. I'm more than happy with that. What if your wife calls you…or your son?"

"Then I'll go into another room to take their call. It's easy as that, my darling!"

A couple of gins and red wines later we went up to bed. We made love for hours. It was like the previous two nights, and our time at the lodge too. He never failed to gaze into my eyes throughout our love-making. It was tender, loving and it made me over emotional.

With his wife and son not due back until the following Saturday, he ended up staying with me for the rest of the week. As the weekend approached too quickly I started to grow a little morose. I knew it would all come to an end.

CHAPTER 27

Coming home from work every night without Jim was proving difficult. I was frequently getting upset and missing his presence dreadfully. We'd settled into a routine during the time we shared together. I wish I could be cocooned up with him for ever. My heart ached for him. We proved to ourselves that we're good together. I loved the way he always held me so tight up to him. One morning over breakfast he told me that if he woke during the night and found himself facing away he rolled over so that he could fold me in his arms. He would reduce me to tears at the flip of a switch with the thoughtful things he did, not to mention his beautiful words. At times, I had to shake my head as if to prove to myself that I wasn't dreaming. It was surreal. I struggled to understand how the guy I once thought I hated could be so kind, compassionate and caring. It seemed as if he'd undergone a personality swap; a transformation. Though he'd stressed on several occasions recently, that he'd never hated me at all, I was still coming to terms with all that happened.

Some days I positively dreaded waking up to find us both

back in the office and dreaded enemies as we used to be. Thankfully, it was real, yet if I thought too deep for too long I would fret that something would bad happen and the bubble would burst.

As we couldn't see each other outside of work we started a pretence of staying back at the office a couple of nights. After the staff left Jim would bring me home and stay for two or three hours. We never wasted a second of that precious time. On those nights we made love and stayed in bed until it was time for him to leave. Once our appetites were satiated we would lay there in each other's arms. He never once closed his eyes when we made love. The fierce eye contact between us served to make our love-making sessions more intense and passionate. I loved gazing into his eyes. At times I almost imagine I can see deep into his soul. It was beautiful. I'd never had a man who loved making eye contact the way Jim did; not even David.

Except for Monday and Friday evenings, we usually varied our 'working' nights so as not to form any set pattern that others may notice. I was happier knowing that we weren't conducting our affair at the office. On the couple of occasions we did, it had felt criminal. The thought of Ted ever returning from a holiday and calling in the office to pick some files up was a worrying factor. Being the over-thinker I'd always been, I was concerned that the staff may take note that I always seemed to be staying late when James was, or vice versa. The one who concerned me the most was Christina. Whenever Jim and I happened to be in a room at the same time she was around, I felt sure she watched the pair of us very carefully. It was the quizzical expressions. She was brilliant at picking up the vibes of others. I'm sure Jim hadn't noticed, but men tend not to be as intuitive as women. I wasn't going to bring the matter to his attention in case it caused him any undue worry. Knowing him as I'd grown to, he would probably say it was all part of my overactive imagination.

From the way he is with me and the things he says, I get the impression that he is starting to look on our relationship as something worth keeping. Whether this means he will leave his wife one day, I'm not sure. I'm certainly not going to ask. Unless he's lying to me, he doesn't love her but as yet, the 'L' word hasn't been uttered by either of us.

Our love-making I could only describe as perfection. He treats me like a lady and with the utmost respect. It's a long time since I was turned on by a man but there's something about Jim that just does it for me. He's perfect. A different type of perfect if I'm to compare him to David, but I try not to do that. They are so different, and yet the way Jim treats me now, is not unlike the way David treated me in our short time together. They care, they love and I can't speak for other women they may have had in their lives, but I can't complain about either of them. David is well and truly locked away in my heart forever. I will always love him and remember him forever, but Jim is my life. I am hoping that this time, my heart is going to be well looked after with no more hurt. Hopefully!

CHAPTER 28

*I*t was twelve weeks since I last saw Simon and it had flown past. Throughout that time I'd barely given him a second thought. A pattern developed with his messaging and phone calls; one that became all too predictable. He spent an odd couple of days each week furiously texting and leaving numerous voice messages. The number of missed calls was beyond ridiculous, it was insane. A couple of days like this each week were always followed by several more of telephone silence. I could imagine his fury at being ignored by me. I felt guilty for being the one who was doing the ignoring yet I didn't want to get embroiled in bitter arguments. Also, I knew my softer side would cave in if he kept making demands to see me. I knew with one hundred percent certainty that he would coax and push. It's in his nature. Unless he decided to look for sexual activity elsewhere, he would be feeling needy. His sex drive is higher than that of most men I've ever encountered.

My phone rang rather late one Thursday night. I was on the borderline between awake and asleep. I groaned and reached out in the dark to grab my phone off the bedside cabinet. It was him. For the past couple of days I considered calling him but each time I was on the verge of ringing, I chickened out. Desperate for sleep but knowing he would keep trying if he was alone, it was now or never. I swiped to accept the call. Before I got chance to speak, he barked out his greeting.

"About fucking time for God's sake! Where have you been all these weeks? I've messaged you thousands of times, called you hundreds of times and you've ignored the lot. I've needed you, sweetie."

"Don't exaggerate, Simon. I've been busy. I already told you I've had things to deal with."

"Okay! You made your point. I just want to know when I can see you, Helen. I *need* to see you!"

I sighed in frustration. His idea of 'I need to see' would no doubt mean 'I want a fuck'. My hackles were up in seconds. I was infuriated. It was an immense effort to try to keep the anger from my voice but somehow I managed it.

"How come you're calling me this late? Where are you? At home with your wife?" Instantly berating myself at the blatant sarcasm I spewed out, I was quietly confident that it would go over his head or he didn't hear it. Not paying attention was a major fault of his.

"I'm in the usual hotel in London. Of course I wouldn't be phoning you if I was at home. You know me better than that, Helen. So when can I see you? Stop being difficult."

Thinking carefully before answering, I knew I *had* to see him but decided it would be better all-round if he didn't come to my house. I've always been of the opinion that if one is breaking bad news to somebody, it is undoubtedly preferable to do it where you can walk away afterwards. It isn't easy to get someone out of your home if they want to stay and argue the toss. I took several deep breaths before speaking.

"When are you next staying in the city? I'll come across to the hotel to see you."

"I'm staying in the city next Tuesday night. Why can't I come to see you this weekend? It's nice and cosy at yours."

"This weekend is not possible. I have things planned."

I cringed after I said it, feeling guilty for lying.

"What sort of things do you have planned? Can't they be cancelled?"

"Since when do I have to answer to you as to what events I have planned? I'm a single woman. I don't have to answer to anybody. I'm not cancelling my plans, Simon. Why should I miss out just because you demand to see me?"

"Helen, I don't expect you to 'toe the fucking line'. I hoped that if it was nothing important you had on…"

"Well it *is* important to me. If I make plans to do something I stick with it, because it's something I wanted to do in the first place. I'm not cancelling. I'll see you next Tuesday and not before."

"Okay. Then I'll have to wait. Come to the hotel for seven. Don't be late!"

With that, he disconnected the call.

Irritating, obnoxious bastard!

I flung the phone in the corner of my room in disgust. I stayed awake half the night flitting between anger and worry. Worrying about what the fuck I was going to say to him. I didn't want to appear a nasty bitch. Simon had done a lot for me and he was a true friend. I constantly remind myself that had it not been for him, I would never have met David. There'd been times when I was jealous to hear that Simon would be going back home on a weekend. I now realise that it was the loneliness that made me feel that way. I'd mistakenly thought I was in love with him. I do love him, but only as a close friend…with benefits. He loves his wife, I know that, but if I'm to predict his reaction when I end our 'fuck buddy' status, he is going to be hurt and a little angry too. I ended up catching four hours sleep, but for the next few days, I struggled again with concentration at work.

Tuesday came around all too soon. Had it not been for spending five minutes in Jim's office, I would have struggled to get through the day. It cheered me up to spend even the briefest of moments with him. The anticipation and excitement of knowing that we would be staying back late at work one night also helped considerably. Once I got this thing with Simon out of the way and was honest with him, I could put our relationship behind me. I had Wednesday night to look forward to with Jim.

I dressed down for the occasion. I didn't want to give him the opportunity to come out with his normal spiel. I toned down my make-up, wore a mid-calf skirt and chose a blouse which buttoned up to my neck. The image smacked of a Victorian look… and certainly not me! I was hoping not to hear 'oh my god sweetie, you look stunning' or 'why do you always look so fucking inviting?' I'd grown tired of his lines.

I entered the hotel feeling as if my face was on fire. My legs were like jelly as I walked along the corridor to his room. He'd text me earlier to confirm that it was indeed the same room number. I gave a little rap on the door.

"Helen! Come in." His voice boomed.

His eyes roved over my body. I noticed the swift 'taking in' of my attire and he raised his eyebrows in surprise, but only for a split second. For once there was no comment from him, negative or otherwise. He leaned forward for a kiss and I turned my face, forcing him to plant his lips on my cheek. I could tell it unsettled him for his next words were tentative.

"Can I get you a drink?"

"I'll have coffee, thanks!" I answered, expecting and getting, the raised eyebrows once again.

He hesitated a little, clearly unsure what to say next.

"Just an observation, sweet pea. If you don't mind me saying, you're looking very…business-like this evening. What is all this about? Where's your overnight bag?"

I wasn't keen to start a row this soon so I stuck to my plan.

"Make me that coffee, Simon. I need to talk to you."

He scowled. I could see from his expression that he had an inkling something was coming that he wouldn't relish hearing. He was already suspicious; a questioning look on his face. He walked away without another word and went across the room to switch the kettle on. He poured himself a large glass of red wine and prepared a cup for me using the hotel's complimentary sachets. Five minutes later he sat down in the arm chair opposite me and took a large slug from his glass.

"I'm waiting, Helen. Tell me what this is about. I've suspected there's something going on with you. You've never ignored me before…not to this extent."

I stared at him for quite a few minutes, without any further comments from him. I felt terrible for what I was about to do but eventually I found the courage.

"Okay. This isn't easy for me, Simon. I should have seen you weeks ago. I know that."

"I know there's a reason you've been avoiding me. I'm not stupid."

"Simon, you knew this day would come. You've said it once or twice yourself. Our rela…no, 'fuck buddy' status… this is where it has to come to an end. I'm seeing someone. I'm sorry."

"Oh."

He looked away from me, staring into space for a minute or so and it was painful to watch the sadness descend on him. My insides churned. It hurt me to see the sad but puzzled look on his face. I wanted him to throw things, get angry, man handle me out of the room; anything but the sadness. When he did speak again it wasn't what I expected to hear.

"Why does it have to end, Helen? I'm married and I cheat. You can be with this…this person and still see me."

I gaped at him in shock, unable to believe what he expected of me. My shock quickly turned to anger.

"No! We can *not*! I can't go through my life being 'the other woman'. It's not what I want out of life. I want to be with somebody in a *real* relationship. Someone to go home to every night, wake up with every morning, someone who is always there for me; to eat a meal with every evening, to go on holiday with. I'm sick of being alone and having nobody to do things with, go places with. You can never give me those things and I *never* expected those things from you. Did you expect I was going to remain single my whole life so you could have me as your permanent 'bit on the side'?"

It was his turn to look gobsmacked. There was no mistaking the hurt in his eyes. His fire had been extinguished.

"So who is he then? I take it he's the one who can do all those things for you, or hasn't it quite got to that stage yet? You want me out of the way before it does?"

"Yes. He is the one. That is why I have come here tonight; to tell you face to face. Or would you rather I'd broken my news over the phone?"

He considered me for a moment.

"No. I would rather you weren't fucking breaking this news to me at all. But what can I do about it? You seem to know what you want! I've always known that we wouldn't last forever, but I always hoped. Despite sounding bitter, I am happy for you. I've always cared for you, you know that. I'll just say one thing, if I may? If this guy ever hurts you in any way or breaks your heart, I'll break his fucking neck for him."

"Don't make me laugh, Simon. You wouldn't dirty your hands. You'd probably get Harry to do it for you."

"That's the same thing, sweet-pea. I'm Harry's boss, so ultimately I would be the one responsible."

"There'll be no need for anybody to end up with a broken neck. Jim would never hurt me. That much I do know. He loves me too much to ever hurt me."

As I said those words, I hoped to God I was right. The last thing I could imagine was that now I'd hurt Simon, was to want him back as my fuck buddy and to see the look on his face, the 'I told you so'. I couldn't face that.

He sat and stared at me for what felt like an age. I could see that although he was trying to hide exactly what he was feeling, he was shell-shocked. I felt the need to try and smooth things over between us. I care for him, I always have. Our sexual shenanigans aside, he'd been a terrific friend to me. I still couldn't forget how I ended up being a whore, but it was always at the forefront of my mind that I wouldn't have met David if he hadn't done. He helped see me through the court case, sorted out my accommodation in London and Harry also played his part, picking me up and running around. He was a terrific friend and I hoped that after I dumped him, he would remain my friend.

"Simon, I am sorry. I truly am. But can I just say that you have always been there for me as a friend, and I value that more than you think I do. We had some amazing sex together. It was always exciting and you have been an awesome fuck buddy."

"But where is it going to go with this...new relationship? Is he going to make you happy long term? Do you intend making it a permanent arrangement...you know, marriage and the likes? Come on, give me an answer. How confident are you that it will go the distance?"

"All the signs are good. We have a brilliant rapport. He's a good man. I'm fairly confident, but like with anything new, you just never know. We shall see."

"Is the sex good?"

I couldn't believe what I was hearing. The bloody cheek of him.

"Simon! That is none of your business. It's personal."

"Well maybe I shouldn't have blurted that out the way I did. I assume he must be good anyway, because I know how you enjoy good sex. Stupid question. My apologies."

He softened. I think he was unsure what to do next. After a slight hesitation he walked over to me and folded his arms around me.

"Stay with me tonight, Helen. Please…just one last time and I won't ask again."

I wasn't prepared for that. I pushed him away with some force and gaped at him, my mouth wide open. He staggered backwards and caught his foot on the leg of the coffee table. I didn't feel any sympathy.

"NO! No more, Simon. I'm not going to betray him. Not for you, not for anyone."

I grabbed my coat from the back of the chair and made for the door. He followed close on my heels.

"Don't leave here on bad terms, Helen. I shouldn't have asked. You made things perfectly clear when you arrived. I'm sorry. I don't want to lose you as a friend as well. I think the world of you. You know I do."

I sighed heavily and turned to face him once more.

"I know. I already said you have always been a brilliant friend to me. Without you, I would probably still be in Paris and as miserable as fuck. I've plenty to be grateful to you for, Simon. I don't want to fall out with you but you over stepped the mark. Show me some respect. Accept that I need to find happiness."

His apologetic look was sincere.

"I do. It won't happen again. I'll always look out for you though. I won't stop that…ever."

He came towards me once more and kissed me on both cheeks before letting me walk out of his room. I didn't look back.

I slept better knowing I did the right thing by Jim *and* Simon. I didn't have to worry any more about him sending me texts or putting undue pressure on. I was confident I got the message across.

CHAPTER 29

$\mathcal{A}$nother post-it note adorned my computer screen asking me to give Jim a quick call. I was thrown into an instant panic mode fearing that he was going to cancel our late evening's 'work'. When I woke up earlier I'd been intoxicated with the thought of spending time with him. The previous Tuesday was when we last got together... it had been a long nine days.

Mentally preparing myself for disappointing news I took a few deep breaths before I picked up the phone and dialled his extension. When he picked up, his whispered words were so quiet I barely heard them. It didn't help that he was tapping a pen or pencil. The sound seemed to have more volume than his words.

"Are you okay, Helen?"

"Yes. I'm fine. What's the matter, Jim?"

My heart was racing. Past experiences had taught me that questions enquiring as to your well-being usually came before being gently let down. I was wrong, thank goodness.

"Nothing's wrong, darling. I just want to tell you that I'm looking forward to seeing you later."

My stomach did a back-flip and I could feel a grin spread across my face in relief.

"I'm dying to see you too. I'm glad we're still on! I thought I was about to be side-lined!"

"Helen! As if I would do that to you! See you later!" He chuckled before putting down the phone at his end.

Feeling much happier that it was still going to happen, I sat with a smile on my face for ages. The rest of the day became tedious and drawn out.

On arriving at my house, he closed the front door behind us and turned the key. He grabbed my hand and led me upstairs before I had chance to head through to the kitchen. We laid on the bed fully-clothed and as we kissed, he slowly removed my skirt and top.

"Why does the time drag when I'm not with you? I hate when I can't see you." He asked me.

"I know. It's been Hell. I struggle every night and have done since the week you stayed here."

He hushed my next words with his kisses as I playfully ran my fingers through his blonde locks. I felt alive when he was with me; having him hold me close as he always does. We took our time fondling each other, exploring every crevice in our foreplay. The excitement soon peaked and I gasped in delight as he pushed his cock deep inside me. Every inch of him throbbed within me. It felt amazing. His eyes burned into mine and it added to the excitement I felt from the physical connection. He could induce an orgasm with his intense stare. Those bluey grey eyes sparkled.

Our love-making, although extremely fulfilling didn't last long. We were so eager, we'd given it our full energy. Once satiated, he stayed close by my side, not once removing his arms from around me.

"Talk to me, Helen!"

I laughed, taken by surprise. Usually we were happy to lay there in silence.

"Okay. What would you like to talk about?"

"You. I don't know much about you. Tell me anything that I don't already know. We've not done much in the way of getting to know each other, have we?"

"No, we haven't. We've been too busy either hating each other or making-love!" I guffawed and he joined in briefly, before becoming serious again.

"I've told you before. I never hated you, Helen!"

"Okay! Let's not go down that well-worn track. I'll tell you about my childhood, okay?"

"I'm fascinated. I want to know everything! Don't leave anything out or else I'll know."

We snuggled tight under the duvet and I had his full attention...keen to learn more. I spent the next half an hour telling him about my parents, sobbing silently at times as I related some of my beautiful memories of them. He'd had his head a little further away on the pillow but moved closer and kissed away my tears. I was touched by the gesture and it brought about a second outpouring. It was inconceivable to think that I was once of the opinion that he was heartless. Every occasion we spend together he continually shows himself to be the complete opposite. He leaves me speechless. I wasn't prepared for his next demand.

"Tell me about the men you've had in your life. No sordid details. I would love to understand how you have evaded capture up to now."

I couldn't believe he was asking this. I had to take it step by step and not blurt everything out. It would give me chance to filter out certain things.

"I didn't really have a steady boyfriend until uni. I dated a few, but that's all they were...dates. During my second year at uni I started seeing a guy called Gavin.

He eventually moved into my student flat. I thought it was going well. I got called away one day when Dad had his first heart attack so I had to go home for a week or two. When I went back, he hadn't expected me turning up. He was there…shagging my best friend. I quit uni after that. I'd never been hurt like that before. I couldn't cope. Two people who I thought had loved me. I was devastated."

"You quit uni? I was under the impression that you got your degree?"

"No. I started attending interviews. Ted took me on and you know the rest."

"After I finished my exams I started seeing Anthony…and ended up marrying him. My biggest regret to date…*bastard*. You know about his drug issue and why he's in prison, but you don't know the rest of it."

"There's more?"

"Oh yes, plenty more to tell. I ended it with him when I came home and caught him with a rent boy. I moved into the spare bedroom but continued to live in the same house. The next…"

I stopped to take a deep breath wondering if I should end the conversation at that point. He wanted to know everything so I changed my mind, wanting to get it out of the way so hopefully it won't get brought up again.

"The next issue was the most traumatic for me. I went out shopping with the girls one day. We decided to carry on and make a night of it. We went to a pub in Soho and had a fantastic night. When I got home I was a little worse for wear. He woke me up in the early hours. He ripped my clothes off me…raped me and blacked my eye. My parents were abroad on holiday so I moved into theirs for two weeks and called into work sick. Nobody at work knows about this Jim so discretion, right?"

"Oh course. I wouldn't dream of breaking a confidence, Helen."

"I returned home just before my parents came back from holiday. I didn't want them to know, because *he* worked for my father. I thought it would only cause awkwardness. My father's heart couldn't have taken it."

"But why did you go back to him? That was madness on your part."

"Because I already knew about the drug thing. I was determined to watch and wait until the time was right. Which I did. Just one more story about him…I went home halfway through those two weeks to get some more clothes. I walked into the house and there was bodies everywhere. Looks like they'd had an orgy of sorts. Naked and half-dressed they were. Empty spirit bottles everywhere, evidence of lines of coke, and he was in bed with two naked females."

"What did you say?" he asked in astonishment.

"Not a great deal. I made them aware of my presence and gave the two girls something to think about when I told them that Anthony had been shagging young men. I warned them of the dangers of unprotected sex. They couldn't get out of the house fast enough."

"Bloody Hell. What a twat!"

"I did right to stay though. When my parents died, I was in bits. Even though we weren't together as a couple, he sorted out all the funeral arrangements for me and other things too. I was incapable of organising anything."

"So a nasty marriage break-up and your parents gone. You must be incredibly strong to have coped with all that!"

"I'm not without my problems, Jim! I don't know if anybody from the office has told you about my O.C.D?"

"No, they haven't. Helen, I don't know what to say to all this."

My laugh was full of irony.

"Who was next then?"

I thought long and hard for a few minutes, wondering whether I should tell him about David. Being laid naked in bed and having just made love, it didn't seem appropriate to mention him. Jim was drinking it all in, eager to know more. Maybe, by knowing more about me as a person would lead him to a better understanding of me. He was also easy to talk to…empathetic, non-judgmental and caring.

"Within six months of my parents dying, I met David. We never lived together or anything. He spent most of his time abroad. We saw each other for a while and it was getting deeper. After a lovely weekend together, he ended our relationship out of the blue. He came out with things like it wouldn't work because of the distance. Apparently, his two marriages had ended because of him working away. That wasn't what he wanted for me. I was broken-hearted. I truly loved him. I saw his obituary in the newspaper about thirteen weeks after he ended it…he had pancreatic cancer. Then I was in for a bigger shock. I received a letter from his solicitor asking me to go along and see him. David had written me a love letter from his death bed."

By the time I related all the tragic circumstances, I noticed he had wet eyes. I reached over and brushed his tears away with my fingers. He was not embarrassed in the slightest.

"Tears for you, Helen. For everything you've gone through."

I sensed that he wanted to move on with the conversation, fearful that I might break down again.

"Has there been anyone since David?"

Having to think quickly, I realised there was nothing to be gained by mentioning André or Simon. Rather than lie I said the easiest thing I could think of.

"I've dated a couple of people…no-one special."

He looked at me aghast.

"Are you telling me I'm not special, babe? I'm mortally wounded."

"Okay. I'll correct that then. There's been nobody special until *you*."

"I'm just an afterthought then? God Helen, you know how to kick a man when he's on his back."

I laughed.

"You're laid on your side, dickhead!"

He joined me in laughter before kissing me urgently. I saw him cast a glance at the alarm clock out of the side of his eyes. He groaned loudly.

"Ten to fucking ten. I want to make love to you again, my darling Helen, but it's time for me to hit the road."

It tugged on my heartstrings as I watched his rear lights disappear around the corner and into the next street. If only he didn't have to go. For once, I could have him wake up next to me, and have an early morning cuddle before setting out for work. I felt so alone each time he left. If only I could have that text when he reached home, just to say 'I'm home safely.' Even that would be something. It would have been incredibly horny to sext each other from our beds. A late night 'I love you' would be music to my ears and to my heart. I seem to spend my life waiting…waiting for the right man, waiting for his words, waiting to be happy. That is all I ask…someone to genuinely love me…someone to stick around. Who knows with the guys from my past? I wasn't one to stick around once I wasn't getting anything back from a relationship. I was the one who always walked away, except where David was concerned. He walked away…but I suppose for the right reasons. He thought he was doing the right thing by me.

CHAPTER 30

$\mathcal{S}$unday morning I was awake and downstairs far too early. I carried my first cup of coffee of the day through to the living room and sat with the cat purring loudly on my lap as I mulled things over and over in my head. I was desperately worried about what Catherine and Ruby would feel about my announcement of being in a relationship with Jim on a permanent basis. I didn't want them to think that I would ever be able to forget about David. I told them on many occasions exactly how much I loved him...and still do. I know they won't expect me to spend the rest of my days single, but what would they think to be a suitable gap between losing somebody and moving on. Its three months away from being two years since David died. Is that a suitable time; respectable, respectful? I don't have a clue, but I feel that I'm ready for this new stage in my life.

Thank goodness they don't know about my past relationship with André and that is something which they will never get to hear about from me. As for my recently finished relationship as Simon's 'fuck buddy', that is also something that will remain a secret between him and myself. To my knowledge, the only person who knows, or indeed has his suspicions is Harry. Whether Simon has told him for sure or not, I don't know as I've never asked. I think it's probably for the best that I don't know. Thankfully, Harry is loyal to Simon and not foolish enough to ever reveal that to anybody.

I want Catherine and Ruby to hear the news about Jim directly from me. They are my priority. I regard them as my family and David always wanted us to get to know each other. I don't want to lose them as my surrogate little sisters no matter who I am in a relationship with.

As regards making our news public knowledge at the Hopkins Partnership, we will of course relay our news to Ted Hopkins first and foremost. Provided that Ted doesn't have a problem with it, only then would we make the announcement to the rest of the staff when we feel the time is right. There'll be raised eyebrows I know, taking into account that all the staff are aware that we were originally at loggerheads.

Late morning, I went upstairs and showered and it was while I was in the shower the thought came to me. To see how the land would lie with the girls, the only thing I can think of is to speak with Heidi...in person.

Once I built up enough courage I called Heidi in the hopes she would be at home. I dreaded if she wasn't there. Given more time to think about it, I know I'd probably think of a hundred reasons why I shouldn't approach her. Feeling incredibly nervous as the phone rang, my stomach started churning and I wished I'd eaten earlier. The thoughts of food though were quickly gone as Heidi answered the call after about seven rings.

"Hello?"

"Hi, Heidi. It's Helen. I hope you don't mind me calling?"

"Helen. How lovely to hear your voice. Are you okay? Did you want to speak with Ruby and Catherine? Ruby's upstairs as usual but Catherine is out with Gary as is the norm for a weekend."

"No, not this time. It's you I wanted to speak with Heidi. Are you free any time soon to maybe meet up? I could do with someone to talk to. No, I'll rephrase that. I have something to tell you and some questions to ask you...if that's okay?"

"I've told you a few times already, Helen. You can call me whenever you want to. It's not a problem. I'm always here. Are you okay? Is something worrying you? If you need any help...?"

"I'm fine. It's nothing too urgent."

"Good."

There was a silence and I thought I could hear something which sounded like pages being turned over in a diary and then she spoke again.

"How about next weekend? Richard's away on business, Catherine is going to Gary's parents for the weekend and if I'm not mistaken Ruby is also away with a few college friends...not that it matters if they're not, we can still meet up."

"That's perfect. Thank you so much."

"Helen, it will...hey, why don't you come and stay on Saturday night? We can have a few drinks and you can talk as much as you want to. I'm your friend, Helen."

It was surreal and sounded fantastic. The way things were turning out, Heidi treated me like a close friend.

"Oh my God. Thank you. That sounds lovely. I'd love to. A good long chat is what I need. I have so much to tell you. Much as I think the world of the girls I'm glad they're not there, because what I want to tell you does have something to do with them."

I heard a deep sigh at the end of the phone. I could picture a look of worry on her face, tension in her shoulders.

"It's nothing to worry about. They've done nothing wrong. I just want your opinion on something that's important to me. I would value your views as to what Catherine and Ruby would think. I'm not saying anything else now until I see you."

"Right, okay. I panicked there. Come over whenever you're ready on Saturday. Morning will be fine if you want to make a full day of it. I'll feed us at lunchtime and we could eat out at night. Whatever you're comfortable with. Just call me when you set off."

The minute our conversation ended I started stressing about what she would think of me. Would she think it was too soon to be getting involved in another relationship? I know for a fact that if *she* thinks it's too soon, I'll be reluctant to break the news to Catherine and Ruby. What I'll do if they don't approve, I don't have a clue.

The week went by in a rush. After a fabulous lunch of creamed mushrooms on bruschetta, Heidi and I made ourselves comfortable in two squishy armchairs in her study. She sent me through to the study with a bottle of tonic water in each hand and she followed close behind carrying a tray with two glasses and a bottle of gin. She placed them on her desk and got straight into it without wasting any time. I was stunned.

"Right, start talking. I'm listening and you have my full attention."

"Oh, Heidi. This is so difficult for me. It may come as a shock to you or it may not. I want your honest opinion. Will you promise me that?"

"Yes. Without a doubt. Come on...you've kept me waiting long enough."

She smiled a genuine smile of encouragement. It was time to tell her.

"Okay. I've met somebody, Heidi. And I..."

"Helen, that's fantastic news!" She was up and in seconds flat had her arms around me in a gigantic hug. I hugged her back. Sitting back down a minute later, she leaned forwards eagerly.

"Tell me about him. I want to hear all the details, sordid ones too." She laughed. Her expression never changed. She genuinely looked happy for me.

"First of all, before I tell you anything about him, I would like to know how *you* feel about it. I'm worried about what the girls will think. Is it too soon after David? What is a respectable time lapse? It worries me."

"I can see exactly why you called me to meet up now. You don't need to explain. You want to know how Catherine and Ruby are going to feel, don't you?"

"Yes, I do. I love the girls, you know that. But David is their father. It's heading for two years since he died. Will they think it's too soon? Do *you* think it's too soon?" I gave her my most serious stare, intense, willing her to give me the answers I wanted to hear.

I was shaking. My hand trembled as I raised the glass to my mouth and gulped the whole lot down. Heidi followed suit and immediately poured us both another one. She laughed and handed me the re-filled glass.

"Bless you. You must have needed that one. I take it your nerves are a bit fraught."

"You could say that, yes!" We laughed.

"Okay. I'll answer your question. Grief is a very personal thing and everybody reacts differently. Some people would feel that once they've lost a partner they could never move on to anybody else, and yet it's not wrong to do so. I know of widows who have got into another relationship within six months. Some don't even wait that long, as shocking as that seems. You are young and as long as *you* feel it is the right time to be involved with another man…then no-one else should judge you for it. Their opinions are of no importance. It's your life, Helen. Live it for you, not others. I think you're doing the right thing. If he makes you happy, then it's right."

"Thank you. But those are your thoughts, Heidi. How about Catherine and Ruby? They mean the world to me and I have no wish to upset them with my news. If they would find it upsetting and fall out with me, then I won't do it."

"Helen, you can't mean that. You have your life to live."

"David wanted me to get to know them. I've done that and I love spending time with them. We all get along fine and I don't want that to change. It scares me. So…as their mother…how do *you* think they will take this news? It's very important to me."

I held my breath as she watched me carefully and considered her next words. Finally she spoke.

"You can breathe, Helen. You may be surprised to hear this, but I can safely say that you have nothing to worry about. The girls and I had this conversation some time ago. It was back in January after we spent the weekend at yours."

I was somewhat taken aback to hear her utter those words.

"You did? Really? What was said?"

"I seriously can't remember whether it was Ruby or Catherine who started the conversation. One of them started it by saying that she hoped you would meet somebody really nice one day, somebody who would make you happy again. That was followed by…I think it could have been Catherine, saying that you deserved to be happy and it was inevitable that someone as pretty as you would definitely meet the right person. Also, they said that you are far too young to be alone forever. I think that's how the conversation went if I remember rightly."

"Well, that's lovely. Those were nice things to say, but did they imagine that I would meet someone this soon? How do you think they will be after only two years?"

"Two years is a respectable time. If I'm to predict their reactions accurately, I would say that they'll be thrilled for you, Helen. They won't think it's too soon. You have nothing to worry about, trust me!"

I felt really emotional hearing her say those words and I hoped she was right. I needed them to be happy for me and also, not to think I have forgotten about David. She handed me the box of tissues off her desk. I dried my eyes and I think she regarded that particular topic as being over. I decided it was time to offer more.

"You wanted to hear all about him so…"

"Helen, let's leave it for now. Fancy some shopping? You can tell me all about him later…if you still want to."

We didn't have far to go to reach the shops. A short walk from their house and we were in Kensington High Street. We spent a lovely few hours until the shops closed for the day. We mainly indulged in serious browsing but we made half a dozen purchases each. We chose a superb little bistro where we ate before heading back.

"Okay, we've eaten, had some retail therapy and now we're armed with our gins, start telling me about him. I'll start you off. What's his name? What does he do for a living?"

"He's called James…Jim. He's my fellow junior partner at the Hopkins Partnership. He joined us last year just before I came back from Paris."

Other than a quick flicker of surprise that I worked with him, she waited for me to continue. My nerves kicked in again and I didn't know where to start. There was things I could tell her and things I couldn't. I didn't want her to know about our lack of professionalism by mentioning events that occurred in the office. When the words finally came I was matter of fact.

"When I first got to know him we were dreaded enemies. We almost hated each other."

"Why? How come you hated one another?"

"I don't know. I found him arrogant at first. It felt as if he hated me, which of course, he didn't. Although we held some animosity towards each other when we came in contact, there was also a sexual attraction going on. I hated myself more, because even though he could be horrible, I couldn't stop wanting him. It's difficult to explain."

"So what changed between you?" She quickly added. "You can tell me anything. I don't judge people, Helen."

"Before I tell you about when things changed, I'll tell you a little more. There was a couple of incidents at work…a couple of nights I stayed back late to work, not realising he was also still there. Shall we just say that on both those occasions he made a pass at me." Seeing her reaction, I quickly added. "Nothing happened. Nothing significant at least. I sort of fobbed him off and got angry. Truthfully, it was anger at me. I was furious with myself because I pushed him away. I wanted it to go further, Heidi. I felt bad."

"So…things changed…when? How?"

"Ted, our senior partner, sent us both to Manchester for a tax seminar, an overnight stay. I was dreading it. We travelled there and back together…in his car."

"Come on, Helen. More information please. What happened?"

The curiosity and excitement showed in her face…like a child waiting to hear something naughty.

"After the first afternoon lectures, I was planning to order room service and watch a film. He kind of told me I was having dinner with him and his old uni buddy who was also attending. I was pushed into it. We had a lovely night. Jim seemed like a different person. He made me laugh, they both did. The evening passed by too fast. Then he asked me to his room for a nightcap…and it all happened from there."

"I take it you slept with him, Helen? Was it good? I bet you couldn't believe it after all those months of hating him?"

"It was fantastic. I never thought, after David…you understand? But Jim made me feel good about myself. He was lovely, and attentive too. He's married…unhappily, I might add. She has apparently, had several affairs over the years, so he doesn't feel guilty. He's going to leave her. He's got to break the news to his son first but thinks he'll be fine about it. Jim says he's sick of living in an atmosphere for the last few years."

"I take it you've somehow managed to still keep seeing him for it to reach this stage. It won't have been easy for you both."

"It happened a couple of times in the office, like when we both 'worked late'. I felt terrible afterwards on both occasions. What we do now is, we stay back until all the staff have gone, then Jim takes me home in his car and stays three or four hours. It's only one night a week. Weekends are virtually impossible for him as he likes to spend time with his son; football matches and bowling, normal teenage boy stuff. On one occasion we spent a weekend together. His wife and son went to her mother's for a week or so at half-term. Jim booked us a lovely lodge for the weekend and when he took me home he ended up staying all that week. It was lovely. He's just gorgeous. I love him, Heidi."

"You know something, Helen? There's been a remarkable difference in you. I noticed when you first arrived. Despite your nerves about how we would all judge you for moving on, there's been a glow to you that I've never seen before. I can tell that this guy, Jim, makes you happy. I couldn't be more pleased for you. The girls will also see the difference. They will be really chuffed for you, honestly."

Again, she hugged me and I couldn't begin to explain how she was making me feel. I had a family to call my own. My love for this lady reached a new level.

From my revelations about Jim, we swiftly moved on to talking about David. I had one question I'd been meaning to ask the girls but I was presented with the opportunity so I took it.

"Tell me about Joanna, David's second wife. Did you and the girls meet her? What was she like as a person? I can see why David would have fallen for you. You're so lovely, just like he was. I can't imagine him ever falling for someone who isn't nice. I wondered if she came under the same category as you...stunning?"

She looked taken aback that I mentioned Joanna. I pondered a moment to think maybe she didn't come up for discussion very often.

"Yes. We met her. She was beautiful. She was always nice enough to Catherine and Ruby, but they weren't very keen. They didn't hate her or anything, they were just...indifferent, I suppose? Is that the word I'm looking for? She was high-maintenance, even more high-maintenance than most high-maintenance females. They weren't bothered by her is the best I can do to describe the situation. I'd say she was definitely after David's money. She did quite nicely from their divorce, or so the girls told me."

I finally had my answer. As she had said about the girls being indifferent, I was so glad I had never got around to asking Catherine and Ruby about her.

We slowly got drunk over the course of the evening and chattered non-stop, even though she selected a film for us to watch. It was lovely to get to know this beautiful lady away from her daughters. I think she was more open and honest than I imagined her to be. I felt that we had developed a strong bond over the months from when I first met her.

I returned home mid Sunday afternoon and I couldn't feel any happier if I tried. There had been several more times when Heidi commented about how made up Catherine and Ruby would be that I had found somebody who made me happy. Being a little suspicious at times, I couldn't help but wonder if Heidi would have some influence over how they would feel or if it would all be based on their own opinions. I went to bed feeling deliriously happy.

CHAPTER 31

*J*im and I had being having our weekly 'private sessions' for several months. On those occasions I waited for everyone to leave the office and walked around the corner to where he would be waiting in his car. Luck was on our side and to our knowledge none of the staff had ever seen us together or were aware of what was going on. I occasionally received an odd wink from him in the corridor and we tried to share a business-like detachment during our dealings with each other at work. There were times when he called me to pop into his office, or I called him to ask if I could see him for a couple of minutes. We usually ended up kissing behind his office door, him holding me tight as always even if it was only for half a minute. It wasn't much but it kept us going until the next time we could see each other properly. The weekends were the hardest part for me, knowing that we could not see or contact each other. And definitely no stealing kisses behind his office door.

Wednesday night arrived and it seemed as if nobody wanted to go home. I couldn't concentrate beyond five o'clock and stood watching at the window, wishing they would hurry up. I'd been in Jim's office earlier, one of our little chats over a coffee. He kissed me on arrival and then even longer as I left. He pulled me up close and pushed his lower body into me. I wished he would stop doing that. His arousal was mine too and as it had been the previous Tuesday when we 'worked late' I was ready for him, eager to have him inside me, his intense piercing gaze into my eyes and more importantly his arms around me…just being with him.

I paced backwards and forwards between my desk and the window and finally at ten minutes to six the first three left and walked past my window; Christina, Gillian and Gemma. Ted wasn't working today so that left Cindy, Nina, Janet and Leanne. All the trainees were out on audits as usual and would be heading straight home from the client premises.

It was quarter past bloody six when the door closed behind Nina.

Almost on cue, Jim stuck his head around my office door.

"Are we ready then, Helen? Let's get out of here. I want you."

"Don't tell me that yet, Jim. Shouldn't we give them a little longer to get away please? We don't want to be seen, do we?"

"Okay. Fair enough. I'll just go back to my office and send a quick four line email and I'll be right back with you."

"No worries. I'll tidy my mess up."

As good as his word, he was back in no time.

"Is it safe for us to walk down the road together, do you think? I'll try and keep my hands to myself. In fact, I'll have a little grope now to keep me going until we get back to your house."

With that, his lips were on mine. Nothing untoward

followed, though I'd expected it. He pulled me close and kissed me for a couple of minutes.

"Right. That will keep me going for now. Just keep your hands to yourself while I'm driving, won't you?"

I laughed.

"Hey! Don't accuse me of sexual harassment, Mister. You're the one who struggles to keep your hands to yourself. Besides which, I'm planning on living for many years yet. I have no wish to cause a car accident of any description. You're a cheeky bugger, Jim!"

"You love me just the way I am though, don't you?"

I picked up on it straight away and was startled.

Did he just mention the 'L' word?

I couldn't ever recall him saying that before and wondered what prompted it.

Back at my house, I was heading to the kitchen and planned to pour us both a drink. As I reached to switch on the kitchen light, I felt his hand over mine.

He whispered.

"Leave us in the dark, babe? I'm not going to look in your eyes just yet. I want to feel you in the dark, close my eyes and imagine each inch, every curve…your breasts, your bottom, your waist. I want to get that vision in my head first. Then we'll go upstairs and I want the lamp on. I want to verify that what I imagined in the dark is true to form in the light. Only then will I look in your eyes again. Down to your soul. I want you to bear your soul to me, Helen. I want to know every-thing…every wonderful thing about your mind. Who you are, what makes you tick, what makes you who you are? I need that. I need you. I want you, baby."

We stayed in the darkened kitchen for some time, undressing each other and exploring bodies. It was exciting. Feeling skin, tenderly touching torsos and exploring sexual parts without taking the further steps, which would mean indulging in foreplay. Finally, we took our naked bodies up to the bedroom. Just inside the doorway, he picked me up in his arms and laid me gently on the bed. He switched on the bedside lamp and gave me that intense stare, a smile on his lips.

"Helen, I need to make love to you now."

"Jim, can I ask you something?"

"Of course you can. Because it's you, you can ask me anything you want, babe."

"Will you fuck me first? Can we have wild, anything goes sex, please?"

He raised his eyebrows, surprised by my request.

"Really? If that's what you want we'll do it. Just for you."

"But…"

"There's a but?"

"Yes. The but is…you can make love to me after we've gone a little crazy, is that okay?"

"As long as we always make love afterwards, there's nothing wrong with letting our animal instincts loose for a while."

"Right. Are you ready for this?"

"Yep! Do it. Do it hard, Jim."

At that, he quickly rolled me over. I knelt, on all fours, knowing what he would choose to do first. He was hard and I felt him push into my pussy with force before raging into me. I screamed out, but it felt good. I was on fire. For months we had done nothing more than make love, but I just wanted the wild side to take over tonight.

"Is…this…hard enough…for you…babe?"

"Fuck…yes! It feels so good."

His arms came around my hips and he massaged my clit. I was racked with a tremendous powerful orgasm. My body juddered uncontrollably for a minute. I felt as if I was about to explode, it was overwhelming and delicious. Every nerve inside me was on edge. The fire in me was like a raging inferno. I wanted more…much more, and he delivered. We kept changing positions. When he raised my legs over his shoulders, the feeling of his cock buried as deep inside me as it could go was sensational. He gazed down into my eyes as always, sweat dripping down his nose and onto mine. He raged at my body for all he was worth, determined to keep my fire burning brightly. Every thrust was powerful. Tendrils of excitement continued to course their way through my body until I felt that I couldn't cope with the intensity much longer. With one hand under my bottom he thumbed over my puckered rear, taunting me with the threat of anal penetration in the next few seconds, but much as it excited me, I wanted more from him. Not anal sex. I wanted him to cease the pounding and slow it down. I wanted his body laid close to mine, him on top, making slow gentle moves; making love to me. Fucking was amazing but having Jim make love to me was on a higher plane. I found I couldn't even describe the feeling it filled me with.

"Jim?"

"You want me to make love to you now, babe! I know you do. I can feel it in my heart, sweetheart."

He obliged. We slowed our animal instincts and he laid on top of me. Slow, sensual love-making began in earnest. His gentle but meaningful moves commenced. Slow was good. His eyes melted into mine, the look of love and I heard him utter the words for the first time.

"I love you, Helen Rushforth!"

And like a baby, I cried. Those words made me feel so light as if I was floating. I felt so happy and I didn't want this moment to end.

"I love you too. You make me so happy, Jim."

He kissed away my tears and we giggled together in the knowledge of having each other, of being together. We finished our love-making soon after and I wanted to lie there in his arms forever. I didn't want him to ever let go.

The pointers on my alarm clock kept doing the circle. It was getting close to the time where Jim would have to leave for home. He nuzzled into my neck, gently nibbling away and there wasn't a better feeling in the world, having been up so close; our bodies almost as one. My eyes started to grow heavy and suddenly I could feel the bedding start to shift close to my body.

"I guess I had better make a move. I hate leaving you, babe!" He leaned over and kissed me once more.

"Jim, what are we going…"

He placed a finger over my lips, hushing me.

"Don't, babe. I'm going to have to figure everything out, what to do next."

What he meant by that I didn't know. Worry started to set in once more, as had been the pattern of my life. Ten minutes later he was gone. I couldn't wait for the next morning when I would see him at work.

Sadly, I never got to see him next day in the office. I didn't even pass him in the corridor. He was busy with clients all day. A day turned into a week and then two. The realisation dawned on me. I quickly came to the conclusion that he was avoiding me. He'd said those words and had not really meant them. At first I tried my hardest not to get upset, persuading myself that maybe he needed time to think. However, once those two weeks had passed there wasn't a word from him, I realised it was over. There was no relationship. He'd simply ended up having an affair. Perhaps he lied to me about the relationship he had with his wife. Maybe the whole thing about her cheating was an excuse for him to seek revenge on her. I'd been had.

On the second weekend since I last I saw, I broke my heart. I arrived home from work after what had been a horrible day on Friday. Jim hadn't been around most of the day, he was out on one of his regular visits to his main client. I had decided earlier on waking, to go in his office and confront him; ask him why he was staying away from me, yet I couldn't bring myself to do it. He was making his feelings all too clear and apparently, didn't want anything to do with me anymore.

I felt such an idiot. I regretted telling Heidi that I had a man in my life. I'm only glad I hadn't yet had the chance to tell the girls. I'd spoken with Heidi and she said she won't tell them. I succeeded in making myself look foolish, but that was only a secondary feeling. My heart was broken in two. Since David died, I'd never felt so miserable. Love evaded me yet again and I felt as if I was in mourning; yet again, mourning something that I never really had. It was becoming a habit. I stayed in bed the whole weekend and cried. I tried to watch something on television and ended up staring through the screen. Everything I tried to watch made me even more miserable. I caught a glimpse of myself in the bathroom mirror on Sunday night and quickly looked away. My eyes were a mess, my hair was a mess and for once I didn't care. I wanted Jim. Nothing else was going to make me happy, nothing but him. Surprisingly I slept on and off both on Saturday and Sunday. When my alarm rang first thing on Monday morning, I got straight out of bed and into the shower to get ready for work. After showering, I did the only thing I could think of to do…I flung myself on the bed and cried some more. The thought of being in the office and having him ignore me…but maybe ignoring would be better than having no contact at all. At nine I called the office to say I wouldn't be in for the week, I was starting with flu.

All week I checked my phone constantly, hoping to find a message from him or a missed call. After the week was over I was convinced he would know I'd been ill but didn't even care enough to send me a text to say 'I hope you're okay, Helen!' Well, fuck him. I would return to work on Monday morning, head held high, lippy on and show him that I was over it. Deep down, I knew I wasn't. I would never be over him.

I was feeling very foolish.

For fuck's sake, why did I tell Heidi about Jim and I being in a relationship? I'd jinxed us!

CHAPTER 32

I gave a loud sigh of relief as I unlocked the door to my flat. It was a wonderful feeling to be back home in Fulham after spending fourteen horrendous weeks up North. The only thing missing as I hauled my suitcase through the door was Bella's usual greeting. I'll go to pick her up from Mum and Dad's tomorrow.

When I took up the challenge from my company to go to York and help get another office opened, I thought it would help to get Helen out of my mind. I know that what I've being doing is wrong. I feel certain that she must already have a boyfriend or partner in tow. If I'm honest with myself, I know for sure what the final outcome will be.

I busied myself making a cuppa, glad that I remembered to call into a corner shop and grab some milk on my walk home from the station. While the kettle was coming to the boil I rummaged in my case and dumped the dirty clothes in the washer, though there was no rush to set it going. I've got a week off work to look forward to now, as well as a handsome bonus in my next month's pay. At least that was a positive to take from the experience.

As I sat down to have my coffee and a quick snack, I reflected on my time away.

It was a rewarding and proud moment to see the new office take shape. Contractors had been in and decorated before Tony and I even arrived there. What we had been required to do was order carpets, furniture and drawing boards. After that it was down to us to organise telephone and internet connections and start advertising for suitable candidates. We would also be doing the interviews. Feeling rather proud of ourselves, we accomplished everything we set out to do and returned to London happy that the mission had been successful. A triumph...but a nightmare all the same!

What a frustrating time the interviewing had been. Tony was tasked with finding a receptionist and an office manager, my job on the other hand, was to employ three draughtsmen. From looking at their C.V.'s I initially thought it was going to be a breeze as the resumes were impressive, but nothing could have been further from the truth. There were several who struggled to string two words together during their answers to the questions. One or two didn't have a clue how to dress smartly or understand the importance of personal hygiene. Luckily, three of them had been exactly the type I was hoping to find; talented, intelligent, common sense and ambitious. During the extra time we spent there helping them get settled in, we discovered that our instincts had been correct.

Each day after the office closed at five thirty, Tony and I visited a wide variety of pubs around the city centre, but we'd stayed sensible from Sunday through to Thursday nights and never had more than three or four pints after our evening meal. The weekends had been a little more exciting. We visited a couple of night clubs to see what talent was on offer.

With my head constantly battling to rid the thoughts of Helen, I did what I thought was best and looked around each weekend for attractive girls who were out to get laid. Hoping that it was a way forward, I indulged in two or three drunken one-night stands. Tony *was happily married and always left the clubs early and like the faithful doormat he is, returned to his room at our low budget hotel.*

Several weekends in a row I managed to get the attention of a female or two. To be fair, they had all been pretty enough although one could have done with losing a few excess pounds. I took all but one of them back to my hotel room. My first one, a pretty little brunette who made the move on me first, seemed to have second thoughts when I got her back to my room and as soon as I started to undress her, she changed her mind and left. But the following weekend my luck changed. After a good hour or longer chatting up a girl who was well over six foot in stature, I was getting some-where. She wasn't the least bit shy and kept rubbing herself up against my crotch. I felt myself getting hard every time she made the movement. As the time rolled around to one am I suggested she accompany me back to my hotel, but as she lived in a flat above one of the stores in the city centre and not too far away, it seemed like the best option.

She giggled all the way up the stairs like some high school girl. As it turned out she was probably more desperate for the shag than I was. Before the door was even closed she removed my clothing, slinging every last item around her living room like a wild one. I don't know whether she expected the foreplay, love-making and flowers the next day, but that wasn't what I had in mind. She took my cock straight to the back of her throat and proceeded to give me a blow job. As good as it felt, it wasn't doing it for me in the slight-est. I pulled my cock out of her mouth and rammed hard into her wetness. It felt good but I couldn't bear to look at her little pixie face and short bobbed hair. I closed my eyes and once the images of Helen came into my mind, I loosened up and enjoyed fucking her. Within five minutes of depositing my cum deep inside her, I got dressed and made my way back to the hotel. I feel awful for having used the girl, but any thoughts of hanging around longer than I needed might have given her the wrong idea. During the time I spent chatting her up, I sensed that she was looking for something in the way of a relationship and nothing could have been further from my mind. I was there to get laid not get myself bamboozled into a relationship. The only girl I wanted was Helen.

I sat for ages before going to bed, thinking back on my experiences up North. I felt defeated, and physically sick. The time I spent away had done me no good whatsoever. Every girl I shagged while I was away had failed in helping me to get Helen out of my head. Sexual gratification but without the desired effect. Not one of the females had managed to hold my attention while I had sex with them. Despite their pretty faces and sexy bodies my mind was constantly on Helen. It was her face I saw each time I closed my eyes, her body I was fondling and fucking...every time without fail.

As I lay in bed waiting for sleep to come, I made up my mind. I will give it one last try. If I fail...well, I don't want to think about failing. It was driving me crazy and the only way I will ever find out is to see her and ask if I could possibly ever stand a chance. Once I hear the words come from her lips, whether it be yes or no, only then will I admit defeat.

CHAPTER 33

*B*eing back at work had helped a little in how I was feeling emotionally. I was aware that I was at times being a moody cow with people. It wasn't like me at all; it had never been my nature to be that way. I instantly regretted every snappy outburst. Many of the staff were my friends for fuck's sake. I knew I shouldn't be treating them like this.

Christina, always the first to notice when something isn't right proved true to form.

"Helen, what's matter? Something's eating away at you, I can see it. You can tell me in confidence. I won't repeat anything. I know when to keep quiet and when not to tell anybody, as unlikely as that may seem. I know I'm a gobby cow, but I can keep secrets."

"Thanks for your concern, Christina, but there really isn't anything to tell. I'm tired. Most nights I don't sleep well. Add to that, I'm feeling lonely at the moment. That just about sums it up."

"You have us, Helen. If you fancy it we could all go out

one night, just say the word. The girls will be up for it, I'm sure."

"Careful, I may take you up on that. After all, you wouldn't want this miserable bitch putting the mockers on a fun night out, would you? I'm not exactly feeling sociable right now."

"But you've been like that before and we've always cheered you up somehow."

"I don't know what the hell the matter is with me right now. I'll get there. Are you serious about a night out? If so, you can count me in!"

"Excellent. I'll see how many I can round up."

With that she was gone...out of the door in a rush, no doubt to get on the case. The depression started to set in again; wishing I hadn't agreed to a night out. It was the last thing I wanted. I dug deep into my work and tried my best to keep my mind off Jim, even though I knew he was a few yards away down the corridor. I brightened up for a short while, thinking that perhaps he was missing me too. Then I instantly talked myself out of it. If he truly missed me why wasn't he making an effort?

It was four weeks since I last spoke with him. I never felt more morbid in my life. My heart positively ached for him, my body pined for him. It didn't seem as if my body would ever have him near me again though. All I could think about was his love-making and how it melted my heart. I was struck with a moment of horror as my head sifted through the memories of our sordid sessions with Chris and I sank into a deeper depression!

That's why he doesn't want me anymore! The fact that I enjoyed doing all that...SHIT!!

Late one night, I was desperately lonely. It crossed my mind that I could do with some company to take my mind off Jim. I got the urge to message Simon. Looking at the clock to discover it was heading towards midnight, I talked myself out of that idea. Usually Mondays were his first day back in the city after spending the weekend with his wife. He was often at a hotel in the earlier part of the week. But what if I got it wrong and he was still back home in Essex. I already hurt him. I couldn't also be responsible for causing any issues between him and his wife if I got it totally wrong. I switched off the bedroom light and decided to try for the sleep which seemed to evade me.

The next morning as I arrived at work, I walked through reception and into the corridor. Jim was heading towards me, probably on his way to the men's toilet. He smiled at me somewhat sheepishly, and feeling childish and petty, I met his gaze, looked through him as if he didn't exist and looked quickly away. From the corner of my eye I watched his smile fade. I know it was ridiculous behaviour but I couldn't stop myself. I was so angry that he suddenly felt a smile would be appropriate. Did he not realise how I was feeling? He didn't have a fucking clue and in that moment I hated him…yet still loved him and wanted his arms around me again.

When I got to my office, I made my mind up. I would send Simon a message. I could use some company. I needed to release some of the sexual tension that was building up inside me and it wasn't forthcoming from Jim.

Once Cindy had done her rounds with morning coffee, I took a short break from the computer screen. I picked up my phone and tapped out a message to Simon.

Hello Simon,

How are you? Well I hope? Haven't seen you in ages so just wondered if things are okay?

Hugs, Helen xx

It was mid-afternoon before I heard back from him. I never expected him to reply immediately as I knew he was a busy man and it was highly likely that he could be in court.

Hi, Helen,

Can't say much right now as I'm running to a deadline on something. Will message you tonight, if that's okay? I'm in the hotel, usual one.

Hugs back

SS the LL xx LOL

It was something. Whether he would expect my message to mean I wanted my fuck buddy back I hadn't a clue. Knowing Simon, he would never stop trying. Being the typical lawyer that he is, they do rather like to get their own way.

Jim happened to be leaving the office at the same time as I was. It was embarrassing and I didn't know where to look as he held the door open for me. Nobody was around and just as I was about to walk out, he spoke rather quietly.

"Helen, I…"

I didn't turn around to face him. I couldn't. It would hurt to look into his eyes and not be able to experience that closeness that I'd always felt with him. I muttered my response.

"Don't speak to me, James. I'm not coping. Don't make it harder."

Before he had a chance to respond to my words, I fled. I made the station in record time and didn't once look back to see if he watched me until I rounded the corner. I didn't wish to know. I was near to tears all the way home. Maybe my call from Simon would give me the opportunity for a distraction. I hoped so. I needed a little escape in my life and felt as if I couldn't go on like this again. My O.C.D. had slowly started to creep into my life again. Nothing over the top, but it could soon head that way.

Just on the off chance that Simon might want to come over if he felt that he was likely to be in the market for a fuck, I decided to get myself into the shower and get ready for him. By seven o'clock I'd showered, dried my hair and donned sexy undies. With nothing but sex on my mind I even took the liberty of getting my small selection of vibrators out of the bedside drawer. They had remained unused in there for some time now and I know he would relish the thought of using them to prolong a fucking session. He always used them before stuffing his cock into me; he loved watching me wrap my lips around the objects, simulating a blow job. It was always a big turn on for him. As I placed them carefully next to the bed I could feel myself getting damp. My thoughts immediately turned back to Jim. He had never used sex toys on me. That chance had gone out of the window now. I managed to fight back some tears that started to sting my eyes and the lump in my throat but it didn't stop me questioning my motives as to why I wanted Simon here when it was Jim who I really needed with me.

I went downstairs once I was ready and poured myself an enormous measure of gin with very little tonic in it. One of Simon's type of measures. He'd be proud of me. I thought it would help get me in the mood for some serious fucking and literally drown my sorrows because it wasn't Jim that I was getting ready for. I then wondered why Simon mentioned in his last message that he was at his usual hotel. Maybe he expected that I would go to him?

It was twenty after seven when I received a message from him.

I'll call you in ten sweetie if okay? S xx

I sent back a message instantly.

Okay, that's fine. Xx

Immediately I hit send, I regretted it and my insides churned. My neck and shoulders ached as I felt the tension take hold. When my phone rang less than eight minutes later, I stared hard at the caller display...Simon calling. I let it ring and ring. Tears formed in my eyes. His was not the name I wanted to see there. I wanted it to be Jim calling but it wasn't. I didn't want Simon here at all...let alone for him to fuck me. I wanted Jim; wanted to have him make love to me again and never stop. I craved for him to be here and to gaze into my eyes the way he did.

I never answered the call. I wept like never before. It wouldn't have been fair to Simon to let him think that he was back in favour when he wasn't. It would be cruel to let him fuck me when it was Jim I craved.

I received another message after I ignored six calls from Simon.

I guess you might have a visitor, Helen. Hope to speak to you soon. I miss you. Simon xx

I went to bed early, totally disgusted at myself for having led him on. I couldn't bring myself to reply that I missed him too, as that would be another lie. Since becoming involved with Jim, I'd not once missed Simon. Totally broken-hearted and craving the man I love but couldn't have, the grief kicked in. Weeping endlessly for hours, I wondered how long it would take me to get over losing Jim.

CHAPTER 34

*I*t was Friday again, and a week since I returned home from my few month's working in York. I'd not succeeded in getting Helen out of my head yet. I'm getting desperate now to put an end to the stalking. I'd made myself ill lately. Even my parents had make comments since I arrived back home.

"You're not looking after yourself, son." It wasn't often my father had much to say, but he looked concerned.

"Something seems to be wrong with you. You're always tetchy these days. Is there something on your mind you want to talk about? Are you feeling depressed? You've not got money worries have you? Are you in debt? You'd better tell me if so. We know how expensive it can be living alone with all the bills to pay. We can help get you sorted out."

My mother as usual bombarded me with the questions one after the other. Dad had never been one to ask questions; his reputation was more for stating the facts.

I ended up telling her that there was a female I was interested in and I was stressing because I wanted to ask her out and get to know her better.

"Oh. Is that it? Well, you'll never know unless you ask her, will *you? It's all down to you. If she's who you want, she won't know that unless you tell her."*

"Yes, mother. I've told you now and...I intend to do something about it."

That conversation played back and forth through my head for the last few days. Heaven only knows what she would have to say had I told her 'I've been stalking her for months and I haven't had the balls to do anything about it.' I can imagine her answer.

'You're a stalker? That is a criminal offence, son. You need to be seeing someone...a therapist, a psychologist or...someone. You can't carry on doing that. It's insane.'

Being economical with the truth had been the only thing I could do. Every time I went back to that conversation my stress levels soared to the point that I would hyper-ventilating and suffer extreme nausea in the process.

My day at home dragged as I waited for night to arrive. I couldn't settle to watch the television or do any jobs around the house. Not that it needed anything doing. Having spent the last four days at home, I was pretty much on top of it all. Even the top of my cooker sparkled. I'd been to the gym, tried reading a new book I started on the train last Friday night, but I was reading the same paragraphs again and again.

Before heading off to Maida Vale, I called into the office and returned the laptop which was loaned to me for my spell up North. Remembering that Monday would be here all too soon, I hadn't hung about. I could hear all the staff news once I was properly back at work, not now during my long overdue time off.

I was eager to catch the train to Maida Vale. I wanted to be there before she was. I could have spent a little more time in the office and in the end I regretted not doing so. I got there far too early and as I didn't fancy going into a pub for a pint or two, I walked up and down the streets and did a circuit or two of a local park. I would have loved a pint but wanted to be fully alert with a clear mind if I was able to talk to Helen tonight. The night was fresh with a chill breeze; another reason to get this over and done with. In a few weeks' time the freezing, snowy and rainy weather would be back with us. I'd had enough of that to last me a lifetime. I shudder when I think about the nights I spent in the shop doorway opposite Helen's office. I walked home numb to the fucking bones on more than a few occasions. Tonight would see the last of those days, one way or the other.

Obsessively checking my watch every few seconds, I suspected that Helen's train would be arriving in ten minutes. I didn't want to be at the street corner when she came round. I watched from a fairly safe distance but from where I had the best view. I was not going to hang about forever this time. I would give her five minutes once she went into her house and then follow her down the street.

The ten minute wait felt like an hour. I was muttering expletives under my breath. In that exceedingly long ten minutes I called myself a 'dickhead', 'twat', bastard, fuckwit, useless wimp, knob head and even the 'C' word; not one of my preferred cuss words. I cursed myself to Hell and back. I cursed Helen too. Cursed her for not knowing how I feel about her, cursed her as if she was to blame for my unhealthy obsession with her...which, in a way, she is.

Glancing up from my watch to the station exit, I saw her and I was shocked. She didn't look too good. Her posture, usually upright and confident, had changed; her shoulders seemed slumped and her head hung down. She looked troubled. I was in a quandary. Was I about to add to whatever it is that's troubling her? I don't know. No backing out, I'm going to chance it. She headed down the cobbles to her cottage and I crossed the road back to my usual place on the corner. I'd stood for less than five minutes and I started to make my move, one foot in front of the other, ready to follow...when everything went black...

CHAPTER 35

*I*t seems like I've waited forever for this moment, but it's finally happening. At last I'm going to get my revenge.

My body is shaking with anticipation and excitement. It's so fucked up, I know it is. My adrenalin is flowing, everything is coursing through me...even the blood flow. I've got a hard-on to be proud of and... I'm planning on using it. It will likely be the last opportunity I'll get for a long while. I'll beat her about until she has no fight left in her, then I'm going to take what's mine. I want her to be...not fully conscious, but aware! I want her to understand exactly how she made me feel. I need her to experience what I'm going to do to her. I want her to be in so much pain that she begs me to end her life even before I'm ready to. I want her to recognise who I am, and specifically why I'm doing it. The bitch will be aware I came back for revenge. Nobody deserves it more than she does.

I wonder who'll inherit her fortune when she's dead. It's a pity she divorced me. I could have had some fun finding a few whores and rent boys for a short while before I end up back in prison...for murder this time. What does it matter anyway? There'll be no more employment for me. No company will employ me now.

My parents, the dear John and Eileen who Helen believed hated her, (and she was right about that fact), disowned me after the court case. They only came along to court to see if Helen had lied and if I was still their innocent son. My mother would have loved her to be wrong and seen all the charges get dropped. Helen was right about my mother. I was in the wrong and by rights, I should have defended my wife against her. I was afraid to do that though. I always knew how nasty she could be but I hadn't wanted to be the one who wronged her. Still, I'll not tell Helen that...there would be nothing to be gained.

I'll only have the prison sex to look forward to after tonight is over. That can be fun at times, though!

I set off...ready to head down the street to her house. I hope she looks nice for me.

CHAPTER 36

ork dragged at a sloth pace the whole week. I'd seen Jim on two or three occasions and it had been horrible. Every time, my heart would break all over again. I felt overwhelmed with feelings of rejection and sadness. It got that bad I dreaded the sickly feeling; scared I would vomit or perhaps faint. He'd smiled at me every time but I couldn't bring myself to return the smile.

Why smile? I want to talk to you!

I was struggling to keep control. I wanted to scream out at him. 'Why did you say you loved me and then ignore me since? Why treat me like this? You won't even talk to me. What have I done wrong?' Because we were at work I needed to be brave and hold back. It wouldn't be professional to cause a scene.

Every night I made sure I finished work before most of the other staff. I couldn't put myself in a position where he and I were the only two left in the building. Trying to speak to him and demand some answers was out of the question. I was fearful, scared that he would actually say the words I dreaded hearing; afraid I wouldn't hear what I was hoping for. I'd then have to sit on the train in a tear-stained mess.

I hadn't cried lately...neither at work nor at home. Mostly I feel devoid of emotion and have no more tears left to cry. It's mind-numbing. Despite the last few weeks of him not communicating with me, I know deep down in my heart that he still loves me. I'm scared he can't bring himself to do anything about it because of the effect it would no doubt have on his son. I feel in my heart he wants to be here with me but just wish he would at least tell me where I stand, because I don't know anymore. As hard as it would be if he told me he made a mistake and doesn't love me, at least then I could learn to accept the truth and move on. But this is Hell and I'm not coping.

I didn't know how I would have coped without Heidi. I phoned her a couple of weeks back and poured my heart out. I told her how foolish I felt. She repeated herself several times throughout our conversation.

"Helen, if it was to be bad news from him, you would know in your heart. He has big decisions to make and I expect he's finding it hard. It's never easy when you have to break up a home and many people do it without thinking seriously about the consequences. When I ended my marriage to David, I didn't take it lightly believe me, but I felt like a total bitch..."

"But you're not a bitch. You're a lovely person..." I cut in.

"I certainly felt like a bitch though. Jim is probably feeling the same. Don't write him off, Helen. Give him time."

I digested those words in my mind over and over again but still couldn't comprehend why he wasn't at the very least, speaking to me. I couldn't rid myself of the images of him smiling at me in the office. Why smile? Why not just explain if he was finding things to be too challenging?

Daydreaming again instead of getting on with my work, I

looked at the time on my computer screen...twenty minutes before five. Noticing I had half a dozen emails waiting for a response, I decided to answer them and hopefully it would be time to go home.

On the train half an hour later, the rumbles from my stomach reminded me that I had eaten very little all week. I knew I needed to have something when I got home, maybe a couple of slices of toast. It wasn't healthy or wise to go without food.

I was relieved to be home and lock the door, shutting the world out. I could switch off and mope around as much as I wanted with nobody there to bear witness. Being true to my body, the first thing I did was sort out some beans on toast and it made me realise just how hungry I'd been. I demolished the lot and pottered around in the kitchen for fifteen minutes or so before I parked my bottom down on the sofa. Trying not to torment myself with further thoughts about how much I wanted Jim, I picked up my latest book and started to read.

After a brief session of losing myself in the novel, I jumped when somebody gave a loud rap or two on the front door. My heart pounded and I froze. I wasn't expecting a visit from anybody. I knew it couldn't be Simon. I doubt he'd turn up unannounced. The one occasion he'd done that was last Christmas Eve when he decided to surprise me with presents. Then my heart almost stopped, I had a sudden thought that perhaps it could be Jim. Maybe he'd decided to come and talk after I ignored his smile in the corridor a few hours earlier. Standing, I fluffed up my hair with my fingers before hurrying to the front door. I made sure to put a smile on my face before I opened it.

As I opened the door wider, I was dismayed to catch a split second glimpse of Anthony's face. The force of his fist met my face with a sharp blow. I didn't have time or the inclination to react. The pain was bad and the blow knocked me backwards and on to the floor. He didn't let up. More pain kept coming as he started to kick me in the ribs. The kicking unexpectedly stopped. My panties and tights were being tugged roughly down the top of my thighs, his finger-nails raking at my skin. I could feel the pain despite my wooziness. I wondered if I was having a bad dream about the time he raped me. The pain was real though; this was no nightmare.

My eyes started to swim in and out of focus and I knew I was about to faint. In what seemed like an age of enduring his kicks and blows, I was vaguely aware that someone was dragging him off me. I couldn't focus. Everything became a blur. I could hear voices. Someone cradled by head in their lap. Gentle hands covered my genitals with my skirt. I experienced a brief return to lucidity and couldn't understand where Anthony was. As I lay wondering if he'd run off...the darkness took hold of me.

CHAPTER 37

*F*riday night came round again and I left work an hour earlier than normal. My plan was to be at Maida Vale station before she arrived home. To make a change, rather than stand on the corner directly next to the arch, I was in a discreet position at the opposite side of the road. It was a long wait. I had at least an hour to waste before she would be getting off her train. I'd assumed that she would leave work at a reasonable hour being the start of a weekend. From my many nights of observation I've discovered that she's pretty consistent. I've spent more than a few long sessions waiting in the cold though, on nights when she was clearly busy and had needed to stay back late.

I decided to go and kill a little time at the pub I visited on a previous occasion. I ordered a pint with a whisky chaser and sat in a quiet corner hoping to get some thinking time. I needed to get clear in my head what I was going to say. My belly churned with loud protests. I knew my thoughts and my nervousness were the guilty parties in causing it to heave. The quiet time I'd hoped for wasn't meant to be, sadly. A young guy in a hoodie came across to the table where I sat and tried to engage me in conversation about football; or more specifically, Tottenham Hotspur. Not being a football fanatic, I knew very little. My face must have looked blank at the questions he bombarded me with. Of course, men who are obsessed with football who live and breathe it every day of the week do tend to think that those who don't follow the sport to be weird.

Okay, so I'm weird then.

Eventually he must have realised my mind was elsewhere. I wasn't up to the conversation. He moved to the other end of the bar to engage with another couple of guys. Before long, I noticed the three of them having an enthusiastic and animated conversation. Whether they were fellow Spurs supporters, I neither knew nor cared. I hadn't been rude to him in any way. I just wanted him out of my face and to leave me with my thoughts.

Once he wandered off, I got back to my ponderings while I slowly sipped at my pint. I finished the pint and went up to the bar for another. The whisky still sat at the table. I originally intended to wash the pint down with it, but hadn't planned to have a second one.

Three quarters of an hour later I went outside and back over the road to the corner under the archway. I stood for ten minutes, giving myself a 'grow some balls' pep talk while staring down the Mews as if I expected something magical to happen any minute. My stomach hadn't ceased its nervous churning and it had nothing to do with the couple of drinks I consumed. I badly wanted to vomit. If anything magical was going to happen, it would be down to me to bring it about.

I paced up and down the streets several times and as it got nearer to the time I expected her to arrive, I took up position again and propped myself against a wall. Holding up the newspaper that I bought on the way to work, I hoped it would hide my face. It turned out I had only five minutes to wait. I saw her as she exited the tube station. From what I could see in the dark, she looked stunning as ever. Her long dark hair was twisted around and held in position by a hair clip. She was wearing a dark, mid-calf coat. An image of her long legs hidden beneath it came to mind. I *watched as she turned into Elgin Mews and hurried along down the cobbles, probably eager to get out of the cold.*

With my mind firmly made up, as it had been for a couple of weeks, I would be knocking on her door shortly. I couldn't act just yet, it was too soon. I wanted to give her time to get in, get something to eat and then settle for the night. I tried to come up with some plan of attack as to what I was going to say, but still nothing sprang to mind. I would have to wing it. I tried not to imagine the look on her face when she finally opened the front door to see me standing there. How would I even begin to explain what I was doing there or how I managed to know where she resides? Should I tell her about all these months that I've been stalking her? No. I think not. That would be a huge mistake. We hadn't parted on the best of terms the last time I saw her. That amazing memory of me fucking her in the park returned. I had to get that thought out of my head and damn fucking quick.

She'd think I'm a freak if I revealed anything about my after-work wanderings. Maybe I am, but I've just become so fucking obsessed with her. I'm in love with her, I know I am. That is also something that I don't feel will be appropriate to mention. To reveal something like that would no doubt be sufficient to scare her away for good.

The time has definitely come where I can leave it no longer. I have to make my move now. I can't go on stalking her forever, I know that. I need this to go right. I want a chance with her. If there is no chance, I need to find out now, then leave her alone and start to move on with my life.

On the last visit here, my mind was made up. I was full of confidence that night, and was on the verge of heading down the street from my position on the corner near the arch. The next thing I knew I woke up in fucking hospital. Apparently, someone found me laid unconscious on the pavement and called for an ambulance. I sustained an injury from a blow to my head. It hadn't been a heavy blow but hard enough to render me unconscious. According to the nurses who attended me, there was a cut on which they used sterile strips to pull the skin back together. My egg-sized bump had gone down after a couple of days. There was no copious blood loss or anything. I'd been very lucky. The whole episode scared me sufficiently to want to be more careful though.

I was extremely distressed with the whole episode. Who had hit me on the head and why? I came to the conclusion that I was just in the wrong place at the wrong time and it was a mugging but then reminded myself that I had nothing on me worth pinching. I checked my clothes at the first opportunity but I never carried cash other than a maximum of five pounds in small change. My credit and debit cards weren't taken and my mobile phone was still in my coat pocket. If I was the victim of an intended mugging then the mugger must have been pissed off when he discovered there was nothing to take. I wondered if they moved on to try their luck else-where, but still couldn't understand why the phone hadn't been taken. After all, mobile phones could always be sold to get money for drugs.

The whole incident made me determined to get this over with. I'm going to do it tonight...find out where I stand. No more hanging around street corners putting myself in danger.

My attention was suddenly drawn to the far end of the street. A guy had just entered the street from Lanark Road and was walking down the cobbles at Helen's side of the street. He was walking in an arrogant manner... determined, but shifty. Thinking he looked suspicious, I didn't take my eyes off him. I hoped he was going to walk past Helen's house and exit onto the street where I'm stood. It could be that he was taking a shortcut from one road to the other. My worst fears were realised. He came to an abrupt halt right outside Helen's front door. He paused for a minute. With my heart racing, I watched him knock on her door and the sound carried. My mind went crazy in that moment. I was consumed by thoughts that he was a boyfriend or lover. Was I to be flouted again at the last fucking hurdle? I couldn't believe it. I could feel my anger building towards the stranger. As I was about to turn away and acknowledge defeat once and for all, I saw him look up. Obviously, someone opened the door to him. His elbow was drawn back and he made a swift striking blow with his fist. He had punched her...or, someone else.

Not giving it a second thought, I set off down the cobbles at a run, thankful that I was wearing soft soled shoes. There wasn't a sound from me. By the time I reached the front door it was closed. Relieved the key hadn't been turned in the lock, I barged my way into her house without a care. As I entered the hallway, I saw them both. Helen was laid on the tiles in the hallway and the guy was kicking shit out of her body. She was barely conscious. Her underwear had been dragged down her scratched thighs. Blood poured from her forehead and nose. Her eyes weren't focussed. It was clear what his intention had been. Her nose looked broken and there was a cut near her left eye.

Fixated on his mission, it was a few seconds before he realised someone stood right behind him. His body tensed. Before he got a chance to swing around to face me, I grabbed a hand full of his hair and yanked his head backwards towards me. With my free hand I punched him hard in the back of his kidneys. He screamed out in pain. Helen moaned in pain. I cast a quick glance towards her. She couldn't see what was happening because of the blood which seeped into her eyes. I was just about to give another blow into his back when somebody grabbed my arms from behind.

"Leave the bastard to me. Call an ambulance for Miss Rushforth!"

I turned to face the newcomer. He had a shaved head and he was enormous. I noticed he wore an ear-ring in his right ear. He wasn't boyfriend material. I didn't get chance to ask who he was. He thrust his mobile phone into my hands and got a firm grip around Helen's attacker.

"Phone the fucking ambulance, now! When you've done that, call the cops. They'll want this fucker!"

He barked at me without another glance, his attention taken up with wrestling the guy to the ground and sitting on him.

"Who the fuck is he?" I dared to ask, scared of getting my head bitten off. I guessed he was not the type of guy to mess with.

"I'll tell you who the bastard is. 'E's 'er fucking ex-'usband, that's who 'e is...Anthony Pawson. 'E just got out of prison recently. Must 'ave enjoyed himself in there. Looks like 'e can't wait to go back."

I tried to take in what he was saying. This big guy who was crushing Helen's attacker wasn't an innocent passer-by. He knew too much about Helen and her ex-husband to be a mere stranger. How come he was in the area at the right time? It crossed my mind that perhaps he could be Helen's lover but I kept talking myself out of it. The thought was ludicrous!

Fingers shaking, I did as he ordered. I called 999 stating that we required an ambulance and the police. Someone answered immediately. I set out to explain that a lady was beaten up by her ex-husband who was recently released from prison.

"So who are you?" The big guy demanded to know. "And 'ow come you're 'ere?"

"I'm...I was a school friend of Helens. I was calling in to pay her a visit. I entered the street to see this...him, knocking at her door. Then I saw him punch her in the face and ran down the street when I realised what was happening. I came in to find...this..."

He scanned my face carefully, trying to decide if he trusted me and if I was telling the truth. Not much more was said between us as the police arrived, the blues and twos attracting attention in the street. They took one look at Helen and asked if an ambulance was on its way. We assured them it was, and after placing handcuffs on the piece of scum, they sat for a while taking statements from the big guy and myself as to what exactly happened. Five minutes later we were interrupted again when the ambulance pulled up. After careful examination of Helen, they loaded her onto a stretcher and into the ambulance.

"Which hospital will you be taking her to?" I asked of the para-medics. "I would like to visit her later and make sure she's going to be alright."

"It will be St John and St Elizabeth Hospital. Go to A &e E and ask if you can see her once she's been examined. She's sustained quite a blow to the head and fading in and out of consciousness. She'll probably be kept in for a night or two."

A bigger police vehicle arrived, a van. They quickly bundled the bastard into the back and drove off. The first two cops continued taking the statements from me and the other guy...Harry Allen was the name he gave them. Once they left Helen's house, Harry turned to face me again.

"You going to visit Miss Rushworth then? I'll follow you if that's okay? We'll 'ave to lock this place up and one of us needs to give 'er the 'ouse keys back."

"Yes. I'm going to see her...I have to. Seeing her kicked about like that...it was horrible. You said you're called Harry. Can I ask you what you were doing here tonight, Harry? I'm puzzled. You know too much about her...and that piece of shit, the ex-husband. What you told me doesn't quite make sense?"

"Okay. I'll tell you. First there's something else I 'ave to confess. When you ended up in 'ospital a couple of weeks back, it was me what knocked you out and called the ambulance. Sorry mate, but I thought you was that bastard staring down the street at 'er 'ouse. Couldn't tell in the dark. We knew 'e was out o' nick. I were keeping watch. We was expecting 'im to visit. You was in the wrong place."

It was hard to take in what he was saying. He just admitted to knocking me out! Who the hell was he? I could feel the anger rise in the pit of my stomach.

"Wait a minute. You...you knocked me out? And what did you gain from that? Why were you here that night too? I'm not getting it. And...we? Who exactly is 'we'?"

I could see that in return he was getting angry with me. Surely *he couldn't begrudge me wanting to know why he hit me over the head. I had a right to be fucking angry...but him?"*

"Okay. My boss...Mr Banks is the 'we'...me n' 'im. 'E prosecuted that arsehole for drug offences and 'e got banged up...with Miss Rushforth's 'elp. With 'is lawyer connections, 'e hears things...from inside the nick. Favours 'e calls in, you understand. Mr Banks 'eard from 'is...grass, that the bastard was goin for 'er...for giving evidence against 'im. Boss told me to keep an eye out down 'ere and that's what I've bin doing. Bin here for the last three week keeping watch, since...just before I 'it you. Someone watching down the street towards 'er 'ouse...I thought it was 'im. I already said I'm sorry, mate."

After some careful consideration I believed his story. It stung that he thought I could possibly be a jail bird, but I softened towards him. He seemed genuine enough. After all, he kept the bastard quiet until the police arrived. I doubt whether I would have been able to achieve the same. He had some muscle on him for sure.

"Okay, Harry! As you no doubt heard, I'm Alex...Alex Baker-Thompson. I was planning to call in to see Helen tonight. I haven't seen her for two or three years. I've only recently found out where she lives. Tonight has come as a fucking shock to me. The last thing I expected was to see her being viciously punched and kicked like that. I hope she's going to be alright."

Between the two of us we cleaned up the blood that had started to congeal in the hallway. Once we made the place look less than the crime scene it was, I explained to him that I came to Maida Vale on the train, so he wouldn't be able to follow me as he suggested earlier. He offered to give me a lift to the hospital and drop me home afterwards. After locking the door behind us, he pocketed the keys.

"I'll give these to Miss Rushforth."

I was pissed off. It meant that he would be there all the time I was. I wouldn't get chance for a private word or two with her. What a fucking night!

CHAPTER 38

I was afraid to open my eyes for a while immediately after I woke up. I kept my eyelids squeezed tight together. There was no need for me to open them to remember what happened. For a few seconds, I was terrified that I was in my house and that he was still there. I remembered I sort of fainted; a loss of consciousness. As I laid there, various recollections kept flitting through my head. I recalled there had been an issue with my sight. Everything seemed red. My whole body was in pain from the vicious kicks I took to the ribs and tops of my thighs. I felt as though I'd been hit by a freight train. Screwing my face up in agony, the sharp pain in my head from earlier returned. It was excruciating. Something felt wrong with my nose too. I could tell there's some padding and a large plaster across it; it's touching my bottom eyelashes.

I heard voices. One, I know is Harry. The other voice is familiar. I've heard it before but my head hurt too much to think who it could be. After forcing my eyes closed for an age, I opened them. I wasn't surprised to find myself in a hospital bed with the curtain drawn around me. I tried hard to focus on Harry but my vision is blurred. When my eyes cleared he smiled down at me. I groaned as I tried to speak but my cheeks and mouth ached with the effort. I couldn't understand what he was doing here.

"Har…Harry? What…happened…?"

"Try not to speak, Miss Rushforth. It's paining you. There's someone else 'ere to see you an'all…over there."

He pointed to the other side of the bed but try as I might, my attempt to turn my head or roll my body over to face the other person was unbearable with the pain. If Harry was here, logic told me to expect the other person to be Simon. Harry beckoned to the person behind me. I heard footsteps walk around the bottom of the bed and worked hard to try and see who it was. My eyes were struggling. Things were going out of focus again.

"Hello, Helen. No need to talk. I just want to make sure you're okay."

The voice was soft and became familiar. Everything still seemed hazy. I puzzled over why the other visitor would be here and where he fit into the events.

"Alex? What are…you…?"

"Miss Rushforth, don't talk." Harry spoke again.

"I'll explain what 'appened. Close your eyes if it's easier for you. Do you remember what 'appened back at your 'ouse? Your ex-'usband? Just nod if you do."

I nodded, yes. I could remember opening my door and seeing Anthony standing there with his fist poised, a second before it made contact with my face. I wouldn't ever forget it…or the pain. My nose felt like it shattered. I recall him pushing me further back in the hall and landing on my back. After that everything seems vague. There was odd moments when things were lucid. I know I'd struggled and tried to wriggle free as he raised my skirt and started dragging my panties down my legs. I did my utmost to fight back and make things difficult for him. The pain in my ribs as he lashed out with his foot was unbearable. Every time I opened my eyes to get a better look all I could see was red.

"Right, okay. 'E was let out of prison three week ago. I've bin keeping watch on your 'ouse every night since then. Boss asked me to do that. We doubted 'e'd try during the day. This man 'ere...Alex, your school mate, saw your 'usband...sorry, ex-'usband, knock on the door and the first blow. 'E came running to your rescue and barged into the 'ouse. 'E were kicking shit out of you, pulling your underwear down. I turned up a couple of minutes later and pulled Alex off 'im. I sat on the bastard until cops turned up. Alex 'eld you in 'is arms and...erm...covered you up."

I was mystified as to what Alex was doing anywhere near my house, but it hurt my head to try and make sense of anything. Harry nodded towards Alex then fished in his coat pocket.

"Alex 'ere called the ambulance and the cops. I've got your 'ouse key 'ere."

He dangled the bunch of keys in front of me and reached over to put it on the cabinet next to my bed.

"I'll leave it 'ere. We locked up. Cleaned the blood off your 'all floor an'all."

"But...I don't...get it."

It was Alex who spoke next, as I stared hard at him.

"You've had a big shock, Helen. You need to recover from all this. I will come and see you when you're home. I'll explain why I was in the area, that's if you don't mind? Now just rest. Don't try to make sense of it right now. Will that be alright?"

I tried hard to think straight. Alex wanted to come to visit me. It seemed strange. The last time I saw him we had sex in a park...in Ascot. I hadn't exactly been very nice to him that night. But I suddenly recalled why he was here at the hospital. He saved me from ending up dead by Anthony's hands.

"Yeah. Yes. It will be…nice…to see…you again…Al..Alex. Th…thank you…for what…you did…tonight. Much…appreciated."

I closed my eyes again. I was exhausted. I didn't want to be here in hospital; I wanted to be back in my own home. I was angry as well as in pain. The anger seemed to be making the pain worse, not anger at these two. I was fucking angry with Simon. He bloody knew the bastard was out of prison to have sent Harry to keep a watch on the street. Why the fuck he couldn't have told me, I didn't understand. If I'd been forewarned I wouldn't have opened the door to him, or to anyone. *He* had a lot of fucking explaining to do. No doubt he would visit me in hospital. Harry would report back to him on the night's events. Letting go of my anger for a few minutes, I started to worry about my nose. It throbbed angrily. I suspected it was broken. The doctor and nurses who attended me in A and E hadn't mentioned much about any of my injuries. I was hoping I would get a full explanation in the morning. I need to calm down before Simon comes in to visit. I was hopping mad and could imagine myself flying off the handle with him when I see him. My eyes started to get heavy. I tried to open them long enough to say goodbye to Harry and Alex and thank them for their help, but it was an effort to try and prise my eye lids apart. Sleep came easily as I'd been given a sedative.

When I woke up again the clock on the wall told me that is was gone two in the morning. Harry and Alex must have been long gone. Still pondering over why Alex had been in my street, I couldn't help but wonder what Anthony might have done to me had Alex not been around. If it had been five minutes after that before Harry realised something was wrong it might have been too late.

Harry came back in to see me the following morning. I was quite surprised he came back, and it was touching that he brought me some essential toiletries. I wish I'd had them earlier on before two lady police officers came to visit me. They took some pictures of my facial injuries, the bruising on my ribs where he kicked me and the scratches on my thighs where he all but clawed my underwear down.

"I don't know if they're the right brands Miss, but I figured any'd be better than none at all."

Harry...the gentle giant. He was a legend. He'd gone even further up in my estimation for his kindness.

"Oh, Harry. How thoughtful of you. Thank you so much."

I had expected Simon, but of course if he was busy in court there was no way would he be able to just abandon his client.

"The Boss would 'ave come to see you if 'e wasn't busy in court. 'E sends 'is...err..best wishes and 'opes you're soon well again, Miss Rushforth. 'E said 'e'll come and visit once you get back 'ome. He's fuc...sorry! 'E's furious about your ex-'usband. I know 'e expected that 'e'd try to see you and do some name calling, but never imagined for one minute that 'e'd try beat you black n' blue and attempt to...you know. 'E's 'opping. 'Ow long they keeping you in 'ere, Miss? 'Ave they said?"

"Harry, I've told you plenty of times to call me Helen. Miss Rushforth is just...you know! I was hoping Simon would have called in today. I'm angry too, Harry. I'm angry with him for not letting me know that the fucking scumbag was out of prison. I'm livid. *That's* why he's keeping his distance. He's hoping I'll calm down. It doesn't matter whether it's a day or a month, he can't hide from me forever. He's going to get it in the neck."

"I get you're angry, Miss. I really do. That young man what came to your rescue before me...beside 'imself with worry 'e was. 'E...pulled your underwear in place and covered you up after I got the bastard pinned down. Covered your dignity, 'e did. I thought 'e was going to barf when we cleaned your 'allway. 'E couldn't get over all that blood."

He started to look a little embarrassed and looked around the room as if he was looking for something to focus on, perhaps an alternative talking point instead of dwelling on the pitiful state they found me in. Things were ticking over in my head again. It seems I owe Alex a big apology. He must have changed over the last couple of years. I would never have had him labelled as thoughtful but I doubted he had ever faced anything like this. I changed the subject first. Harry gave an audible sigh of relief.

"The doctor came and examined me this morning, Harry. I think I have to stay in here one more night but should be allowed home tomorrow. My nose is broken but he told me it should be alright. I might end up with a slight bump on it, but it's hard to tell until the swelling has fully gone down. I feel okay, but my ribs are bruised too."

As an afterthought I asked him a big favour.

"Harry, do you have your mobile phone on you? I assume mine is still back home on the kitchen counter. Work will be wondering where I am come Monday morning. I need to let them know I'll be spending a week at home."

He fumbled in his jacket pocket and handed me his iphone.

"'Ere you go, Miss. Keep this 'un until you get 'ome. You need to be in contact with people in the meantime. I 'ave another in my car I keep for emergencies. Got my list of contacts in there too so it's not a problem."

"Thank you, Harry. Would you mind popping down the corridor and bringing us both a drink. I'd love a coffee and I can phone someone from work while you're gone."

"I'll do that. I'd best be gone after I've 'ad a drink with you though. I've one or two errands to run for the Boss."

Off he went to get the drinks and I placed my first call. Cindy answered her mobile after only a couple of rings. There was silence at her end while I told her about Anthony's attack.

"Bloody Hell, Helen. I don't know what to say. I'm just glad you're okay...well, sort of okay. I'll see if I can get some of the girls to come in and visit with me tonight. Will that be okay?"

"Cindy...there's really no need. I'll be home tom..."

"Don't be silly. It sucks being stuck in a hospital with no visitors. Don't worry, me and...whoever wants to come will be over to see you later. I'll call them and see if anybody's free on a Saturday evening. You rest up."

There was no arguing with her. I knew she'd be here along with whoever she could get hold of. There were no set visiting hours so it would be fine. We said our goodbyes. The next call I placed was to Catherine. She also suggested coming to visit me with Ruby and maybe Heidi that same night. I suggested they wait until I got out of hospital because I was going to be inundated with the girls from work.

Bless Harry. He gave me a good ten minutes. I could see him lurking with our drinks in the corridor. I waved him back through.

We sat and chatted for about twenty minutes until he finished with his cup of tea. He hadn't really known a great deal about Anthony, so I spent the time filling him in on the things he didn't know. The behaviour towards me by his parents. The rape, the gang bang, the rent boy and the system that he set up for the dumping and collection of the envelopes full of cocaine.

"Seems like your poor Dad set you up with a wrong 'un, Miss. A right bad apple."

"Harry, do you have a family…kids?"

"I do, Miss. A four year old girl and two boys, twins who are eighteen. They just started university few weeks back. Little girl is the apple of my eye. 'Aving this job for the Boss, gives me plenty of time with 'er. My wife 'as an important job and she earns good money." He laughed. "I know I'm a bit of a rough 'un, but I got me a lovely lady, Miss Rushforth. Twenty years we bin together now.

I looked at him in a new light. I'd always known him as a rough diamond and I knew that Simon always placed his trust in him. What I'd never had the image of was Harry as a happily married man with a family. My respect for him had gone beyond where it had been before. I always was amused by his company even though it had only been for minutes at a time.

Once Harry left I turned over onto my side, I felt drained and was still in a lot of pain. I didn't expect sleep to come but it was well past mid-afternoon when I woke. I had slept through dinner but I wasn't feeling like eating anyway, so it was no great loss. Remembering that some of the girls from the office would be visiting later, I summoned one of the nurses.

"I need to take a shower. Can I ask…is it possible that any of your team would have a little bit of foundation I could use, please? I want to try and look a bit more respectable when my colleagues from work arrive tonight."

She laughed.

"All that you've been through…and you're bothered about your friends seeing you without make-up! Tut tut! I'll see what I can do. You sure you'll be okay in the shower? You've got extensive bruising. If you need any help, ring the bell. We don't want you falling on the tiles."

She headed off down the corridor chuckling to herself. I gathered up the towel from the bedside cupboard and the bag of toiletries that Harry had brought in and headed for the nearest bathroom. The pains in my ribs were pure agony. Dreading what I would see, I slowly shuffled over to take a look in the mirror. I was horrified. My eyes were a manky shade of black tinged with yellow. I peeled the sticking plaster and padding off my nose. I was surprised and pleased to see that it didn't look as bad as I expected. I ran my finger from my forehead right down to the tip of my nose. There was the slightest of bumps, and I turned my head for a sideways profile. I didn't see that it looked much different to the nose I always had. Taking a closer look at my eyes, I realised that unless the nurse could find me some concealer type of foundation, there was no way I would be able to cover the dark bruising.

I stood under the flow of the shower longer than I normally would, but the heat of the water was soothing on my aching body. I wasn't in a rush to get out and once I started to towel myself dry I regretted not staying in longer. It hurt like a bitch and I winced as I rubbed the towel over my skin. If my father could see me now, see what Anthony had done to me, he would have taken him on with his bare hands. I couldn't blame him for the ways things had turned out. Anthony fooled everyone, myself included.

Back on the ward, afternoon drinks were being poured. The nurse I asked for foundation was helping the auxiliary nurse serve the teas. Seeing me head for my little side room, she rushed off and arrived back minutes later with a tube of foundation and some blusher.

"I couldn't lay my hands on any brushes. You'll have to use your hands, sorry. I hope it helps but somehow I doubt it, honey. Besides, your friends will only be concerned for you, not your lack of make-up."

"Perhaps you're right. But it will make me feel a little better. Thank you so much."

A little later, after the evening meal, I headed back to the bathroom and after a couple of carefully applied applications and a little blusher, I felt a little better about my appearance. I couldn't cover the bruises fully but the two coats had toned down the darkness, making it slightly less obvious...but only from a distance.

It was almost six when through the glass in the door, I saw Cindy, Christina, Gemma, Leanne and Janet stop at the nurses station, looking all around them for a sign of me. A nurse approached the station and pointed in the general direction of my room. They walked in, looks of concern plastered over their faces. Christina held a massive bouquet of flowers and Gemma handed me a gift bag.

"Helen, oh my God, I can't believe it." Christina's eyes glazed over as she leaned in and gave me a gentle hug. The other girls did the same, scared to hurt me. Fearing questions that I wasn't in the right frame of mind to answer, I grinned.

"I don't want to talk about it, I'll warn you. It's a nightmare I want to forget. What are you going to do to keep me amused and cheer me up?"

"James said to tell you that he hopes you're soon up and about again, Helen. That was nice of him, wasn't it?" Feeling ungrateful, I couldn't help my selfish thoughts kick in.

Then why isn't he here with me?

With the exception of Christina, who had to rush off after half an hour to take her daughter and friends somewhere on a night out, they stayed for a couple of hours. They kept the chatter going between them and it raised my spirits. No-one pushed for information on Anthony's attack, thankfully. By the time they left, I was drained again. My snooze earlier in the afternoon had no effect on my ability to sleep that night.

After I used Harry's mobile to call a cab, I left the hospital mid-morning. The same nurse who brought me the make-up kindly loaned me a thick cardigan so that I could cover the blood-stained clothes I was wearing when admitted. Having no bag and therefore no money, I had to promise the taxi-driver that I had the money to pay him when I got home. Two minutes after he pulled up outside the house, I was back out with the cash to pay him. Five minutes later I was in my pyjamas and dressing gown. The clothes I had worn earlier were double-bagged and in the trash.

After charging up my mobile phone, which for the last two nights had been sat on my kitchen worktop, I checked for missed calls and messages. There was a message from Jim.

Helen, I'm shocked and sorry to hear what has happened. I hope you're soon well again. Jim xx

I dismissed it. There was no mention of him being worried or wanting to be at my side. I was numb, beyond crying. I looked forward to seeing the girls and Heidi later in the day.

More flowers and gifts followed from them. For a couple of hours they fussed and fretted over me. They didn't want to outstay their welcome though and pointing out that I looked tired around nine, they made their excuses and left. I sat in an armchair and broke my heart. I didn't realise how severe the trauma was going to be; coming back home to remember being attacked in my hallway. The next morning, I called out a security company to add some additional safety features; a reputable company that the Hopkins Partnership had used in the past. It was a little too late. I knew that Anthony would already be back in prison.

CHAPTER 39

*I*t was ten thirty in the morning when I heard a knock at the front door. I assumed it would be Simon. He hasn't visited once, not even since I left hospital on Sunday afternoon. I dragged my aching muscles from the sofa and went to answer the door. It was him. He thrust the most enormous bunch of blooms in my face. My anger was there in a second. So he thought flowers would get him off the hook? Not holding back my fury, I snatched the flowers out of his hands and threw them onto the road.

"Flowers, huh? SO YOU THINK FLOWERS ARE GOING TO MAKE UP FOR WHAT YOU'VE FUCKING DONE? OR RATHER…WHAT YOU DIDN'T FUCKING DO?"

He took a couple of steps back, startled and frightened by my outburst. I didn't give a shit and carried on with the verbal attack.

"WHY DIDN'T YOU TELL ME HE WAS OUT? HOW COME HE'S OUT? HE'S BARELY SERVED FIFTEEN FUCKING MONTHS!"

I was on a roll and had no intention of stopping my tirade of abuse towards him.

"HE BEAT ME BLACK AND FUCKING BLUE… ALMOST RAPED ME AGAIN, BUT FOR…BUT FOR…"

I screamed at the top of my voice, my anger at him taking priority over all else. I knew I needed to stop bellowing at him. My emotions were over the top. Then the tears started. He stepped forward and folded his arms around me. He gently pushed me backwards into the hall, leaving the flowers on the pavement. I couldn't hold them back, my cheeks were drenched. He came in and closed the door.

"Helen…I…I'm so sorry. I wish I had told you now. You could have got out of the house and stayed in a hotel for a couple of weeks. I could have had Harry tail him for a while and find out what the scroat was up to. I didn't think he would be after you so soon after getting out. God knows how he found out where you live. I am truly sorry, Helen."

He held me tight as I sobbed uncontrollably into the sleeve of his expensive suit jacket. He patted my back and didn't say another word until my sobs died away. He released me from his grip, grabbed my hand and walked me through to the living room.

"Go and make us a cuppa, sweetie. I'll retrieve the flowers from the street…unless anyone has picked them up and walked with them."

It kept me occupied for five minutes making a coffee for him. I needed something stronger so opted for the gin bottle.

"You shouldn't be having that if you're still on tablets, Helen."

"Don't preach at me! I can do without the fucking lecture, thank you."

"Okay, okay. I get you. Calm down."

"I'm not an alcoholic, Simon. Don't look at me like that. It's just been rather a shitty week for me, wouldn't you say?"

"Sorry. Sorry, sweetie. I didn't mean to be thoughtless. Right, come and sit down and tell me about this guy who rescued you...Alex is it? Harry tells me he's a good guy. Tell me about him."

"There's nothing to tell. He's an old friend from school. He recently found out where I live. I don't know how yet but no doubt he'll tell me. He's coming to see me on Saturday afternoon...coming to see if I'm okay. Apparently he was pretty cut up about turning up here and seeing what he saw. He's a good guy. I haven't always been what you'd call pleasant to him. I feel guilty now after what he did for me the other night."

"It's a bloody good job he was around if you ask me. Things could have got nasty if he hadn't turned up when he did. Yet I hear Harry was only a couple of minutes after him."

He gave an audible sigh. I was still scowling at him.

"Anyway, just so you know, he's back inside, and he'll end up having to serve the full sentence now. We could go for further charges to be brought against him...attempted rape, grievous bodily harm, call it what you will...attempted murder even. I'll leave it up to you. You maybe have no wish to want to go through that again, Helen."

"No. I don't. I don't ever want to set eyes on the bastard again. I may have to move from this cottage. He might come back for me one day. He knows where I live. I can't live like this, being scared to open my own front door."

"I don't think there's any need for drastic action like that. We can get an injunction slapped on him. He can be arrested for being within so many metres/miles of your house. But right now, don't worry! He is already back inside for having broken the conditions of his parole. We'll sort it, Helen. You need to rest and recover, so don't start worrying your pretty head about anything. You don't need it. I want you to get better. Where's your man through all this? The one you dumped me for? Why isn't he here supporting you?"

I couldn't tell him that Jim and I were no longer together; couldn't bear for him to criticise Jim in any way, as he surely would. There was only one person who was allowed to dis the guy I love and that's me! I had no doubt that he would also start pushing for our 'fuck buddy' status to recommence and I was done with that! I had to defend Jim, no matter of how he broke my heart.

"He's keeping the office running. You know Ted's almost retired now. He's always holidaying or golfing. I can't be in the office, so Jim has to be there to keep things running. He'll be here at the first opportunity. He phones me two or three times a day to check up on me."

After I finished my gin I calmed down. Simon was giving me plenty to think about. I didn't want to be alone. Maybe I should get a dog. Nothing was more important now than seeing to my personal protection. I'd made excuses to Simon why Jim wasn't here with me, not wanting to tell him the truth. I was touched by a moment of feeling quite sad about the way it turned out, but it is what it is. Serves me right for falling in love with a man who isn't free.

Simon stayed with me for a couple of hours before he left to go back to his office. On several occasions he tried to take my mind off things by drawing me into general conversations, but I wasn't really up to making small talk. I was glad when he left and I could sit with my own thoughts or watch a film on T.V; something to try and get out of my *own* head for once.

I looked forward to Alex's visit on Saturday. I've a few questions to throw at him, and I hope he'll be able to answer them.

CHAPTER 40

I 'd been pacing the floor since five thirty. Even though I slept well I hadn't contemplated being up this early. I tried my hardest to get a few extra hours of sleep but it had proved pointless. After fifteen minutes of staring at the ceiling I got up to watch a film...another action film that served no purpose. The television was playing to the room at large and I was oblivious to what film or programme periodically flashed colours around my darkened living room.

I feel physically sick. I'm going out later to visit Helen. She's back at home after her stay in hospital. I won't have to label myself as a stalker any more after today. She knows about this visit. It's already planned and she knows to expect me around eleven. My mind is in turmoil. I feel as if my head is about to explode.

Here I am again with the question I have been unable to answer; what am I going to say to her? Other than explaining more about the night I caught her bastard of an ex-husband attacking her and probably with the intent of raping her, I don't know what else there is to say.

I cast my mind back to the time I bumped into her through work. Her company had come to do the audit where I was employed *and we chatted each time I saw her. I was elated when she agreed to meet up with me again. We shared some lovely times together as friends until I blew it. I tried to shove my hand into her undies one day. Nobody's fault but mine why we stopped seeing each other after that. Not having the patience to wait until she was ready, I pushed her into something she didn't want at that stage. She walked away. If it's possible to really hate yourself, I would have to say that after that night, I detested myself more than anything or anybody. I fucked up, big style.*

Our next moment came a few short years later. I was out with a crowd of mates at Jigz nightclub in Ascot and spotted her in the middle of the dance floor. She was out with colleagues from work. I pushed and fought through the masses of people dancing and approached her. Encouraged by the fact that she smiled at me, I led her off the dance floor and out into the night so that we could chat. We walked away from the deafening white noise of the club where it was barely possible to think let alone talk. I can't remember what prompted her to grab my hand and thrust it down her panties. I didn't protest when she subsequently got my cock out and almost started to give me a blow job at the side of what is a busy road. I led her into a little park and from there on, we indulged in the most amazing sex I ever had. Where the prudish Helen had gone and this insatiable nymphomaniac emerged from was totally beyond me. I never experienced anything since that could come anywhere near surpassing it.

I can see that it was that night that completely screwed my head up. To have had the best sex ever and then half an hour later be told 'I don't feel anything for you, Alex.'

For a while, I went through periods of hating her. There were times I even fantasised about killing her for not liking me. The number of times I uttered 'you fucking bitch' under my breath and out loud in the privacy of my own home were off the scale. I went through Hell for months after and it still haunts me. I got through it. I dated plenty of females, expecting and hoping to find someone who could set me on fire the way she did that night in the park. Sadly, I've never found anyone who comes close to the category that she falls under.

Eventually, I thought I got her out of my head for good...right up to the point where she ended up on the same flight back from Paris that I was on. She arrived late for the plane, being the last person to board but she disappeared behind the curtain that separated first and economy class. It was a bitch of a flight having to relive everything I thought I had got through...and feeling my cock stiffen beneath my denims. That flight resurrected my obsession with her.

Through an early morning's unhealthy caffeine intake, I let all these memories take over. Back and forth they went until I felt good for nothing.

I hope this morning is going to be different. I'm not going to tell her that I've been stalking her on and off for nearly a year. I will not tell her about my feelings for her, nor am I going to ask her to be my girlfriend or that I regularly dream about fucking her. This is my last opportunity so I'm not going to blow it. Taking it slow is my only option or I can see myself being shown the door.

I'm going to go in the house, ask her how she's doing, show compassion and do what I can to get her on side. I won't be over-friendly or patronising. I'll call and get some flowers to take for her. Hopefully, she won't read too much into a floral gift. After that it'll be casual conversation all the way. I'm determined not to overstay my welcome...an hour, two at the most. I'll get up and leave when I feel an appropriate moment presents itself.

What had seemed a long time to wait when I first got up, actually passed fairly swiftly. It was ten o'clock before I knew it and I headed to get showered and dressed. I decided against driving over there after my last effort. I struggled to find anywhere to park but ended up driving away after I saw her with those girls and the blonde-haired woman. I would catch the tube. I should be able to buy a bunch of flowers at one of the stalls inside the station.

I was pissed off to find that there was no flowers to be had at any of the stations so I grabbed a box of chocolates and couple of 'women's magazines' that I hoped would be her sort of reading; 'Vogue' and 'Hello'. I had a few misgivings after I paid for them. Somehow I couldn't imagine Helen would be interested in celebrity gossip and pictures. I rather fancied I was right about 'Vogue' though. She always looks like she belongs in a magazine like that with her looks, figure and beautifully fashioned clothes.

I walked out of Maida Vale station and under the archway to Elgin Mews and was visited by a sudden urge to run. My head was screaming 'just what the fuck are you doing? My heart was at full gallop. An acidic taste of vomit rose up in my throat. Maybe if I had grabbed a bowl of cereal for breakfast it would have helped to settle my stomach. It was the constant churning that had made my mind up to leave food alone. I was scared in case it made me feel worse. Fuck, whatever I did was never right. Yet here I am, about to take the plunge with something that had...never felt right. I'm here now so I might as well see it through.

'Best behaviour'.

Poised on her doorstep, I took a few deep breaths and knocked. I panicked. I was ten minutes earlier than had been arranged. I hope she doesn't mind. I could hear an inner door open and footsteps crossed what I remembered to be the short distance to the front door. Feeling a little self-conscious, I plastered a smile on my face ready to face her.

The door opened...but it wasn't Helen. It was the guy I saw leaving her office a couple of times. He's the one with whom I felt there had been a big fall out. What was he doing here? My jaw dropped as he stood aside to let me pass through.

CHAPTER 41

On waking Saturday morning, I instantly remembered that Alex was visiting at eleven. I felt a little unnerved and dreaded the memory of that night with him, returning to haunt me. I lay in bed for a while thinking of the things I wanted to ask him. I needed answers. I want to know exactly what he saw when he arrived at my door. I know there's nothing to be gained from knowing what the bastard did but I can't help it. I wonder if by knowing it will be able to rid me of the fear. He's locked away again so I don't want to feel scared. I've spoken with Simon. What he anticipates what will happen is that he will be made to serve his original full sentence now that he's broken the terms of his parole.

After lying in bed too long being maudlin, I got up and gave Harry his breakfast. It would be unlikely that I could make myself a cup of coffee without my little beast tormenting me as I moved around.

I didn't linger long in the kitchen after I fed him. I carried my drink through to the living room and switched the television on for background noise. Sipping away at my coffee, I reminded myself to ask Alex how he came to find out where

I live and why he was in the area that night. I was suspicious and feel certain he couldn't have just been passing by. He was in the area for some reason and I suspect he decided to visit me. I was puzzled as to why that might be, as the last time we came into contact it hadn't ended well for him. The memories and words I have never been able to forget. We had the time of our lives in a park. I acted like a tart and when we walked back to the nightclub he asked if we could see each other again. I was viciously blunt with him and told him I had no feelings for him. It must have hurt! Then he saves me from being half-killed at my ex-husband's hands. I struggled to comprehend the whole situation.

I mooched around until nine thirty and then felt an urgency to go and get myself in the shower and dressed before he arrived. I hoped he was only visiting to see my progress, anything other than that I can't bear to think about. As I sponged myself down under the hot water, my ribs where Anthony kicked me several times caused me extreme pain and my body jerked. Looking in the mirror afterwards, I was pleasantly surprised to see that the bruising was almost gone from my nose and eyes at last. I looked like new. It shouldn't be hard with foundation to cover up what little bruising remained.

As I sat and applied concealer and followed that with thick foundation I was pleased with the result. I didn't bother with much else other than blusher and a tiny amount of mascara. I looked human again. I ran the hairdryer through my hair and chose some denims and a loose sweatshirt. It pained my ribs if I wore anything too fitted.

I had a bit of time to kill so I sat propped on the bed with my pillows and read a magazine that had been on my bedside table for the last month. I lost myself in a true reader's story about her cheating husband. I felt her pain as the words rung true. Looking at the clock and seeing it was still forty minutes before Alex was due, I started to read another article. Two minutes into it, there was a knock at my front door. Not impressed that he was early, I slapped the magazine back onto the table and headed downstairs. I had to calm down from my irritation at the fact that I might still have been in the shower and not ready for visitors. I couldn't have a go at him after what he'd done.

I opened the door dreading how it would go and not knowing what I was going to say. But it wasn't Alex. Jim stood there, his handsome face looking tired and drawn with worry.

"Jim?"

"Surely you're not surprised to see me? Were you expecting somebody else, Helen?"

I was shaking. Confusion crept into my head. Why was he here after all this time?

"I am actually. The guy who turned up and stopped *him* from half-killing and raping me is calling in to see me. I thought it was him arrived early."

"I see. How are you, sweetie? You look as beautiful as ever."

Smooth as ever. It bounced off my shoulders as I prepared to go on the defensive.

"Come in!"

I turned to walk away but after he closed the door he grabbed my hand and spun me around to face him. His arms were around me in an instant. I tensed.

"Helen, I've been dying to see you since I heard. I've been worried sick about you. I came to the hospital during the day, before the girls visited you. I peered through the glass in your door and you were sleeping so I left. I've wanted to see you since, but feared that you may be inundated with visitors."

"Oh!"

"Helen, please don't be like that with me. I want to kiss you!"

Being petty and not wanting to break down the defence I had put into place, I turned my face away. His kiss landed on my right cheek.

"What exactly are you here for, James? To put me through Hell again?"

"Can we talk please, sweetie? I'm not here to hurt you or 'put you through Hell'. There are things I need to tell you. We can't have a full on discussion in your hall."

Still feeling icy towards him, I peeled his arms from around me and walked through to the kitchen. Tendrils of suspicion and doubt crept into my mind. He was hot on my heels.

"How long have we got? Before your *friend* arrives?"

"Don't say *'friend'* in that tone, James. He *is* only a friend; an old school-friend. Nothing more than that. He's due here at eleven."

"Maybe we should have our chat after he's gone. I have a lot to say to you."

"After he's gone? And what makes you think I have anything to say? I might ask you to leave before he gets here. Since we're over, I don't see any reason for you to stay."

I watched his face. He looked stung, as if I just slapped him. He was horrified and I wondered if it was more by my attitude towards him rather than the words I used.

"Can we get one thing straight please, Helen? Did you ever hear me say that we're through? I don't think you did, because I know I never once uttered those words. That idea came from your head."

"Okay, you didn't use those particular words, but then again you don't need to. Your absence from my life has left me in no doubt as to what your feelings are."

"That's your interpretation, Helen. Like I said, nothing

more than the thoughts you have in your head. What I said to you was that I needed not to see you for a while. I did the right thing by staying away; living without any proper contact with you."

I couldn't keep the sarcasm out of my voice as I spat out my reply.

"Ah! So you discovered that you don't need me in your life? I guessed as much. You can go now, James."

He stood open-mouthed, not knowing what else to say until the knock came at the door. It would be Alex. James was nearer the door to the hall and before I could make a move, he headed to answer the knock.

"Hello! I take it you're Alex? Come in, please. Helen's just through here."

Alex stepped into the hall and noticed me stood in the living room. His face was flushed and he looked shell-shocked.

"Hi, Alex. Thank you for coming. It's nice to see you again."

He looked embarrassed but managed to stutter a greeting.

"Hi…hi, Helen. How are you? You look better than…than the last time I saw you."

Remembering my manners I set out to introduce the two. I indicated Jim.

"I'd better introduce you both. Jim, this is Alex. Alex, this is Jim. Jim is…"

He quickly butted in. The words spilled out of his mouth and he came to me and put his arm tightly around my shoulder and maintained a tight grip.

"I'm Jim…Helen's partner!"

I couldn't believe what I heard. He continued to hold on to me like a possession. Determined not to make a scene or contradict what he just said, I smiled up at him briefly. Hopefully what he would read as an 'I'll deal with you later' look.

Looking back at Alex, I noticed he was carrying a couple of magazines and chocolates. Seeing the glance I gave them he held them out to me.

"Sorry it's not much. I bought you these in the station, Helen. I hope they're of some interest. Something for you to read while you're unable to work."

"That's a lovely thought, Alex. Thank you. You didn't need to bring anything but yourself. I am already very much in your debt for...for what you did. Can I offer you a drink after you've travelled over here? You must be ready for one."

"Okay. I wouldn't mind coffee please, if it's not much trouble. I've...it's only a quick visit to see how you are getting on. You look as if you're on the mend, thank goodness."

Unexpectedly, Jim offered to go and make drinks, and I wondered if it was to somehow avoid being asked to leave; to make sure that he would be staying until after Alex's visit was over.

"Sit down, Helen. Alex, have a seat. I'll make the coffee. Helen should be resting."

I gestured for Alex to take a seat and sat opposite him.

"Tell me about that night, Alex."

Watching him carefully I could see he was uncomfortable. His hands were shaking and the redness of his face hadn't faded since he walked in the room. It seemed as if he was finding the visit to be torturous. Instinct told me that he wished he was elsewhere. I'd never thought of Alex as shy. I couldn't understand why he didn't even make eye contact with me. He was struggling for words too.

"I...I...don't think...think there's...any...any more to tell. It...it was exactly as your...friend...the one called Harry...t...told you."

I waited patiently for more, but further words were not forthcoming. This was not the Alex I know. Feeling the need to get him talking some more, I offered a further prompt with my next question.

"How come you were down my street that night? I don't mean to pry but…Hell, I'm glad you were. I dread to think of my fate if you hadn't been in the area."

He appeared to be carefully planning his answer, twiddling his fingers together and when he eventually spoke he cleared his throat every few seconds.

"I…I…ahem. I was…was on the same train…ahem…as you one night a few months ago. I had…ahem…had to…go and visit…someone I know. You…you came out of the station…just ahead of…of me. I…I watched…you…walk down the street…and come to this…this cottage. That…that night…ahem…I had been visiting…my friend again…ahem… and I thought…I thought…ahem…I would look you up…and say hello."

My head was spinning. I was aware that my mouth must be gaping wide open.

"You…you were coming here…to see me?"

"Ahem…Yes!"

"I…I can't believe it. Ob…obviously you were meant to be here that night. I'm a big believer in fate."

He turned to make eye contact, but only briefly.

"Meant…meant to be here…to…to save you, Helen. That…that must have…been my mission."

Jim walked back in the room with a tray of coffee at that point. Seeing the shock on my face, there was a question in his eyes.

"Helen? What's matter, sweetie?"

"Al…Alex found out where I lived by accident one night when he got off the train just after me. He saw me come down the street and unlock my door. Last week…the night… he'd been to visit a friend and thought he would look me up to say hello. It…it was supposed to happen that way. Jim it's insane, isn't it? Visiting me…on a night when I needed help."

He looked over and beamed at Alex.

"Thank you, Alex. I can't thank you enough, my friend. If you hadn't been here that night, my beautiful Helen…well, I dread to think…"

I was quick to pick up on his remark and I found myself being enveloped in a deep warmth. I smiled…until I saw Alex's face. He wasn't looking at either Jim or myself and if I wasn't mistaken he looked ready to run out on us.

Jim knelt down on the floor and poured the coffee. He handed a cup to Alex first.

"Th…thank you. I'll…ahem…I'll just drink this…and leave you two in peace. Helen…needs to rest still. I'm…just glad I could…help!"

It proved hard to engage him in any conversation. I could tell he wasn't up to talking. He made a valiant effort but other than a few mumbles, Alex seemed to have nothing further to say. Halfway down his cup of coffee he placed it back on the coffee table and pulled the sleeve of his coat back to glance at his watch.

"I'll…just drink this and…go and see my friend. He…he's just down the next street. Well…it's…it's been nice seeing you…looking well, Helen."

"I'm so grateful, Alex. Right place, right time, eh?"

With that, he stood up, drank the last of his coffee and placed the cup back on the coffee table.

"I…I'll go now. You…rest up, Helen."

Jim walked to the door with him. I heard them say goodbye to each other as he opened the door to let him out. Coming back into the living room he gave me a twisted, wry smile and raised his eyebrows.

"Well, well. If I'm not mistaken, that young man was

uncomfortable because I was here. I feel his short visit proved to be an ordeal for him."

"What?"

"He fancies you, Helen. He thought, you being alone that night, that you didn't have a partner. That's why he was eager to visit you. Don't you think?"

I searched my mind for other memories, the way Alex usually was, and I had to admit, his behaviour was totally out of character.

"It *is* strange. I've never seen him like that before. I've known him since we were kids and he's never been stuck for something to say. You're possibly right, Jim."

He came and sat at the side of me, making that intense eye contact; the contact I had missed so much.

"Helen, I...you called me Jim again."

"So...'my partner', 'my beautiful Helen' and 'he thought that I didn't have a partner'. Jim?"

"Yes. I'm glad you picked up on those words. That's why I'm here, Helen. I know you've been hurting. Believe me, I haven't wanted to put you through all the shit. Seriously! I know how upset you've been. It hurt me to see you like that. I've stayed away from you for one reason. I had to see how bad it would hurt *me* to stay away from you. I had to be sure. I discovered how much it hurts...it was pure fucking evil. My mind was already made up when...when that guy attacked you. When I heard the news from the others, I wanted to come and see you straight away. But I couldn't...because I knew you were having lots of visitors. And obviously I couldn't talk to you when you were asleep in the hospital. Today has been my first opportunity."

"What? Opportunity for what, James?"

"We're going to be together, Helen. I haven't stopped loving you. These past few weeks my love for you has deepened. I want to be here with you, permanently. I'm leaving

Cheryl. She doesn't know it yet. She won't even care. I have to tell Jack and I'm going to do that tomorrow. She's out for a spa day with her 'friend'. That means she's out shagging the latest guy she's got in tow."

He paused for a minute to let me take in what he was saying. Smiling didn't seem appropriate and it was hard to keep one off my face. If what he was saying is true, I can't appear to be delighted about the fact that he's breaking up the family home. It entered my head to feel sorry for her.

"Does she still love you, Jim?"

"I doubt it. I'm positive she doesn't. If my instinct serves me well, she'll show me the door. It's an opportunity to bring her men friends to the house instead of shagging them in the back seat of their cars. My worries are not about her. It's Jack I feel for, but I know he hates living in what he's always called a war zone. With me happy and his Mum doing what she pleases, it'll do wonders for his mental health and wellbeing! I hope so!"

"Oh, Jim! I can't help feeling this is because of me. I feel bad for them!"

"Don't! Whether you had come along or not, I would never have seen it through. Once Jack gets to uni, I couldn't stay no matter what! It's never been a proper marriage."

"I…I thought…when you weren't speaking with me, it was because…because of what we did with Chris; because…I enjoyed it at the time! I…"

"Helen, never! I wouldn't do that, I promise! Please don't forget, the three of us were paralytic that first night, in Manchester. We were all out of control. And don't forget, I was the one who put the idea into your head…the suggestion that we do it again, if that was what you wanted. I'm to blame."

"I thought I did want it, until…until it started happening again."

"The point is...we stopped it. You stopped it. We both realised it wasn't what we wanted anymore. We wanted each other, we still do, Helen...don't we?"

He took me in his arms and squeezed me tight to him. His lips met mine and I felt so happy. For the first time in ages I was happy. Five minutes of kissing and I don't know how but we ended up in my bedroom. I gasped out loud as his cock nudged into me for the first time in weeks. He was gentle as ever.

"If you feel any pain whatsoever, darling, tell me and I'll stop. I won't enjoy it if you're hurting in any way."

"I'll be okay! Promise!"

I felt inebriated. The room was spinning and my emotions took over. He thrust into me time and again and with each movement it seemed as if he was drumming the truth into me, pressuring me to finally believe in us, that this is our future. Jim and I together. We released our cum together and with my orgasm, I also let go of the emotions that had built up inside me for so many weeks. He watched my tears and through glazed eyes I could see his love and passion.

"I love you so much, Helen Rushforth!"

"I love you the same, Jim Mortimer!"

Our statements prompted a fit of laughter from the pair of us.

"It's going to be like this for us every day. Just think about that, Helen. Let that thought consume you for the next week or two until I pick my moment to do the deed. It will be done before you know it."

He stayed for most of the afternoon. Sitting close by and holding me close as if he didn't want to let go, I could feel his breath in my hair and one hand grasped mine tight. We were quiet as there was nothing much to say. I know I was caught up in the enormity of it all; pure elation for Jim and I, total sadness that yet another separation would be added to the statistics. I wondered how his son would feel. I feared for the impact, if any, in our work place. Things would be whispered behind our backs, eyebrows would be raised and no doubt I would be labelled 'marriage wrecker'. I hoped Jim would put those ideas to rest with whoever dared say it.

When it was time for him to leave, I went into the hall to let him out. After holding me for one last time, he pulled me close, whispering in my ear.

"When you come back to work I won't be avoiding you anymore, Helen. Text me on a night if you need to. I don't care anymore. I'll send you texts back. Bear in mind, one night I will be calling you to say 'it's done' and then you can expect me on your doorstep pronto. I won't stick around after I've told her."

"I'm coming back to work on Monday, Jim."

"What? So soon? Helen, you…"

"I need to be there, Jim. Do you think I can hang around here every day stressing about what you have got ahead of you? Besides, I'm fine. Aching ribs, that's all…I'll manage!"

"Okay. If you can't cope with the train journey, message me. I'll come for you and bring you home. Like I said, I don't care…they'll all know soon enough."

"Go! I'll see you Monday morning."

After showering, I threw my dressing gown on and that was how I spent the rest of the day. I reclined on the sofa with coffee constantly on the go. Alcohol didn't appeal, I wanted to be fully compos mentis to enjoy my thoughts and my happiness. I wanted to smile until my cheeks hurt. I haven't had enough of those moments in my life.

CHAPTER 42

*W*hen the door opened and I saw him standing there, the one I originally thought she argued with in the office, I wanted to vomit on the spot. I was gutted. My nerves were already wrung out with the effort it took for me to make the visit. I wanted to turn around and start running and not stop until my legs couldn't go on. Despite my doubts, he showed good manners and invited me in to the house. I couldn't think of much to say. I felt like a useless prick!

And Christ Almighty! When Helen introduced us, he couldn't help but add, 'I'm her partner.' I took that exactly in the context he intended. He'd warned me off for fuck's sake. Like what was I going to do while he was there...he'd staked his claim!

Once a conversation got under way, Helen asked me what happened that night. She wanted any further facts I could add to what I had already told her. She already knew what I'd seen when I walked in the door. I didn't feel like talking to her with him being there. I could have said much more but I didn't. I didn't want to make conversation now that my heart wasn't in it. I lied too; when she asked how come I was in the vicinity. I was truthful about calling in to say hi. What else could I have said? I made up some *whacking great untruth about a friend living in the next street and that I happened to be in the area. I picked up on all his big hints, everything that spelt it out. 'My beautiful Helen', 'my partner' both had been warnings.*

How she would have loved to hear the truth. 'Oh, yes I saw you on a plane back from Paris. I've stalked you ever since. I phoned around accountancy firms and found out where you worked. I stood freezing my bollocks off in a shop doorway opposite where you work, for months. I disguised myself and followed you to the station, got on the same train as you. I actually came in my pants as I watched you sitting there, stunning as always, and day dreamed about fucking you. I stood on your street corner watching many times, and being the coward I am I couldn't do anything about it. I wanted to come and claim you for months and my attempts have been thwarted not only by my cowardice but by people coming and going to your house. Then I finally took the plunge, Helen. I fought back my cowardice. I summoned up the courage...and saved you...for this guy, your partner, to have! Do you know how fucking humiliating that is? Do you?' I can imagine the look on her face if I had blurted all that out in a splash of verbal diarrhoea.

That twat had casually walked back through to the living room with a tray of coffee. I fought the urge to take the tray from his hands and viciously smack it around his head. But, no...I accepted the coffee gracefully and had to sit there enduring the lot; seething one minute, feeling hurt the next. I couldn't bear to look at either of them. In their eyes I'm some fucking super hero for doing my part. I helped a damsel in distress...well, whoopy fucking doo for me! Super-hero indeed! I'm a stalker, a liar, a coward and one fucking great waste of space!

Well, it's finally over! Defeated at the final hurdle! I can honestly say that it hasn't come as a great shock. I told myself at the beginning that someone like Helen would have a special person in her life. I should have stayed away from her and been content with never getting to find out that my suspicions were correct. What the fuck has it all achieved?

Before I boarded the train in Maida Vale, I looked at the track longingly. The temptation to climb down and just lay there and wait for my fate was overwhelming, but there was too many damned people milling about. Busybodies who would coax me back, call an ambulance, suggest I get professional help for my depression and pat me on the back knowingly. They'd sympathise with the loser in their midst. I know exactly what I am, without that shit to deal with.

I've got a cupboard full of booze in the kitchen. I'll drink myself into oblivion tonight. Who knows, I might even flush down a full packet of paracetamol and take a chance. If I don't wake up, so be it. But if I go ahead and do it, at least I won't have to obsess about someone I can't have, a lady who has a life to live!

CHAPTER 43

ed was finally back in the office after another holiday. He'd been gallivanting around some British golf courses on his annual 'boy's holiday', a fortnight touring and playing a round on many of England's finest golf courses.

He stuck his head around my office door just after nine.

"Helen, can you and Jim be in my office for eleven, please?"

"Of course, Ted. Do you want me to mention it to James for you?"

"Yes, please if you wouldn't mind, my dear!"

"Not a problem. I'll be there. I can't speak for James, of course."

I felt a tingle of excitement at the prospect. At last we could get it out into the open and without either of us having to approach him first. As soon as he closed my door, I rang Jim's extension. After a couple of rings he picked up.

"Helen?"

"Jim, Ted wants to see us both at eleven. Our chance to tell him!"

"Oh, right. What does he want us for?"

"He didn't say!"

"I dare say we'll find out. Once he's said what he has to say, we'll tell him, or I'll tell him if you're feeling shy?"

"Oh, my God! I can't begin to imagine what he'll think. I..."

"Don't stress, Helen. It'll be fine. I dare say he'll be shocked, but I can't see any problems. Get some work done. No stressing!"

"That's easier said than done!"

But he'd already hung up.

Two hours later, he tapped on my office door. I went to join him in the corridor. He quickly glanced down both ends of the corridor. Nobody was around so he grabbed my hand and gave it a quick squeeze. He gave me a confident smile. He knocked and we heard Ted's deep voice.

"Come in!"

We went to the two seats he obviously placed in readiness, side by side facing his desk.

"Ah! You're both here. Good. Take a seat. It's just a brief meeting and I promise not to keep you too long. I've been looking at the calendar and I have come to a decision. Christmas is coming at us with alarming speed. I'm adding a couple of extra days to our normal Festive break."

Jim looked over at me to see what my reaction was. I shrugged my shoulders.

"That seems fair. What's the plan, Ted?"

"We'll finish work at lunchtime on Thursday twenty second of December and go for our Christmas Dinner. I've still to sort the venue out. I must look into that later and find us somewhere nice to eat. We'll be returning to work on Tuesday the third of January. That will give us a total of eleven days. I'm sure the staff will be delighted. Would you mind letting everyone know, Helen? An email will suffice."

"Yes. I'll do it this afternoon. Was that all you wanted us for, Ted?"

"I can't think of anything else, unless of course either of you have any matters to bring to my attention."

Jim piped up.

"Only one thing for me to mention, Ted. I've booked in the audit for Computer Wares Limited for the first week in April. You said you wanted to know when."

"Excellent. Thanks for that, Jim. I'll make a note in my diary. I would like to pay them a visit while our technicians are there. Well, I think that's it. Thank you both. I've no wish to hold you up any longer than necessary!"

Jim stood first and I got to my feet seconds later and moved a little closer to him. I looked at Jim in the hopes that he would do the talking. He gave me a slight nod.

"Can we just take a few more minutes of your time please, Ted? I have... sorry, Helen and I have something we'd like to share with you."

Ted raised his eyes to look over the top of his glasses, immediately agog.

"Go ahead, Jim!"

Jim reached out and took my hand in his. Ted's eyes followed the hand movement with interest. I noticed his raised eyebrows.

"Ted, we would just like to inform you that Helen and I are...in a relationship. I've started moving a few things into Helen's house and by the end of next week we will be... erm...co-habiting."

Ted looked over at me first. He gave me a kind and lingering smile, before turning to face Jim. It was another few minutes however, before he spoke and it was a question he directed to the pair of us.

"Are you both happy? No, don't answer that. Of course

you are or else things would not have reached the moving in stage."

Jim answered first.

"I'm very happy."

"Me too." I piped up after Jim.

"That's good. I've known since you started working here, Jim, that your situation at home was not a happy one. Helen, I know that you have had more than your fair share of troublesome and heart-breaking times. Your joint decision to be together is not really any business of mine as such. I would though, like to thank you for telling me. I appreciate that. The only thing I have to add, is that if you are both happy, then I am delighted for you. I mean that sincerely."

With that, he walked around his desk towards us and shook Jim's hand first before folding his arms around me.

"My dear, Helen, nobody deserves happiness more than you. I'm thrilled for you."

"Thank you for being so understanding, Ted."

He let me go and I heaved a sigh of relief that it was out in the open.

"So, just one little matter to mention to you."

We looked at him, wondering what was coming next. The obvious thought came to mind just before he started to speak.

"Can I just say that I hope this will not affect your working relationship. You know what I'm saying. If you have any differences outside of work..."

Jim quickly cut in.

"That goes without saying, Ted. We won't! Let's say... there's a much better atmosphere between us these days."

We laughed. Whether Jim intended it to be funny, I'm not sure. But it was a good outcome.

As we made to depart from Ted's office, we reached the

door and both spun around on hearing a mumble from Ted. "My plan worked then!"

It had barely been audible. I wasn't sure whether I heard correctly. Jim also looked puzzled, as if his ears had deceived him. We both looked at our senior partner in shock as we found him pretending to be engrossed with something on his laptop.

"Pardon?" Jim's eyes were wide in astonishment.

"What?" I asked.

Ted looked up, his pretence blatant.

"My plan! Sending you to Manchester together. If I'm not mistaken, it was after the seminar that the iceberg thawed. Would I be right in my assumption?"

I could feel the colour rise up from my neck and throat to my forehead. Did I just hear that right? The shock on Jim's face confirmed that we both did.

"Yes. That's correct." He answered, looking nonchalant.

"I've seen the difference in you both. Neither of you needed to attend that seminar, I guess you realised it back then? It was a little plan that formed in my mind when the paperwork arrived on my desk. The tension between the two of you since Helen returned to the partnership was visible for all to see. I know there were issues between you. But I saw something else there. Something that perhaps neither of you could see. Now, if you would be so kind as to send Cindy through with a coffee for me, please."

We turned to the door once more before he added.

"Oh. One more thing. How do you propose to inform the staff of…of your new arrangements? Whatever you decide, it's your call. It's your news to break, not mine! I'll speak with you tomorrow."

Just before lunch, Jim sent out an email to everybody in the office, asking if all staff could gather in his office for a few minutes after lunch break was over.

Most of them were already assembled when I walked in. The last one to arrive was a very flustered looking Christina.

"Have I missed anything?" She asked.

"Glad you could make it, Christina. Better late than never." He smiled at her before turning to address them all.

"Right, now that Christina is here, I have an announcement to make."

I didn't know where to look. I knew that in the next few seconds all eyes would likely be on me.

"The reason why I called you in today won't take long to explain. You'll be back at your desks in a minute or two. What I...what Helen and I would like you all to know, is that we are in a relationship. From next week we will be living together."

I was right. All eyes were on me in an instant; raised eyebrows, looks of shock and disbelief and smiles all round. Christina gave me a knowing look and nodded her head slowly in a self-satisfied manner. I could see that our news had come as no shock to her in the slightest.

As we left Jim's office, she pulled me to a side in the corridor.

"I knew it. I've been watching you two for months. You may have fooled the others but there's no fooling me. I saw it in your eyes. I saw it in him. He's been much better lately. What the fu...sorry! What the Hell happened in Manchester, Helen? That's when everything changed. Even before the seminar, I noticed the sexual tension between you. All I can say is...what took you so bloody long? All the flowers were from him, weren't they? That's the only reason they didn't have cards with them."

She grinned, self-satisfied and proud that she'd worked it all out.

"Really? You noticed everything? What is it with you?

Why do you always seem to know? Are you bloody psychic or something?"

Her eyes twinkled with mischief.

"I might be!"

She gave one of her great snorting laughs. I cringed, wondering what Ted would be thinking tucked away in his office. He couldn't possibly fail to have heard it!

CHAPTER 44

our days after we disclosed the news of our relationship to Ted and the staff, Jim moved in. He arrived driving a small rental vehicle. I expected him to turn up in something much larger, but the little van contained *all* of his personal possessions...a guitar, a stereo system, boxes full of books, CD's and DVD's plus several suitcases full of his clothes and suits.

"Using my car would have taken three or four journeys. She was there when I left so I was relieved I'd hired the van. I couldn't do with seeing the gloating expression on her face; to have her watch me every time I needed to go back for another car load. I wanted to get my stuff and be away from there as fast as I could. She's not bothered in the slightest, in fact she looked smug and self-satisfied. Wouldn't mind betting that by the time I drove away, she'd be on the phone making arrangements with one of her...shags!" He explained.

It didn't take us long to unload the van. We hauled everything into the garage and placed it in one of the far corners until he returned. After a quick coffee, he headed back out to return the van to the rental place and collect his own car.

"Was Jack there when you left?" I asked him cautiously.

"He was…and he was beaming. He gave me a big hug and said he'd see us soon. I know he'll be alright. At least he doesn't have to listen to the bickering and sarcasm anymore; basically, he won't miss the bad atmosphere. He's fine, Helen. He told me over and again that it was the right thing to do, for everyone's sanity. I asked him to come over and meet you and he said he's looking forward to it. Is that okay, darling? If he comes over to visit? I've given him your address."

"Of *course* it's okay. He's your son, Jim. You don't have to ask. He's welcome here any time he wants. This is your home and he will always be welcome."

"You might regret saying that when you get to meet him." He laughed.

"Jim! What a thing to say about your son!" I scolded.

"Only joking, babe. I'm proud of him I really am, especially the way he is handling this. He's mature… and sensible for a kid his age. And a nice guy too!" He quickly added.

"I'm sure he is and I can't wait to meet him, Jim."

I floated around the house all weekend, dizzy with happiness. Singing along with the radio, I danced around the kitchen from time to time as I prepared each meal. I wanted to shout it from the rooftops. My man had moved in. It was my dream come true; *he* was a dream come true! He's in my life now and hopefully for it will be for good. Now I can sleep contented, knowing that he won't leave me to go home. He's already home. Routine didn't exist in those forty eight hours. We ate our meals at odd times, made love wherever and whenever we wanted. If we weren't indulging in our intense love-making sessions, I lounged around in my dressing gown and Jim wore nothing but his boxer shorts. It was idyllic.

Monday morning arrived and my euphoria continued. Though I'd always used the tube for my commute to work, it made sense to travel into the car with Jim each morning. I'd only used my car on the rare occasions when I had client visits. Jim however, made regular visits to his client; one of our larger accounts, so always needed his vehicle at the ready. Walking down the street hand in hand with him, I couldn't keep the smile from my face. Fifty yards or so before we reached the office, Christina bounded up behind us, effervescent as ever.

"Good morning, love...ermm...lovely people!" She sang out.

I swung round to face her cheeky grin and chuckled.

"You were about to say 'lovers', weren't you, Christina? Come on, admit it!"

"No! Well, yes I was. But you are, aren't you? Lovers, that is!"

Jim and I looked at each other speechless as she scurried ahead to open the door. He shook his head in disbelief.

"Bloody Hell, we might be in for a full week of that, Helen! Don't know if I'll survive it!"

"You will...*we* will!"

As the week progressed, Jim was out of the office for much of the time, so he hadn't needed to 'survive it'. Except for the young technicians, the girls who'd always been my friends called into my office at some point or other. I succumbed to several lots of tears and with a lump in my throat as they made comments about how happy I looked and wished us both well. Also, Ted had stopped me in the corridor and without any words being exchanged, gave me a colossal bear hug and kissed me on the cheek. He'd pushed me away from him to look into my eyes, gave me a mischievous wink and carried on walking. I wanted to say something, maybe a 'thank you, Ted' but the words wouldn't come. Of all the years I'd worked for him, this was my happiest week.

During that week we went to bed earlier one night, it was Thursday and only half past nine. After several glasses of wine, we were extremely chilled and finding it hard to keep our hands off each other. It was a case of make love in front of the fire, or go to bed where we could fall asleep in each other's arms straight after. We opted for the latter.

We showered and laid on the bed naked. Taking in his stunning torso, I revelled in it. He was all mine. We kissed and were about to make our first moves when there was a thunderous knocking at the front door.

"Are you expecting visitors, Helen?"

"Not at all. I haven't a clue who it could be."

"I'll go! My new duty; to answer your door."

"It's our door now, Jim! Not only mine!" I scolded.

He grabbed his dressing gown, unpacked just twenty short minutes ago, and headed downstairs to answer the frantic knocking. I heard his voice, probably loud as a warning to me.

"Jack? Come in! What's wrong?"

I could hear a mumbled reply. Not wanting his son to think the obvious, I got dressed again; jeans and a sweatshirt. Maybe that way he would think Jim was just out of the shower and not that we'd been 'at it'.

When I went downstairs to the living room I noticed the suitcase tucked in a corner in the hall. Memories came flooding back. Ruby had arrived in the same manner earlier in the year. Jack was already seated on the sofa and Jim stood firing questions at him. I walked straight up to him and noticed instantly how much like Jim he was.

"Hello, Jack. Pleased to meet you. I'm Helen!"

"Hello, Helen!" He took hold of my hand and shook it enthusiastically.

He looked extremely embarrassed and I wanted to put him at ease straight away.

Jim looked at me with a shrug of his shoulders.

"Helen, I…Jack's turned up here because…"

I cut him off, delighted to see father and son together. My eyes flitted between the two, comparing their looks and their mannerisms.

"I haven't a clue why he's turned up Jim, but there's no need for explanations. He's your son and he can stay as long as he likes…"

"But…"

"Rubbish! Take him upstairs. I saw the suitcase. Let him choose which room he wants. I don't need to know anything."

"Are you sure, Helen? It's a big ask."

"It's not a big ask. Now…shut up. Get him settled in his room and I'll make something to eat. What food do you like, Jack?"

Jim looked at me and back at his son.

"I eat…well, most things really." His reply was almost apologetic.

"Okay. I'll sort something. It'll only be quick, but if you're hungry I don't suppose you care? Once you've eaten we can talk."

Jim stared at me, mouth and eyes wide open.

"Helen, we could order a pizza or something, you don't need to start cooking."

"Will you shut up and take him upstairs to sort a room out?"

"Okay, okay!" He grinned at me and despite his 'buts' and 'are-you-sures' I could see his evident delight to have Jack with us.

I busied myself in the kitchen for ten minutes or so. The quickest thing I could find was a microwave pasta sauce and I put a serving of penne on to boil. It wouldn't take long. Once it was ready, I ended up lowering the oven temperature to keep it hot. They were still upstairs so I expect they were having a father and son chat. Thoughts of what had occurred at his home whizzed around in my head. I wondered if he'd had a row with his mother at all. Ten minutes after the food was ready they both came thundering downstairs. I took Jack's tray of food through to the living room and made myself comfortable. Jim was making the place look untidy, pacing around the lounge, back and forth.

"Jim, sit down. Tell me what's happened one of you, please."

I expected his dad to do all the talking but was surprised to note that Jack stepped in. It pleased me that he didn't need Jim to speak for him.

"Nothing's happened as such. It's just that since Dad moved out, my mother has had…a couple of blokes back to the house and I don't like it. She's a fucking embarrassment…"

"Jack, don't speak about her like that. She's still your mother, no matter what her faults are."

"Sorry Dad, but she's behaving like a tart. I can't ask any friends around anymore. It's really embarrassing to have your mother behave like she does. She even comes on to *my friends*."

"I can imagine. I know it's not easy for you, Jack. It never has been."

"But Dad you haven't heard the worst thing yet. She and Uncle Paul have been texting each other. I don't know if he's next on the list. Mind you, where he's concerned I don't suppose she would dare bring him to the house, in case I run and tell you."

"What? If she hasn't brought him to the house how do you even know about it?

"Well, she went to the bathroom one night and left her

phone on the arm of the sofa. I took a quick look. Trust me, you don't want to know the content of the messages."

"Jack, you shouldn't have done that. That was wrong."

"I know I shouldn't. I wish I hadn't. And I can't *un*see it now."

"Jim, what? Who's Paul?"

He sighed heavily and turned away. Jack stared down at his size nines and twiddled his thumbs. He clenched his teeth together in a grimace and screwed his eyes up. I got the impression he was regretting his outspokenness. Turning back to face his son, Jim saw his anguish and was swift to put him at ease.

"It's okay, Jack. I don't blame you for mentioning it. So you saw the messages…better than find him coming out of her bedroom one morning, wouldn't you say?" He turned to face me.

"Let me explain, Helen. Paul is my wayward brother. We haven't spoken in years. To be honest, they deserve each other. He can't keep it in his trousers. A match made in Heaven they'd be. It's typical of him. He's always been like that. Maybe they should get together and have an open marriage. They'd love it."

Though he had every right to be bitter, there was no trace of it in his voice. He just stated the facts.

"Dad, aren't you angry?"

"Of course I'm not fucking angry. When it comes down to the nitty gritty, where's the point? He won't…they won't ever change."

"Hell, what a mess!" I piped up, unable to think of anything else to say.

"Okay. We'll see how it goes for a few weeks, Jack. If you and Helen get on alri…"

"Jim! We're going to get along just fine, aren't we, Jack? You can live here with us if that's what you'd like to do?"

"Helen, aren't you jumping in at the deep end here?"

"No. No, I'm not. He's your son. I can see how close you two are and you've always told me so, Jim. Of course he must stay. He doesn't have to go back to his Mum's unless he really wants to."

"Thank you, Helen." They both said it at the same time. Father and son in stereo. My Jim and his son. My family.

One afternoon at work, I took the opportunity to call Heidi and give her an update on the 'Jim and I' situation. I swear I heard a few sobs from her at the end of the line as she expressed her delight.

"I'm ecstatic for you! I told you it wasn't over, Helen! You should have had more faith. It's obvious the guy loves you."

She listened with enthusiasm and egged me on to disclose all the details of how the events unfolded, with the odd 'Phew!' and 'Oh my God!'s thrown in here and there. As luck would have it, both Catherine and Ruby happened to be home, so I was able to speak with them too. Heidi had been as good as her word and left me to tell them about Jim. It wasn't exactly what I planned; I would have preferred to break the news to them in person, but everything had happened so quickly. Thankfully, my fears had been groundless and they were both thrilled with the news. Well, Ruby's exact feelings came out as 'Cool'. Fifteen minutes later and with our news up to date, Heidi came back on the phone.

"Helen, one more thing. I've just been talking to Richard while you spoke with the girls. We would like you all...you, Jim and Jack to join us for the Christmas period...if you'd like to, of course? We want you to stay. Please say yes! Let's have a big family Christmas. Because you *are* family, Helen!"

My mouth opened wide but the words wouldn't come. I couldn't think of what to say so I wept and blotted my tears dry with a tissue.

"Helen? Are you still there?"

"Yes. I'm here! Sorry for going quiet on you. I was a little taken aback. Heidi, thank you so much. You are so sweet and thoughtful. I would love to spend Christmas with you all, but I must…"

"Yes, I know. You want to run it by Jim…and I'm aware you have Jack to consider too. That's understandable, Helen. Give me a quick text or call tomorrow, whether it's to say 'yay' or 'nay'. But we'll understand if you want to spend your first festive season with just the three of you. We can do it next year instead."

After thanking her for the umpteenth time and promising to let her know about Christmas, we ended the call.

At home, we quickly settled into something of a routine and I loved every minute of each day. Jack was a pleasure to have around. He was hilarious, a constant joker and has a great banter with Jim. He regales us with some of the most bizarre stories about his college friends and their behaviour during class. Like his father, his personality is endearing; warm, caring, loyal and helpful. I was rapidly becoming fond of him. I can see Jim enjoys having him live with us and beams with pride…rightly so. As Jim and I sit downstairs either watching TV or chatting, we often hear the stereo blasting away in Jack's room as he's studying. The normal family life I craved is mine and my cheeks ache from smiling. I love to hear the laughter of father and son when he's in the living room watching T.V. with us. Jim and I don't have the freedom to make love wherever we want in the house now, yet I'm so happy that it doesn't even enter my head. It doesn't matter about being wild anymore. I have everything I want… my family.

During the first couple of weeks after he moved in with us, his mother never contacted Jack once. Other than the one occasion Jim drove him over to hers to pick up more of his clothes and personal items, Jack hadn't even been near the house. She wasn't at home when he went to collect his things. Jim was relieved. He'd expected her to be there…and that he would come under fire for 'stealing' their son from her. What mother wouldn't care? I felt for Jack, as it seemed she doesn't.

CHAPTER 45

I'm finding it a mammoth task to keep a grip on things. My mind is in overload and I'm way too excitable; my stomach is churning until I could almost vomit. I haven't a clue what I'm supposed to be doing half of the time. To sum it up, I feel hyper…like I'd overdosed on sugar for the last week or so. There's only two weeks to go until Christmas and Jim, Jack and myself are spending the whole festive period at Heidi and Richard's place. Catherine and Ruby will of course, be there too. The plan is that we'll head over to their house on Christmas Eve and will stay until the day after Boxing Day. I've not been this excited since my early years; the magical Christmases with my parents.

Since our phone call just a few short weeks ago, when Heidi had invited us over, I'd been in a constant dreamlike state. I was flattered to have been asked and stunned when she referred to me as 'family', but to top that I've been insanely giddy once Jim agreed 'yes, we'll go'.

Jim and Jack will be meeting the whole family for the first time, and it's my first opportunity to meet Richard. Jack was invited to his grandparents along with his mother, but he'd declined and opted to spend the festive season with a family of total strangers. After I spoke about them all over our evening meal, Jack expressed his eagerness to meet Ruby and Catherine, even though they're slightly older than he is. His eyes sparkled as we made our plans. The last couple of lonely Christmases, I'd exchanged presents with Ruby and Catherine. This year we would also swap gifts with Heidi and Richard.

At the first chance since Heidi asked us, we headed into the city and spent the day shopping around looking for a few novelty items for each of them. It was a great day. We started our day out at The London Eye and followed on with lunch in a fabulous bistro. Jack, even though he didn't know any of them, offered up advice on where to shop for unusual gifts. He was in his element.

"Do you think Ruby would like something like this, Helen? He asked, holding up a lacy black thong in an underwear shop.

"Jack! I would never have expected that of you." I laughed, unable to believe that a young guy would wave around a very scanty pair of undies in the middle of a shop heaving with customers and without a hint of embarrassment.

"Just a thought!" He was doubled up laughing. "Or how about this one?" He snatched up a white crotchless pair in his free hand.

"Put them back and let's get some bloody shopping done." Jim reprimanded, though I could see from his smirk that he found Jack's antics highly amusing.

I couldn't recall the last time I'd had such fun while shopping. It was lovely to mooch around the shops, have a laugh, shop for nice things and generally take in the frost day and infectious Christmas spirit. It was inconceivable that this would be my biggest family Christmas ever. During my Christmases with Mum and Dad, we usually alternated between having relations over to ours or we would go to one of their homes on Christmas Day. Since Mum and Dad died, I'd had only myself to think about. During my little exile in Paris, I spent Christmas alone grieving, not bothering to get washed and drowning my sorrows. I had been aware only that it was the festive season, but didn't actually realise which of those days was Christmas Day. It was a sad existence. The following year, I'd had a surprise visit from Simon on Christmas Eve. He'd stayed with me until Christmas morning but I spent the rest of the day alone. Ruby and Catherine made the season more enjoyable when they'd joined me for a few days after Boxing Day. It had been a pleasure to have their company. This year would be remarkably different.

I imagined the scene at Heidi and Richard's home, a house with seven bedrooms, fully decorated for the season. It was going to be awesome.

Back at the office, it was business as usual and one of our busiest times of the year. Somehow we all managed to wade our way through the oppressive workload. Finally it was the last day. We finished work at one o'clock, piled into the two seven-seater cabs and headed to the restaurant Ted had booked for our Christmas Fayre. A fine dining experience!

Once everybody was armed with their first glass of wine, they proposed a first toast to Jim and I, wishing us all the best for our new life together. Hilary, Ted's wife was with us again. For me, it meant the world to sit close up to Jim as his life partner instead of just…a partner in business. All eyes were on us from the start of the meal. As the afternoon passed, each time I looked up I would catch one or two of them peering over at us and smiling. It occurred to me to wonder how many of them actually had their suspicions about us, other than Christina. Since we'd made our announcement, every time she saw Jim and I together, she couldn't help but show her self-satisfied smile. The smile that said 'I knew all along!'

By the time the other staff left the restaurant, there was only Jim and myself left with Ted and Hilary. Hilary was beaming at us just like her husband. I'd sensed throughout the afternoon that Ted wanted to say something; he was twitching with impatience, but with the staff all headed for home now, he wouldn't hold back much longer.

Sure enough within the next couple of minutes, he came out with his speech. Jim must have been expecting it too, he moved closer and placed his arm firmly around my shoulders.

"Jim. Helen. I have to say that this has been my favourite Christmas party in all the years I've been in practice. You two together...well it makes me happy. Helen, I have seen you through some very traumatic times. I think the world of you, you know that. At times I have felt so helpless though. I've watched you go through so much and there has been nothing I could do to help. I helped where I could, but I couldn't make everything right for you. Sadly, it's a fact of life. Every-body has to go through hurt and grief alone, even though people are there routing for them. Though you weren't aware of my plan, I knew it was the right thing to do. You are so right for each other and the only people who couldn't see it were you two...the people themselves. I knew from the beginning. The vibes that you were both giving off in your animosity towards each other were...well, you both wear your heart on your sleeve. You're quite a shallow pair." He laughed and Hilary joined in too, before adding her input.

"Ted has told me all along...I've listened to this story about you two since the day you returned to the practice, Helen. He never stopped staying it...Jim and Helen will get together one day...and he was right. I'm genuinely happy for you both, I really am. Helen, I've never seen you looking so relaxed, happy and beautiful…and with nothing on your mind for once."

Ted's speech was a beautiful end to the day.

One our way home in the taxi we ordered, Jim had his arm around me on the back seat and whispered in my ear.

"Were we really that transparent, Helen? I would never have thought for one minute that I was."

I grinned and planted a kiss on his forehead.

"You're drunk, Mr Mortimer. I didn't think I was transparent either, but apparently we must have been. They all seemed to have a clue what would happen. Remind me never to fall out with you, or they will all know about it before we do."

On Christmas Eve, Heidi arrived to collect us in Richard's Range Rover. We were laden down with three night's worth of luggage, our contributions to the food and drink for the two full days, our gift bags for them, plus our gifts for each other. She greeted Jim and Jack graciously.

"I hope you're looking after our beautiful Helen, Jim? The girls and I will never forgive you if you don't." She held up a threatening fist and laughed.

"Well with a threat like that how could I do anything other than look after her? But I think we've done a pretty good job up to now, don't you Jack?" We all laughed. "Seriously Heidi, I am…well, Jack and I are thrilled to be a part of your family Christmas. I've heard so much about you all."

"We're looking forward to having you all, honestly." She walked over to give me the biggest hug ever. She glowed with happiness.

"Hope you're ready for our Christmas Eve? The girls are demanding a trivial pursuit night and a Christmas Eve box. Oh, did I tell you that Catherine's boyfriend……is joining us after Christmas Dinner? His parents insisted he at least stay with them for Christmas Dinner and after that he can please himself."

"Wow! We've also brought Christmas Eve boxes. It should be fun. Jim, are you any good at trivial pursuit? I don't really know you well at all do I, if I need to ask that?"

"I'm the best. If you want to win you'd better partner me."

"But I might not want to partner you, Mr Cocky. I partner you in the office and at home. Tonight, we might have to change that for once!"

It was a jovial mood already and we'd barely finished putting our things into Richard's car. I was glad she'd thought of it. It wouldn't have fit into the boot of Jim's BMW and certainly not in my Merc.

As we pulled up outside their house twenty minutes later, I gasped with excitement seeing all the fairy lights in the windows. The girls and Richard flung open the door and hurried down the steps to greet us. My heart melted at seeing my new family and being able to be with them for Christmas. A sudden thought entered my head.

We need a larger home!

I already had plans to returning the favour next year.

"Jim, we need a bigger home. We're going to need to move before next year. This is our family and they're coming to us next year."

He put his arm around my shoulder as he joined me on the pavement to meet Richard, Ruby and Catherine. Jack followed close behind us. This was going to be the best Christmas ever. My first one with my new family.

EPILOGUE

*E*leven Months *later...*

    I'm daydreaming again...lost in my private thoughts as I stare out of the window at the winter sun so low in the sky. I felt my dressing gown slip down off my left shoulder and tickle the top of my arm. As irritating as I usually find it, I'm ignoring it for the time being. I'm not going to allow anything to interrupt my musing.

I have a thousand or more emotions and thoughts running through my head. I need to take this quiet time to savour each and every one. Even the most negative emotions need taking down; bringing to the forefront, feeling the vast hurt for one last time and then ...committing it to a small corner of my grey cells. I hope it will be the deepest and darkest crevice, one in which I can contain all my bad forever...lock the door on it and never let it surface again. I won't have time in future for the bad, the hurt, the scars and the negativity that has skipped so freely through my life... dancing, cavorting, hurting and taunting me at so many and such inopportune moments throughout my years.

It's as if I'm currently detached from reality. I'm vaguely

aware of the voices in the background; murmured conversations…but I quickly blot them out…

'Don't let them in, Helen! Have your moment…exorcise those demons!'

Just as swiftly…I can't hear them anymore; the whispers that faded away. The hurt is safely stashed away now. I'm back to experiencing the guilt again, and there's so much of it…

First and foremost, and in particular, something which bears relevance to my current situation, came the gnawing guilt I felt when I aborted Gavin's baby. But only with regard to my parents. That tiny foetus would have formed within me in time and become my parent's first grandchild. I can feel the lump in my throat and the sting of tears as I blink them away. I'd deprived them of ever being able to hold their grandchild in their arms, of being able to spoil that baby. Yet at the time, I never could have imagined that they would die so tragically, it was incomprehensible. Had I had any inkling that I would soon go through the grief of losing them both, I think I would have *not* gone ahead with the abortion. I would have willingly endured the pregnancy, at least so they could have that experience that they had one day hoped for. I can't forget the guilt of having lied to them. Thinking again though, I hadn't really lied to them. I had just *not* told them I was pregnant and had booked in to have an abortion. Economical with the truth, that's it. Not lying.

Still locked in my shell, I cast my mind back even further to my school days. I questioned myself as to whether I had anything to feel guilty about. I can't think of anything; not one thing. The bullying I had endured? No. I never gave the bullies any reason whatsoever. What about the fact that I could almost have been deemed to be the school bike? No. Nothing to feel guilty about there; I was growing up, experimenting. Was that wrong of me? I don't think so. My mind flitted forwards from school, to the university days and the fact that I had no guilt when it came to Gavin and Bobbie and their betrayal.

I fast forward once more to the thoughts on my marriage. Again, not guilty! There was nothing to chastise myself for with regard to that...that total sham. I wasn't guilty for involving the police over Anthony's involvement in drugs. It had been the right thing to do. But then again, maybe I should have done it much sooner than I did. I only involved the police when the time was convenient for me to up and leave him. So, yes, I was guilty of being selfish. The timing had needed to suit me. My Dad came immediately to mind. Perhaps I should have made him aware of Anthony's behaviour towards me and his involvement with drugs. Maybe if he had the knowledge, he would have dispensed with Anthony's role in his company. Perhaps he wouldn't have had heart problems and both my parents could even be here now...

No, my guilt mostly came from events that unfolded in my life since their deaths. Helen the accountant turned cleaner, turned call-girl. The perverted and depraved needs of my clients and how I accommodated them. That 'thing' led from another after all...it had been brought about by Simon. Not forgetting the fact that he subsequently became my fuck buddy and he's happily married. Those married clients I had entertained and for the purpose of fulfilling my own selfish sexual needs, my...yes, it was nothing more than sexual gratification. The way I treated Alex after he fucked me in the park that night...only to blurt out that I didn't have feelings for him. Then he saved me from Anthony's vicious attack. The way I had been towards Andrè too...using him when I wasn't over David's death. That had been torturous for him. I tried hard...but I couldn't ever have loved him. And then came the manner in which I attempted to run away instead of being honest with him. He had deserved the truth at least. Maybe if I'd been honest with him, Ruby would have had no need for an abortion. Maybe he wouldn't have had sex with her to get back at David. Who knows?

Then there's the constant guilt I feel over the Linda Brownlow business. I don't feel any guilt whatsoever where her son is concerned; he deserved his prison sentence. But Linda is his mother when all is said and done. Afterwards, she'd felt she couldn't return to the Hopkins Partnership. I still feel bad for her and probably always will.

I mustn't forget Jim. He was married. I don't bear any guilt for being with him, but for his wife, even though she had several affairs during their time together. I know though, that Jim shares that guilt with me.

The last few years of my life just flashed through my head, like what we are led to believe happens when people are about to die...their lives flash before their eyes in the moments leading up to tragic deaths. I however, am not about to die. I've relived these moments, visiting them one last time and now I will tuck them away...hopefully forever. At least, that's my intention.

I slowly drift back from my musings to the voices in the room, but I've fully returned to them all now; back to reality. Jim is staring down in amazement at the beautiful little miracle laid asleep in his arms, cute little murmurings coming from her lips at times. Jack is standing behind his father, looking over his shoulder at his new baby sister. I think he's still in shock, poor Jack. He'd returned home from uni to find me gripped in the pain of an agonising labour. Suspecting something wasn't right, he'd called an ambulance before getting in touch with Jim at work. Jim arrived at the hospital just in time as I was being wheeled down to surgery for an emergency Caesarean. At my request, I was awake during the whole procedure. In no time at all, our beautiful baby girl emerged into our world. They passed her to Jim until I'd been stitched up. It was love at first sight; father and daughter!

Heidi, Richard, Catherine and Ruby are sitting squashed together at the bottom of my bed. Ten days from now, they'll join us for Christmas at our new home in Virginia Water. We only moved in two months ago, but thankfully the house didn't need any major work. It has seven bedrooms so we can happily accommodate everybody for our second big family Christmas with the four of them. I'd sold the Maida Vale house, the Paris apartment and the villa in Marbella to enable us to afford it, but I have no regrets.

Our original Christmas plans had been a little dubious for a while with the baby being due on the twenty-fifth of December. For once in my life I'd been organised this year and my shopping was finished by mid-November. I didn't want to take any chances on leaving it all until the last minute.

Simon, who'd been here for the past half an hour stood up and headed for the door, ready to leave. He'd brought in a large bouquet of blooms and together with several others they adorned the table at the bottom of my bed. I've no doubt the nurses will remove them all at some point soon as apparently, it's not healthy.

"I'm so happy for you, Helen. Jim, she's truly a little beauty and so like her mummy."

He smiled again in the direction of our baby girl, Madison Rose Mortimer. We called her Rose for my beautiful Mum. Jim still gazes down at her in disbelief and wonderment. Simon gave me the slightest of nods, a wink and then he was gone.

Jim managed to tear his eyes away from our baby girl for a second.

"Helen, I've brought some cards that I was given this

morning when I called into the office. Also, there was one through our letter-box, it's been re-directed from Elgin Mews. I found it first thing when I came downstairs. They're on your table. See who they're from."

There was a dozen cards in all. Christina and her family, Cindy, Nina, Gemma, Leanne, Ted and Hilary and some others. The final one, which had a postage stamp on and was addressed to our old home, I opened last. I was stunned to find a short letter inside.

Helen,

Congratulations on the birth of your baby. (I found a neutral card as I have no way of knowing whether you've had a boy or girl.) I hope your little family brings you happiness. I've seen you in the distance on several occasions and just wanted to say that pregnancy suits you. You always looked beautiful. I did a wonderful thing the night I saved you. I just wanted to tell you that.

Alex x

Alex had seen me in the distance on a few occasions? I wondered if he'd been visiting his friend again and spotted me down Elgin Mews or near the tube station before we moved house. It's thanks to Alex that I'm still here to tell the tale and I'm living the life I am with Jim, Jack and now baby Madison. I suddenly remembered that Harry had also been around that night, so perhaps I would have survived Anthony's attack on me. After all, Harry arrived at my house shortly after Alex. As much as I've put my anger at Simon behind me, the thought still crosses my mind that had he forewarned me that Anthony was out of prison, I could have taken a few precautions. Though I would never have had any inkling that he would even consider attempting to attack me. Rather naïve of me I suppose with everything else he put me through.

I look across the room to where Jim sits cradling our

daughter and I can't stop smiling. There is a look of pure love in his eyes as he gives me a smile before gazing back down at her. Heidi thrust the box of tissues onto my lap as I feel the tears well up yet again. She knows me so well.

"Here you go, Helen. Tissues at the ready. It's an emotional time all round for you. Get those tears out now. Your hormones are still all over the shop and you need to be rid of them all before Christmas, because the only thing on the menu this year is laughter...and lots of it!"

"Thanks Heidi! I'm not sure it's hormones though. I'm crying because..." I sniffled and blew my nose a little too noisily. "...because...I never thought it was possible to be this happy! Madison, Jim, Jack and you four have all made my life complete. I love you all so much. The family I've craved for a long time."

"And we all love you too, Helen! David would be delighted for you and Jim and your precious little daughter, I know he would!"

"Are you okay, darling? It looks like you're going to flood the place if you cry much more!" Jim asked.

Standing up, he headed to Heidi and she took the baby from him, happy to have yet another cuddle. He came and sat beside me, folded me in his arms and played his fingers through my hair as I sobbed.

"I'm fine, Jim. Really, I am! I'm just happier than I can put into words right now!"

He pulled me towards him and gave me a tight squeeze around the shoulders. He gave me a lingering kiss on the lips and there was so much love and warmth in his eyes, I felt as if my heart would melt. We both leaned over towards Heidi and stared down at our tiny creation. I know that Jim and I will do everything to make sure our daughter is loved in the way I always had been. In the back of my mind I'm sure that my parents will be watching down over us. I can feel their pride and I'm sure they'll approve of Jim. I feel safe with him around. He takes care of me in every way possible. We love each other so much...and we make each other happy. David is forever locked away in a corner of my heart. These people gathered around me in my hospital room are my family and I couldn't wish for nicer people to have further life journeys with; a truly loving, caring family. I've been searching for a long time and now I've finally found them. I can forget about the scars!

THE END

ABOUT THE AUTHOR

Eva Bielby was born and raised in North Yorkshire in the North East of England. From the age of seven, she became a member of her local library, and was backwards and forwards perusing the children's section at least twice a week. Eva still lives in her birth town with her son and daughter, and their respective families being in close proximity.

Having worked in accounts offices since leaving school, Eva passed her accountancy qualifications when her children were very young. She has spent over thirty years of her working life as a company accountant.

Eva has always been interested in writing and has written many poems over the years. She started writing seriously in 2014 when she completed the first part of the erotic Goings On series. Book 2 followed in 2015. These two books have now been revamped and given new titles, 'The Hurt' and 'The Healing'. Book 3 is completed and will soon be released as 'The Scars'. Being a reader of many genres of novels, Eva would also love to write a suspense thriller in the future, and possibly a comedy, which she would carry out under an alternative pseudonym,

Eva has many hobbies, which include playing badminton and going on long country walks. She has a keen interest in spiritualism/mediumship, and has attended several workshops to develop her skills further.

Eva loves nothing better than to have fun with her

grandchildren. During quieter moments, she enjoys a cryptic crossword, sudoku and gardening.

Milton Keynes UK
Ingram Content Group UK Ltd.
UKHW020624021023
429777UK00014B/704